Praise for Adam Baron and the Billy Rucker series

'Urban Noir has arrived in London, and Adam Baron is one of its finest proponents' *Independent on Sunday*

'There's much to like here. A well drawn hero, a great sense of and pleasure in London itself . . . Baron is the nearest thing to a British Dennis Lehane' *Time Out*

'Excellent . . . Best of all is his goose-pimpling choice of rain-soaked, wind-chapped London locations' *Literary Review*

'Rucker is an intelligent, reflective hero, a man well worth keeping an eye on' *Sunday Times*

'A tale of intrigue in a setting which brings to life some of the seedier parts of London . . . Baron is getting very good at London noir' *Sunday Telegraph*

'A satisfying page-turner with plenty of twists and genuine literary quality' *Time Out*

'Tense and readable' *Company*

'Baron takes a cool, noir look at contemporary London: the media, the beautiful game, the bars and back alleys, and tells a tale of corruption and ruthless betrayal' *Manchester Evening News*

SuperJack

Adam Baron is an actor and comedian as well as a writer for TV and radio.

SuperJack is the third novel in his series featuring Billy Rucker, following *Shut Eye* and *Hold Back the Night* (both available in Pan Books).

By the same author

Shut Eye
Hold Back the Night

Adam Baron

SuperJack

PAN BOOKS

First published 2002 by Macmillan

This edition published 2003 by Pan Books
an imprint of Pan Macmillan Ltd
Pan Macmillan, 20 New Wharf Road, London N1 9RR
Basingstoke and Oxford
Associated companies throughout the world
www.panmacmillan.com

ISBN 0 330 48741 8

A CIP catalogue record for this book is available from
the British Library.

Phototypeset by Intype London Limited
Printed and bound in Great Britain by
Mackays of Chatham plc, Chatham, Kent

For Paul and Simon, distant relatives

Acknowledgements

Naomi, of course, comes first. Your rare beauty, quick mind and generous spirit inspire a thousand stories. Thanks are then due to the Delaps, my new family, who continue to amaze me with their faith, love and confidence. My old family are pretty inspiring too, from top to bottom and at the sides as well, but especially when playing Max Bruch at eighty or slagging me off in newspapers at thirty-seven. Both require bravado and panache, two things any writer should admire. Susannah Zeff once again provided the gold dust of clear feedback in the days of doubt, while Andy Watts' work-rate continues to make me feel lazy and useless and hence forces me back to the rock-face. Thanks to Ben, Becky and Annie for taking it upon yourselves to bat on my team. A mention also for Vicky Tennant's kind words, Marston Bloom for taking it on the chin and coming out smiling, and the wonderful Clays – I thought it was gone for ever.

Beverley Cousins and Elizabeth Allen make finishing a book a real pleasure – it means I get to see them and work with them again. Likewise, profound and heartfelt thanks to Lisanne Radice and Jane Gregory, who both know when a gentle word softly spoken isn't going to do any damn good at all. If you were jockeys you'd be banned for overuse of the whip, but I loves ya.

We only sing when we're fishing.

Part One

Part One

Chapter One

It was early in the morning of Karen Mills' wedding day. She'd spent the night at home in her flat, with her mother and elder sister, and had slept very well, which she took to be a good sign. The night before her first wedding she'd been so nervous she'd stayed awake all night, and when she looked back on it, it all made sense. Something inside of her was trying to warn her. But not this time. She had a beautiful sleep and even dreamed of her future husband. He'd been picking flowers for her and piling them into her arms. Her arms were full but he wouldn't stop, just laughing and running off into the woods for more. At just after eight, Karen Mills had woken up smiling.

Karen's mum was up and making coffee. Karen got out of bed and had a long leisurely bath. She saw Simon, sitting at the other end of it, her shower cap on his bald head, mucking about. She went through the day, in her head, making sure nothing was awry, trying to remember the short speech that Simon had insisted she make. Everything seemed in order. In fact it was perfect, the sort of day that would completely blot out six miserable, wasted years. Only one thing niggled at her, and it was so tiny that a call from her mother, asking her if she wanted any toast, was able to knock it right out of her mind.

It was only when she was dressed that it came to her again. Her sister was teasing her hair and her father, who had arrived at ten, was chiding them both about being late. Her mother told him not to fret. Karen suddenly thought of her neighbour. Alison. She tried to brush the thought away again by trying on her veil for the eighth time, but it was no use. Just a small niggle, but she wanted today to be perfect. Not like last time, that bastard ignoring her only twenty minutes after the service. That look he gave Karen's young cousin, the crumpled, terrified feeling Karen had had. She told her sister that her hair was fine, handed her veil to her mother and told her father she wouldn't be long.

Alison lived across the hall, the other side of the lifts. She'd only been there a few months but if she'd moved in earlier Karen was sure she would have invited her. They got on so well, she felt as if Alison was one of her oldest friends. Not that they had anything in common, mind. Alison was beautiful and glamorous, if a bit common, as her mother would say. She was all parties and nightclubs, Karen wouldn't have thought Alison would have been interested in her at all. But she was, and the two of them had spent many a night over the last few weeks, sipping white wine together in Karen's flat, chatting about nothing or watching TV. Alison was just so easy to be with. It had been great for Karen because, apart from Simon, she didn't have that many friends who came round to see her.

The invitations, however, had gone out almost

before Karen and Alison had got to know each other, and even then her dad had balked at the numbers. It was a shame, because Alison had seemed very down over the last week, not going out at all, hardly leaving her flat. An invite might have cheered her up. In the weeks running up to the big day Karen would have liked to invite her in person, but had thought Alison might have been offended, because it was too late and she might have felt tacked on. The day before, Karen had even gone round, but she'd heard voices from inside Alison's flat and hadn't been brave enough to interrupt.

But now Karen didn't care. She was going to ask her to come to the reception, to beg her to come. And if Alison couldn't make it, well, never mind. She could give her a kiss, wish her the best of luck, and Karen would have ironed out every last little thing for her second shot at the perfect day.

At ten fifteen a.m. Karen rustled past the lift into the corridor on the other side, where there were four more apartments. Then, she stopped. The furthest door, Alison's, was ajar. Karen knocked lightly, but got no reply. She was about to go, but reasoned that Alison must be in. She could see that the lights were on. She was slightly puzzled by this. It was a bright morning and on that side of the building the sun came straight in. Odd. She gave another knock and then, very slowly, calling her friend's name, she pushed the door right open.

His daughter's screams brought Brian Mills running. In his impatience he'd watched her enter the flat along the corridor, and so knew where she was. Taking a second to register the noise, he frowned, then hurried towards her. He found Karen, just inside the doorway of the flat he'd seen her enter, screaming and shaking, taking small steps backwards. To begin with, he had no idea why.

Taking her ruffled shoulders in his hands Brian Mills moved his daughter aside and stepped forward. And then he could see. Everything inside him stopped. After a second he felt his gorge rise but managed to check it. It happened again though and this time he wasn't so lucky. He threw up all over his sleeves and the trousers of his morning suit and his shoes and the carpet and down the side and back of his daughter's wedding dress.

Karen Mills didn't get married that day.

Chapter Two

I suppose it began one morning in late February. I say suppose because it's difficult to know just exactly when something has started, the point before which there's nothing to say. It's like when you fall in love with someone. People ask you how long you've been going out, and it's very difficult to answer. Did it begin when you met? Or when you first went to bed? Or when you looked her in the eyes, and heard yourself saying I love you? Who knows? So I'm not sure where the story of Jack Draper starts, but I do know that it was on a cold bright morning in late February that my connection with him began. And because I'm telling it, that's where I'll start telling it.

He was one of Nicky's friends. Nicky called me at my office, just after nine thirty, on a Monday. I rent a small, bare space on the third floor of a former carpet factory near Highbury Fields that was built to last in the 30s and has long since been converted into a warren of design studios and small business premises. I'd like to report that I was deep into a case when my friend called, using my years of experience and heaven-sent intuition to bring a particularly difficult problem to a neat and satisfying conclusion. But I wasn't. I was gazing out of the window. It was a cold, fresh day, with a thin icing of snow on the ground, and I was in a good mood. Apart from the return on the desk behind me I didn't have anything very taxing to do that day, and I was looking forward to a walk through Highbury Fields later. Then a meal with Shulpa. I'd been meaning to get the tax return done for weeks, and was both proud and amazed that I'd sprung out of bed before eight that morning and was already halfway through it.

I'd meant to finish the return in one go, but I'd had to stand up. My office is heated by a radiator that looks like it should be on the inside of a submarine and which only has two settings – off, or inferno. I'd stopped what I was doing to open the window. The window looks out the back of the building across tree-tops and neatly laid out gardens, directly east towards Dalston and Hackney. I stood, with my hand on the latch. A bird was sitting on the branch of a chestnut tree, a huge spreading beast that my neighbours to the left complain about because it blocks their light. The bird was grey and white, reminiscent of the wagtails I remembered as a kid, but much bigger, and with a clearer, whiter chest. It was a bright, crisp day, and it stood out well against the thin plating of snow, blown against the broad, twisting trunk of the tree.

The size of the bird surprised me. It must have been about ten inches tall. I was sure I'd never seen that kind of bird before. It was only a foot away, side on, with no idea I was there. The bird was preening, burying its beak in its feathers as though it were trying to stab itself. I've never been that interested in birds but found both its actions and proximity mesmerizing. I don't know why. I stood, watching the bird and trying

8

not to move. The window, however, is directly over the radiator, and my Levis were heating up alarmingly. I tried to turn the latch silently, but the bird heard me and hopped further into the branches, though I could still see it. Then it looked back my way, through a twist of black twig knuckles. I was very still and it kept its position. With the welcome chill of the air I could hear its call. 'Check-check, check-check,' it said, and I smiled. Good advice for any private investigator. I was just wondering what kind of a bird it was when the phone rang.

The large bird flew down through the frost-covered branches and disappeared. I turned back to my desk again, picking up the receiver, trying to keep the image of the bird in my head.

'Mr Rucker, I presume.' It was a high-pitched voice, and straining. 'My name is Lady Frogface Devine, Duchess of Faversham, and there's a body in the drawing room. My nephew, I'm afraid, Viscount Brownose. I'm pretty sure the butler did it but can you drive down here to Frogface Hall, in a classic English automobile, and solve the whole thing before lunch? The vicar's coming, you see. *I* wanted Hercule Poirot but Lord Frogface says he won't have any damn Frenchman in the house.'

It was good to hear Nicky's voice, even if it was pure Dick Emery. I hadn't seen my good friend since a couple of weeks ago, when something had happened that had worried me. Seriously worried me. Nicky had assured me at the time that it was nothing, and I'd somehow been persuaded to take him at his word, but I still wasn't happy about it by a long, long way. Since then Nicky had sounded edgy, and it was good to hear him so cheerful now. I told him it was about time he returned my calls and he apologized for being slack, and then apologized again. His tone changing from playful imitation to something slightly more serious; he told me that it wasn't really a social call. He asked if he'd ever mentioned an old friend of his to me.

'A guy called Jack,' he said. 'Jack Draper?'

I stood with the receiver in my hand and smiled. I didn't have to think about it. I said he had. I turned and looked out of the window, thinking the bird may have come back. It hadn't.

'You were at school together, right?'

'Right,' Nicky said.

'All the way through?'

'Right. We sat next to each other in the infants.'

'And you played in the same team. You won the National Schools Cup when you were seventeen. And you scored more goals than him, and if it weren't for your dad then you'd have been a big football star too. No doubt about it. Most people thought you were better than Jack, actually. The games teacher said so. If only you'd been allowed to go to the Leeds trial. But your dad didn't think being a footballer was anywhere near good enough for a bright young Asian boy like you so you ended up running a bar while he gets to kick a ball around for a living and writes a column in the *Observer* Sport and goes to parties with Denise van Outen . . .'

'Okay.' Nicky laughed. 'Okay. I see I have mentioned him.'

'You have. And by the way, did you see that goal he got last week? I caught it on *Football Focus*.'

'Everyone in the country must have seen it by now,'

Nicky said. 'Never mind *Football Focus* it was on the *Nine O'clock News.*'

I saw it again. It was further than Beckham's, right over the keeper's head. Goal of the season, no doubt about it. And Draper, so cool, hadn't even celebrated. He'd even had another go, from just as far, ten minutes later, this time hitting the bar. I'd seen a picture of him, on the back page of the *Guardian*. Not the goal, though. At the end of the game Draper had jogged to the side of the pitch, taken his left boot off, and given it to a kid in a wheelchair.

'Super Jack,' I said. 'But why do you mention him?'

'I think he might be in trouble,' Nicky said. 'Serious trouble.'

I've known Nicky six, maybe seven years, ever since I happened to wander into his bar one night. I'd spent a very long day flatfooting it round housing estates near Old Street, looking for a twelve-year-old boy who I'd never managed to find though the police eventually had, two weeks later. Face down in a skip. I'd decided to walk back to my flat on Exmouth Market and had been in as dire need of oiling as an It girl's four-year-old Range Rover. I was new to the area then, and so didn't know the Old Ludensian, which is on St John Street down near Smithfield. I liked the laid-back, classic look of the place immediately and the state of the Guinness didn't harm the effect. The owner, Nicky, and I got talking and that was it. As far as I can remember he'd wanted to know why I'd ordered the whiskey I had, which was outrageously expensive and worth every penny, an Irish brand called Middletons, a bottle of which I'd noticed high up on a corner shelf when I was halfway through my pint. I'd told him it was my absolute favourite and was then pretty impressed by the fact that he waved away the barman, set the bottle between us, and poured me out a tumblerful for nothing. It was his favourite too, he said, as we touched glasses, and he never charged anyone who was classy enough to ask for it by name.

I was pretty puzzled by Nicky at the time, and I remain so. A kind and gentle Bollywood charmer, a man who the word 'handsome', not a word you hear much any more, was coined for, a generous man with a quick smile and the kind of dress sense you wouldn't even have if you bought exactly the same clothes as him. I don't know if guys in their thirties can have best friends but if they can then I suppose that's what Nicky is. I certainly see him more often than anyone else I know. We talk for hours, we drink for more, I even persuaded him to swap his Guccis for Gortex on a hiking trip to the bonny Isle of Skye one time. There's an affinity, something inexplicable but almost tangible, that hangs in the air between us when we meet up. I know a lot of people and Nicky, running a bar, knows ten times as many, but our friendship is different, don't ask me why, don't ask me how. It's maintained by an honesty that comes from an inability to hide anything from each other for long anyway, and the occasional favour, such as the time that a minor crim whose wife Nicky had been overfamiliar with was threatening to spoil his irritatingly good looks. I got a minor crim friend of my own to 'persuade' him not to. In return Nicky has never let me pay for a drink in the Old Ludensian and has extended this kindness to anyone

I've ever taken there. Nicky and I are friends, and we do things for each other, and I was more than glad to hear from him at last. I told Nicky I'd go down and see him that night, so we could talk about his friend's problem.

'I'll try to get Jack to come too,' Nicky said, before he rang off. 'Though I doubt he will. He doesn't think he needs anyone's help.'

'But you do?'

'I don't know. Probably. His wife certainly does. She's pretty shaken up.'

'Really?'

'I don't want to go over it now. Tell me what you think later on.'

'Will do,' I said.

'Great. By the way, how's that sister of mine? Still running you ragged? You better be careful, Billy, she'll have you in an early grave.'

I laughed. Nicky was talking about Shulpa, his younger sister, who I'd met some months back, at Nicky's birthday party. We'd spent that night together and many since then, each one more intense than the last. Shulpa burst into my mind like a doll out of a jack-in-a-box.

'Nonsense,' I said. 'It's good for me, all these parties, going out all the time. It's keeping me young. But, I have to admit, she's bloody hard to keep up with.'

'Tell me about it. I can't any more so I don't even try. In fact, I never could. You could run a city on the energy she puts out just planning where she wants to go. I wish you the best of luck.'

'Thank you, Nicky, that's very kind.'

I was about to ring off but I had a thought. 'By the

way, Lady Devine,' I said. 'I think I can solve your troublesome murder before the vicar gets round. I can do it right now in fact, without even having to get into my classic ten-year-old Mazda. Hercule Poirot is Belgian not French, as any duchess would know. I therefore surmise that you're not Lady Frogface Devine at all. You're an impostor, and so is your husband, which explains his reluctance to entertain a great detective on the premises of Frogface Hall. I think you killed Viscount Brownose yourself, because he had discovered your secret and was blackmailing you.'

'The shame,' Dick Emery said, 'the shame.'

I hung up, smiled to myself and looked at my tax return again. But it was no use – I'd done my best, I'd started on it once. Show me a man with the resolve to start on a tax form twice in one day. Robert the Bruce was only trying to take back a country. I slid it under some other paperwork and sat for a second, wondering what sort of trouble a footballer and B-list celebrity like Jack Draper could be in that would warrant my help. I was very curious, especially as it wasn't him asking me to look into it but people around him. I wouldn't know, though, not until later, so I shrugged the thought aside. I thought of the last time I'd seen Nicky. I saw a man, one of the biggest men I'd ever seen, and I saw the look on his face. Nicky sounded better today but there was still something in his voice, something I couldn't quite get at. Again I closed the window on it. Maybe it really was nothing. I closed the real window, looking out through the empty black branches, laced with snow. The chestnut had been bound with barbed wire towards the top, to stop kids from trying to climb up onto the roof. The tree looked like it was being slowly strangled and I realized that that was exactly what Nicky's voice had sounded like. I turned the radiator off and walked out into the hall.

Chapter Three

I spent the rest of the day searching for two runaways. This is what I do. Ever since leaving the police force, more than seven years ago now, I've been a private investigator specializing in locating children who have made the break from their home environment long before it was usual for them to do so. I do other work as well, but it's the kids who take up most of my time, their parents paying me to find and keep tabs on them, to let them know if they're okay. I don't often tell the people who employ me where the kids they're looking for are, though. Kids don't usually choose a life of hostels, begging, cold, rain, violence, drug abuse and prostitution over a warm and loving home environment, and I realized pretty early on that if I led parents to their offspring, I could never be sure what I was sending the kids back to. So it is usually mothers who employ me, telling me not to say anything to any fathers there may be. I send pictures, and I try to speak to the child in question, to try to get an idea of how they are.

The kids I was looking for today were both fifteen-year-old girls from a Cornish residential home, who'd disappeared on an arranged school visit to London two months ago. The director of the home wanted news of them and as there was no funding available for services such as mine she was paying me out of her own salary. But I didn't find them. I'd been given a tip that they might be trawling for business at King's Cross Station, and while I did find two girls doing this, who vaguely fitted their description, it wasn't them. The ones I eventually spotted, skinny, pale, freezing in cheap thin fleeces, pulling on damp roll-ups, approaching lone men off the train, were from Leeds not Cornwall and they weren't fifteen. They were quite a lot younger than that. I watched them both for a while, until they'd each scored a punter and gone off towards the car park across the Pancras Road. I took their pictures anyway and left them there.

By the time I'd finished and walked out onto the forecourt of the station it was about seven. The buoyancy that had sprung me out of bed that morning was a forgotten dream. The night was dark, the streets pretty quiet but for the occasional drunk and the odd human pharmacy, guys trying to look natural propping up bus stands and phone boxes, as if there were nothing at all unusual in simply hanging out on the street at the beginning of a deep, bitter February night. I moved past them, getting a look of dim recognition turning to back-burner hate from one guy, his thick puffa making him look like a six-foot robin. It was far colder than the city usually ever gets and I pulled my gloves on as I blanked his look and walked quickly up King's Cross Road to now very trendy Exmouth Market, Clerkenwell, where I live in a former photographic studio that I'd acquired seven or eight years ago. A studio which would now cost me about ten times more than I could afford – *if* I had to pay for it.

Just not being in King's Cross felt good. I know it's an up-and-coming area and all that but it still goes on, everything that ever happened there still happens. You just have to be cursed with the ability to see it. Hookers don't dress like hookers, especially not in the winter. Street style and heroin chic have become so mainstream that the guys passing crack pellets mouth to mouth to ancient eighteen-year-olds appear no different than kids on weekend leave from Eton being picked up by their girlfriends. In contrast to a day of that, Rosebery Avenue, just a step away, was a long and winding oasis.

My flat is on a side street the other side of the market to the Avenue but I didn't go there. I had a chicken in the fridge but I couldn't face handling cold, raw meat for some reason, so once I'd made it up from the Cross I stepped into Fred's, a bar on the corner of the market that I use a lot, where I found a table. I'd actually bought the chicken to cook for Shulpa, but when I'd called her earlier she'd cancelled, and as much as it was a relief not to have to cook it was also a relief to be on my own. That may sound uncharitable, and it wasn't that I didn't like Shulpa, but I was in a definite mood to relax and Nicky was right – Shulpa was not exactly relaxing. Feisty, yes. Vivacious, yes. Beautiful, attractive, exciting, yes. But relaxing, forget it. We'd been going out for three or four very hectic months and not seeing her for an evening, having a bite to eat and a quiet drink, felt like opening a deckchair in the eye of a tornado.

Fred's was filling up and I was lucky to get a table. I let out a long, slow breath, didn't bother with the menu and ordered. I thought about the girls I'd seen, the children really, walking away to the car park through the crowd of tourists and commuters and people trying to make it home. They were like ghosts we live among but choose not to see. I blinked my eyes a few times and then I couldn't see them either. After fifteen minutes of staring into space, letting a glass of red spread a welcome wave of heaviness through my bones that made the rest of the day seep out, a bean burger with chilli salsa and salad was brought to me by my good friend Alberto, a lugubrious Italian in his mid-thirties still struggling to make his name in the art world.

I thanked Alberto for the food and asked him how he was and he told me terrible. He was thinking of chucking it all in, going back to Genoa to work in his father's paint factory. I tried not to smile (though it felt good to want to) having heard variations on this theme many times before, and I told him to stick at it. I'd rolled out this line several times before too, but I was actually being sincere. I hoped Alberto would get noticed because the time I went to a private view he was putting on I liked his work a lot. There was also the fact that he was, while a nice guy, a truly terrible waiter. I'd much rather *meet* him for a coffee than wait for him to bring me one.

There was nothing at all to make me think that it was going to be anything other than an ordinary night. King's Cross gradually got pushed more than just a mile away as Alberto chatted for a while and a half the way he does, until some other customers finally got his attention and I got on with my burger, wishing too late that I'd ordered chips with it. Between bites I glanced around the modern, half-filled bar, taking in the blond-wood chairs, the questionable paintings, the faces of some of the people I sort of recognized, trying to decide if a girl sitting at a table opposite, occasionally glancing my way, was attractive or not. I spent ten minutes doing this, wondering what it was about her that interested me so much, before I realized that while she didn't look anything like Shulpa, there was something in her manner that put me in mind of her. I found myself wishing that, actually, Shulpa hadn't cancelled. I had a very sudden and very violent need for her, a need for her to blot everything else out. Again Shulpa appeared like a jack-in-a-box from nowhere, but this time it wasn't in my mind but my whole body. Fuck the deckchair, I wanted the tornado.

The effect was instant and embarrassing. I saw the smile I was gradually getting used to and the way it changed as Shulpa pursed her lips together, her eyes shining with mock wickedness. I'd joked with Nicky about his sister before but the way I felt about her wasn't funny. I couldn't figure it. Only days before I'd met her I'd finished a relationship that I'd thought and hoped would be my last, but Shulpa somehow had reached right into me. It had started out as a physical thing but had now got to the point where I needed to think where it was going. More confusingly, sometimes I seemed to wake up from her, to wonder what I was doing in the same room as my friend's sister, let alone in the same relationship.

Whatever, the rest of the evening seemed empty without Shulpa in it. I turned back to my bean burger. I'd finish it and then call her. If her friend had left I'd drive over to her place. If she hadn't I'd drive over there anyway. Nicky's chum could wait till the morning.

I could see a very beautiful end to a cold and frustrating day. But as I was finishing the burger off, a little more rapidly than my mother would have approved, I noticed a man, coming into the bar, casting his eyes over the restaurant.

I did a double take Fred Flintstone would have been proud of, almost missing my mouth. He was wearing an expensive fleece and black jeans, a Stone Island coat over one arm. He had a brown, A4 envelope in his hand. I'd never met him before, and on another day I might not have recognized him, but as it happened I knew instantly who he was, and was very surprised to see him there. I noticed a guy to my right clocking him too.

The bar was really filling up now. Fred's attracts a mix of suited-up journalists from the *Guardian* or Emap, young designers from the *Face* and *Arena*, all equally in uniform – theirs supplied by the Carhartt company – and other youngish, professional types. I waited a second, thinking that it might just have been coincidence. But Draper was hurriedly looking around the place, and it wasn't for a table. He was trying to spot someone. It had to be me. For a second I saw Shulpa again and I thought about ducking out of sight. But I didn't. After shaking off the surprise like a dog on a riverbank, I stood up. He turned my way. He saw me standing there, took a moment to see that I fitted the description he must have had of me, and nodded. I nodded too and sat back down. Then I waited as he struggled through the knot of chairs and tables, past the girl I'd been swapping glances with.

As he made his way towards me, a little out of breath, Jack Draper nodded to a couple of people. He was a tall man with a big face and a look of total confidence that I didn't find very attractive but which, I knew, put me in the minority. He had that look I'd seen a couple of times: I know I'm famous. A man who could afford to be humble. I told myself that it wasn't necessarily a bad thing, it must be weird walking into a room full of strangers who all know who you are. Draper was in his early thirties, a good six two and muscular with it. He had a big, square, open face with deep-set, hard brown eyes, so dark they were almost black, which made me think he had some Welsh in him. His jaw looked like a set of goalposts. Draper had a full head of thick black hair with a cowlick the girls probably died for. The whole lot was brushed forward and cut to look ragged by someone probably called Lionel, a style that didn't really seem to belong to him, that looked a little too young. The girls no doubt loved it, though, and it wasn't just them; Draper was head to head with Ginola, pushing another brand of shampoo for men. He'd have had a mullet, I said to myself as he ran his fingers back through it, ten years ago he'd have had a mullet.

Before long Draper was standing with two large hands on the back of the chair opposite me, looking down.

'Billy?' he said to me. He had a fairly deep voice, pretty neutral with a hint of Midlands in it. It felt strange to be looking up at this man I'd seen on the television, in the papers. Something about him just looked so, well, *famous*.

'Billy Rucker?'

I nodded. 'And you're Jack?' I said. 'Jack Draper.' I was going to say 'the footballer'. Instead I said, 'Nicky's friend?'

Draper nodded. 'Yeah,' he said, 'that's right. Hi.'

'Hi.'

Draper hovered above me, looking like he didn't quite know what he was doing there. And wishing he wasn't.

'Listen,' he said, after a second or two. 'I was just talking to Nick. Down at his bar. I . . . I need to speak to someone and he recommended you. He said you'd be able to help me. I left messages on both your machines but he said I might catch you here. I gather you're going down there anyway, but I'm pretty busy later. You don't mind me finding you like this?'

'Not at all.' I shrugged. I did mind. I wanted to go to bed – preferably to Shulpa's, though my own would have been welcome too. But I was a little curious. Nicky had said Jack might not even come later on, but here he was hunting me out three hours early.

'Sit down,' I said. 'You want a drink?'

'Just a Coke.'

Draper sat, hanging his coat over the back of his chair. He kept the brown envelope in front of him, folding his arms over it. I moved my plate aside and finished the last mouthful of wine in my glass. Alberto was walking by so I gave a tug on his apron and ordered the Coke, asking him to bring me an espresso too. He nodded but kept walking, before sitting at a table of three girls, each one of whom he kissed three times at least.

I turned back to Draper and smiled. He was looking right at me, an impatient, held look that was a little unsettling. He was being urgent and blasé at the same time, like a fourteen-year-old on a date. Draper's brow was heavy and concentrated, as though he were squinting into the sun, making him look older than his years. I wondered if that was the effect that being a striker had on you. You could tell by the way he carried himself that he was fit, but he also had the drawn, somehow unhealthy looking pallor of a natural athlete. The red razor rash smeared across his throat looked out of place.

'I can make an appointment if you like.'

'No, no.' I shook my head, wishing that I'd said sure, how about tomorrow? I smiled again. 'No, I don't mind. What is it? What can I do for you? It's good to meet you at last, by the way. Nicky often talks about you, says you two were the most lethal strike force Leicester has ever seen.'

Draper smiled at the memory, but without really smiling. All the while he gave off something. Shulpa would have said he had a radiance, that he knew how to channel his energy. To me it was as if he were asking a question by just sitting there, without saying anything. He made me want to check to see if I had any spots of food on my face.

'Says he always scored more goals than you, though.'

'I think he did.' Jack nodded. He let the thought in, but not far. 'He wasn't bad, Nick. Not strong enough, though. Too lanky.' He turned quickly to the bar before turning back to me.

'We all right here?' he said suddenly.

'Unless you have the trout.'

'Sorry?'

'Nothing. Yes, we're fine here.' There was a pause for a second. Draper's right leg was moving up and down, very slightly but very quickly, and I don't know if he was aware of it. I could feel his directness again. There was also an awkwardness between us. An immediate but unmistakable sense of being out of sync, as strong as when you meet a girl and there's an instant rapport, it just happens straight away. I wondered if it was all coming from me. I tried to ignore it.

'Well then, what is it?' I said again. 'What can I do for you?'

'It's these,' Draper said quickly, and he pushed the envelope that rested in front of him across the table towards me.

Draper sat back again, very still, and turned his head to the left as I put my hand in the envelope and slid its contents out onto the table in front of me. It seemed a bit strange to be looking at them, with no preamble, no introduction, nothing. It was almost as if Nicky had okayed me, so Draper didn't need to know any more, didn't want to go any further than the matter in hand. Usually, I get asked all sorts of questions.

Draper continued to ignore the pictures I was looking at, taking the chance to turn his phone off before sitting with his arms folded waiting, his face side on to me, his leg still going. He kept sneaking glances at his watch. I took my time looking through the material I'd found, nodding to myself now and then, and then I asked him what had been going on. Beyond him, I noticed the girl again. She was definitely attractive, with eyes that glanced my way like pretty toes dipped into an unknown pool.

25

Draper turned towards me and leaned on his elbows. 'You know I play for Orient, right?'

I'd actually thought it was Palace but I didn't have time to say so.

'Well, it's been going well for me. Finally.' He raised his eyes and crossed his fingers as though the heavens had been particularly unkind to him, but he was just pulling God round. 'I've been free of injury for about fourteen months and I'm going more than a goal a game now. People say it's only second division but it doesn't matter where you are when you're scoring. People take notice of you, start taking you seriously. It doesn't matter where you are if the ball goes in.'

I nodded. Being a striker was like being a boxer. In spite of anything any fight coach or football manager said to the contrary there was a very easy way of telling whether you were any good or not. If you put the other man down or the ball in the net you were good, simple.

'You know I started off at Leeds?'

'I do,' I said. I nodded and did my best natural laugh. The man was a friend of a friend even if he did have an unfeasibly large face and hair you could see your own in. He deserved my attention, at least. 'Nicky always goes on about having to miss the trial. Because of his dad. His big chance, he says . . .'

'Well, I started at Leeds when I was eighteen, though I didn't often get in the side. But that was okay, I was young and I was learning. Then I did get in and I could feel it, you know, I began to feel I belonged. That I more than belonged. I'd come on for the last ten and I got a couple of goals. I started twice. But the manager left. Dave Harvey. They binned him even though the team were beginning to do okay.'

I nodded. I was pretty sure I didn't need to go through Draper's CV, but if he wanted to tell me his life story that was fine.

'The new one was a *twat*. He put me on the back burner again. He wanted to keep me, he said, when I was finally granted an audience, but the two Dutchmen he brought with him meant I'd hardly get a look-in. He just wanted me for cover and to give his two Perrier-drinking stars a kick up the arse. He was a patronizing cunt as well, he thought English footballers were a bag of shite. And where the hell's he now? Two clubs have given him the boot and I drank a glass of champagne each time.

'Anyway. I wanted to play so I went down a division to West Brom, followed Dave Harvey who I knew would put me in the side *and* let me play where I wanted. I scored eight goals in eleven games. That's where I first got my nickname. It sounded pretty good with a whole stand singing it I can tell you – even if it was in a Brummie accent. But I was only there two months when I did my cruciate. That's the ligament at the back of your knee . . .'

'I know what a cruciate is.'

'Well, that was the end of that year. And most of the next. What a fucking nightmare. When that healed I finished the season, played in a few reserve games but we got relegated before I was back in the first team. They kept Harvey on and I could have stayed too but Wolves came in for me. They're a big club and I jumped at it. I was fine for a bit, playing up with Bully, even pushing him out now and then, but I did my groin. Then the gaffer, Don Hughes, put me back in before I was ready, the bastard, because we were chasing the play-offs. I've not been right since, to be honest, not until now. Little knocks, then different managers who didn't have any faith in me. Different clubs. People don't understand how long it takes to get back, if you're not given the chance to . . .'

Alberto appeared with Jack's Coke and set it down in front of him. Draper gave his famous person's thank-you nod to the waiter and I tried not to smile at the fact that Alberto had no idea who he was. Draper looked at me, trying to remember where he'd got to. I couldn't help him. I hadn't been listening really. I was looking at the pictures he'd brought me. As Alberto moved away I realized he'd forgotten my coffee.

'So the last thing I need is this. Not now. This is my chance, you know, to show people I belong at the top. And I do belong there. I don't want to stay at Orient, obviously, but it's a good platform for me. I've been knocking 'em in from all over the park.' He couldn't help a slight smirk creeping across his lips as he said that. 'But the last couple of games I've been off, I haven't been right, thinking about . . . that. Still scoring, but not feeling right. I'm not getting any younger. This is my chance, I know it, and I want that sorted, I really need to find out which bastards—'

Draper was getting overexcited and I stopped him. It was my turn to look around the restaurant. 'Jack,' I said. 'Slow down. When did this all start? How long have you been getting these? The pictures? You haven't even told me how you got them.' I put the prints on the table while Draper took a breath, his impatience flooding out of him like a wave.

'A month or so.' He shook his head, as if he'd just been given offside. 'A bit more. They've just been coming in the mail. Plain envelopes, nothing else in them. To start with I just thought it was weird, a fan or something. It freaked the missus out but I wasn't that bothered.'

'So why did you decide to find me today? Nicky said you weren't keen on getting anyone's help.'

'It's the last one. My wife, she kind of insisted I speak to you. Or someone. That last one. She told me I had to get it sorted.'

'Right,' I said. 'When did that happen?'

'That was today. I took the picture myself, just for proof. It's the last straw.'

'I can see how it would be.'

'I mean, that's sick, isn't it?'

'It's not usual.'

'It's fucking sick and I want it sorted. The others, that's spooky but I know how to handle myself. But I don't know what to make of this kind of shit.'

Draper picked the photo up from the table. It was a Polaroid and he stared at it, his mouth open, shaking his head. The rest of the shots on the table were black and white, taken with a zoom. They looked like the sort of prints someone like me would take – *if* I ever did any divorce work that is, something I've so far been successful in avoiding. But maybe someday I'd be forced into it, like playing for Leyton Orient when you'd once been the new star at Elland Road.

There were six pictures in all and the first two featured Draper. In one he was on a suburban street, getting into a car, a blue Jeep Renegade. The second showed him walking away from a house, probably on the same street. There followed a shot of a street sign, one of a number plate, presumably Jack's Renegade, and one of the Renegade leaving from the front gate of Leyton Orient football club. The last one was of a woman, an attractive woman in her mid to late twenties pushing a pram. I raised an eyebrow as I turned it round in my fingers.

'Louise,' Draper said, nodding. 'And Tommy, our little boy. I was freaked out enough when I got that one, and that's when I did tell Nicky about it and he suggested you. I wanted to wait a bit, though, I thought things would become clearer first, I'd be contacted, told what it was someone was trying to prove. That they knew where I lived? Big fucking deal, I'd have said. But they didn't, I didn't hear anything. Then this happened.'

He handed back the Polaroid and for some reason I had another look at it. I don't know why. I knew what it showed and it wasn't exactly a pleasant thing to look at even after your dinner. It was in colour, naturally, and was of the back door of a house, or garden flat. There was nothing at all unusual about the door, which was a stained wood with four frosted panes, but there was definitely something unusual about what was stuck on it. Hanging from a nail was a head shot of Jack in his kit, taken from a magazine. The picture was hanging upside down, Jack's big, inverted grin more like a grimace. Also fixed on the nail was the severed head of what looked to have been a large, silver tabby cat.

The cat was staring into the lens like a misplaced and very lifelike gargoyle. I couldn't remember actually having seen a dead cat before and was surprised by the slightly comic look on its face, a small pink tongue poking out of its mouth. I wasn't laughing, though. It was a pretty gruesome sight, made more so by the fact that there was quite a lot of blood staining the picture beneath it, running down Draper's up-turned face to the door underneath.

I slid the photo under the others, then looked back across the table. Jack looked like a manager knocked out of the cup by an own goal.

'My neighbour's boy found it. Can you believe that? He's always coming round – my wife'll give him a glass of milk. She babysits him sometimes too and I kick a ball around with him in the garden and stuff. Hasn't got a mum. He came round after school. Louise had come in the front door and she hadn't seen it. Can you imagine what running into that sort of thing'll do to a ten-year-old kid?'

I wasn't sure, actually. Kids can be an amazingly resilient bunch. My younger brother Luke and I cer-tainly had to be, or else there wouldn't have been a whole lot of us left. Not with Rucker senior around. But I've also heard that one single trauma can affect your life for ever, if it happens at the wrong time.

I nodded. 'And you want me to look into who's behind all this?'

'I don't want Rolf Harris to come round and see if he can cure the poor fucking thing! Yes. There's been no notes or anything, no indication at all. I've got a couple of ideas, the photos possibly but I can't believe they'd actually do *that!*

I had another look at the picture and thought about it. Jack was shaking his head. His leg had stopped moving but he was tapping the corner of the table with his thumbnail instead. I picked up the shot of his wife and child.

'You know they may be unrelated?' I said. 'The cat's head, that could just be kids. Who are your local rivals?'

'At Orient? West Ham are the nearest but we don't compete. We wish.'

'But it could be rival fans?'

He shrugged. 'I suppose, but . . .'

'And the other?'

'Well, I've pissed off a few people in the press, other players and stuff. Other people. I've made a list, but how the hell I'll ever know who it was . . .'

'And the police? What are they doing? Someone obviously knows your movements and where you live. With this last thing I can't see them failing to put someone out to watch you, keep an eye on your wife at least. The pictures on their own, I'm not sure, but they would have to take it seriously now. Who are you dealing with?'

I reached into my jacket for a pen. My notebook was in my bag, but as I bent down to it I stopped. The look on Draper's face told me I wouldn't be needing it. He let out a breath and turned his head to the side. Then he picked up his Coke. I left my bag where it was.

'You haven't told them.'

My tone must have given away what I was thinking. Draper met my eye but he didn't say anything.

'You're afraid it'll get out. Yes? There'll be headlines.' Still, he didn't speak. I shrugged. 'What does it matter? You'll just get better known, you'll just get more for that column you write.'

'I don't want to be a fucking journalist! Listen, I

can't go to the Bill. It will get out. That's why I'm using you. Because Nick said you were good, *and* I could trust you.'

There was a slight hint of a threat in his voice that I decided to ignore. I gave him a look that said, 'Go on.' He leaned forward, making an effort to lower his voice.

'I'm looking to move, okay. My agent tells me some of the big boys are interested. I need someone to sort it, and not say anything.'

I shook my head. 'It's your choice. But it's the police you should contact. More than likely the sight of a squad car will scare off someone with a grudge, or local kids. And if it is more serious, and the two things are related, well, that makes it doubly important. They have pictures of your wife. Doesn't that worry you?'

'Of course it worries me. This is all about my wife!' The volume had gone up again. The guy to my right, who had clocked Draper, looked round. 'And my kid. Do you think the likes of Man U would go near me if they thought I was hassle? Football's all squeaky clean now, it's all role models and shit. Listen, I've thought this out, okay? It's my last chance, it's the last chance for Louise and for Tommy. A year or two at United or Villa or some place like that and I'm sorted. My contract's up at the end of the season and so I won't cost anything. I know someone will come in for me – if I'm not any sort of risk – and pay me big money. That's why I need you.'

'Well,' I said, shaking my head, 'All I could do is look into it, which would still leave you wide open, or else keep watch on your house. I couldn't even do that alone, not effectively, twenty-four hours, and even if I could you wouldn't necessarily learn anything. You need someone to watch yourself and your wife all day, and someone else to find out what's going on. You really need the police. And if not them then a big company, someone like the TBG Agency, with enough people to cover you *and* do some delving—'

'And it would get to the press even quicker.'

'So, let it. And let it sort itself out,' I said. 'Then it'll be over and people will see it's not your fault, you've done nothing wrong.'

'By which time my cruciate's gone again! Or I can't find the net because of it all and this time that's it. I'm thirty-two years old. It *can't* come out, it just can't. So I'm asking you!'

By now, he was almost shouting at me. I didn't like it.

'I'm sorry,' I said. 'But I don't want to give you a false idea—'

'Hey,' he said. 'Wait a minute. It's not like I'm asking a favour here. I'm going to pay. I thought that's what you did – investigate things for money?'

He pulled out a clip of notes from his back pocket and started pulling some off it. I didn't like that any better than the shouting.

'I'm working more than enough at the moment,' I said, and felt pretty stupid as soon as I'd said it.

'Oh? I'll pay you double. Listen, this is my family I'm talking about. All I'm asking is that you keep an eye on our house.'

'And like I told you, how can I do even that twenty-four hours a day? I suppose I could get someone in, just to sit and watch—'

'I don't want anyone else involved. Nick vouched for you but . . .'

'Well, there you go then. I'm sorry, I don't think I can help. And it seems to me that if you actually did care about your wife's safety you wouldn't give a lorry load of shit what the papers said.'

I sat back and folded my arms. The conversation had somehow got away from me. The man opposite me took a deep breath and shook his head. He looked like he just couldn't quite believe he wasn't getting his way. But he was also scared. His eyes looked pinched, I could see the effects of pressure on him. He frowned to himself and suddenly it was as if I didn't exist. I could see him wracking his brains, starting over, trying to think of another way to fix it. I let out a breath and shook my head.

I was about to tell him okay. I'd spend some time outside his house. I'd look out for his wife, tell him to send her to a friend's or something. Then I could wait *in* the house, see if anyone else came by with any more offerings. Maybe I'd catch them delivering the rest of the cat. I'd have to find that book I got for Christmas once. I held my palms up and tried to catch his eye. I was about to say his name when he stood up.

'Well, fuck you,' he said. More people heard him, and turned. The girl at the table opposite plunged her eyes right in. 'It wasn't a counsellor I wanted but a private detective. I'll just have to find one who wants to detect things. Nick told me you were a good guy, but I can see he's lost his judgment over the years. I hope the next time you've got a problem someone tells you that you don't give a shit about your family.'

I sighed. 'Listen,' I said, 'Jack . . .'

But before I could get out of my chair he was gone.

Chapter Four

It didn't make me feel very good. When I thought about it I could understand his feelings. He wasn't a bad person. He was just trying to juggle the various aspects of his life, which now included a very worrying new element. He didn't want to turn the matter over to the police because he was scared that if he tried to put any one of the balls down he'd drop the whole lot. I could see why he didn't want to blow his big chance. And the reason why I'd told him no had nothing to do with what I'd told him, not really. I just didn't like him, that was all. I didn't exactly know why. Maybe it had something to do with being well known and admired – and knowing it. I also knew that he'd been out with Shulpa when they were young but it couldn't possibly have been that. Could it? It wouldn't have been the first surprise I'd had since meeting Nicky's sister. Whatever it was, he got my back up.

I pushed my chair behind me and stood up. I was annoyed. I still couldn't see how I'd let the conversation run away like that. Draper was a friend of Nicky's, I should have handled it better than that. I was also pretty interested in what he'd told me – looking into what was going on was bound to be a bit more stimulating than taking pictures of young girls in the cold looking for businessmen to jerk off. Oh well. I looked for Alberto but couldn't see him. I slid a ten-pound note underneath the saucer, then sighed to myself and dropped two pound coins next to it. I moved towards the exit faintly aware that I'd just created trouble for myself. The place was pretty well rammed by now and my table was pounced on with the speed of a SWAT team by a couple who'd obviously been keeping me under tight surveillance for some time. I made my way through the smoke and the hub-bub and stepped out onto the market.

It was dark, but not quite as cold-seeming, though a feather-fine rain had decided to fall. The light snow from the morning had transformed into patches of wet, spawn-like slurry that glowed orange from the street lamps. I stood for a second, breathing the damp, fetid air, listening to the amorphous rumbling in the bar behind me. I pictured Shulpa again. A cab trundled past and my hand itched in my coat pocket but I left it there. I strolled down the street towards my flat.

Thoughts of my bed floated into my head like rose petals on a warm breeze. I wasn't going to call Shulpa, or go round. I needed space from her. It was all moving too fast. I felt myself slipping away into something that I wasn't exactly sure about, as if one part of myself was leaving the rest of me behind. I knew which part it was. I followed the rose petals to my door. It would be the first time I'd been alone in my bed for almost a week and as soon as I'd made the decision I knew it was the right one. I was lost in thoughts of sliding in between crisp cold sheets when a football came scooting across the wet street towards me. I stopped it with my right foot and looked up at three young kids twenty yards ahead of me, all of them wearing Arsenal shirts, with sweatshirts underneath. Two of them were in red but the last one wore yellow. That kid must have come over from somewhere else to play. The kids were looking at me, all of them with their hands on their hips.

I kicked the ball back to them and the one in the yellow shirt trapped it with his instep and performed a neat turn. When I got level with them he said, 'You an Arsenal fan?'

I stopped, folded my arms. 'No,' I said.

'What are you then?'

I smiled. 'Forest.'

The three kids thought that was pretty funny.

'We just saw Jack Draper,' the kid in the yellow said.

'Yeah? Really? Give you any tips, did he?'

'Nah, told us to fuck off. Wanker.'

I smiled. Poor old Jack, he would have to learn how to deal with his public at Man U a whole lot better than that.

The kid in the away strip had his foot on the ball. I made as if to walk past him, up towards my flat, but then ducked left and tried to take the ball off him. He was too quick. He ran his foot over and knocked it to his friend. He put his hands back on his hips and shook his head while his mates ran off.

'You're as bad as he is. Leyton fucking Orient!'

I shook my head. 'See you,' I said, laughing.

'*Au revoir*,' the kid said.

Upstairs in my flat I called the Ludensian to explain

what had happened. I wanted Nicky to let Jack know that I would help him, as long as he knew that I might not be able to do him any good. And I still thought he was being pretty irresponsible. I didn't want to put Nicky in the middle of something, and then feel embarrassed if he happened to mention one of us to the other. I could see a time when I was sat in the Ludensian, talking to Nicky, and Jack dropped by. I called the Ludensian but Toby said Nicky wasn't there. He'd left after just Jack Draper had, Toby told me. I tried his mobile but he was one of those people who had a mobile they never turned on. I left a message.

I was tired as a marathon runner's dog. I turned the TV on and stretched out on my futon in front of a review programme. Mark Lawson and friends were discussing a musical some bright spark had written about homelessness, and again I thought of the two girls I'd seen today, wondering if there was something I should have done, rather than simply watching them walk away. It wasn't the first time I'd had thoughts like that and I never knew if the decisions I made were the right ones. People have asked me why it is that I specialize in locating stray kids, but though I can give reasons enough I don't really know. My age is certainly on my side – I can get into the sorts of places kids drawn to London like to hang out, and I don't look like a pervert if I have to spend time inside video arcades or tube stations or skulking round the back streets of Soho peering into shop doorways at obviously young shapes huddling together beneath boxes and newspapers and stained sleeping bags. There is also the fact that I specialize, and as no one else who advertises seems to do that, I usually find myself with more than enough to do.

The real reason may be a little more complicated than expediency. The girl who came before Shulpa, who I'd thought wouldn't have anyone coming after her, used to say that it was because of the way I felt as a kid myself, that I sympathize with them now. She could have been right. When I left the police I did nothing for a while, and then I asked myself why I'd gone into it in the first place. Naïve as it sounds now, and it sounded naïve after only two or three days on the job as a matter of fact, I joined because I wanted to help people. I never wanted to nick single mothers on council estates for shoplifting in supermarkets, I wanted to catch people who caused other people pain. She used to say that an inbuilt sense of injustice had become a defining part of me, because of the way my father behaved towards my brother and me. And our mother. I'm no psychologist, but she may have been right. She was right about a lot of things, or at least she used to be. Who the hell knew what she was like now?

Images of Sharon came to me like a slide show. Thinking about her I suddenly wondered what she would say about Shulpa and me. I wondered if she'd be happy for me, or resentful, or not give a shit either way. I wondered if the word 'rebound' would figure in her conversation. I didn't know. And as much as I daydreamed about running into her, having that excuse to talk, maybe go for a cup of tea, casually tell her about my new girlfriend, I certainly wasn't going to do anything to find out.

Back on the TV the subject was a Tate Modern

retrospective on Tracy Emin and I sat in front of the debate for a while before obeying the strange impulse to put some washing on. Who said modern art didn't have a purpose? I bundled my sheets into the machine and came back and they were still talking, and I suddenly wished Tracy Emin was on the show too and that she be allowed to comment on Tony Parsons' shirt. The conversation moved on to a play I had no intention of seeing and I hit the off button. I sat on my futon for a while and then fetched fresh sheets for it. I paused for a second, remembering where I'd been when I'd bought the sheets, why I'd chosen that colour, and nearly decided not to bother. But they were the only spare ones I had, so I had to use them. I cleaned my teeth before getting under the crisp, fresh covers, telling myself to take it easy with Shulpa for a while. I turned the light out, and pictured a long dark corridor it would take me at least eight hours to get to the end of.

Chapter Five

But it was no use. After the morning I'd spent, getting up early for tax reasons, and then the day I'd spent, I thought I'd slide off faster than an autumn leaf down a running weir. But I didn't, and at first I didn't know why. My Jungle-loving neighbour had moved out a while ago and Alberto had been careful enough of my sleeping patterns not to give me an espresso. I just took it as one of those things, and turned a light on. I read for a while but I couldn't concentrate – as much, I felt, due to Mr Kureishi as to me. I poured myself a good slug of John Powers to see if that would do anything. Then I tried stretching, as though the exhaustion I knew I felt was blocked in me somehow and needed tapping. Sometimes I did find it hard to sleep after a particularly heavy day and stretching often helped.

But not this time. It couldn't dispel the picture in my head. Eventually, it came to me. It was that, nothing else, that was bolting my mind open. I tried to ignore it, reasoning that because I'd identified what it was that was keeping me awake, it wouldn't any more. I was wrong. I said fuck out loud and stood, calling myself an idiot, and then I picked up my jeans from the back of my reading chair.

I pulled my jeans on like a reluctant schoolboy and

looked around for a tee-shirt, with the picture still
stuck in my mind. I pulled on the socks I'd taken off
earlier and slid my feet back into my Red Wings,
yanking hard at the laces. All the time I could see a
woman pushing a pram. I thought about what I saw as
Jack Draper's selfishness in not going to the police,
then of my own stubbornness in not agreeing to help
him, and wondered how it would make me feel if, on
a bizarre off-chance and because of these two things,
these two very male things, something terrible happened to the woman in the picture. And her baby.
Something, any number of things. Especially if it happened before I could register my willingness to help
in the matter. I would feel worse than terrible and
Draper would always, *always* blame me and Nicky
would say it wasn't my fault at all but secretly wonder
why the hell I'd been so negative and . . .

I stopped what I was doing and sighed. I knew I
was being less than reasonable. If Draper hadn't found
me in Fred's, then tonight would have passed without
my involvement anyway. But I couldn't help it. People
who can cut a cat's head off and nail it to a door are
probably capable of quite a bit more besides. There
was no way I was going to sleep, no way, not wondering what they could be up to now. There was a
night, a night eight years ago when I could have done
something, something as simple as picking up a telephone. And I hadn't done it. And every two weeks I
go to a hospital north of London and look at the result
of my not doing so. At least every two weeks, for eight
years, looking at a face that can't look back at me.
My brother's face, getting slowly older in strange and
obscene parallel with my own. And now this thing was

there, nagging at me, like knowing you've set the alarm the night before something important but still turning the light back on to check anyway. You just have to do it. I pulled the tee-shirt over my head and reached for my jacket.

Still swearing at myself I jogged downstairs and through the now steady drizzle to my old, brown Mazda, which hummed into life with no fuss at all due to the recent service which had almost certainly cost more than the damn thing was worth. I was wide awake and I stopped to think for a second. All I had was the name of a road, having seen it in one of the photographs. That, and the make of a car. I had no sort of plan. I'd think of one on the way. I pulled out towards Old Street and twenty minutes later I was cruising past the thin, naked skeletons of market stalls dripping with rain outside Whitechapel Tube Station.

The rain was a lot less tentative now, picked up by a rising wind and blown in broad sheets across the street in front of me, making it hard to see. As I took a right it smacked hard, straight into my windscreen, laced with the odd rock of hail. I slowed, making sure I had the right street. I did; Stepney Green. I closed my *A to Z* and left it on the passenger seat. I pulled forward, slowly. I was on a wide road with a long series of gardens running down the middle surrounded by tall, black iron railings. I didn't have a house number for Jack Draper and his family, only the street name, and I cruised down at a crawl, casting my eyes around for the blue Renegade that someone as yet unknown had snapped him in. I slowed even more, and then moved forward along the black tarmac, streaked tiger-skin orange from the street lights, checking out the vehicles parked on either side of me.

I still didn't know what I was going to do. Quickly I decided that if I found Draper's house then I'd knock on his door and apologize for the way things had gone. Bite my tongue as we kissed and made up. Then, if he wanted me to help him we'd work out where we should go from there. And if I didn't find the house? Well, I'd just have to park up and wait until morning, trying to keep warm, making sure no one on the street was up to anything they shouldn't be. I shivered at the thought and said a short but very sincere prayer, hoping that the latter would not be the case.

I'm not a God-fearing man but every now and then He must do favours for strangers because my prayer came true, almost immediately. The rain was continuing to assault my windscreen but somehow my eyes were drawn by a slight movement. At the top of the street, to my right, a row of Georgian houses curved down towards a red-brick building with an old sign telling me that it was called Dunstan House, and had been put up in 1899. I was still looking for Jack's Renegade but my eyes went to a door, a red door opening in one of the houses closest to the block. I pulled in to the left and slowed. Somehow, I instantly knew that I'd found the place I was looking for.

That's when I should have gone home.

Through the thick rush of water sluicing down my windscreen I saw the door open and a woman emerge. The woman had a sports bag slung over her shoulder and a covered carrycot held low in her left hand. She was moving quickly, slanted over to one side though her head was directly forward. She looked annoyed.

She was followed out by a man who I could instantly see was Jack Draper.

There was a space to my left and I pulled into it, my eyes never leaving the scene in front of me. Jack was remonstrating with the woman, his big shoulders being pounded by the rain as he tried to get an umbrella open at the same time. The rain was too loud for me to make out what Jack was saying but he wasn't getting much of a response from his wife, who was striding in front of him with her head down and her mouth shut tight. She marched along the pavement taking small, fast steps. She was moving away from me, now crossing the street to the same side I was parked.

Jack had got the umbrella open now and was trying without much success to hold it above his quickly moving wife and their baby. He had to step behind her when a car swooshed by. His wife still hadn't said anything to him, though Jack was quite obviously pleading with her. It was as if he wasn't there. She snapped a quick look over her shoulder to check for further traffic and then started marching along the line of parked cars. As she did so, I caught sight of the Renegade, up ahead of her. I thought she was making for it, but instead she stopped just before it and used her right hand to open the hatchback boot of a small, soap-mould Fiat. Jack stood holding the umbrella over her, not really knowing where to stand, looking like he just wanted to pick her up and bodily carry her back inside, while his wife, Louise, I suddenly remembered, slung her bag into the boot and then slammed the lid down hard.

I watched as Jack's wife secured their baby's

carrycot onto the back seat of the small car. I didn't know they could double up like that. She didn't say a single word to Jack that I could see, and after a while he gave up, just helping her and then standing in the road with his hands on his hips. He put the umbrella in the car and then I watched as his wife, acting as though Jack were invisible, simply stepped into the car and drove away, down towards Canary Wharf, towering above the sodden trees at the far end of the street. When the car was out of sight I looked back to see Draper, still with his hands on his hips, facing the empty road his wife had driven down, ignoring the rain as it plastered his hair onto the side of his face and streamed down his neck into his tee-shirt.

I had to admit I felt sorry for him. If I'd agreed to help, I didn't think this would be happening. Jack shook his head and turned away. I put my hand on the door handle, about to jump out and call to him, but before I could do it he turned, in a flash, and through the rain I caught a low, dull thump as he sent his famous left foot hard into the back passenger door of the Renegade. From where I was I couldn't see if he'd put a dent in it, though it did look like he might have. He turned away immediately and stomped back to his house. I took my hand off the handle and watched as he slammed the door behind him.

That's when I should have gone home. The rain let up a touch and then came down harder, like a flurry of jabs from my friend Des, just when you think he's tiring. I turned my wipers on and watched the house. I'd leave him a while and then ring his doorbell. I wouldn't tell him that I'd been sitting outside. No one likes witnesses to their domestic disputes. Telling him that I'd just seen his wife leave wouldn't endear me to him overmuch. Not that I cared that much about what he thought – it wasn't him but the picture of his wife that had dragged me out in that miserable night. But I didn't want another fight with him. I'd give him a little while to cool off, though, before telling him I'd help him out if he still wanted. Then he could call his wife and make it up with her and I could go back home, knowing she was safe at her mother's or somewhere. And I could forget about them both – at least until morning. I'd think about Shulpa instead, what her methods of curing my insomnia might have been.

It felt good to see the end of this nonsense and I felt myself relax into my seat. My windscreen was starting to steam up and I turned the fan on it. I yawned and stretched, keeping an eye on Draper's house. I flipped open the glove compartment, looking for my Chet Baker CD to while away the minutes. I couldn't find it. I slid Roberta Flack in instead, getting through about half of 'The First Time That Ever I Saw Your Face' before I had to hit the eject. Those lines about the sun rising in her eyes. I filled my head with thoughts of Shulpa instead. I couldn't believe how lucky I'd been to find her so soon. I pictured her deep black eyes. I tried to figure out what it was about her. She was so not the kind of girl I ever imagined I'd be with. I remembered meeting her, at Nicky's birthday party. I remembered the smell of her, that most of all. I could almost feel it now. How it got to me, how it would be there in my flat, hours after she'd left. Other things. The way she bit on her bottom lip without knowing it. How she'd almost completely scrubbed me clean of the feelings I'd been going through when I'd first met her, feelings that only ever seemed to surface when I was alone. I shook my head, wondering what the hell she was hanging around with me for. A private detective with no real prospects who didn't earn as much in a week as you'd need to pay for the dresses she usually wore. I wasn't arguing but I couldn't help wondering. I used to do this with Sharon too, only in a different way . . .

It hadn't occurred to me that Draper would be coming out of his house again that night and even though he was right in front of me he'd crossed the road and was a yard away from his Jeep before the blip from his alarm brought me back into the street. It must have been the heat from the fan. I sure as hell wouldn't have had any trouble sleeping by now. I pushed myself upright. But before I could collect myself he was in the car and pulling away fast, up towards the Mile End Road. He was past me before I could wave at him. I hit my horn but he took no notice.

'Fuck.'

Shulpa vanished, like she did in the very early morning sometimes, leaving me a pillow to wake up to. I started the Mazda. I yanked the wheel and turned round, having to make a three pointer out of it. Then I pulled off, my left tyre mounting the pavement with a jolt. I wondered if Draper would do a U-turn, and follow his wife. Instead he made it through an amber, turning left towards Whitechapel. I sat at the light, tapping my thumbs, come on, come on, and saw him pull a right onto a cut-through leading up towards Bethnal Green.

I shook my head and swore at myself quite inventively as I tried to catch Draper through Bethnal Green, then up towards Hackney. How much easier would it have been to say sure, I'll help, though I'm probably not your best option? Two fifty a day okay? Fine. If you ever get any tickets for the Cup Final . . . I felt like a man who hadn't been bothered to tie up his boy's kite properly and was now chasing it through a field of nettles. All I wanted to do was talk to the man. Draper drove fast along Bethnal Green High Street and took a right towards Hoxton. He seemed to be in a hurry. I drove on, trying to catch him, wanting to let him know that I'd help him, wanting to tell him not to panic. He took a left and then a right and when I took that too I thought I'd lost him. I pulled up. I turned my wipers up to maximum. The rain was crashing into my windscreen like a wave of kamikaze pilots. Through them I just caught Draper's tail lights cutting a left onto Hoxton Square itself, and I followed them.

This would be my chance. He couldn't go round the square that quick. I could get right behind him and then flash him or hop out at a red light and tap on his window. A quick chat, say I'd do what I could. Then, with his wife safe at her mother's or somewhere I'd go home, to my bed, to the tunnel I'd been looking down. Shorter now but very welcome nonetheless. I pulled onto Hoxton Square and felt myself relax again, as the brake lights on Draper's Renegade flared misty red, only twenty yards ahead of me.

The unmarked Sierra behind me only had to give a short flash of blue for me to realize that it was there. My whole body jumped, none of it in the same direction. My foot hit the brake and my eyes went to the mirror. I squinted into the blue light filling my car then looked at the road again. What the hell had I done? The car slowed and I changed down automatically, before pulling to the side of the road and killing the engine. I looked in my mirror again. The lights were off, but the Sierra had pulled in behind me.

I wasn't that inventive this time. 'Cunt,' I said. 'Cunt. *Cunt.*'

I sat with my hands on the wheel. The rain sounded like I was in a tent and I wished to fuck that I was, far away. All of a sudden I laughed. What else was going to happen? Eventually I pulled myself together and dragged myself out, the way you should, keeping my eye on the Renegade, which was manoeuvring to park thirty yards away across the square. Through shafts of rain I could see Draper at the wheel. I thought about the defenders he tormented every week. Was this what it was like trying to get hold of him?

I stood in front of the man, my palms to the sky. He was tall, young and not that bright-looking.

'Your brake lights, sir,' he explained. 'Did you know one of them wasn't working?'

He stood there in a mac, seemingly oblivious to the rain crashing down onto his hat and well-protected shoulders. In the car behind him I could see his partner, looking bored, whistling to himself. I had a brief flash of the mechanic, giving me my car keys back following my service. I had a brief flash of what I was going to do to him.

The rain on my head was cold and hard. I looked at the light then back at the officer. I did my best amazed. I told the officer that I had *no idea* about the light, and thanked him profusely for bringing the matter to my attention. I'd get it fixed, first thing. He could be sure. Over his shoulder I could see Jack Draper, pushing the buzzer on a block of expensive-looking converted flats. He wasn't getting a reply. I made to return to my car.

He wasn't going to let me do that.

'You also seemed to be in a bit of a *hurry*, sir. Not very sensible, is it, in this weather?'

I agreed with him wholeheartedly. Shaking my head I told him, while not attempting to excuse myself in any way at all, that I was tired and just wanted to get home. I went further. I thanked him for stopping me, for letting me know that I was not driving safely, assuring him that I'd take it very easy indeed the rest of the way. He nodded patiently.

'That would be best, sir. You haven't been drinking at all, have you?'

'No.'

'Not at lunch perhaps, any time today?'

'No. Nothing. Absolutely nothing at all.'

Unlike mine, his coat was completely waterproof. He wasn't in a hurry. In less than a minute I was soaked and freezing. Jack was still leaning on the door-bell. Then I saw him reach into his pocket. For an address? Had he got the wrong flat? I asked the policeman if that was all. He didn't answer. Instead, he checked the Mazda over carefully and methodically, and I had to admire his attention to detail. He certainly took his time, but eventually he was done, having found nothing else wrong with it – except, of course, that it was a piece of shit. I looked at him expectantly.

'Oh, I'm going to have to write you a ticket, I'm afraid, sir.' He looked quite outraged at the mere idea of letting me off it.

'Mind if we sit in your vehicle to do it, no point in getting wet now, is there?'

I walked back to the car, pretty sure I could see a smile on his face. I gave up being nice to him. His partner still looked bored. Across the square, Jack was gone. He must have been buzzed in. I unlocked my passenger door. The officer brought at least a gallon of water into my car and wrote me the ticket. Then he left me, my back damp against the seat-back, my jeans tightening round my legs.

'Twat,' I said, not exactly sure who I was thinking of.

I sat with my arms folded and watched him in the mirror, getting back in the squad car, next to his chum. Now he definitely was laughing. They both were. I waited, hoping the Sierra would pull away, but they were obviously waiting for me. I revved the engine but they still sat there. Eventually I pulled off and drove round the square with the car behind me. I pulled off onto Coronet Street while the police car made its way towards Old Street. Then I headed back into Hoxton Square and parked exactly where I'd just been stopped.

By the clock in my car I could see that it was now after two. How had it got that late? I checked my mirror, opened the door and got out. I stepped off the pavement and headed across the road. I was sure as hell going to speak to Jack Draper. And I was going to do it tonight, if it was the last thing I did. I was cold and wet and very pissed off. Not a sense of humour failure. A total meltdown. No longer feeling the rain, I marched over to the apartment building.

In a modern porch-way up four broad steps I stared at two columns of big, round, silver buttons, thirty-two in all, trying to decide which flat Jack Draper had entered. Number thirty-two was at the bottom of the last column and there was a droplet of water on it, with a few splashes on the silver underneath. It had to be that one. The steps were wet beneath it, just where Draper had been standing. I pressed it, and waited. Nothing. I pressed it again. I was just wondering if I *could* have got the wrong one when I heard a noise behind me. A very well-dressed but very drunk woman, trying to keep hold of an umbrella, was waddling towards the steps. Using the rail to steady herself she made it to the door, seemingly oblivious to me. As if I were not there, she searched her purse for her keys, finding them remarkably quickly. I followed her through the door and towards the lift, stepping round her when she turned to enter one of the ground-floor apartments. There were four buttons, plus a basement. I hit the top one and waited.

That's when I should have gone home. As the lift set off I could hear the lift to my left, coming down. The lift was very slow, and I could feel the cold, the rain having got right through to my tee-shirt. I was glad when it slowed and stopped, at four. I stepped out into a brightly lit lobby, with two corridors leading directly away from each other. Not corridors, really, but an open, covered walkway. A sign pointed towards thirty-one and thirty-two, but I wouldn't have needed them because a muddle of wet footprints on the cement floor led to them just as well. With the gait of a farmer walking up to a cornered fox I started to add to them.

But I stopped almost immediately. I heard a blip, a blip I recognized. A lot of people have car alarms but somehow they tend not to sound alike. I turned. There was a window in the lobby, next to the lift, and I stepped towards it, a frown forming on my forehead. I heard an engine being gunned into life and a set of tyres squalling against wet tarmac. I took the last step quickly and was just in time to see the top of the Renegade, lurching away from the pavement below, swinging towards the line of cars parked opposite it, just managing to compensate in time. In a second it had swerved away from them. Then it was out of the square.

I stood still for a second, my hands by my sides, nothing on my face. Slowly, I turned back to face the harshly lit corridor, leaning back on the wall. No. I couldn't believe it. It wasn't happening. I took a step to my left but the thought of chasing Jack Draper back out into the rain came and went faster than he had. It just wasn't worth it. I stood still for a moment, my mouth open. Less than an hour ago I'd been in bed. Now I was cold and soaked, standing in a block of flats I had no business being in, with a fine to pay and my documents to produce within the week, documents I wasn't sure were absolutely up to date. Marvellous. I scraped my nails back over my scalp and shook my head. I glanced up at the corridor. It was a short passageway broken up by two doors and I didn't pay much attention to it until a shiver ran down my entire body like a king snake hurrying down a rock face. It was nothing to do with the rain.

There were two doors ahead of me and I looked at them. I didn't move. I couldn't. One of them was ajar. I didn't have to be told that it was number thirty-two. I stood a second longer, just looking at it. It was only open an inch, maybe less. A light was on but I couldn't see inside. I couldn't see anything. But I knew. Sometimes you just do. Sometimes it just settles on you, or rather in you, settles in your stomach and in your bowels, an ice-cold sheet, lead heavy. And then you are bound to it. Bound to it because you've sensed it, bound to it because you recognized it before you saw it, bound because you're the sort of person who *could* recognize it. And it sickens you. It sickens you because of what it is, and because you're the sort of person who knew it. My throat turned over. My stomach pulled like a lurcher on a short lead.

And that's when I really should have gone home. Because I knew it. But I didn't. Instead I moved forward along the walkway, my eyes on the crack in the door. Instead I pushed the door open with my sleeve, and looked into the apartment.

It was a pleasant apartment, kind of golden, with more fake wood flooring and a thick cream rug, uplighters and lamps spreading a soft glow over smooth yellow walls. There were two inviting armchairs facing me from across the room with a coffee table separating them from a broad, high-backed putty-coloured sofa. And over the back of the sofa was a mess of hair, of golden hair to match the light.

I didn't bother with a hello. It was too quiet. Even the furniture looked too static, as if it were tense, scared to move. Instead of going home I walked round the sofa and looked at her. She was leaning back, her arms by her sides. The wounds she had were in her stomach, all over her chest and on her breasts, on her arms and her shoulders, her thighs and on her face. Many, many of them. Some slashes, some short

57

some longer, puncture marks mostly. There was a lot of blood. Her open dressing gown was soaked in it and the cushions beneath her and the cream rug. One of her nipples had been torn, nearly torn right off. It hung to the side by a thread, like an open bottle cap.

Her left eye was open. I couldn't tell if her right eye was open or shut. I turned away. A long thin knife had been rammed into it up to the hilt.

Chapter Six

At seven next morning I was sitting in a small café on Rosebery Avenue called Zack's Snacks, a place used at that time of day by cab drivers and postal workers. I was squeezed on a table next to two middle-aged women just off the night shift in the sorting office opposite. I was drinking coffee and waiting for a couple of slices of toast I was never going to eat. Images were running through my head like luggage through an airport scanner. Photographs, a cat's head, a woman leaving with her baby. A body. A face, streaked with blood and tissue. The images were completely separate from each other, with no connection that I could see, each one more disturbing than the last. I looked into the shining black surface of my coffee instead.

I felt hollow and flat, my insides pulled like a sturgeon's. I drank the coffee but I could hardly taste it. I ran a hand over my face and it didn't feel like mine. A man sitting opposite me was reading the *Sun*. I watched him, his mouth moving slowly, a piece of egg flapping from his bottom lip. When he'd finished he left the paper face down on the table between us, got up and left. I pulled the paper towards me and, because it was the *Sun*, didn't bother with the front page, turning straight to the back. There'd been a few games last night. It would be something to read, to look at. I read the whole of the back page, taking nothing in, and that's why I didn't see the caption to begin with, the caption on the front page telling me to turn to the centre – if I wanted to read about the latest goings-on in the life of a man that I knew.

I stayed in the room Jack Draper had fled from about three minutes. Three minutes that felt like forty. The feeling I'd had was right, but it didn't keep out the shock. Everything stopped in me. It seemed strange to think it, but even though she was dead she looked so vulnerable. Naked, hurt. There were marks on her hands, she'd obviously tried to defend herself. I wanted to cover her, to keep her warm. To draw that knife out of her face. I had an impulse to pull her gown closed. I couldn't do it, but I wanted to, if only to keep myself from imagining the frenzy, the rush of violence that must have left her like this. I turned my head away from her. To the door. Then the feeling of horror, of a nauseating, clock-heavy grief, gave way to something else.

I wanted to get out of there. The impulse rushed through me like a short espresso but I fought it, moving over and pushing the door shut instead. I'd been stopped in the area by the police. Nothing in itself, but someone bright might not take too long to make a connection between myself and Jack Draper. I knew I might have to face some questions later and if that was the case I needed to get some answers first.

The door clicked shut, a sound far too loud in that quiet. Again I fought the panic, the impulse to simply get out as quick as I could. I turned and looked back into the room. Then I went through the place, quickly, but as slowly as I could make myself. I stayed long enough to discover the name of the girl on the sofa, long enough to take a look in a couple of drawers and a longer one at a photographic collage hung behind glass in the flat's small kitchen area. There were lots of pictures, some of a little girl, some of teenagers on a beach, some of a middle-aged man I took to be her father. Most, however, were of groups of people, smiling, huddling into frame, drinks in their hands, having a good time. I focused on one shot, the most recent-looking and also the clearest I could see. It was of a golden-haired girl with an oval face, a rash of freckles like spilled rice running over and around a nose so perfect I wondered if she'd had help with it. She was dressed in a sleeveless silver sheath, at what looked like a pretty swanky party, with a lot of men around her, none of whom I recognized. The men looked happy. So did the girl. I stared at the girl's face. I wanted to know what she looked like, to fix her in my mind. On the sofa, it wasn't easy to tell that.

Back in the living room I took a very quick skirt around the sofa, looking for anything that might have been left. I checked beneath the sofa and on top of it, lifting a couple of cushions, spattered with whirls of red as though Jackson Pollack had killed her. I didn't see anything. Finally, I must have spent ten seconds simply looking down at her. I tried to look at a corpse, a matrix of events, of clues that could help me reel back the threads that had unravelled to leave her there. Not at a girl, a young woman lying dead and stupid-looking with a knife in her eye socket, the cheek below it covered in blackish blood and whatever it is that makes up the creamy, effulgent mess that is usually on the inside of someone's eye. I blinked away, having seen something clear and gelatinous clinging to the hilt of the knife.

I stared at her other eye, open, still wide, empty but for a little picture of me, looking down at her from a thousand miles away. Then I blinked again and bent down, my eyes pressing into her wounds. I didn't touch her. I didn't try to check for rigor or feel for her temperature, to see how cold she'd become. I did take a breath, quite consciously, getting urine, then blood, and excreta. Not old. I looked at the wounds she had, and tried to estimate how tall she was. Not more than about five four. In almost all of the cases the blade had come down on her.

The last thing I looked at was her hair, spread out on the back of the sofa, almost as if she were preparing for a photo shoot. In the kitchen there was a shot of her lying on an armchair, her hair splashed out like that. A little girl, dressed as a nurse, a square plastic case in her hand with a bright red cross on. There was a look on her ten-toothed face of pure, unrestrained glee.

I turned away. Now it really was time to go. I walked across the room and stood by the door until I was sure I couldn't hear anything, then turned the handle. I looked back at her one more time, now just a mess of gold over the sofa back. I found it hard to leave, as though I were abandoning her. Eventually, though, I turned, and stepped out into the hallway. I used the stairs. I left the building by the rear door and took the long way back to my car, entering the square from the furthest corner to the flat. I didn't pass any-one. I got into the Mazda, shut the door and let out a breath. I started her up and pulled away, trying not to drive on my brakes. It didn't take me long to get back. My bed was there waiting for me but I didn't sleep. I didn't even try. Instead I stood beneath the shower, scrubbing every inch of my body. At seven the sun still hadn't risen but I walked down onto the market anyway.

My eyes moved over a report of a Man U defeat in the second group phase of the Champions' League. There was a big picture of Roy Keane with his head in his hands, after what was a very expensive miss – in every sense of the word. It didn't matter, though, the report stated, because two teams qualified to go on to the knockout competition and United were bound to be one of those. I looked at the table. So far there had been two stages of group matches in the European Cup and it seemed to me that it was almost impossible to get knocked out of the damn thing. Just more games that didn't matter for the TV companies to sell.

Zack and his staff were inundated and the toast I didn't care about was taking a while. The women to my left were talking about their supervisor, who they both fancied doing a bit of sorting with. They were laughing and joking, tired and easy after work, but to me their voices sounded like they were coming out of a radio. Nothing around me was real. I drained my coffee and held my cup up for another. I was strung out and tired, with cramps in my belly and an electric hum singing in my head. I wanted the women to shut the fuck up. I wanted to scream don't you know what has only just happened? Don't you know what I have seen? Zack filled my cup in passing and I sat it down but didn't touch it.

Next to the Man U report was a piece on the latest record wage demand from the current hot-shot striker in the Premiership, which made Roy Keane's weekly take home look like pocket money. I went backwards through the paper until I got to the racing, which is a foreign language to me. My thoughts jerked back like a sprung door to Alison Everly, still staring into nothing. My one regret was leaving her there, but I consoled myself with the knowledge that I'd called it in. I'd decided against 999 because they recorded all calls, as well as giving the caller's location. Instead I'd left a short, heavily muffled message on the machine of an old police colleague of mine, who would think it was one of his snitches. With any luck he'd find the message when he got up for his early shift.

Just as I hadn't been able to go home without telling someone about her, I couldn't imagine being able to sit back and do nothing about what had happened to Alison Everly. I didn't plan on making it a personal crusade, but I did wonder how I felt about telling the police that I'd seen Draper going into her building. I knew I would do it, if time went by and they didn't come up with anything. I didn't care whose friend he was. I didn't know that Draper had done it – he'd been there, yes, but then so had I, and it wasn't me – but he had to have some sort of link to her. What the hell could she have done for him to kill her? I pictured what Nicky would say when I told him that I was going to turn his friend in.

A small cloud billowed towards me from the woman on my left. I turned the paper over, wondering what shattering piece of crucial world news the editor of the paper had chosen to flag his publication with that day. A picture of Chris Evans greeted me. He was arm in arm with a woman I didn't recognize, but the editor had assumed I would have. I didn't stop to find out who she was, though. Nor did I wonder why anyone should care that she was going out with Mr Evans except for her mother because in a box at the bottom of the page was the face of another girl, a girl I did recognize. It stopped me like I'd walked into a glass wall.

I couldn't believe what my eyes were telling me.

I stared at her face. I don't know how long. I suddenly realized that I'd stopped breathing. I turned to the centre pages. She was there too, dressed in a bikini, lying on a bed, her head in her hands. Her golden hair was swept over one side of her head like a wave in a Japanese painting. She had an uncertain look on her face, a mixture, it seemed to me, of hurt and guilt. You couldn't see her freckles.

HE JUST USED ME

The woman to my left was saying something. She was asking me to pass her the sugar. It sounded like the fifth time she'd said it.

'You all right, love? Look like you've seen a ghost.'

More pictures were spread over the two pages, most of them of Alison. In the top right corner was a small shot of a couple, posing with their baby. Below was a head shot of a man with very shiny hair, grinning, the collars of his football shirt just visible.

MY NIGHTS OF LOVE WITH FOOTBALLER
JACK DRAPER

I shook my head and apologized. I slid the shaker over and looked back at the newspaper. A very clear and obvious connection. I looked at the pictures and read the article twice before my mind went back to the conversation I'd had with Nicky, in my office. Less than twenty-four hours ago Nicky and I had joked around a bit until he had eventually told me that his friend Jack Draper might be in some sort of trouble.

Draper's big, square face smiled back at me.

He was now.

Part Two

Part Two

Chapter Seven

One very long day later I was sitting in a well-kept if slightly chintzy living room, looking at some notes I'd made and waiting for a cup of coffee. I heard feet on the stairs and a young boy came round the banister, aged around nine or ten.

He stopped still when he saw me.

'Who are you?'

'I'm a friend of Mrs Draper's,' I said. 'You?'

'I live next door. My name's Michael.' He was a well-spoken, intense little boy, with a slight lisp. He looked at me for a second, before pushing his thick, clear plastic glasses up his nose. 'I've been playing Jack's Dreamcast. My dad won't let me have one. He doesn't know I play Jack's. They're Jack's medals.'

The little boy pointed at a glass case in the corner, full of cups, medals, two or three scarves. He'd said it like Jack was a World War Two veteran.

I turned back to him.

'Impressive.'

'He said he'd get us tickets. In the Cup, when New-castle come. March the 5th. He said he was going to show Alan Shearer how to do it.'

I smiled. Not difficult, these days. 'It'll be a great game.'

'It will.' He paused again, and looked sad. 'My daddy's a doctor. He's no good at football. I wish he was like Jack. Jack's taught me loads of tricks. Are you a friend of Jack's as well as Mrs Draper?'

'Yes,' I said. 'Yes.' The kid looked at his feet.

'They say he killed a girl, don't they? They say he stabbed her. Stabbed her to death.'

'Yes.' I nodded. 'Yes. They do say that.'

'At school they all say it. Everyone. They call him Jack Raper. But I say they're wrong. I got in a fight.' He paused again and looked nervous. He didn't really want to ask, but he went ahead.

'*Did* he do it?'

'I don't know,' I said. 'I don't know about that. No one does.'

'He's hiding, isn't he, Jack is? No one's seen him. Do you know where he is?'

'No,' I said. I could hear Mrs Draper in the kitchen, about to walk through to us. 'No. I'm afraid that nobody knows that either.'

When I left Zack's it was after eight. I was still in a kind of daze. It had got light without me noticing. I walked past Fred's and saw Draper again, wound up tight, tapping his thumb on the table. I saw how he had snapped, jumping up, telling me to fuck off. All because I'd told him I couldn't help him. Again I wondered what would have happened if I'd just said sure, I'll help, though I'm probably not your best option. Would he then have gone off to the flat on Hoxton Square and done what he had?

The morning was cold and I hadn't bothered with

a coat. I climbed the stairs to my flat, amazed at how suddenly my life had flipped on me. I shook my head and made a few phone calls, one of which was to Nicky, but again I only got his voicemail. I was confused. There was just too much to take in. I wasn't ready for it. I shook the whole lot away and managed to get my head down for an hour. I had a dream in which I went to see my brother, Luke, in the hospital that has been his home for the last eight years. It's rare that I dream and this one was clearer than any I could remember. Luke was lying on his bed, as he always is, not moving, not speaking, his grey eyelids closed to the world, only his shallow breathing and the monitors to the right of his head giving any indication that he is still alive. I dreamed that I was telling him about my new girlfriend, about Shulpa, telling him what she was like. The only thing was that Shulpa was standing there beside me, completely naked, and I was discussing her as if she weren't there, telling Luke to open his eyes, he really wouldn't want to miss *that*. Even in my dream I felt sleazy. Waking up felt like an escape even though I craved sleep. I got up quickly and plunged my face into a sink of cold water.

It hadn't gone away. None of it. It was all still there, waiting for me to decide what the hell I was going to do. I tried Nicky but again I couldn't get hold of him. My hand hovered over the phone a few times, my finger over the nine. But I didn't call the police. There was time for that. Rushing it wouldn't do a lot for Alison Everly. I needed to think, to talk to Nicky. Instead I made one last call, to the *Independent* newspaper, and then, glad of having made some sort of decision, I grabbed my car keys and walked downstairs.

I parked the Mazda next to a sleek modern Jag on the west edge of the large, green space, and looked at my watch. It was just after eleven. I clicked through the events of last night again until I came to the picture of Alison in the *Sun*. There most definitely had to be a connection between the photographs I'd seen and Draper's actions, of Alison lying dead, then in a centre-fold, but what it was, was a mystery to me. I didn't know why Draper had really come to see me or if it had anything to do with Alison. I didn't know anything, except that I wished, beyond measure, that I'd eaten somewhere else last night.

I sat for a minute, yawning. The sleep I'd had had only reminded my body that such a state was possible, it hadn't helped. I slapped the side of my face a few times and looked out of the window. I didn't imagine I would be the only person looking for Jack Draper and I craned my head around for journalists. Draper was the kind of footballer Vinnie Jones used to be, with a far higher profile than his footballing achievements would have got him. There would be plenty of hacks who'd want his reaction to having been caught with a pretty 'model', though I didn't imagine there would be any who wanted to ask him the sort of questions I wanted to ask him. Not yet. They'd just want to push his nose in it, go through the same routine they usually did. Kiss and sell, it was becoming a regular industry, with standard procedures. They probably taught it at journalism school. First, put aside any sense of right and wrong. Then get the man himself, after which the missus. I saw her, Jack's wife, stomping off into the night. Had he told her? Had the editor phoned him, out of 'courtesy', to warn him? Had he then gone and hacked at Alison in a frenzy, for doing it to him? I didn't know. I peered through my windscreen, out over the grass. There were no photographers that I could see but I couldn't be sure until I got out there.

The area of Wanstead Flats I was looking at was an uninspiring piece of land surrounded by a flyover, a row of shops and some large Victorian houses. I pushed open the door of the Mazda. A long cold claw of wind reached straight in and I pulled it shut again. In the distance, I could see a haze of small figures running around between some football posts and what looked to me like portable five-a-side goals. I thought about staying where I was, waiting until they broke, but I had no idea how long that would be. I locked the car then walked quickly across the crunchy grass towards the group of tiny figures, the sound of men shouting reaching me through the crisp air, backed by the dull whump of feet on leather.

A friend of mine on the *Independent* sports desk had told me where Leyton Orient train. I'd caught her there, not long after leaving Zack's. I worried a bit about asking her, and she had sniffed around a bit, but I couldn't think of any other way to find out. No one was answering at the club, and with their lead striker in the paper they probably wouldn't have been too keen to tell me anyway.

The day was definitely cold rather than fresh, a frigid east wind whipping my collar against my neck and playing havoc with the crosses several of the men in front of me were trying to practise. Others were doing sprints or practising skills, while two goalkeepers were diving around after the balls some younger lads were throwing. I dug my hands in my pockets, looking from face to face. Then I just watched them, with interest, never having seen a team train before.

No one seemed to notice me or be put off by my presence. There was a big pile of kit on the halfway line and I saw a gaunt Asian-looking man in his sixties standing next to it, with light skin to match a black cashmere overcoat, belted over a thin frame. He was watching the action, next to a younger man wearing what looked to me like a chauffeur's cap. The players all certainly seemed to be working very hard, and I wondered if this guy's presence might have had something to do with it.

After ten minutes the players all stopped what they were doing and stood, catching their breaths, their hands on their hips, steam coming off them like racehorses. I thought the session was over but instead the manager, a bull terrier of a Scot with a bobble hat and a limited vocabulary, handed out red bibs and organized the players into two teams of ten, which went up against each other for another twenty minutes.

Draper wasn't there. I suddenly realized that it was a bit of a long shot that he would be. I stood watching the game anyway, trying to focus on what was in front of me. It was a mixture of some surprisingly good stuff and some pretty woeful rubbish. I picked out a couple of skilful midfield players and one lad in his teens, a winger with a hell of a lot of pace and almost as much touch, but who didn't know quite when to pass it. I winced when I saw him clattered by a lumbering centre back whose tackle was a good second too late. I was surprised by the tackling in general, which was more full-on than I'd thought would be the case on a training ground.

The manager played on one team but that didn't stop him screaming at the other, urging them to greater effort, telling them to run off the ball more, create more spaces. When a defender miss hit a back pass, letting the manager's team score, he didn't congratulate the young lad who'd dribbled round the keeper, instead turning on the defender.

'Useless cunt,' he spat. 'Who do think you are, Gary fucking Neville?'

He got a laugh for that but he wasn't trying to be funny. He continued to give his squad the benefit of his instruction for another ten minutes, before calling a halt to the proceedings. The red team won, both goals scored by the nippy teenager, a black kid with a big lightning flash shaved into the back of his scalp.

Both teams made their way to the pile of kit. I left it a minute and then walked towards them. The manager was zipping himself into a coat that made him look like a giant caterpillar – with arms. His face was as red as a skinned tomato. All around him players were pulling on sweatpants, coats, hats.

'Mr Janner?'

My friend on the *Indy* had given me his name. He carried on with what he was doing, not even glancing at me.

'You're a bit late, son. Most of your lot have been and gone. So why don't you piss off, eh?'

I couldn't help smiling to myself. I didn't know what kind of man Janner was but watching him train had warmed me to him. There was something about the way he abused his players that told me he really cared for them. I looked down at him.

'I'm not a journalist, Mr Janner.'

"Course you're not, lad. And I'm not a wee Jock with a foul temper this bright morning. Go on with yer, before I set big Willy our centre back on you.'

'I saw what he could do.'

'Then you'll know not to mess around wi' me, eh? Now scurry along, I've nothing to tell yer.'

He was packing up a sports bag. I stood in front of him. 'I'm not a journalist, really.'

'Then what are you?'

I thought about that. It would take too long.

'My name's Billy,' I said. 'I'm a friend of Jack Draper's.'

Finally, he looked at me, his chin going towards his throat. I couldn't tell whether he believed me or not.

'Are you now? Then I wished you'd have advised the daft little prick not to go screwing wee lasses with mouths bigger than their titties.'

'You've seen the *Sun*, then?'

'Oh aye, we've all seen it. We get it for the stock markets, you know.'

Again I smiled, until a picture of Alison came to me. 'I take it he never showed this morning.'

'You take it correctly. And when I speak to him, he'll take it correctly too. Not that I really blame him. About an hour ago there were more lenses here than in Dolland and fucking Aitchison.'

I smiled again. 'Did he phone, say anything?'

'Not a dicky.' He zipped up his bag and called to one of the teenagers I'd seen helping out the goalkeepers.

'Right,' I said. I looked around. 'What did you tell the press?'

It was his turn to smile. 'To fuck off. What else? When that didn't work I said he was at the football ground, getting physio.'

'And is he?'

'No. I don't know where he is. Having a long talk with his missus if he's any sense. Now is that all?'

The young lad picked up his bag and Janner, not waiting for a reply, followed a loose line of players, lumbering over to a squat concrete building I took to be a shower block. I followed.

'The young lad's good,' I said. 'The goal-scorer.'

He was up ahead of us, plugged into a Walkman, limping slightly with the knock he'd had.

'Potentially.'

'Been on yet at all, in the first team?'

'A couple of times, twenty minutes at the end. He did okay. Not sure he's quite ready yet.'

I nodded. 'You might have to find out for sure, though,' I said, 'and soon. Next game's Thursday, isn't it? I think you're going to have to play him.'

Janner laughed. 'Because our Jack's put his plug in the wrong socket? Oh no. I'll let him miss a session because of it but play, he will—'

'No,' I said, 'he won't be playing.'

It was my intention that something in my voice should stop Janner and it did so. He came to an abrupt halt and turned to me. He put his hands on his hips and let the last few people trail past us. Then he let out a breath.

'What do you know?' he said. He sounded weary, instantly resigned. 'What the fuck's happened?'

'You'll find out soon enough. Just tell me, how did he meet her?'

'I dunno,' Janner said, putting his hand to his forehead. He could tell I was serious and he took the worry straight into him. I could see him working it, instantly reorganizing his team. 'She modelled some kit in our programme, so the lads say. I think that was it. But why do you care?'

'You'll find out soon enough, really.'

He seemed to accept that. He let out another breath and shook his head. The wind played with the bobble on his hat like the swingball Luke used to beat me at as kids.

'Fifteen goals in twelve starts. Super bloody Jack! Best signing I ever made. Cost next to nothing. And there was me, already cleared a space on my sideboard for the Manager of the Month shield. I knew it was too good to last. What a fucking morning. Draper'll be out, you're telling me? Really?'

I pointed forward. 'Better get someone to look at that lad's leg. And if you speak to Draper, get him to call me. Billy. Okay? It's important.'

'Aye. Aye. And thanks, I suppose. Oh fuck, *fuck* it. Squires,' he screamed. 'Squires! Stop rotting your brain with that tuneless fucking druggie music and come over here. And cut that limp out, you sorry little pansy, or you'll not start against Crewe. Do you hear me?'

The lad turned. When he realized what Janner was telling him beneath the bluster he couldn't stop a huge grin splitting his young face.

'And you'd better learn to pass the twatting ball too, or else I'll be sending you back to your knife-wielding ghetto friends in fucking Harlesden or whichever crime-ridden filth-hole you were lucky enough to be plucked from by Mr Korai. You hear me, son?'

'Yes, boss.' Still the grin. He got a clip round the back of his head.

'Lightning you reckon you are, lad? Let's hope you're not fucking well struck by it, eh?'

I walked back to my car. When I got there the Jag I'd parked next to was turning round. The man in the back was looking out of it, a pad in his hand. He was writing something. As I dug out my keys he looked at me and our eyes met for a second. His eyes were dark and deep, with no expression at all. I held his look until the Jag swept round and pulled away.

I got out of the wind and drove through East London, slower going back, listening to a local news station to see if they had anything on a murder in Hoxton. They didn't, yet. I listened to a long piece on football, focusing on the fact that attendances were dropping all over the country. Has the bubble burst? the announcer asked. All the while I was thinking about Draper, the things he'd tried to tell me in Fred's. That bollocks about not wanting the police in on it because he cared about his wife and his child, he just wanted to protect his Big Move. It was crap, all of it. He just didn't want anyone around him who might let the papers know he was playing away, as he would have put it. He didn't want anyone finding out about Alison. He'd wanted me because he either thought I wouldn't discover anything or else, being Nicky's friend, I'd keep schtum. All he cared about was that it didn't come out, and then it did.

I was pretty sure Draper hadn't known he'd be in next day's papers when he'd found me in Fred's. Coming to see me then would have been the last thing on his mind. I saw him leaving the bar again and went through what must have happened next. He'd gone home and he did find out, somehow, and he'd either told his wife or she'd found out some other way. Either way. She'd left him, taking their baby. And then he flipped. He went round and put a knife in Alison for doing it to him. Or else he went round just to yell at her, call her bitch, and then he'd lost it. Whichever, he'd been so angry he hadn't been able to control himself, he hadn't been able to stop until she was dead three times over.

I got to Stepney Green in about twenty minutes. I didn't know if Draper would be home, but I didn't have any intention of stopping to find out. I just wanted to see the state of play. Once again I drove down slowly past the damp, green gardens. There were a lot of cars parked opposite Draper's house as well as a couple of powerful, plastic-looking motorbikes. As I'd expected, a group of men with long lenses were slouched on the railings outside looking bored. Draper either wasn't in or else he wasn't coming out, but the gang looked like they had all the time in the world. I moved on, looking away from the 'journalists' to the road. No patrol cars, no unmarked vehicles that I could see. They can't have made the connection yet or if they had, they hadn't told the press. But it wouldn't be long before some copper made himself a ton or so by tipping off a friend. I wondered how many lenses would be pointing at the door of number fourteen then.

Chapter Eight

Forty minutes later I was in my office. I'd gone back to check the post and my machine, see if I had any more work. The trip out of Wanstead Flats hadn't made anything any clearer to me. The last twelve hours still seemed like some sort of sick joke someone had played on me. I gazed out of the window, remembering the conversation I'd had with Nicky, how unaware I'd been as to what it was going to lead to. I heard his voice again; choked, false. I still couldn't believe I hadn't seen him. He must have got the messages I'd left him, why the hell wasn't he getting back to me?

The branches of the chestnut weren't empty but it was only a sparrow that was perched on the branch nearest the window and I was a little disappointed. I wondered if common birds knew they weren't special, that no one wanted to look at them. I stared at the little creature, the wind tearing into its breast feathers. How did I know it was common? It could have been a rare Botswanan eagle sparrow I was looking at, it could have been the spot of the century. I saw myself, on the front cover of *Bird Spotters' World*, signing autographs for bearded men, getting a lot of action from girls in windcheaters.

The small red light in the top corner told me that

there was only one message on my machine. I'd hoped it would be Nicky but when I hit play a female voice rang round the room, the volume a little too loud. I didn't recognize the voice. I was bending down to the radiator dial but when I realized who the voice belonged to I straightened right up again. She wasn't the last person I'd expected to call me. I hadn't expected her to call me at all.

'Hello. Mr Rucker?' Silence. 'My name . . . My name is Louise Draper. I believe my husband spoke to you. I . . . I'd like you to call me. My number is 7790 8022. Can you call me, please?'

Her voice was as taut as an electric fence. Unlike her husband's there was no north in it that I could hear; no accent, just stress. I stood, looking down at the phone. The first thing I wondered was how she'd got my number. Her husband? Nicky? I picked up the receiver and put it down. I had an instant and jarring hunch that I should walk down the hall, get a pastry from the café and chat for an hour with my friends Mike and Ally who run the place. Then go to a museum, or for a swim maybe at Ironmonger Row. Catch a matinee at the Screen on the Green. The receiver looked at me. No. Leave the phone where it is. I picked it up again and dialled. I was relieved when a machine kicked in but when I started to speak the line clicked open.

'Hello. Hello. Mr Rucker?'

I owned up to that.

'I'm sorry,' she said. 'It's just the newspapers, they've been calling all morning.' If her voice on the message had sounded strained, now it was ready to snap. 'They just keep calling back, calling and calling.

Jesus. Anyway. I've left the machine on. Thank you for returning my call.'

'That's okay.' I didn't tell her I nearly hadn't. I didn't tell her that the last thing I wanted to do was spend any more time chasing around after her husband. She didn't know where that had led me.

'You spoke to Jack, didn't you? Yesterday.'

'We spoke,' I agreed. 'He asked me for some help but we didn't sort anything out.'

'I know. I know.' I could hear her thinking. 'You were right. I told him. He should have gone to the police. Listen,' she said, 'can you come and see me?'

In the background I heard a doorbell ringing. I heard someone calling her name. I held the phone from my face and tried to picture Louise Draper, standing in her living room, the pack I'd seen outside. Did she know? Did she know yet? I couldn't tell by her voice. She sounded terrible but so would any wife whose husband's picture was next to that of his mistress, centre page in the *Sun*. Did she know that Alison had suffered a whole lot more than she had?

'Can you tell me what it's about?' I said. 'I should say that I don't do divorce work, anything like that . . .'

'It's not that. I wouldn't need you to watch him, would I, to catch him at it? A bit late for that. Something. I can't talk over the phone. Something has happened.' She did know. I could tell she did. She just didn't know I knew too. 'Listen. It's not about what's in the papers today. Oh, Christ.' Her voice started to dissolve but she didn't let it. 'Can you just come . . . ?'

'I don't know,' I said. 'Really.'

'Please, Mr Rucker. You know Nicky, don't you? Please.' The doorbell rang again. I thought I could hear the clatter of the letter box. 'Oh shit. Shit.' She paused again and I heard her taking three deep breaths. 'You'll see something on the news. I can't tell you. Today or tomorrow. After that, can you come and see me? I'm not going to waste your time, not like Jack did. Please.'

Behind her voice was another, obviously coming through the letter box. Caring, patient. 'Mrs Drapa? Mrs Drapa. Please. Do you have any reaction? Do you have a message for your husband? Is there anything you want to say to the giwl, Mrs Drapa?' I heard the creak of the receiver, shifting in her hand.

'Please,' she said. 'You'll know what I mean. Please.'

She put the phone down.

I sat back in my chair and stretched, feeling slightly nauseous due to a dramatic imbalance between sleep and coffee. I thought about trying to steal some kip on the sofabed but there was too much going on in my head, a rave was being held in there without me having issued a licence. So. There would be something on the news. Mrs Draper was right there. I figured that Alison would have been found by now. It would only be a matter of time before someone would realize who she was. It may even have already happened. I imagined the operation that would be in progress, the wheels that would be turning. Alison was probably on her way to the morgue even now. Hoxton Square would be full of squad cars. People just curious would be hanging around, looking up at the building that was cordoned off with yellow tape, wondering what had happened, whether they'd get a glimpse. The papers would get onto it soon. The neighbours would be getting knocked up by serious-faced noddies. The search for Draper would begin. Alison's flat would be crawling with forensics officers, photographers, detectives hoping that this would be the one to put them on the map.

I leaned forward on my desk, looking at the framed print of my brother that was propped up in front of me, and put myself in their carefully covered shoes. I was there, my first murder, nine, ten years ago, looking down at the body of an old Chinese woman, clubbed to death for her pension, we'd thought, until we'd seen the swastikas on the bathroom mirror. I was back with the tension, the hyper-reality. I'd had that urge, that electric urge to get in there, to find out, to *detect*. I shook my head. I didn't have it now. All I wanted was to fade into the background, to close my eyes and go to sleep. Hopefully I wouldn't even have to put Draper there, the police would do that. I was well out of it. I heard Louise Draper, pleading with me to go to see her. I saw myself standing up in Alison Everly's vacant eye. I thought of the reason I'd joined the police force, why I'd wanted to be one of those men hovering round her corpse. Not to nick single mothers for shoplifting in supermarkets. For people like Alison. But no. I wasn't a policeman any more. I'd stumbled in on her, that was all. I could still see Alison looking at me. I shook my head, stood up and walked out into the hall.

The café that serves the building is four doors away from me, made up of a compact unit with a tiny kitchen attached. It's a pleasant, light space with four small tables covered in bright laminated tablecloths, an overabundance of pot ferns giving it a rainforest feel. The people who run it are even more pleasant; a young couple called Mike and Ally who had got married a couple of months ago, and I'd only recently shaken the hangover. Ally's family had come over from Milan and Mike's family had come over from West London and it had been the warmest and most riotous wedding I'd ever been to. Ally had looked so beautiful that Mike had hardly been able to speak when he saw her. He'd blubbed through his speech like a TV evangelist outside a cheap motel.

I'd been very happy for Mike and Ally, especially because I knew that in the six months prior to getting engaged they'd had quite a few problems. They'd spent five years living together in one small space and working together in another and I knew it was getting to them, largely because of the strain they sometimes showed on their faces or the sounds of raised voices that occasionally rang out into the hall once they'd shut up for the day. But they'd worked through their difficulties, and it had made me see that it was actually possible to do this. Sharon and I, the girl I'd been seeing for the two years prior to their wedding, hadn't been able to. Our problems had grown into a wall until we'd lost sight of each other. But Ally and Mike showed that you can come out the other side, if you want to bad enough. I often wondered whether knowing this would be any help to Shulpa and me.

Ally was behind the small counter on the left, opening a box of Kit Kats, using long red nails instead of scissors. A stack of sandwiches sat next to her. Ally is a very pretty olive-skinned Milanese who met Mike when she was looking for a studio in the building for the jewellery she never got time to make any more. She took a place somewhere else, but kept coming back to look at spaces there, pretending she was interested. Every time, she stopped into Mike's for a coffee.

'On your own?'

Ally looked up and smiled. 'Hi, Billy! How are you?' Ally's voice is like rich, expensive chocolate. She leaned forward and I kissed both of her cheeks. 'No, Mike's in the back.'

'Doing the bleeding washing up as usual, mate!' I could hear Mike, splashing around behind his wife. 'Love, honour and *obey*. Why did I have to go and bloody say that? Why couldn't I have just stopped after the first two, eh?'

I called out hi while Ally smiled and shook her head. She pushed a crinkle of shiny black hair behind a silver earring I knew she'd designed herself. I smiled too and lowered my voice.

'And how is he?' I said to her, nodding towards the kitchen. 'Still not speaking to you?'

Mike came and stood beside his wife, wiping his hands with a tea towel. He'd heard what I'd said. Ally didn't look at him.

'Barely,' she said. 'But what can I do?'

'Nothing,' I told her. 'There's nothing you can do.'

Ally suddenly turned to Mike, dismissively. He folded his arms and raised both eyebrows.

'See? Look at him. He blames me. *Me!?!* I don't think he'll ever stop blaming me.' She put out her bottom lip, like a child. Mike's expression didn't change.

'Don't let it worry you,' I said. 'He knows that it wasn't your fault. Deep down, he *knows* that.'

She shook her head. 'I hope you're right, Billy. I hope you're right.'

Mike said, 'Never. It was down to you. It had to be.'

Ally's hands shot towards the ceiling. Then she set about arranging the Kit Kats.

'What I tell you? I don't even like the game. I don't really care about Inter! Not really. But when he asks me who I was supporting I couldn't lie to him, could I?'

'No. Of course not.'

'Of course I want Inter. I don't even know why he took me. And why shouldn't I cheer when we scored?'

'Why? Because we were at Stamford Bridge, in the home end, that's bleeding why! We were surrounded by the faithful. You even had a blue scarf on!'

'It was cold! Sitting outside for hours. What do I care which colour it is. Milan is my home town! Of course I wanted them to win – even if it was against his beloved Chelsea.'

'And he couldn't accept that?'

'Before, yes. He was okay – because he thought Chelsea would win. But when we won, and they were knocked out of this stupid European League thing, he says it was because of me! He says he goes to the match now and his friends give him a hard time for marrying a Milanese woman. And I say to him, you should have married that nice little girl from Acton who came to the wedding and cried every time she looked at you. Anyway.' She turned to Mike. 'Why you care, huh? Tell me. Why do you care about this? It was all Italians playing in the game anyway, and both of the managers. What does it matter which team of Italians wins?'

Mike had his wife's slim neck in his hands when I left them.

'You're a witness! You're a witness!' Ally called out as I walked down the hall.

The rest of the day was spent like many others before it, on the concourse of King's Cross Station, leaning against pillars, standing at food concessions or in W.H. Smith's, my camera in my bag. It wasn't long before the two girls I was looking for made their appearance; they came and stood exactly where Joe Nineteen had told me they would. They were a touch more sassy than the two who had been there yesterday, both a little older. They looked like any kids would have done and I had to check the pictures I had of them pretty carefully. No, it was them. Just standing there you would have thought they were waiting for some mates or something. Normal teenagers would probably not have started talking to a German businessman, though, fresh off the train. And they wouldn't have gone off in a cab with him.

I took the girls' pictures before they disappeared and even managed to speak to them, asking them for a light, handing out some fags I'd bought for the purpose, telling them I was just waiting for my girlfriend who was coming down from Edinburgh. The girls seemed okay to me, they didn't have that dead, grey cast to them. I looked but couldn't see any needle tracks. They had a toughness to them, which seemed to say, 'This isn't getting to me, I'm in charge of this.' They appeared to be feeding themselves well enough. It was only when I asked them where they came from that hesitation entered their eyes. One of them looked especially knocked by the question. Like a child learning to ride a bike, who suddenly realizes she isn't being held onto any more.

I left the film I'd taken with Carl at the repro shop I use, and stayed chatting for a while. I asked after his boyfriend and he said he was fine and asked after Shulpa and I said she was fine too. I knew I was glossing over a lot and I expected he was too, but though we were friendly, it seldom went much beyond a casual chat. I enjoyed seeing him, though. I was glad that my normal life seemed to be retaking some sort of hold of me. I'd successfully put all thoughts of Alison Everly to one side, just as I had my tax form, until leaping out of bed to tackle it the day before.

But back at my flat, I couldn't ignore her any more. It was a little after six. I tried Nicky's mobile one more time but again it was off. I wanted to tell him the decision that had been making itself in my head while I was at King's Cross. That when the police had picked Draper up, and they came looking for me, I was going to tell them I'd seen Draper going into Alison's building. If the police didn't come calling I'd leave it a bit and see what I could dig up – out of pure curiosity, and because whether I liked it or not, seeing Alison had connected me to what had happened to her. But I wouldn't leave it for ever. If it looked like Draper was going to walk away from it, because no one had seen him there, then I was going to finger him. Not that I thought I'd have to. Suddenly, I realized: the two coppers who'd stopped me were bound to have noticed his car. They may even have spotted him. I didn't think they'd need me to make a case against Jack Draper.

I stood in my kitchen looking into the fridge. The chicken was still there but I had no urge to do anything about it. I didn't really know why I'd bought it actually, Shulpa always seemed to want to try the latest new restaurant. All I wanted to do was have a cup of tea and then go to sleep. I shut the door and flipped the kettle on and then just stood, looking out of the window towards the market, watching people walking quickly down towards Farringdon Tube or hurrying into the Penny Black. Then I just seemed to come to, to wake up almost, to realize where I was, as if the time before that moment had been some sort of illusion. I shook my head and blinked. The last two days had come upon me like a freak wave and completely taken me out. Now I found myself standing on dry ground, looking around at my kitchen as if I were a potential house buyer. It was because, right at that moment, there was nothing I could possibly do, there was no one to go and see. I'd tried to find Draper and until Alison's murder was public knowledge that was all I could do. I didn't have a clue where else to look. I felt exonerated somehow, excused, and it felt good – even though I was tired I was filled with a bizarre elation. I used to get this feeling on the force sometimes after working really hard. It was usually when we'd gone so far and were waiting for forensics to move, and couldn't do a thing until they had. A feeling of getting your head above water. There was also the fact that after the initial cold horror of seeing the corpse of a murder victim, and of trying to work out who had left it there, there often came the thrill, the almost vicious thrill of simply being able to walk away from it, of taking another breath. Of being able to leave it lying there. Of it not being you.

I made some tea and suddenly I was hungry. I left a message on Shulpa's machine, asking her if she was busy that night, if she wanted to do something, get a bite to eat. She liked hanging out in Soho so I took a chance and booked a table at Spiga on Wardour Street, hoping I hadn't forgotten about some other arrangement she'd made. I sat for a second, as the girl checked to see what was free, thinking about Shulpa sitting opposite me sucking the flesh from olive pips. The dream I'd had of her came back and it made me feel a little ashamed of myself as well as arousing me at the same time. Again I thought of times on the force, nights following the start of a murder inquiry. How the tension between male and female officers was suddenly shot with a thousand volts. I needed Shulpa. I needed to feel her teeth biting into my lips, feel myself inside her, as far as I could go. I needed to say, 'You're dead, Alison, I'm not, look at me, I'm not like you.' I was back at my mother's funeral. Halfway through the wake one of the girls she'd worked with let me take her upstairs and screw her over the sink in the bathroom, her half-stifled screams rising above the respectful murmur coming up through the floor below.

The phone rang towards the end of a game in the UEFA cup, Liverpool walking all over a team from Finland who looked like they'd have trouble on Hackney marshes let alone Anfield. Looking at Owen made me think of Draper. That would have been him. I saw the goal he'd scored again, and thought of another couple I remembered him getting. Draper had a strange look about him when he knocked one in. He didn't go mad, pull his shirt over his head or point to the name on the back of it. He just looked slightly fucked off, justified, like a man let out on appeal. He didn't let the other players near him, taking his own time to get back to the circle, like a circus lion out of his cage. It was almost as if he expected to score, and he would score, just as long as everyone else did their jobs, something he clearly felt they seldom did.

I reached over, grabbed the phone and said my name, as the shot moved to John Barnes in the studio wearing a suit that a blind man wouldn't have chosen. I repeated my name but there was no answer. I said it again but still no response.

'Shulpa?'

It was a mobile, I could tell that; background noise bathed in static. I thought for a second that there was no one there, the phone had got knocked on by accident, in Shulpa's bag or something.

'Shulpa? Hello?'

I shrugged, about to hang up, disappointed not to be listening to a deep soft voice telling me how much she wanted to see me. I smiled, just thinking about her doing that. I flicked channels, getting a *Rising Damp* repeat on 4. The phone rested in my hand. Alan was telling Rigsby to calm down. There was a killer on the loose. *Calm down?! Calm down?! What do you meeaaan?!* But then I heard a voice. It mumbled a word, a word that sounded like my name. It was faint, hardly there, but I could tell it was a man's voice and all of a sudden I sat up.

My hand gripped the receiver. 'Jack, is that you?'

'Billy,' the voice said. It was louder now, but still a whisper. No, not a whisper. You whisper when you're trying to be quiet. This person was speaking as loud as he could.

'Hello . . .'

'Billy.' It was a huge struggle. There was an unnatural wetness to the voice, disguising it. I didn't think it was on purpose. Something was wrong.

'Billy . . !'

Then I knew who it was. And I had a feeling, an ice-cold clenched feeling that had been waiting patiently in the pit of my stomach for two whole weeks. In a second it had flared right through me.

'Nicky . . !'

'Thank God . . !'

He coughed, and spat.

'Can you help me, Billy?'

'Of course. Nicky. Nicky! Speak to me.' Nothing. 'Nicky, keep talking.'

I thought I heard his voice again but I couldn't be sure. I shouted a few more times. I didn't get a response. I heard what sounded like scraping, and then nothing.

The line went dead.

Chapter Nine

Running out onto the street I smacked straight into an old man walking past my flat. He looked frail and resentful as he kept his balance and I felt instantly terrible. But I didn't have time for it. When I got to my car I saw that I'd been blocked in, by a van on one end and an empty black cab on the other. I didn't have time for that either. The cab took most of it. I got out eventually, and put my foot down.

I knew he was in a bad way. There was blood in his throat. I knew it as soon as I put the phone down. I dialled him back immediately but there was no reply. I didn't have a clue how to find him.

Before rushing out, the first thing I'd done was call Nicky's bar, the Old Ludensian. Toby, his head barman, came on the line.

'No. Haven't seen him.' Toby was casual. 'He went out at lunch and never came back.'

'Did he tell you where he was going?'

'No. Just said he'd be back. And he isn't.'

'Have you looked upstairs?'

'No, should I? Is there something wrong?'

'If you could have a look, please, Toby.'

Toby checked the flat out and came back on the line to say it was empty.

I called Nicky's home number, knowing he wouldn't be picking up. He'd sounded like he was outside. I thought he may have left some sort of message on his machine but he hadn't. Finally, I called Shulpa. She'd just got in from work, hadn't even played her messages yet. I asked her if she'd seen her brother and she told me no. I asked her if she knew what he was doing today but she didn't, she hadn't seen him for a week. I tried to be calm but she picked up on the stress in my voice.

'What's happened? Billy, what's happened to Nick?'

'I don't know. He called on his mobile, didn't sound very good. I tried to get him to tell me where he was but he rang off. Shulpa, do you have a key to his flat?'

'No,' she said. 'But he keeps one at the bar. It's with the cellar keys. He's loaned me it a few times.'

'Right. I'll go and get it. It's as good a place to start as any.'

'Shall I come? I want to. I'll meet you there . . .'

'No,' I said. 'He knows your number. If he tries me again and I'm out he may try you.'

Shulpa agreed to stay at home. I dialled Nicky's mobile again but it just kept ringing.

I knew it. I fucking well *knew* it. I got to Nicky's bar in five minutes. I persuaded Toby to let me take all the keys I could find. How was I to know which was which? Toby was nervous about it but he didn't argue. It wouldn't have mattered if he had. I left the car outside and ran up to Nicky's flat. Nicky lives in a former council block near Ironmonger Row baths, ten minutes' walk from the bottom end of St John Street, where his bar is. About a year ago he'd noticed two properties for sale, next door to one another, and bought them both. The conversion he'd had done cost more than both flats together. I got into Nicky's flat quickly, after trying only two keys that didn't work.

Nicky wasn't there. I called his mobile again and got nothing. I looked around. A feeling of raging annoyance at myself kept trying to beat itself into me but I held it back, knowing it wouldn't do any good. I turned the place upside down. There were no notes by the phone, no memos on the fridge, nothing to tell me where he was. I couldn't find anything in his desk diary. The day had an asterisk on it but other than that it was a blank. The message light on his machine was flashing but the only message was from me. I changed the message, telling Nicky to tell me where he was if he called there. His remote access code was printed on a label inside the machine and I put the label in my wallet.

I didn't know which way to turn next. I dialled my machine, and my office machine, in case he'd called me again. He hadn't, there was nothing from anyone on either. I paced round his flat, hunting around, lifting magazines, looking in cupboards for the sake of it, picking up things I'd picked up before. I couldn't believe it. Why hadn't I forced him to tell me what was going on . . . ?

I made myself stand for a minute, leaning against a thin metal support in Nicky's cavernous living room. Maybe if I could work out what was going on it would help me find him. Was it something to do with Draper? I waited for some inspiration but nothing came. I felt helpless, frustrated. I took Nicky's keys and walked out onto his balcony, locking his door behind me.

The only thing I could think to do was see if his

car was there. Nicky rents a lock-up garage at the rear of the building. I ran down the stairs and out of the rear door, leaving it wedged open so I could get in again quickly if I needed to. Outside it was dark, the sky clear and purple black with stars like fine stab wounds. I jogged through a well-lit communal space complete with small squares of grass, concrete walkways doused in salt and a child's swing set. Ignoring the cold I made my way round the other side of the building and came out by some high-sided aluminium wheelie bins. The garages were in a square beyond them, with an entrance where the last garage in the square would have been.

I carried on jogging into the square. There were only a few limp bulbs fixed on the garage roofs and there wasn't a lot of light. All I could see was junk, stacked against garages that were obviously out of use; old furniture, a knackered fridge, things the bin men wouldn't take. There were cars parked outside about a third of the garage doors, their owners either driving two vehicles or using the space for other storage. I'd been to Nicky's garage a few times and knew it was on the far side. I made my way round, hoping I'd remember which one it was, running my eyes along the row of garages, all practically identical to each other. I thought I had it. Number thirty-four. I stopped outside it, my mind going back to the times Nicky had driven me back there, what I'd seen when I came out of it, which direction his flat was in.

I looked back at the apartment block, five storeys of pale yellow window lights like rows of bad teeth. Yes, I was positive. I stood in the middle of the door, not really knowing what to do. It was closed, the thin black sheet of steel pulled over and down. I looked back round the square, my hands on my hips. Then I leaned on the door and nearly fell when it moved. It was open, the bottom pushed out towards me.

I didn't know whether Nicky locked his garage as a matter of course, but today he hadn't. If he was using the car, and he kept nothing else in there, this wouldn't have been hard to believe. Personally, I would have still locked it – you never know what someone is going to do in a space like that if they find it empty – but Nicky may not have wanted to unlock it before putting his car away. No, that didn't make sense, he would have had to get out of his car to open the door anyway. I stepped backwards and pushed the door over.

I was surprised to see Nicky's car standing there. Why have a garage and not lock it? I fumbled for a switch and pushed it down, sending a square of light reaching out into the dark. I looked the car over, the light adding a soft sheen to the dark paintwork. I still couldn't figure it. Nicky must just have forgotten to lock up, but I couldn't imagine that. How could he have, when he had had to pull the door closed anyway? The lock was in the handle he must have used. I was trying to work out what had happened when I heard a sound behind me.

I was startled, but it was only a mobile ringing. I ignored it and looked around. The car seemed okay. A flashing red light from the dash told me Nicky had locked and alarmed it. Looking in through the windows I could see nothing awry. I slid along the narrow gap on the left side to the front and looked for signs of an accident. Nothing. I bent to look underneath – nothing there either. I stood up, shaking my head, and looked out at the tongue of damp orange sticking out from the garage into the darkness.

And as I did so, a drop fell from the bottom of the pull-over door, landing with a quiet 'tick', just outside the garage. I stared down at it. It hadn't been raining. I was walking towards it when it was followed by another, which this time hung almost to a thread before it broke, and fell. I didn't understand. Then I did. No, it hadn't been raining. I looked at my hands. The thumb, palm and forefinger of my right hand were sticky with blood. I looked up to the door again where another droplet fell from the lip of the garage door, the door I'd pushed over to get in.

Now I could see small dark spots on the ground outside, illuminated by the light from the garage like a Weegee shot. I ran outside and called his name. I looked behind cars, amongst the junk, in the farthest, unlit corners. There were shadows everywhere, the whole far side was obscured by darkness. I couldn't see him. I looked some more. Then I cursed myself and ran upstairs to his flat. When I'd got in there I dialled his mobile number and ran back down again. I could hear it as soon as I opened the back door.

'Nicky. Nicky!'

He didn't answer, but his phone was still calling to me from the darkness like an abandoned chick. I made myself shut up but I needn't have bothered because there was silence as it went to voicemail. I zigzagged to where the sound had been coming from and after a couple of minutes I found him. He was slumped on the far side, half underneath an old rusting Transit with four piles of bricks instead of wheels. He was face down, his mobile beneath his left cheekbone.

SUPERJACK

I put the phone in my back pocket as I bent down to my friend.

He wasn't moving.

Chapter Ten

Two weeks earlier I'd had no idea that everything wasn't its usual easy-going self in the life of my friend. I'd been in my flat with Shulpa. It was a Sunday, and I'd taken her to a Turkish place off the Caledonian Road, somewhere I hadn't eaten in years. I like going out for dinner on a Sunday night, but it has to be a Sunday night kind of a place, and the restaurant we went to didn't really have it. The manager was rude and the food was only okay, which probably explained why I hadn't been there in ages. You may wonder why I hadn't taken Shulpa to a place that I knew, somewhere definitely worth going, but here I had a problem. Shulpa was my new girlfriend. I've lived in the area for years and every other decent place I could think of had old girlfriend written all over it. They would have had the burnt echoes of other Sunday nights ringing round my head. This was the last thing I wanted and I was candid enough to mention my reservations to Shulpa, who didn't look impressed but said she understood, so we ended up eating indifferent moussaka on Copenhagen Street instead of great squid in Casale Franco, or free-range duck in the Falcon. It was a shame. Splitting up with someone, it doesn't just affect your heart. It's a pain in the arse for your stomach too.

We'd cut our losses and gone back to my flat quite early, and it was probably due to the dissatisfaction we both felt that we didn't stay there very long. Shulpa and I settled on my futon in front of the TV, not intending to go anywhere else, but as the only film worth watching was a repeat of *Apocalypse Now*, and we'd both seen it, we soon got bored.

'Let's go out again.'

Shulpa was already standing up, sliding her long slim feet into the Patrick Cox mules she'd kicked off only ten minutes before. I'd acquired a certain amount of inertia by now, old film or not, but I didn't really have a choice. Something about the girl meant you had to keep up with her. You wanted to keep up with her. There was also the fact that the one thing we didn't seem to be good at doing together was simply hanging out. I never felt completely at ease when we were doing normal, everyday things. There was an intense chemistry between us but somehow it didn't extend to having a quiet couple of drinks together down at the Falcon or O'Hanlon's, where an awkwardness would sit between us like a disapproving chaperone. For her part Shulpa always seemed to want to be doing something more than that anyway. Whenever we were just having coffee, say, or reading the paper, she would get a restless look in her eyes that seemed oddly close to fear. She had this almost insatiable need to fill her life with colour and noise. This need was inspiring most of the time but there was something about it that unsettled me.

'Where to?' I said. 'It's Sunday night . . .'

'Some place in town. You must know somewhere that's open.' Shulpa had dug in her bag and come out with a lipstick, a dark sensual red. I watched her paint it on her full mouth, a little square, a little big for her face. It was only matched by her eyes, the biggest, darkest eyes I've ever seen. 'Give me a few more weeks and I'll have us on every guest list in the South of England. But I've only been here three months. And I've been wasting a lot of that time being a very naughty girl with you.'

'A waste?'

'Pointless. Mere physical gratification.' She was looking in the mirror, and after unzipping the back she let her dress fall to the floor. All of a sudden I didn't want to go anywhere, but she was only putting her bra back on. She smiled when she saw me looking. 'Mmmm. Maybe later. If you're a very lucky boy. In the meantime, I went to the Playroom last week. Why not there?'

She was talking about the latest media hang-out, a club on Beak Street populated by jowly forty-something blokes in generic black Paul Smith suits and coke-thin women so insecure and miserable, the only way they can cope with life is by standing around in exclusive bars trying to make other coke-thin women feel insecure and miserable.

'Maybe,' I said, racking my brains. The only places I could think of were illicit drinking holes below porn shops and dodgy cab offices, run by well-connected crack dealers who make sure there are only two spliffs and a lump of black around when a hundred policemen come charging through the door. Hardly Sunday evening with your girlfriend.

'Why don't we pick Nicky up from the Ludensian, take him along?'

'Okay,' Shulpa said, after a second or two.

Shulpa was being slightly hesitant and I understood why. As I have mentioned, Nicky is, for want of a better phrase, my best friend. He also happens to be Shulpa's elder brother. I find this situation slightly weird and I know that Shulpa does too, if only for the fact that while she tells me she loves her brother, up until now she's never really hung out with him.

'It feels odd,' she tried to explain to me, when we first started going out. 'Sitting in a restaurant with you and him. It makes me feel young, like a baby sister not a woman. I mean, I like the fact that Nicky's my older brother. I'm not sure I want him to be my friend instead.'

I understood how she felt but I hadn't seen Nicky in a while and there was also the fact that he was a member of a place in town where we could go for a quiet drink, without having to elbow our way through to a bar and then shout to be heard over music so loud and monotonous you would think it had been invented by Ainsley Harriot. I hoped he'd be up for it, or else there'd be one or two people at Nicky's Shulpa could talk to, and we'd end up staying there. I knew that the only way I'd be able to deal with the Playroom would be to drink too much and I had to be up by seven. Shulpa did too but, in the months I'd known her, I'd never seen her evince so much as a slight groan the morning after, even though she was one of those women who could, and very often did, put away more than a roomful of sailors on their last day of shore leave.

Nicky's bar is only a ten-minute walk but as we were probably going on after I thought we'd take the car. My old brown Mazda was slumped right outside and I opened Shulpa's door for her and walked round the front. As we took the short drive down the Farringdon Road to Smithfield I glanced across at Shulpa, sitting in the seat beside me. The seat had a long slash across the back, caused by someone who had been keen to put a long slash in me, and on the dash in front of her she'd put the remains of the sandwich that had been my lunch, which she'd decided not to sit on. She hadn't found a place for the still half-full styrene coffee cup that had been next to it, though, so she held that between her legs, trying not to spill any. Her legs themselves were very much in evidence, Shulpa having zipped herself back up into a tight black dress that was definitely not Sunday night and made it pretty clear to anyone who was interested that she was not coke-thin. Usually, quite a few people were interested.

It's only five minutes down to the Old Ludensian. Now that I thought of it I was glad we'd come out again but I was hoping we could persuade Shulpa that a drink or two at the bar with Nicky, Chet Baker and a couple of the staff for company was enough. Shulpa could flirt with Toby, the head barman, while Nicky and I stacked the chairs on the tables and then we'd sit around over a bottle or two.

I left the Mazda double-parked at the widened-out bottom of St John Street, making sure that both the cars inside of me had enough room to get out. The night was mild for February and I left my coat on the back seat. I took the coffee cup from Shulpa, the sandwich off the dash, and put them on the roof while

I locked up. There was a wastepaper bin on the pavement and I dropped both items into it, managing to get some of the coffee on my hands. I wiped them on the bottom of my jeans, turning my head to look towards the Old Ludensian across the broad, quiet street. It was about eleven by now and the lights were up. There didn't appear to be many people left in the bar. While I was still wiping my hands dry Shulpa, who hadn't bothered putting her coat on either, hugged her arms together and skipped across the empty street. I stood up and followed her towards the door, wedged open to encourage the last of the stragglers to make their way home. I was ten yards behind Shulpa and I expected her to keep on going straight through, but instead she stopped. She hesitated in the doorway and took a step back.

Coming up behind her I could hear shouting. One man shouting over what sounded like a Macy Gray track. I moved past Shulpa and through the door. The full, bright lighting showed me there were only two customers left in the Old Ludensian, both standing a few feet back from the deep, mahogany bar. The bar runs fifty feet down the left-hand side of the room, facing a wide, treated-brick archway leading into a broad space filled with tables and chairs. I could see Toby, wiping tables in there. Nicky was standing behind the bar in front of the two men.

It was one of the two customers doing the yelling. I was too late to get the gist of his argument because just then he finished his spiel. I was, however, in time to see his right hand go back behind his head. It went back quickly and came out quicker and only then did I see that he was gripping a bottle of beer in it, like a club. I only saw it in his hand for a second. It didn't stay there any longer.

I didn't have a chance to move. The beer gunned out of the neck like a Catherine wheel as the bottle rushed towards Nicky's head. For a split second it was sure to hit him but it tumbled over his shoulder, smacking into the mirror behind him. There was an instant explosion, an eruption of glass and beer that burst back from the mirror. It wasn't just the bottle that had gone but the huge mirror too, with its heavy gilt frame. What followed was a shattering thunder, an avalanche caused in crystal, fragments crashing down, glasses flying, bottles going over, glittering shards of glass leaping back up from any hard surface like trout flashing from a running stream. When they were still, the whole place seemed awash with glass.

Shulpa took a breath. I couldn't see Nicky. A duck had taken him below the level of the bar. I was still frozen, my arms were encased in amber. It seemed like seconds. Then they broke free. Without thinking I moved quickly towards the two men, focusing on the one who had thrown the bottle, the nearest to me, checking him out to see if he held anything else. He didn't, not that I could see. The men had both stepped back when the mirror went but now I saw the closest to me moving towards the bar. Neither of the men had seen me standing in the doorway but as I approached them they turned. To my right I could see that Toby had turned as well, a cloth in one hand and a bottle of spray cleaner frozen in the other.

I stopped about three feet from the nearest guy.

'Nicky!'

I didn't get a reply. He must have been right under the mirror.

'I think we leave now. Out of the way.'

'Nicky, you okay?'

My eyes moved towards the bar where I could hear movement, followed by glass shifting, falling to the floor.

'Hey, fucker, out the way. We're leaving.'

His voice was calm and insolent, with an accent I couldn't place. I looked back to him.

'I don't think so. Not just yet. Toby, get upstairs and call the police . . .'

I blocked the guy's path as he came forward and he took a step back. He was about my height, sporting blow-dried hair, a shiny 80s-style double-breasted suit and loafers with a gold strap. He had a scar from a harelip covered by a thin, shaped beard which he probably thought made him look like George Michael. He stepped forward again but again I moved in front of him. He shook his head as if I were very stupid.

'I'll give you chance, get out the fucking way.'

He was running both hands back through his perm. I wasn't going anywhere. I looked him in the eye so he'd know that.

I heard another movement from behind the bar and my eyes must have strayed again because suddenly he was on me, filling the gap between us, getting me off balance before I could take a step back to steady myself. His hands were twisted into my shirt, trying to move me aside. I grabbed hold of his wrists and found myself right up in his face. He looked bored, inconvenienced. Beyond him I noticed his friend, noticed him for the first time. His friend was huge, a dark brooding block carved from Prince of Wales check and hair oil. His smooth brown face was big as a bell. I had a dull, plummeting feeling. I knew I had to deal with the chatty one pretty damn quickly and then look for something heavy. Very. The guy was twenty-odd stone and none of it was flab.

Two hands were gripping hold of my shirt, trying to send me sideways. I let them do it, turning their owner with his own weight, shuddering him into the wide brick arch. It sent some breath out of him but he was still there. He tried a knee in the groin, but I turned my thigh against it. I dug a short left at his kidneys but only got his ribcage and he managed to get a butt in, his hands back on my shirt again, his hard, thin forehead connecting under my cheekbone. At any time I expected his friend to come on. I jammed the guy up against the brickwork again which loosened his hold, and then I pushed his wrists into his lapels. I got a good pivot in and wheeled him round, smacking his face up against the opposite arch. A rose of blood flowered from his nose. I forgot about him. I was looking round for his chum when a voice boomed out from the door.

'That's enough.'

It was deep and clear and instantly commanding. I looked up. The big guy had simply walked by us, like a teacher past a fight in the playground, going to get his cane. He was standing in the doorway, his back to the night, practically filling the frame. It wasn't a cane he was holding, though. He had Shulpa's neck clamped tight in a hand the size of one of Nicky's dinner plates.

I kept an eye on George Michael and stepped back from the archway. Shulpa was frozen. She was looking at me. The guy's other hand was round her waist, pulling her to him. Next to me the smaller guy turned to face me, not bothering to stem the flow of blood from his face. He took a step, halving the distance between us, glass fragments snapping beneath his loafers.

'Forget it.'

The voice from the end of the bar stopped him and though he looked resentful he turned towards it. Then he walked up to the bar. Nicky was standing behind it now, his face like chalk.

'Wanker.'

The guy spat at him through bloodstained teeth. Then he walked the length of the bar and out of the door without looking round. His friend stood for a second, taking a measured, hard look at Nicky. He still had hold of Shulpa's neck, like a lion with a rabbit beneath its paw. His eyes turned to mine. He brought his other hand up from round Shulpa's waist and there was a blade in it. He held it up until it found a light. Then he fanned his other hand open. He ran it slowly along Shulpa's naked shoulder. She tensed as he moved it inside her bra. He bent and kissed the side of her neck, his eyes still fixed on mine. Then he took his hand away and stepped back slowly, out of the door, pulling it closed behind him.

We all of us stood for a second. The mirror had crashed down on top of the stereo and the bar was silent. No Chet Baker tonight. Then Toby seemed to come alive, hurrying to Shulpa to see if she was all right. I went to her too but she was fine, just stunned.

'Quick,' I said. 'The police.'

I reached for the door, got it open and rushed outside. I saw the two guys, across the road, getting into the BMW I'd taken great care not to block in. I ran towards it but I was too late. I turned back into the doorway.

'Tell them it's a dark blue Five Series. Heading up St John Street . . .'

Nicky wasn't paying any attention to me. He was asking his sister if she was sure she was okay, and picking pieces of glass out of his hair. There was blood in it, staining the deep black like the feathers of a dead crow.

Chapter Eleven

He was breathing. I moved the phone from beneath his cheek, turned it off and put it in my back pocket. He was in the shadow of the van and I couldn't see much. I didn't know whether or not to move him but I had to see if he was bleeding, whether there was a flow I needed to staunch. I said his name a few times without getting anything back. As gently as I could I turned him over and got my hands underneath his arms.

I had an image of Draper, his big, smug, semi-famous face telling me his name. If this had anything at all to do with Draper I was going to get to him before the police did and he wouldn't be able to play with himself let alone with Villa. I braced my knees and took Nicky's weight. He came to as I pulled him over to the garage. He let out a cry and made a feeble attempt to struggle until I told him who I was. I heard him begin to retch, and put him down. I helped him over onto his side, then his knees. He began to throw up. He was only wearing a suit, now ripped to shit, and I put my jacket round his shoulders as he heaved his way through it, hugging his sides as he did so. I waited, impatiently. It was still pitch black and I could barely make out his face, I had no idea what sort of state he was in. I didn't find out until I'd managed to get him into the light of the garage, one arm over my shoulder. I half dragged half carried his tall, lean frame into the light and propped him up against the left rear wheel of his Audi.

Now I could see him. He'd been given a very thorough makeover but it hadn't made him pretty. He was minus some teeth, which explained the blood in his throat, and the rest of his face was chopped meat, complete with a knife slash running from his left eye straight down to his jaw. It looked pretty deep. I pulled off my fleece, then my tee-shirt, bunched it up and got him to hold it against the cut. I pulled my fleece back on and asked him for his car keys.

'What for?'

'To take you to the hospital.'

'Just get me upstairs.'

'Uh uh. That cut looks bad. You'll need stitches. Probably broke some ribs too.'

'I don't care. Just get me upstairs. I'll go later. Billy, it's important. I have to do something.'

'Listen—'

'For fuck's sake, Billy! I'll go later, I will.'

I let out a breath and helped him up. I wasn't happy about it, but up in his flat was better than out there in the cold. I'd take a better look at him and then get him to Casualty if I had to beat the shit out of him again to get him there. With his arm over my shoulder we made it round to his building and I got him through the back door. I pressed the button, glad there was no one around as we waited for the lift. When it came we stepped in and I propped Nicky in the corner as we waited for it to rise to five.

The lift in Nicky's building is so slow it's hard to tell which direction it's going. Minutes seemed to go by. I spent them shaking my head, mad at Nicky, angry with him for getting himself beaten up, madder for refusing to go to hospital. But if I was mad at him, I was boiling with rage at myself.

After I'd run back into the Old Ludensian that night Nicky had refused to call the police. It was just a couple of arseholes, he'd said, standing beneath a newly exposed section of framed brickwork. They were just pissed arseholes and they were gone and that was all he cared about. I argued with him but with every passing second there was less and less point.

'Please, Billy, I mean it, forget about it. Anyway, you sure you're okay?'

I was, though I knew I might have a shiner the next day, and so was Shulpa, though she did go very quiet. Toby fetched his fleece and she hugged herself into it, shivering nonetheless. Nicky's head was still bleeding, though, so Shulpa took him upstairs to clean it. When they came back Toby and I were sweeping up the jigsaw of glass from the floor and the bar top but Nicky wasn't having any of that either.

'Tomorrow,' he said. 'Leave it. I'll do it tomorrow.'

I didn't argue. Nicky pulled a bottle of Old Granddad from the shelf and took it to a corner table. Toby turned the lights down and we all had a good go at it. All the while I wanted to ask Nicky what had really gone on but I didn't. At about two the whiskey was gone and then so were we, driving the short distance back to Exmouth Market. Shulpa stayed quiet.

As we lay in bed, however, she turned to me, as soon as the light was out. We made love in a way we never had before. It wasn't fun or wild, we hardly moved, but there was an intensity to Shulpa's need of me, of my body inside her, that was almost frightening.

'Fuck it away,' she said. 'Fuck it all away.'

I held on to her, running a hand through her thick black hair. It was very dark in my flat and as Shulpa held on to me I stared at the shapes there, all gradually emerging like ships through fog. I saw the look in Shulpa's eyes, from the other end of the bar. I saw a huge hand, clamped onto her breast, a steel blade up against the heart-shaped birthmark on Shulpa's slim, pretty neck.

I got Nicky onto the sofa and handed him the phone. I sat on a chair across the spacious room and watched him. Nicky dialled, waited awhile and then began to talk. I didn't know what he was saying because he was speaking Bengali. He went on for about five minutes, a conversation that got increasingly heated. He began coughing at one point and had to stop, and I could hear a very irate voice on the other end, shouting at him, yelling his name. Nicky finished his fit and carried on, repeating one phrase over and over. Eventually the conversation calmed down. Nicky replaced the receiver. Then he just leaned on the coffee table, supporting himself with one arm. He stayed that way, taking deep, painful breaths.

I wasn't feeling too good either. They weren't simple pissheads. I'd known it all along. I thought he was just saying that because Toby and Shulpa were there, I thought he'd tell me next day, the day after. But I'd let Nicky move me away from the knowledge of it like a skilful hostess at a party, steering you from someone they know you're going to hate.

'I'm taking you to the hospital.'

'Okay,' he said. 'Billy, my hero.'

'But before then you're going to tell me what the fuck's going on. And you're not going to bullshit me.'

He was still leaning forward on the table. He wouldn't look at me. The words I'd said were like another boot in his guts. I saw his shoulder begin to shake and his face crease up.

'Oh fuck, Billy. I've been an idiot. I've been such a fucking idiot.'

'Has this got anything to do with Jack Draper?'

'They're going to kill me, Billy. Next time they'll really kill me.'

'Who? Who were those guys? In the bar?'

He started to tell me but before he could get very far his voice began to crumble until it broke like a cliff face being battered by a force-ten gale.

Chapter Twelve

He got through a lot of it in his flat. I listened, interrupting him only once to call Shulpa and let her know that he was, roughly speaking, okay. The rest came out in my car, then before and after the doctors had fixed him up. Nicky had had three ribs broken, plus all of the fingers on his right hand. As well as the two teeth that were still lying out near his garage, two more were wrecked and would have to go. His jaw was dislocated and the rest of his face was bruised as a ripe banana in a spin dryer. The back of his head was severely grazed but his skull wasn't broken. The gash in his face needed fourteen stitches.

'You're going to have a scar,' the doctor said. She didn't sound too sympathetic.

They'd jumped him after he'd pulled the door of his garage down. It was the same two guys as before, in his bar. They'd pushed him against the flimsy metal garage and started with their fists.

'It made a hell of a noise. I thought someone would be bound to come,' Nicky said. 'But they didn't come.'

They left him alone long enough to tell him that this was his last chance. Next time he wouldn't see them, or even hear them. He should welcome the pain they were making him feel because next time there wouldn't be any. Just a bullet in the back of his head.

'You're fucking with us. We thought you were clever. How come you are fucking with us?'

Nicky's protestations fell on deaf ears. The small one, the one with the beard, had pulled a blade and slashed him. Nicky was dragged off behind the Transit van where they spent another ten minutes using their feet, ending their visit by holding his arm still while the bigger guy drove his heel into the back of Nicky's hand.

'He just stepped on it and turned his foot like he was grinding out a fag. I heard my fingers breaking. And then he did it again. I think that's when I started to lose it. I could tell they were kicking me after that but I couldn't feel it. Then I must have passed out. When I came to I didn't know where they'd gone. I thought they might be waiting for me, I thought they might want to get into my flat. So I called you. Did I tell you where I was?'

'You'd passed out again. I had to find you. It didn't take long.'

'Thank God. I thought it was them again.'

'I know.'

'I was so scared, Billy. I thought they'd changed their minds. I thought they'd come back to finish me.'

When the nurse at the Euston Hospital saw the state of him they rushed Nicky through Casualty and I waited an hour, sitting in the flat yellow lighting of the waiting area watching a TV set fixed high up on a bracket out of reach. I switched between the TV above my head and the constant, low-level drama going on around me as people came in after fights, car accidents, sudden internal explosions. The TV was less depressing. I sat through most of *ER* before realizing the irony of it. Then the nurse came over and told me I could see him.

Nicky didn't want to tell me the rest. We were waiting for his X-ray results in an open booth at the end of a long corridor, him sitting up in his bed, me on a chair. He wasn't nervous about being overheard – there was no one in the next booth. He just didn't want to admit what he'd done. When I asked him if it had anything to do with Draper he looked confused and shook his head. I thought I'd leave it till later to tell him what had happened with his friend.

'You never ever asked me how I got the money for the Ludensian,' Nicky said eventually. There was something almost accusatory about the way he said it. 'How come you never asked me that?'

I shrugged. 'I never really wondered. I assumed you borrowed it, got it off a bank. No? That or you inherited some money . . .'

'My father runs a tailor shop. Doesn't even own it. I never went to college. I didn't have anything to go to a bank with.'

'So tell me.'

Nicky lay back on his bed. I knew they'd pumped a lot of Lydocaine into him. He was still in pain and just wanted to sleep, but I wasn't going to let him.

'Tell me.'

'I sold coke,' he said. 'To begin with. When I came to London.' He shifted in his bed, his hands going to his side. Of all the damage he'd suffered I knew that in the days following it would be his ribs that gave him most grief. 'I was charming, I knew how to wear a suit.

120

That was when coke cost money. I went to parties, hung out in what used to be the Zanzibar. I made a lot of money.'

'And you bought the Ludensian?'

'I didn't have anywhere near enough for that! No. Not that I cared. I had enough, but after a few years I just wanted out. I'd nearly been caught a couple of times. Once I had to pay off some copper more than I made in a month. I was using too much of it too. I was looking for something else when someone I knew mentioned that he needed a bar manager for a place he had in Mayfair. He was a client of mine. It seemed like the perfect chance. And it was fine – for a while.'

'But you went back to it?'

'Not really. No. I was happy. I didn't have as much money but I still got invited to the parties, I was having a good time. I was still only in my mid-twenties. Then I was working one day and this little old guy came in, said he wanted to talk to me. I recognized him, he knew the owner, they were very pally. He was Maltese, wore a little pin in his lapel with a cross on it. I thought he was a bit of a joke to be honest. But later, when the owner had left, he pulled me aside. He told me he knew what I used to do. I thought he was trying to blackmail me.'

'And he wasn't?'

'He wanted me to wash some money for him. Through the bar. And not tell the owner. My cut was ten per cent. I didn't want to do it but the way he put it I didn't think I really had a choice. I did it for three years. By the time I finished I was pretty well loaded. And I got the Ludensian.'

'And you told him you were quitting? The Maltese?'

'I didn't need to.' Nicky shifted in his bed again. 'He died. I even went to the funeral. That's when I decided to leave. I just left my job and I didn't hear anything. I kept expecting to but I didn't. Maybe the guy who took over from me carried it on, I don't know. I set up on St John Street, in a shite old pub that I gutted and did up. I knew the former owner and he wanted out. Ten years ago. And it's been fine. Fun at times, boring at times, fucking hard work the rest. But fine.'

'Until they came back.'

'Yes,' Nicky said, 'until they came back.'

'And they made you start up again?'

The ends of the curtain flapped gently as a trolley went by. Nicky closed his eyes and turned away from me. He'd done something and he couldn't quite believe it. I knew what he was going to say. If they'd tried to make him, he would have said something about it weeks ago, he'd have asked me what to do.

'No.' Nicky sounded like a child, standing in front of an old lady's smashed front window. 'They didn't make me. I heard what they had to say and I agreed. Simple. I don't know if they'd have pushed it.'

'If they had we could have done something.'

'I know. But I just said yes. They told me it was a one-off, that I'd clear twenty-five grand in five months and I said yes. Jesus. I didn't even need the money. Not *need* it. I can't believe I did it. I just thought, yeah, cool, twenty-five K, could do with that. It had been so easy before, why not now? And they came round with a suitcase. The next day. A fucking suitcase. A suitcase stuffed with cash. With two hundred and fifty thousand quid.'

No wonder he didn't tell me. He knew what I'd have said.

'I put the money out through the bar, the tills. A bit at a time. I was to give them back ninety per cent of what they'd given me.'

'And what went wrong?'

'Nothing. It was just like before. Piss easy. No one at the bar knew. For weeks it was okay. Business has been great, I was shifting more of it than I thought. The Maltese picked up fifteen K three weeks straight and the initial bundle was a bit lighter each time. It was all going fine.'

'Until?'

'Until it fucking well disappeared.'

'What?'

'All of it, the whole pile. From the bar, underneath the floorboards upstairs. It just fucking vanished and I've no idea where. And now they come calling, once a week. And they want fifteen grand each time. And I haven't got it. And next time when I tell them no that'll be the end of it. They're just going to fucking kill me.'

I didn't know whether or not to be relieved that what Nicky had got himself involved in had nothing to do with his footballing friend. It was probably a relief; as yet, there were no corpses involved. I was about to fill him in on what had happened ever since I met Draper when there were more footsteps and the doctor came into the booth, with a nurse. The doctor removed the dressing from Nicky's face and I watched as she stitched him up, as effectively, it seems, as somebody else already had. She wasn't over gentle. The doctor was a very attractive woman in her late thirties with a V between her eyes that never disappeared and hands that looked older than the rest of her. They were strong hands, but veined, a copper band at her wrist. Her hair was clamped back across a high forehead, a chickenpox square stamped into her pale, almost translucent skin, just below her left temple. She looked at both Nicky and me with an expression blank of concern, laced with flat curiosity and barely disguised distaste. Her look said, 'Men, men do this.'

The doctor asked the nurse to tighten the bandages round Nicky's ribs, then asked me to step outside into the quiet corridor. She took off a pair of heavy, black framed glasses and hung them from her coat pocket.

'How did this happen?'

She was tall, five ten. She had a clipped, precise voice but not harsh, as attractive as she was.

'I don't know, exactly. I only found him. He was mugged. Surely he told you?'

'He told me. Not a pub brawl, then? Some drunken fight?'

'No.' I shook my head, puzzled. 'He was mugged.'

'Funny. His wallet was in his pocket. Muggers tend to take that.' She looked at me very hard. She didn't speak for a second.

'He managed to fight them off.'

'No he didn't. Not with those injuries.'

'I only found him.'

'He could easily have punctured a lung, you know? His ribs getting broken like that. He could have died.'

'But he'll be fine?'

'Yes, I suppose. Eventually. Though he'll definitely have a scar. It was obviously a knife that cut his face. Sharp too, very professional. The sort of thing the police get very interested in. Easier for us than a bottle as it happens but still very unpleasant. His ribs will hurt like hell. But he'll be fine, if he doesn't make a habit of this kind of thing.'

'Right,' I said.

'And you just found him, you say.'

'That's right.' She was still staring at me. I realized why. She was looking at the result of an uppercut from my friend Des two days before. I'd ducked it late and his thumb had hooked underneath my headguard. 'Were you mugged too?'

My hand went to my forehead. 'It's a day old.'

She moved closer, touching a cold thumb to my brow and nodding, grudgingly. She was close to me, her body almost touching. There was a thin gold chain round her neck, a delicate cross resting just below the deep well at the base of her throat. Her breastbone was washed with faint freckles.

'I see. How did you get it?'

'It has nothing to do with this.'

'Convince me.'

'I got it in a boxing ring.'

'Oh, I see. Boxing.' She turned to the left, pushed the curtain aside and told the nurse that she was going to see to another patient. She turned back to me.

'Boxing. My very favourite sport.' Her lips pursed. I thought about answering her but I had nothing to say. I'd noticed before, as she sewed Nicky's cut, that she was wearing a wedding band. I suddenly wondered what her husband was like, whether he had to pretend not to be interested when there was a report on the news about the latest Lewis fight. I had a picture of the house they shared, full of books, mahogany and Radio 3. I had an instant kick of jealousy.

'Take care of your friend,' she said. 'Tough guy.'

I watched her walk down the hall.

I told Nicky about Draper as I drove him home. About how I'd refused to help him but then changed my mind. What happened next. He didn't know what to say. After a while he looked at me.

'He wouldn't do that.'

I didn't answer him.

'He wouldn't. He's . . . he's a lot of things but not that. I've known him years. We fell out for a while, and I realized he was a long way from perfect as a person. A long way. I know he's no angel. He was a twat to Shulpa years ago, but he's not a killer.'

'No one is. Until they kill someone.'

'Not him,' Nicky asserted. 'I know he comes across a bit, I dunno, flash, but did you think he was capable of killing anyone? You've got instincts about that kind of thing. Well?'

I glanced over at Nicky but didn't say anything. We sat for a while, in silence, locked at a red light.

'What will you do? Tell the police? I understand that you'd have to if you got pulled for it yourself, but what if you aren't?'

I didn't really have an answer for that either.

Later, when we got to his flat, helping Nicky onto the sofa, I remembered the phone call. He'd made me take him inside so he could make it.

'Who did you speak to?'

'My father.'

I looked at him.

'In Leicester. He doesn't live at home any more,

but I asked him to go round there. He wasn't very pleased about it. I asked him to tell my mother to go and live with him. Him or one of his sisters. That or pay for her to go to India for a while.'

'Why?'

'They didn't just threaten to kill *me*. I don't know how, but they have my mother's address.'

Chapter Thirteen

At five to nine I was propping up a pillar outside the George on the Pancras Road with my hands in the pockets of a Norwegian ski jacket that I'd found in the sales in August. The morning was cold but the coat was warm and strong with, the sales assistant had been proud to show me, a radar sensor sewn into the arm so that avalanche teams could find me under the snow if that proved to be necessary. Not, I trusted, that I would be needing that particular feature in King's Cross. I hadn't used the jacket to ski in yet and had no idea when I'd be going. When I'd bought it I thought maybe I could go with Nicky but, thinking about it now, he'd already been under one avalanche that year.

I pulled the zip up to my chin and waited as the early morning rush hour moved around me. Rush hour? None of the cars making their way to or from the Westway was moving any faster than a crawl. The pub behind me was dark. The George is that rarity in the area these days, an unreconstructed gin palace that has resisted the stripped floorboards and the roast guinea fowl, clinging on to a lurid burgundy carpet and pickled eggs. I drink in the George now and then but only because the gym I train at is underneath the pub. When I say train I don't just mean lifting weights and using a rowing machine, which I do, I mean fight. I come here to fight other men, other men strange enough to want to come and fight me. But even though I very much needed to put more work into my speed, and my jab still wasn't getting through enough, it wasn't to trade punches that I'd come here that morning. I yawned in spite of the cold and looked at my watch.

My head had been rushing from sleep when the phone woke me. I'd been dreaming again. This time, for some reason, it was of the doctor who had treated Nicky. In my dream she was naked, her chest and stomach covered in open stab wounds, one of her nipples hanging off. She was slapping Nicky, pushing him back down a hospital corridor, punching him with a woman's fist until he cried, cutting his face with her ring. I was there but I wouldn't do anything. I wouldn't help him. When she'd had enough of him she turned to me, her teeth curled in a snarl.

'Come on,' she spat. 'Tough guy. Come on. Come on.'

The machine kicked in but the caller didn't feel the need to say anything. There had been a similar message last night and the electric woman on 1471 informed me that she didn't have the number. It gave me a good idea who the caller was.

My head was still clanging with sleep but I shook myself awake. I sat up and listened to the machine rewinding itself. At that moment my alarm went off. It was after eight and I pushed my duvet aside. Then I had that feeling again, only twice as bad.

Yes, this was really happening.

There were some croissants in my fridge, the kind

you make yourself out of a roll, which you see in the supermarket and buy and then realize how little like croissants they taste, until six months later when you buy them again. I made four and ate them all, listening to the news on Radio 4. They had it now. The woman recently reported to have been having an affair with married footballer Jack Draper had been found dead, in her flat. A spokesman for the Met with a voice flatter than most parts of Holland, confirmed that they were treating the death of model Alison Everly as suspicious, but would give no details of how she had died. I could understand his reticence. When pressed the spokesman admitted that no arrests had yet been made and when pressed further he told the reporter that the police had not spoken to Mr Draper about the incident but were, understandably, very keen to do so. They had not, however, managed to locate him yet.

On my way down to King's Cross I passed at least five newspaper boards flagging Alison Everly's murder, all with Draper's picture on the front. It had snowed again, but already the inch or so of white on the ground was salted and trodden, blackened by tyres and exhaust fumes. Everything seemed very distinct from everything else, as though the city weren't quite put together properly. I didn't know if it was the snow or my state of mind. The sky was a thick heavy grey, dirty as a mail sack.

I looked up from my watch to see Sally's Renault among the snarl of traffic inching its way towards me along the Pancras Road. When she was level she pulled up onto the broad pavement outside the pub, and gave me a short wave. Then she drove round the back.

Within a minute she had reappeared, minus the car, and she apologized for being late.

'You look like you're waiting for this place to open.' She nodded towards the pub behind me.

'The last few days I've had, don't be surprised. I'd happily sit in there for ever.'

'That bad, huh? I thought you sounded a little tense, shall we say, on the phone last night. Why don't you come downstairs and tell Auntie Sally all about it?'

'Thanks. I never had an aunt like you, though. All four of mine had moustaches. Which you don't.'

'No, thankfully. At least not yet. And if I was your aunt, then a certain evening last year would have been even more of a mistake, wouldn't it?'

'Yes,' I said, blushing slightly, 'I see what you mean.'

Sal unlocked the outside door and I followed her down the steps towards the gym. The occasion she was talking about had been eight months ago. It was the night that for various reasons the dam of our friendship had broken and we had ended up in bed together. We'd both been equally surprised by this, Sal because she'd had no physical contact with men for some time, and me because I'd never dreamed I'd end up pulling the clothes off my boxing coach. We'd both worked hard to wall the dam up again pretty quickly after what had happened but the knowledge of what we had done still hovered around us sometimes, like a patient flyweight looking for his chance.

I waited as Sal unlocked the door at the bottom of the steps and then followed her into the empty gym. I'd never been there in the daytime and was surprised at how quiet the place was. Our footsteps and voices rang hollow and tinny in the space that was usually so full of noise. Sal flicked on the master switch, flooding the room with a hard yellow light, and I looked round the square room, smaller-seeming with no one working out in it. I saw how the carpeting was old and worn. The ring in the centre looked shabby. The scuff marks on the floor and the sag of the ropes gave it a tired feel, as if it had had enough. The walls that I'd thought were cream were actually an old yellow. The place needed voices, colour, movement, the squeak of boots on canvas, Sal's voice belting out above the beatbox at warm-up. I found it vaguely distressing to be there, like visiting the house you grew up in, and I wished I'd asked to meet Sal somewhere else. But it was too late. I followed her into the office where she bent down and turned the switch on a gas heater.

'Coffee?'

'Please.'

'Instant, or I can put the machine on if you want fresh.'

'I can wait.'

'For caffeine? You're a strong man. Normally I need it now now now. But I'll wait with you. Sit down.'

'Thanks,' I said.

I took my jacket off and sat on a heavy, old-fashioned office chair with a cracked leather seat, watching as Sally opened a tin of coffee and found some filters. My fight coach and friend was dressed in a sleeveless fleece, a black roll neck and crisp blue combat pants, all snug enough to show that she still did a fair amount of training herself in between putting me through the wringer. Her hair was down, a straight sweep of black running to her shoulders, laced with the occasional embroidered strand of silver. On her left wrist she wore the heavy silver bangle I'd found at Spitalfields in December and given her for Christmas. I'd never seen it on her and it looked good. I wondered if she'd done that on purpose.

I've known Sal ever since wandering into the gym one wet October night five years back to ask her some questions about a missing kid. Back home in Dundee the kid had been a member of an amateur boys' boxing club, and I'd thought he might have been drawn to boxing gyms in London, and Sal's was the third I'd tried. As it turned out it was the things that were happening in the boys' club that had driven the lad away from Dundee, so he was hardly likely to go in search of more of the same. But Sal had helped me out in various ways and we had become friends. To begin with I just wanted somewhere to train, and I spent a month or so simply using the machines and the free weights. Then Sal put some gloves on me and suggested I had a go at the bag. For tension relief, nothing more, she assured me. But it wasn't long before I was eating up Ali biogs, doing more sit-ups per week than I'd done in my entire life, getting better at skipping than a ten-year-old girl and learning different ways not to get my teeth knocked out. At the time I had no idea why I'd taken to the sport so fast and five years later, while I'm a good deal better at it, I'm no nearer an answer. The adrenalin rush is higher than tennis, say, but maybe my love only continues because nothing bad has happened to me in the ring. I've never seen any negative consequences, to me or anyone else. I've never even had my nose broken, something I suspect

Sal of urging a couple of the boys to remedy as soon as possible.

Sal unzipped her fleece and turned the heater down. She knew I wasn't there to gossip but somehow it didn't seem right to begin until we were both set with our coffees in front of us. As the machine heated up she perched on the edge of the table and asked me how I was getting along with Shulpa.

I saw her in the frame of the door again, her face frozen. I hadn't thought about Shulpa. What might happen if she got involved in this. They already had Nicky's mother's address and Shulpa was a lot nearer. The thought stopped me. I knew I had to keep her well clear.

'Fine,' I said. 'Fine.'

'And you're over the other one?'

I smiled. Sal is a remarkably frank woman. When she has a thought you don't have to be David Copperfield to know what it is. She'll tell you. I thought about what she'd asked me. I saw a pair of green eyes, shining like wet grass. I blinked them away.

'Yes.' I nodded. 'Yeah. Really. I keep thinking that I can't be, it hasn't been long enough, not after everything we went through. But I think I am.'

Sal raised an eyebrow, then shrugged. 'Do you ever see her?'

'No. I keep expecting to run into her, visiting Luke especially, but I never do. I think she's stopped going.'

'That's a shame. She was lovely, really lovely. Do you *want* to meet her?'

'I don't know,' I said. 'I really don't know.'

'You could just call her.'

'Yes,' I said. 'I know, Sal.'

The coffee was dripping down into the jug and Sal washed out two cups. I was glad she didn't go any further with her questions than she had. Sal had met the girl she was talking about a few times and had told me before that she'd liked her. She'd never said it, but she wasn't a particular fan of Shulpa, something which I tried not to let worry me, or add to the doubts I sometimes had myself. I knew that Sal had reservations about our relationship and I also knew that they were to a large degree based on Shulpa herself. Women tended not to take to my new love. But they also went further than that. Sally just thought that with Sharon I'd done that thing, that amazing thing they write a lot of books and make a lot of films about. She thought I'd found the person who was right for me. And if you'd asked me at the time I would have been the first to agree with her. But then I did that other thing they write a lot of books and make a lot of films about. Once I'd found her I lost her again.

However much I wanted to change the subject I didn't ask Sal about her love life. Sally's husband died, what, ten years ago now, and she's long since abandoned her attempts to replace him. Instead she puts her energies into running the boxing gym that was his passion and carrying on various aspects of the business that was his livelihood. Until now I'd never delved into that. It was an area of Sally's life that, very early on in our friendship, we had both instinctively decided not to visit. I didn't ask when I saw her break off from training to go into her office with the kind of characters who were always going to get picked out of a line-up, whether they were at the scene or not. I pretended not to notice if a couple of the boys happened to be missing from training, leaving Sally tense, overly buoyant, until they showed up later and she calmed down. I never judged her and I knew she didn't think I did, and nor did it have anything to do with the fact that I used to be on the other side. I just, quite simply, didn't want to get involved.

That, however, was what I was there to change.

Sally pulled her fleece and sweater off and I wondered where to begin. When she turned back to me her face, smiling and soft before, had hardened to a seriousness, a weight I hadn't often seen. It surprised me. It was the same face, broad, strong without being manly, the same full, generous mouth, each fine line round her eyes a chapter in her life story. But it was different. It was like stepping into the ring with the friend you've just loosened up with, looking at him behind his guard. It just wasn't Sal any more.

Sal folded her arms over a copy of the *Sun*, Jack Draper's face on the cover. I moved my eyes away from it and set myself. It took me ten minutes to tell her what Nicky had got himself into. I tried not to miss anything out. I didn't make it sound any better than it was, or any worse for that matter, just giving her the facts. The Maltese guy, buying the bar, the suitcase full of cash and the way I'd found him. Sal sat there all the while, her feet drawn up to her chest, nodding or shaking her head, looking straight at me. She knew Nicky, having met him a couple of times at the Ludensian, and she liked him.

'It took me a while to realize that the charm was actually genuine, though,' she'd said, after leaving the bar one night. 'He's got a very rare quality. He really does *like* people, doesn't he? How many people do you ever meet in London who even ask you anything about yourself, let alone go ahead and listen?'

Sal winced when I told her what they'd done to Nicky, the muscles in her face tightening, but she nodded at the same time, as if it was a natural event. A logical result given the events that had preceded it. It made me wonder something that had never before occurred to me – if she'd ever put in motion anything like that herself. I told Sally what the two guys had promised to do to Nicky's mother and then what they said they'd do to him. Again she nodded, as if there was no other way it could go.

When I'd finished she leaned forward, her lips pursed and her eyes narrowing.

'So, who's got it?'

'I don't know.' I picked up my coffee and drained the cup. I was glad I'd waited.

'But you intend to find out?'

'If I can. That or find a new place to drink. And someone to drink with.'

'And it was under his bedroom floorboards, you say? At the Ludensian.'

'So he tells me. One day it was there, the next, *nada*.'

'I hate to say it but I will. Fucking idiot. And these guys, they're not going to give him any breathing space?'

I shook my head. 'Do you know them? A Maltese outfit?'

A wary, worried look came over Sally's face. We'd never spoken like this. Strange as it seemed to me, it was obviously weird to her too. I could see her wondering how much I assumed about what she did, how much I knew. I could also see her asking – does he really want to go there?

'*Of* them,' she said after a second or two. 'They're pretty quiet, normally, these days at least. They used to run Soho, in the 60s, strange as that might sound. They take a lot of money off their own – there are more Maltese in London than you'd think. They're into smack pretty heavily, though not at street level, several bookies, a casino, probably somewhere behind the odd shady property deal here and there. They're reputed not to take kindly to being interfered with – but you already know that. I'll ask around and get more. As far as I know there's only one Maltese outfit in London now.'

'Thanks.'

'No problem. Is there anything else I can do?'

'Yes,' I said. I sat forward and nodded. 'There is. There's a very, very big thing you can do.'

Sal's expression didn't change for a long time. She pursed her lips.

'Are you sure you want this?'

'It's the only way. I need to buy him some time.'

'You do know it's not just him who'll be in debt, don't you?' There was an appeal in her voice that said, 'Please, think about this.'

'You'll be connected to it, you'll be in it too, Billy.'

'I'm aware of that. But he's my friend. I'm not going to sit back and let someone waste him.'

'You know he could just mortgage his bar?'

'In a week? And have the money ready? I'm going to get him to do that anyway. But for you, not for them. I don't think they'll wait for that. They'll think he's trying to chisel them.'

'It's a lot of money, Billy.'

'And his bar is worth more, a lot more. He'll raise the money on it, just not straight away. It'll take a while.'

'Even so. It's a lot of money. I wouldn't be able to get it all myself. Not this quickly. I'll have to put it together, and that means there'll be people other than myself who'll want it back. And they're not as nice as me, Billy, if you know what I'm saying.'

'I understand.'

'It's not just the Maltese who play rough.'

'Yes, I know that, Sal.'

'I'd hate to have to come to you and ask you for money you didn't have.'

'I know that.'

'I can see why Nicky would need to – but you? Are you sure you want anything to do with this?'

'I am. Nicky's a wreck, he can't do shit. Get me forty-five grand and it gives me three weeks to help him. Nicky will mortgage his bar and we'll pay you back out of that, *if* I can't find out what happened to the stash he had. The rest of the cash from the mortgage will go to the Maltese.'

Sal thought about it but I could tell she didn't like it. She was looking for a way to say no. But the business was fine, she couldn't see anything wrong with that. It was me, being in it. She didn't want me to cross the line my foot was resting on.

'I wouldn't ask, not if I could think of another way. There is no other way.'

'And he'll agree? To mortgage the Old Ludensian? He won't like it, not after building it up the way he has.'

'No,' I said, 'he definitely won't. But I don't see that he has any choice. This way, if I can't get the money back, he might lose it, everything he's ever worked for, paying these guys off. But that's okay. The other way he keeps his bar. He just loses his mother, then the back of his head.'

Sally let out a long breath and nodded. She lifted her shoulders, pretending she was simply thinking figures, cash flow, whether the deal made financial sense to her. She knew she couldn't persuade me.

'It sounds okay, I suppose,' she said eventually.

I sat back in my chair, relieved. Relieved and excited in a way I couldn't understand. I had a tight feeling in the pit of my stomach. I was in it now. I felt an instant and intense connection to Nicky, as if the rest of the world had faded away, like two guys on horses in a John Ford flick. I thanked Sally and asked her when I could have the money.

Sally told me she'd sort something out soon and then we sat, trying to pretend that I hadn't just become a name in her little red book. We talked about this and that. Sally's arms were folded over Jack's face but she didn't mention Draper, having no idea I had anything to do with him. We were a little more like we usually were but Sal was still distanced from me. I think she wanted me to be sure I knew I'd crossed the line. I did know that but I hoped that in three weeks' time or less, I would be able to some degree to step back over it again. The atmosphere stayed brittle. There was now another fighter hovering in the air between us, but this one a little more deadly.

'Why are you *so* keen to help him out?'

'I told you. He's my friend. Naturally I want to help him.'

'Of course. But there's helping, and doing this. Why take it all on yourself?' I didn't say anything. 'He must have other friends.'

Again I was silent.

'Don't tell me you blame yourself!' Sally laughed and I looked away from her.

'That's ridiculous. *And* you know it.'

'I should have stopped it.'

Sally's chin went towards her throat. 'Your friend chooses to be a prize jerk, how can that be your fault?'

'I should have known,' I said quietly. 'No, I did know. I assumed Nicky thought more of me. I assumed he trusted me enough to let me in. But he didn't. And I left it two whole weeks without making him tell me.'

Sal was shaking her head. 'No. It was because he thinks so *much* of you that he couldn't tell you, not that he doesn't value you. He knew he was being greedy. And weak, and stupid. And he didn't want you to think those things about him. Anyone else, not you. That's why he waited until he *had* to tell you. It's tough, Billy, to admit who you are to people. It's easier to go on and pretend and hope it'll work itself out. I bet there are things you've never told him.'

I shook my head. 'Maybe . . .'

'And why didn't you? Because you want to present

to him the side of yourself that you want him to see. Not the crap.'

'Maybe,' I said, and I nodded to myself. I'd never told Nicky about sleeping with Sal. It had happened the night I'd started seeing his sister. I smiled. 'You're right. He knows I box, for instance, but I've never bothered telling him that Des picks me apart most nights, makes me look like Joe Bugner fighting Ali. But when I finally land one on him that gets his arse dusty I'll tell Nicky about it.'

'Exactly. So don't be too hard on yourself.'

'No.'

Sal shifted in her chair and gave me a wry smile. I was reaching for my coat.

'So,' she said. 'You think you can?'

'What?'

'Get the better of Des.' I laughed. 'Dazzling Des Formay? Former pro. The training he does makes you look like a housewife trying to get her figure back for her hubby. And he's quick. Quicker than you.'

I smiled. 'Better see you tomorrow night, then.'

'You had, Mr Rucker, you had. And many, *many* more nights after that.'

Outside a big hand had turned the world upside down and given it a shake. Fat wet snowflakes were twisting in the wind. I thought the snowfall looked out of place in the middle of the city but changed my mind. Through the flurry and the shake, pedestrians scurried for cover, cars edged through lights, hooting, pushing, a laden bus lumbered off, its windows steamed, a jet of diesel blasting out. And in my mind the events of the last few days whirled too. Everything seemed as confused and random as the snowflakes, jostling for space in the white air. But the snow became uniform when it settled and somehow all the rest knitted together too, the cars got through, the people got to work and the buses made it back to the depot. The only difference was that the city never stopped. There was never a time when it was peaceful and still, quiet, unmoving.

I stood for a second watching it all. I'd hate to have to come to you and ask you for money you didn't have. I wondered – if someone owed her and wasn't paying, how far would she go? I saw the drop of blood, taking an age to drip down from the lip of Nicky's garage door. How far would she go if the person not paying her was me?

Everything in Britain seems to be devastated by an inch or two of snow as if nothing like it has ever happened before but I, for one, was prepared. With the peaked hood of my Norwegian ski jacket in place I pounded up the hill to my flat, the Recco system in my sleeve emitting radar messages all the way. All of a sudden it felt very comforting to have it there. Avalanches tend to be caused by people skiing off-piste, bringing down walls of snow in their wake. Since my chat with Sally I realized that now, that was exactly what I was doing.

So. I'd bought Nicky a few weeks. Now I had to decide how to use them. I didn't get a whole lot of time to think about that, though, just the ten minutes it took me to walk back up to Exmouth Market. I didn't take much notice of the bike courier, leaning on the wall of the magazine company next door to my flat. The hood of his orange waterproof was up and a breathing mask covered his face. He was out of my mind as fast as he'd come into it, even though it was still snowing and it was odd that he should be standing there. Can't be an easy job, in this weather. I'd walked past him, about to reach for my keys, when I felt a hand on my shoulder.

'Billy,' Draper said. 'Billy. I have to speak to you.'

Chapter Fourteen

'I didn't fucking do it!'

We were standing in the deep, covered porch of the magazine publishers. He'd wanted to come up to my flat but I'd told him no. God knows why I was even speaking to him. I could have been under surveillance, anything. Draper kept his hood up though he'd pulled his mask down. I told him I didn't want to talk to him.

'I was framed, set up . . .'

'I don't care.'

'What do you mean!? What do you mean, you don't care?'

'Like I told you. I have other things to think about . . .'

'What? That's bullshit, looking for missing kids? Bollocks. You really don't care? It wasn't me, I didn't do it.'

I sighed. 'Do what, Jack?'

'You fucking well know what. I didn't do it. You went to see Janner. I called him. He said someone had been to see him. He wanted to know why you were sure I wouldn't play on Thursday. He wanted to know what you knew.'

'And I want to know what you know. Last time, you didn't exactly tell me much.'

'You didn't give me time.'

'Bullshit. You could have told me you were screwing around any time you liked. But somehow, you forgot to mention that, didn't you?'

'Okay, I wasn't going to tell you. But why the fuck should I have, eh? I didn't think Alison had anything to do with what I wanted you for.'

'And doesn't she?'

'I don't know. No. Yes. How the fuck do I know?'

'You tell me. Come on, Jack. Speak to me. For instance – tell me how you found out about it. About what had happened to her. If you didn't kill her. Hear it on the news, did you? Someone call you?'

I knew how he knew. I'd followed him right to the place. I just wanted to know if he was going to have another go at shitting me.

'How did *you* find out? Janner said you were fishing around long before it was in the news.'

'I used to be a copper. I hear things. Come on.'

'Shit. Shit.' He shook his head, his hands on his hips. His face closed in on mine. 'I *found* her. I was there. I walked in and she was . . . she was cut up, okay? I probably left my prints. Christ. There were loads of them there anyway. It comes out in the paper I was seeing her and then she's dead, she's fucking dead. What the *fuck* am I going to do?'

'Go play for a side in Mexico. Or deal with it. If you didn't kill her—'

'I didn't. I did not kill her!'

'Then why go round there?'

'Why?' He laughed like I was seriously stupid. 'Why the fuck d'you think? I was fucking the girl, okay. I had a bust up with my wife and I went round, I went round to fuck her.'

He stopped me with that. I'd assumed he'd found out about his forthcoming appearance in the *Sun*. I'd assumed he'd gone round because Alison had betrayed him. I didn't know whether to believe him.

'Then why did your wife leave you?'

'What? How . . . ?'

'I was outside your flat. I saw you. She steamed out with your baby and you drove off to Hoxton. I saw you go into Alison's building.'

'Jesus . . .'

He was trying to take it in. What it meant. I didn't let him.

'So why did she leave? Did you tell her about Alison?'

'No, I told her about you. That cat's head freaked her out. She'd said I had to tell the Bill. I persuaded her I'd get you to do it. When I told her you'd turned me down she left. She said you were right.'

'I was.'

'I know. I *know*. And it wasn't because I thought you'd rumble me about seeing Alison. I just wanted it low-key.'

'Oh sure. Right.'

'Oh okay, so I didn't want anyone with a line to the tabloids sniffing round. Of course I didn't want it to get out about Alison. But Christ, you've never banged someone you shouldn't have?'

'Maybe.'

'Maybe bullshit. So. What am I going to do? More to the point what are you going to do? Tell them you saw me going into her place?'

'I won't need to do that, Jack.'

'My prints are there, I know. But I could say they were from before . . .'

'It's not that.'

'What do you mean?'

'I got stopped by the Bill.'

'What?'

'On Hoxton Square. My back light was out. I saw you park. I saw you going into the place while they were booking me. They must have seen you too. They must have.'

'What?! Oh fuck. Oh no.'

He had gone white. He had a serious case of stubble burn again, and it stood out like a silk scarf. His face twitched. I thought he was going to lose it. He took a deep breath that juddered out of him.

'You should have seen her, Billy. She was so messed up. You should have seen what the bastard did to her.'

'Not you, then?'

He didn't answer me. He'd pushed himself right up close to me. He was wired, almost insane. It was either the look of an innocent man staring at fifteen years or that of a guilty man too freaked to believe what he's done, what his anger has led him to.

'They're going to do me for it. They're going to fucking do me for it, aren't they? They saw me, going in? You have to help me. Okay? You *have to help me*, Billy.'

I didn't get a chance to answer. Suddenly Draper's eyes had flicked to the street, to the blizzard. Then he turned his back to it and his eyes found mine, locking straight in. They were asking me. A little confused, I broke his look. I wasn't confused for long. I turned to follow the police car that was slowing to a stop, only five yards from us, slowing to a stop outside my flat.

His eyes found mine again like a jet fighter's lock-on. The question never left them. He took a step back from me. The car had stopped. Slowly, he pulled the cycling mask up to his face. I took a breath. Draper didn't so much as blink. He tightened his hood until all that was left were a pair of dark eyes drilling into mine. I felt like a keeper, looking at the last pen in the shoot-out. Draper took another step back. Suddenly remembering, he held out a package that he was holding.

'I didn't know if I'd find you.'

He pushed the package forward and I looked at it. My hands closed round the padded envelope. Draper stepped back towards the street, his eyes staying fixed on mine. Behind him I could see the doors of the patrol car, opening. Two plain-clothed officers were stepping out of the back. My mouth opened. Draper stopped. He raised his chin. His head twitched towards them and his hands went to his hips as if to say, 'Well, well then?' They were slamming the car doors. I didn't move. After a long second Draper turned away. He took a couple of steps towards a mountain bike standing on the pavement, leaning up against the wall of the building.

As Draper emerged from the porch, the female officer glanced at him. She looked to be having the same thought I'd had. Tough job. Her younger partner wasn't paying any attention. Draper had his back to them. The woman who had been looking at him glanced away. She followed the other officer up to the door of my building and watched as her partner pushed the buzzer. She rubbed her hands together and moved on the spot. Draper got on his bike. I watched the other copper, pushing my bell again, as Jack Draper pedalled off towards Rosebery Avenue, his orange jacket gradually fading into the blizzard.

Chapter Fifteen

They only stayed ten minutes. They hadn't connected me to Draper, something I'd known as soon as I spoke to them. They were too polite. I was just a motorist who happened to have been in the Hoxton Square area, which they knew because I'd been stopped. They did ask me what I was doing there but I wasn't a suspect, they already had one of those. Just trying to get home, I told them. The fact that the police car had followed me into the square and then straight out again, as they'd thought, was also on my side. All the while the envelope Draper had given me sat in the centre of my coffee table between us.

The senior officer, DS Coombes, was a brisk woman with short ginger-brown hair and a thin, fox-like face. Her skin was wafer pale, covered in flat, smeared freckles, her lips non-existent. She had taken off a thin raincoat and was wearing a maroon trouser suit that couldn't have been a worse colour for her, with a gold sateen blouse beneath. A red metal badge in the shape of a ribbon was pinned to her lapel. Her assistant looked like he was on work experience from primary school, his permanent scowl about as intimidating as a plastic truncheon.

Coombes asked me if I'd seen anything suspicious

that night and I laughed – I said it had been raining too hard to see much of anything. She wanted to know if I'd happened to notice a blue Jeep Renegade on the square but I told them there had been too many cars around. I asked her what had happened in the square and she was a little surprised that I didn't know. They told me that a neighbour had found the body of a model, Alison Everly, the morning after I'd been there.

'Jesus,' I said, doing a nice crinkle with my forehead. 'Alison Everly? Don't I know that name?'

Coombes nodded. 'She was in the papers yesterday, sir. Having an affair with a footballer.'

'Right. Yeah, that's it. Draper? Jack Draper? Super . . .'

'That's right.'

'Shit. Sheee-it. And he killed her?'

'We don't know that yet.' Coombes put her notebook away and reached for her coat. 'It's too early to say. But between you and me, sir, I reckon the next team he'll be playing for won't have stripes on their shirts.' A glint came into her eye. 'They'll be arrows.'

I showed Coombes and her colleague out and then watched them through the kitchen window, stepping into the blizzard, clenching their bodies tight as they jogged the few yards to their Escort. A strong wave of guilt flooded through me. So, my former colleague Andy Gold hadn't got my message after all. It was left to a neighbour to find Alison. My mind went back to her. I didn't know who had stumbled across her body, I didn't know what kind of person they were or what they did for a living. All I knew was that the image of Alison lying back on that sofa had twisted my guts into a knot, had forced its way into my dreams and branded itself on my brain. Even though I'd been a policeman, even though I've seen other things like it. I didn't like to think what effect it had had on a friend, just calling round for a coffee, or seeing the door open. Once again I told myself that if I hadn't been there, which I very nearly wasn't, then the neighbour would have found her anyway. Once again I told myself that it had nothing to do with me. I watched the patrol car pull away tentatively into the traffic on Rosebery Avenue, leaving a rectangle of wet black tarmac behind it. The patch had been warmed by the car's engine and the flakes wouldn't settle. They blew onto it and disappeared like they were falling into a grave.

I stood for a second as the car moved off the way Draper had, trying to figure out what I was going to do that day. Yesterday I was pleased that there was nothing I could do yet. Today, it left me frustrated. There wasn't anything I could do for Nicky, not until I had the money from Sally. I needed to do something. I looked at the package in front of me, then opened it. There wasn't much inside, just a short note. In it Draper protested his innocence. He begged me to help him and told me to buy the *Evening Standard*. He also told me to speak to his wife, and gave me a number to call. I thought for a second. Nicky would be resting, I could see him later, tell him what Sally had said. I heard Jack's wife's voice, heard the letter box clapping behind her. I made two calls then grabbed my coat.

When I walked on to the market again the snow had nearly stopped, just the odd flake like empty nags coming home in the National. It was also a touch warmer, though the low grey sky still looked heavy as an alcoholic's suitcase. I walked round to the newsagent on the market and bought all the tabloids, plus the first edition of the *Evening Standard*. I took them to the Sand Bar, a stripped-out coffee place halfway along the market, with big tables, great cakes and staff so miserable the place is usually nice and quiet. Apart from the guy from the second-hand bookshop next door, leaning against the counter, there was no one in. I took a double espresso and some raisin bread over to the far corner, pushed aside a magazine on architecture and went through the papers, starting with the publication that had first featured Alison Everly, the *Sun*.

It would keep me from fretting over Nicky, at least. The tabloids all ran with Draper as lead story, even though the *Standard* had got the fact that his lover had been murdered the day before. That's the way it goes sometimes, with papers put out later in the day than the nationals. It all depends on when the story breaks as to who gets the best of it. The editor of the *Sun* probably felt aggrieved. He'd set the story up, had created the story if you like, building the girl, paying the girl, making her news. Then her body was found at nine the next morning and it fell into the *Standard*'s lap without them having to do anything.

A lot of what the *Sun* and the *Mirror* had was a rehash of what had been in yesterday's *Standard*, and on the television news. In the *Express*, it was the only story on the front page:

FOOTBALLER'S MISTRESS FOUND DEAD

The shot the *Express* had of Alison was different from that which had appeared in the *Sun*. They'd obviously bought it from a photo library. Alison Everly was a model, there were plenty of pictures of her about. It was shot from the side, Alison turning her face to the camera, smiling, her naked arms folded over her breasts. The picture had been cropped just above her hips, but low enough to tell that she wasn't wearing anything.

All of the tabloids went into the past of Alison Everly, noting her choice of career, all copping to the fact that she had appeared in several of the Leyton Orient match programmes modelling team kit. The *Sun* even reproduced one of their own Page Three shots of her, and my eyes ran over the naked breasts of the dead girl. It felt like the worst thing I'd ever done.

None of the papers came out and actually accused Draper of having killed Alison but there was no way that wasn't what they were trying to put across. There were shots of Jack, grinning, next to shots of the outside of Alison's apartment building. All the papers concentrated on the fact that Jack was missing. He hadn't been seen since the killing. The *Mail* reported the police as being anxious to speak to him while the *Star* made the point more vividly.

SUPER JACK WANTED OVER
STRIPPER SLAYING

References were made to Jack's past, to his frustrating injuries, to his 'powder keg' personality on the pitch. There was an interview with Draper's sports agent, who had no comment to make other than that he had not seen his client, nor heard from him, in weeks.

Before putting the tabloids aside I read a reworking of Alison's story in the *Mail*, which supplanted lurid headlines with a very motherly 'caring' tone, obviously trying to point up the horrors of infidelity. Alison's was a tale of sex and seduction, both of which Draper was, apparently, good at; and deceit, which he also managed pretty well. It told of hours of snatched happiness, long nights of loneliness, of dates and promises broken. 'He said he loved me and I believed him,' Alison was quoted as saying. 'But he just wanted my body.' She ended with the line: 'It's not me I'm sorry for really, I'll find someone else. It's his wife.'

There was a picture of Draper's wife in the centre of the page, struggling out of her house with her child. I finished the story, and then just looked at Alison. Her eyes. I thought I saw fear in them, or guilt, but it was probably just because I knew what had happened to her. Again it was overlaid with another face. A little girl, in a nurse's outfit, smiling with pure glee.

Once more, however, it was the *Evening Standard* that was pushing the story on and I could see why Draper wanted me to read it. The piece made both back and front pages and was written by none other than the editor. Like the rest of the tabloids, the *Standard* also noted that Draper was still nowhere. But they had, the editor claimed, come into the possession of notes that Draper had been making for an autobiography. It was another thing he hadn't said anything to me about. The paper didn't print any extracts, knowing that what they had was juice enough for now and they could always use the extracts later.

The *Standard* claimed that the extracts they had made reference to some very sharp practices Draper had been witness to during his career. They told of bungs and bribes, match-fixing and gambling syndicates, of players feigning injury to get their price lowered, having been promised a pay-off by the teams coming in to buy them. The *Standard* went on about the Bosman ruling, which allowed any player to own his own contract. Draper was alleging that after it came into effect big clubs often bribed players in smaller outfits to see their contracts out to the end, so they wouldn't have to pay a fee to sign them. The alleged offences had happened right up until the end of Draper's career, not just at the beginning, and would shock people who believed the game had cleaned up its act. What the paper was really excited about, however, was that in the extracts they had got their hands on Draper did one very important thing. He named names.

I read the article twice, and thought about what Draper had actually tried to find me for. The photographs posted to him, even the cat's head. Had the person responsible gone even further? Draper had said he had a list of names, and then I'd got him so worked up he'd done one before he'd gone through them with me. And now he'd been scared off before I could ask him about it. By the sound of it the list was pretty long. If the *Standard* was to be believed there would hardly be a single person, player or coach, involved in football who wouldn't want to get him into trouble. Had someone from his past really killed Alison, to land him in it? Had he been stitched up? Why not just kill Jack himself? Had he been stitched up or did he just want the world to think that?

I sat back, downed my coffee, and looked at the note Draper had given me. Did I want to get involved in this? Sally had asked me the same thing about Nicky but I'd had no doubts there. I shook my head. I didn't really have a choice here either. The police were polite enough this time but it wouldn't be long before someone linked me to Draper, through Nicky or some-one who'd seen us in Fred's. They'd want some answers as to what I'd really been doing there. I stood up and walked through what was now sleet, to my car.

Chapter Sixteen

There were still quite a few photographers outside number fourteen when I got to Stepney Green. I knew there would also be a police officer or two sitting in one of the seemingly innocent cars opposite the house, in case Jack ran out of socks and came back for some more. A no-win job that, one I'd always hated. There was never any way a missing suspect was going to return home once he knew he was wanted, no way at all, but if he did, and you missed him, you'd be back in a silly blue hat before the day was out. I drove past the house and looked for a place to park.

I'd binned the note Draper had given me but brought the envelope along, stuffed with old carrier bags. I pulled into a quiet cul-de-sac where I was less likely to get a ticket and looked at my watch. Midday. Driving down the street took me straight back to the night before last and yet again I couldn't get the image of Alison Everly out of my head. I felt like a landlord with a tenant he can't evict. She was lying on her sofa, but already I couldn't be sure if I was seeing her as she was, or as she had become inside me, her image from the newspaper lying alongside the body I'd seen. I saw my picture in her eye, as if it would stay there once I had gone. I felt bound to her, bound in a similar way that I am to the kids I look for. As soon as I have their photograph in my hand it's as if there's an instant covenant between us, they're part of me, until I make contact. Some, I never do make contact with. Some just go back home and their parents sometimes remember to tell me. Some just vanish, and I take their pictures out of their files sometimes, just to look at them. They always look back. The thread is still there and there's only one way to cut it. And that's what I was doing on Stepney Green. While I knew that I'd drop everything to get Nicky out of the jam he was in, it didn't really affect the way I felt about Alison.

She was, as the man said, looking at me.

I locked up and walked out of the cul-de-sac and back up the street. Stepney Green is a wide road with a series of gardens running down the middle, guarded by tall black railings. To the right of the gardens a very narrow, cobbled lane separated them from a series of surprisingly beautiful Georgian and Victorian houses, one particularly impressive example of which, four storeys high with a rather grandiose entranceway, was undergoing renovation. It was a strange area to look at, the skyline a mixture of pleasant old brick housing and tatty grey tower blocks where the V2s had landed. I walked on the left of the road, past a row of cheap, 60s shoeboxes, up to the red-brick dwellings I'd noticed on my last visit there. They were put up in 1899 by the East End Building Company. I knew this because of the architectural qualities of the building, the shape and style, as well as the research I had done into the area as part of my detailed and methodical investigative procedures. Not because of the plaque on the wall.

The curtains of number fourteen were closed, both upstairs and down. The house looked empty but I knew it wasn't. I received a little attention as I walked towards the photographers, an even bigger group today, all dressed in the sort of coat I was wearing myself. The attention waned as I made my way through them, up to the door of number sixteen, but it didn't disappear completely. I leaned on the bell.

'Special delivery,' I said, when I heard footsteps on the other side of the newly painted blue door. I turned the package in my hand over. 'For Dr Flowers.'

The door opened and there was Dr Flowers, or at least a man who claimed to be him. He was tall and blond, good-looking in a withdrawn, nervous kind of way. He took the package from me and squinted at it through a pair of tortoiseshells, pretending to read the address.

'Oh yes,' he said. 'Thanks. Do I need to sign?'

'Please.'

'I have to get a pen. Do come in, it's freezing out there.'

The doctor held the door open for me and I took a step forward, glancing at the men gathering on the street next door. None of them was paying any attention to me. I walked into the hallway and the doctor closed the door behind me.

He told me that he was indeed Richard Flowers and we shook hands. 'Good performance?' he asked.

'You should contact the RSC.'

The doctor looked ever so slightly pleased with himself.

'Anything exciting?' He held the package up.

'No,' I said. 'Sorry.'

'Well, never mind. But I'm glad you're here, I have to leave soon.' He looked worried for a second. 'It is Mr Rucker, yes?'

'It is.'

'Right. Come through,' the doctor said. 'I know Louise is waiting.'

I followed the doctor down the hall and into the kitchen, which looked out onto a surprisingly large garden. He unlocked the door and peered out, down towards a high wall at the bottom, topped with broken glass.

'Journalists,' he explained. 'They've tried getting over there. The police warned them off but you never know. Coast is clear now, though. Follow me.'

He led me out of the back door, across the top of the garden, past a herb bed made up mostly of rose-mary, strong enough to give off a mild scent even at that time of the year. There was a short wall separating the property from its neighbour, which gave way to a high fence. Set in the wall was a door, which the doctor pushed open. He put his head through and I could see him looking down towards the end of next door's garden too.

'This way,' he said, after a second.

Louise Draper met us in the small conservatory that had been added on to the kitchen of her own house. I'd looked for traces of blood on the back door, but hadn't been able to see any. Louise was washing some dishes. She looked up with a bright, forced smile, her eyes somewhere completely else, and thanked Richard Flowers for his help. He gave her a quiet smile back, while she stripped the gloves from her hands and untied the apron she was wearing.

'Michael not giving you any trouble?' the doctor asked.

'No,' she assured him. 'You know he never does. I'll send him round. He's upstairs.'

'Right,' the doctor said.

Louise and the doctor chatted for a while, making mutual babysitting arrangements. Her voice was a slight surprise. It was a lot softer than it had sounded over the phone. I stood, vaguely listening, my hands crossed in front of me, looking at Louise, occasionally glancing out of the window at some garden birds, jockeying for position around a small net of nuts hanging from a bird table. I had a brief flash of the bird I'd seen, outside my office window. Then the doctor left, shutting the door behind him quietly, and Louise walked towards me, giving me a slim, long hand to shake. It was a firm hand, which she left in mine a little longer than usual the way some people do. I smiled at her, wondering what she must be thinking after the week she'd had, and took my hand back. She thanked me for calling, for coming round. Then we stood for a second, neither of us speaking.

Louise Draper was a petite, attractive woman, with an awkward, doe-like quality that softened her brittle, doll-like figure. She moved with nervous, skittish gestures, as though there were foxes on the wind, and I didn't know whether to put this down to her character or her situation. I saw her stomping out into the night the way she had, careless of the rain, and could hardly believe it was the same woman. But that was only after receiving strange mail and a rather gruesome delivery.

She was yet to be a wronged wife with a wanted husband and a pack of baying photographers outside.

Louise was dressed in a pair of tight black pedal pushers and a turquoise halter top, a ribbon of taught stomach visible where the two just failed to meet. Her thin, muscular arms looked very naked against the cold, broad windows. Louise had full, deep black hair, the kind you see in slow motion on shampoo ads, setting off the flawless skin that was given a light, amber sheen from what looked like the discreet use of a sunbed, but could easily have been her natural skin tone.

Louise had looked relaxed enough when the doctor was there, but soon began to tense up. The atmosphere stiffened, became more and more brittle. It affected me too. I felt clumsy, bigger than her, and I didn't quite know where to put myself. Louise's eyes flickered constantly, looking at me then moving away before I could get a hold on her. Her eyes were small, light brown with bright blue flecks. Rimmed with red. The face surrounding them was small and just slightly squashed in on itself, as if she'd just woken up. She looked shaky, uncertain, the girlish face that on another day would have put her at college age now making it impossible to say how old she was.

It was a slight relief when Louise walked out into the living room and called out 'Michael!' up the stairs. When she came back into the kitchen she smiled faster than a subliminal advert and asked me if I wanted tea or coffee. I said I was easy, whatever she was having. I watched as she bent down for a cafetière, then as she reached on tiptoes for some cups. She still moved very awkwardly and I was again relieved when she said why don't I wait next door. I gave her a closed-mouth smile and walked into the darkened living room, the curtains closed, where I sat on a long, maroon-coloured sofa. My eyes moved round a well-kept room, the furniture new, the fittings modern Laura Ashley, but still Laura Ashley. The curtains were closed. I'd seen a riding crop protruding from a pair of boots by the back door and on the coffee table in front of me was a copy of *Horse and Rider*.

The doctor's son walked down the stairs and after we'd spoken he went out through the kitchen. Through the door I saw Louise giving him a Kit Kat to take with him, then tousling his hair, making him blush. She walked through with a tray in her hands and I glanced away as she leaned over in front of me to set it on a coffee table, before hitting the switch on an uplighter near the sofa.

'It's decaf I'm afraid,' Louise said, her eyes never leaving me. 'Jack drinks it, he says it's a special brand, but I still hate it. I haven't been able to get any fresh. I'm sorry but I've been a bit of a mess these last few days.'

'That's okay. I drink too much anyway. And I understand.'

Louise sat down on the other end of the sofa, her delicate frame making little impression on the deep cushions. She looked at me, feeling it necessary to try to sustain a smile, as if it were the vicar who'd called. She looked like a child, pretending to be grown up. I gave her a reassuring grin and reached into my bag for my notebook.

There was a baby monitor on the tray and Louise checked the volume before setting it down on top of the magazine. She pressed the plunger on the glass jug and carefully poured beef-smelling coffee into two cups, asking me if I wanted milk. She was affecting an air of nonchalance that wouldn't have got her into drama school. I tried to match it, probably doing just as well.

'A little please, Mrs Draper,' I said, not really caring. 'But no sugar.'

'Right,' she said, her hand going to a small, gold earring. 'That's how I have it too. And it's Louise, okay? Mrs Draper. It's what the police called me.'

I nodded, and promised to call her by her Christian name from now on. We sat along the sofa from each other, Louise side-on to me, her legs pressed tight together, resting her cup on her knees. The sofa was expensive but she didn't look comfortable. She drank her coffee like a child, holding the cup with both hands. There were no goosebumps on her arms but they still looked cold. I wished she'd pull a jumper on. I had the impulse to take them in my hands and rub them for her.

'Before you ask me anything, I should say that I spoke to my, to Jack last night. He called when I was at a friend's. He wouldn't say where he was. He told me to ask you to help him. He said I should give you a thousand pounds if you agreed, but more if you wanted. He didn't tell me how much more.'

I took a sip and nodded, trying not to wince, before putting my cup down on the low table. Should I tell her I'd just seen Jack? I didn't know. 'That won't be necessary,' I said. 'Your husband is a friend of a friend, so if I help it'll be for a favour, not for cash. I don't know what use I'll be, though.' I thought of the things

I could tell the police. They may have clocked his car like I told Draper, or they may not. Either way, they wouldn't help him. 'You see, what I find might do him more harm than good. I don't want his money, because I don't want to hide anything. Do you understand?'

Mrs Draper thought about it then nodded, slowly. She looked down at an impressive rock on her left hand and turned the band that was next to it. 'You mean that you might prove Jack did kill that girl. Just as easily as you might prove he didn't?'

'Yes,' I said. 'Yes. And if he did, then I'm not going to help him. If he did do what it seems he's being accused of, I hope they catch him for it. So I don't want to take his money, only then to do more harm to him than good.'

Louise pursed her lips and nodded slowly. Suddenly, she looked completely lost, tiny on the oversized sofa, like Alice in a nightmare Wonderland. When she saw me looking at her she pulled herself together and set her cup down next to mine. She reached into her purse and pulled out a chequebook.

'Really,' I said. I held up my hands. 'I don't want Jack to pay me. In fact, I won't take his money . . .'

'This is mine,' Louise said quickly. Her voice was struggling for authority like a salmon fighting upstream. 'And though I know Jack wants you to clear his name, so that he can come out of wherever it is he's hiding, that's not what I want. That's not why I called you. Not at all. I want to know the truth. I want to know whether I'm married to a murderer or not. A murderer as well as a bastard. You can understand that, can't you?'

'Yes,' I said quickly, 'that makes sense to me.'

'So it's me who's employing you, not him. Okay?'

'Okay.'

'Good,' Louise said.

I took a deep breath and waited patiently while Louise wrote the cheque. I still didn't know whether to tell her that I'd seen her husband. She handed the cheque to me and I left it on the coffee table. I was about to start asking her some questions, most of them pretty difficult, when she beat me to it.

'So,' she said. Bright and bitter. 'What do you think?'

'About . . .?'

'Jack. The police are pretty certain, I could tell. Yesterday they went through this place like a bunch of archaeologists. And they were all so *amazingly* nice to me. The poor little wifey. I know he went there, you know? That night. He told me.'

I nodded, slowly. 'I know that too.'

'But did he – ' she found it hard to say it, and she took a sharp breath – 'did he kill her? Did he, Mr Rucker? Did . . . did the man I married *kill* someone? Kill them with a knife, like that? I didn't want to ask the police. I didn't want to say anything.'

'What do you think?'

Her eyes had been wide open to me, but now they withdrew, like a schoolgirl being asked why her homework was late. 'I don't know.' She shook her head, looking down at her lap. 'He's never been violent, he's never hit me, anything like that. Not all footballers' wives can say that. Believe me. But what if he had? What would that show? I keep telling myself that of course he couldn't have done it, and then it dawns on me yet again that that's what every wife must say. But you're on the outside. Tell me, honestly, do you think he did it? You must have an opinion.'

I closed my notebook. I couldn't see any point in lying to her. 'I did,' I said. 'Yes. Now, I don't know. He would have had to have been pretty quick. But everything points to him. Motive, opportunity, a probable sighting by a police officer. But I can't know. I'd like to know what the forensics people come up with – and I *might* be able to find out if I'm lucky. One thing I am sure of is that if he stays in hiding everyone'll be convinced that he did it. The police, especially. So if you speak to him . . .'

'Don't worry. I told him to give himself up. But he's never done anything I've said. He's never done anything anyone's said. And somehow, I don't think he ever will,' she added.

Louise hugged her arms together and drew her legs up onto the sofa, tucking them beneath her. She didn't look any less tense, though. I couldn't help thinking about Nicky. Nicky had been assaulted, beaten up and left for dead. I hadn't seen him today but I knew he'd be in a hell of a state when I did. Well, the same thing had happened to Louise Draper. Last week, in spite of the problems she was having, she had been, essentially, fine. Whole. And then her world had come down, knocking her not only sideways but every other direction too, sending fragments of herself spinning off her, fragments she'd never get back. She, too, was being held together by vinegar and brown paper and the signs that she'd been through the mill were as easy to see as the bruises and bandages that adorned my friend.

I turned round to face my new employer and gave

her a look that was meant to prepare her for the conversation we now needed to have. She sat very still, staying very attentive to me. Over the next half hour I asked her a lot of questions: how she'd met her husband, whether he had ever been unfaithful to her before, places she thought he might be hiding. I tried to pitch my voice very evenly, lacing it with cotton wool without overstuffing it, keeping my body still and calm. Louise remained tense at first but gradually began to relax, settling into the sofa. It made it easier to focus on her and sometimes, when her answers began to untangle at the ends into strands I couldn't use, I found that I was doing that rather than listening to her.

On first glance Louise had the body of a teenage girl, but when you looked further you saw the added strength young mothers often display, in the arms and neck, along with a weightier, fuller quality that was all about the way she sat, and moved. My mother had a couple of phrases that would have described her perfectly, better than fit or cute or beautiful or sexy: she was easy to see, my mother would have said. Easy to see or soft on the eyes. I told my eyes to stick to more difficult things. I concentrated on my notebook, focusing on Louise's voice, backed by the sounds of the street; cars driving past, an occasional siren, a helicopter throbbing heavily in the air. The room took on a deep, sombre quality, matched by the dim grey light. Louise sat opposite me, small and alone.

She told me about the letters she'd received. She spoke of her feelings when she'd seen the mess on her door. She answered my questions methodically, taking her time, weighing her answers so she could be of most help. Even when I asked her things that were obviously painful she seemed to accept that they were things I had to know. After a while I took her through the night of the murder. Jack hadn't told her about Alison after meeting me in Fred's. Louise confirmed that she hadn't argued with him about an affair – she knew nothing about it – but over his in-action concerning the letters she was getting, and the cat's head.

'I begged him to go to the police,' she insisted. 'I couldn't understand why he wouldn't. It drove me mad, so I left him. I was just scared, of being here. Of what might happen next, especially with Tommy in the house. Jack went on about his career, not getting the wrong profile, but it didn't mean anything to me.' She gave a short, harsh laugh. 'Then, when I saw the paper the next day, I knew why he didn't want anyone following him around.'

Louise told me that she'd spoken to Jack twice since then. He called her at her sister's in Fulham, later that night, where she'd gone with her child. He'd told her about his affair with Alison.

'He said how sorry he was. Then he told me he was going to disappear for a while. When I asked him why, why wasn't he coming over to beg my forgive-ness, *beg* me to have him back, he told me what had happened.'

'And what was that? According to him?'

'He *said* he went round to end it.' Louise laughed. 'That he knew it was a mistake. He said he drove over to Hoxton Square, and when he got there she was dead. And he knew they'd think it was him. Everyone would. He knew they'd tie him to her. I was hysterical. Then he just broke the connection and was gone. I couldn't believe it. It was like a sick dream. Even now it's hard to believe it. Jack, out there, wanted for murder. Me, in here, those leeches waiting to suck my blood.'

I hadn't given a thought to the men outside but now I did. Louise disappeared back into her coffee and shivered. I looked up at her and put my notebook down.

'Were you surprised?'

'Oh, just a little. I wasn't exactly expecting my husband to call me in the middle of the night and tell me he'd just found a corpse and was going into hiding . . .'

'I mean, surprised – ' I took a breath – 'that he had a mistress?'

'Oh,' she said. 'That. Is that relevant? I mean, to whether he killed her?'

'No. Not really, I suppose. I'm sorry. I'm just trying to build a picture . . .'

Louise waved away my concern and gave a long, bitter sigh. 'No, no, that's okay. Don't worry. I don't even care. Not now. I've ceased to understand why women do care actually, after the initial shock. I just feel so totally *stupid.*'

'But you weren't surprised?'

'No,' she admitted. Her hand went to her ring once more but she took it away immediately. 'No. Jack, screwing someone? I mean, I tried to make it seem like it was, to Jack, when he phoned, but I was only going through the motions. It wasn't a shock.' She gave that laugh again, metallic and hard. 'I've known Jack a very long time. I've never exactly *found out* before, but I've known a couple of times. That's something you should know, Mr Rucker.'

I tried to smile. 'Billy, please. If you're Louise, I'm Billy.'

'That's something you should know then, Billy. We can always tell. Always, even when you think you've got away with it. We pretend we don't know, to you, to ourselves. We *let* you get away with it because it's too much to face. We don't want to feel shit about ourselves. But you're pretty damn transparent, you know. All of you.'

Louise glanced up at me as she said that, a knowing look underlined with something like loathing. There was a silence in the room that hung like a guillotine. Then she laughed, another short, ironic flurry.

'And the other reason why I couldn't really be surprised was that when I met him he was practically engaged. She may have even had a ring, the poor girl. At first it was just sex, for both of us. We saw each other for six months before he broke it off with her. She was devastated apparently, kept calling and calling. I can hardly claim to be surprised that he liked to screw around, when he did a lot of it with me, can I?'

'I don't know,' I said. 'He was still single, wasn't he? It's you he chose to marry. I think you could have expected him to be faithful, even if he wasn't before.'

'Do you? How old-fashioned.' She looked at my left hand. 'You'll make someone a lovely husband. You know what is ironic, though?'

'Tell me.'

'Well, Jack was practically married when I met him, and I didn't think twice about screwing him five nights a week, even once in their flat. But now I hate that bitch.'

'Alison.'

'I hate her. I know I have no right to – it's almost like a punishment, don't you think? – but I do. And it's made worse because she's dead. I try to imagine what she went through, how scared she must have been, but it doesn't do any good. I hate her. I hate her for sleeping with my husband and if he killed her I hate her for that too. I hate her for being in my life, for those wankers outside, for the way I feel.'

'You don't know what Jack told her. You don't know what she felt for him. You don't know enough to blame her.'

'Who said blame? I don't blame her and I don't blame Jack, not really.'

'Who then?'

'Me, I suppose. I had ample knowledge of what he was like. And I still married him, didn't I? So I know enough not to blame her. It's deeper than that. Maybe only a woman could understand. The woman who had my man. He didn't want me, you know? Ever since Tommy. My sister says it was because he was there when Tommy was born, and it was a bit gruesome. I thought it was true about strikers and sex because after Tommy was when he started scoring. But it's not. He was seeing her. *Her.* I hate her. I see her body, her Page Three body in her leopardskin bikini, and I see it covered in blood, all stabbed and dead and it makes me feel so terrible, and so guilty and so mean. Because I still really *hate* her.'

I left a moment for Louise to collect herself, the rhythmic snuffles of her baby's sleeping coming through the monitor the only sound in the room. I didn't know what to say about the things she was feeling, but I did feel sorry for her. She may have hurt someone once but that didn't mean she'd asked for any of this. Wanting to get to the end of my questions I asked her about the book Jack was writing. She told me that the only person who knew about it was his agent, so it must have been him who gave it to the *Standard*. The agent or Jack himself. I asked her why he hadn't published it before.

'Jack was waiting,' Louise said. 'If his career ended, or if it looked like he was going to be staying in the lower leagues, then he said he'd publish it, he'd take the money. If he carried on, got in a Premiership side, then he wouldn't. Not until he retired. I was dead against it from the start. I told him not to show it to Jeff—'

'Jeff?'

'His agent.' I remembered his picture, in the *Daily Mail*. 'I thought that was why we were getting hassled, because someone had found out what was in Jack's book. Jeff had let something slip at a party or something. I still think that's what happened. I never liked Jeff. He's a flash git. He was always taking Jack to parties, never remembered to ask me. I bet Jack met Alison through him. Other players he looks after have been in the tabloids after having affairs. He's flash, he takes them out, he doesn't care what happens to them. If someone did find out about Jack's book, and tried to shut him up, I bet it was Jeff mouthing it round to publishers that got it out.'

'Do you have a copy?'

'No,' she said. 'The police took our computer.'

'Did you ever read it?'

'Yes. Not that I needed to. I lived through it. The transfers that never came off, the months of misery while he was injured. The people he pissed off. I knew you'd ask. I've written a sort of précis for you. You can have it before you go.'

'Great,' I said. 'That'll be very helpful.'

Louise stood up and walked over to a chest of drawers with a beech veneer, opening the top one and pulling out several sides of A4, torn from a spiral-bound pad. She stood for a second, reading them. An empty delivery van rattled by, silencing a blackbird for a second or two before it piped up again. Louise set the pages down in front of me and sat down again. She ran her right hand down the length of her left arm and waited for my next question. The room was very quiet. I didn't have anything else to ask. I was about to tell her so, and thank her, when a light squall from the baby monitor took her attention. Louise picked it up. She waited a second then turned it off and set it on the sofa beside her.

Louise didn't excuse herself, simply standing up and walking to the foot of the stairs. Faintly, from up above, I could hear the child, his plaintiff cries a perfect match for the face turned suddenly towards me. Her small mouth, the slight tremor again. I watched as Louise walked up the stairs, not hurrying, not looking back at me. I watched her feet disappear, listening to her footsteps on the landing.

The child continued to cry for another ten minutes, during which time I sat, telling myself I should wait and say goodbye properly. I wanted to give Louise my number, tell her what to say to Jack if she spoke to him again. I folded the pieces of paper in front of me into my notebook and put it into my bag. Jack's agent, taking his players to parties, some of them getting into trouble. That was interesting. I wrote his name down in my book and glanced around the room again, this time taking in the framed pictures of Jack in various kits, the trophy cabinet in the corner. It was a pleasant room, but somehow I couldn't quite see Jack there. I couldn't actually see him in this house, with this woman. It seemed a little nice, a little homely for him. I laughed. I bet he'd have settled for it now.

After another ten minutes Louise still hadn't returned though I could tell the baby had settled. There were things I had to do. I looked at my watch and stood, then walked to the foot of the stairs.

There were three doors leading off from the landing. The first was ajar and I took a step towards it. I expected to see a cot, with a mother sat next to it. But I didn't. The cot sat on its own and all I could hear was the soft breath of a child. I had the impulse to move forward and look down on it but I was stopped by an image of Draper doing the same thing, his big hands resting on the sides of the cot. I backed out onto the landing, my feet creaking on a floorboard, causing the baby to give a short murmur before settling down again.

The door of the second room was open and I stepped across it. The room was at the back of the house and a pale yellow slice of sunlight cut through the space between myself and Louise. Louise was sitting on the side of the bed naked, her clothes in a neat pile beside her. I stopped, dead. I couldn't move. Louise didn't look up, though she knew I was there in the doorway. She just carried on brushing her hair, the long tresses falling over her slim, golden shoulders. She'd found a knot, and was pulling at it. Before I could stop them my eyes ran over her like wild horses let out of a trailer. It felt so natural for her to be sitting there. For me to be watching her. I still didn't move, not wanting to break the spell. A naked girl, pulling a brush through her hair. When she turned her eyes towards me my stomach turned over like a car that won't start.

There was no expression on her face. She hadn't been surprised by what she'd done. And neither had I, really. We'd both known, as soon as we'd met. Then later, that look she gave me. There was an instant understanding, a knowledge that while we'd been speaking to each other, using words to communicate, other parts of ourselves had been holding a more subtle conversation. Our bodies had been watching each other, becoming more comfortable. Our voices had lowered. Louise had heard the conversation, and accepted it. I'd pretended not to hear it. But in the instant that I saw her there I knew I'd accepted it too.

The only sound was the scraping of the brush through Louise's deep, endless hair. I found myself moving forward. I saw myself taking the brush from her hand, then felt myself kneeling on the bed behind her. I ran the brush through her hair, long, hard strokes, until she shivered and turned into my arms. Our mouths met. She pressed herself against me as though she was freezing to death. I ran my hand down across her back, lifting her arms, kissing the inside of her elbows, folding myself around her. For the briefest of seconds I wondered why I was doing this. An answer began to form but it was washed away before it could take.

She smelled sweet, the same as her baby. Her hands inside my shirt were cold as a running stream. I pulled it over my head and went towards her but she pushed out a hand, holding me away. I thought she'd had second thoughts but instead she lay back, her knees up, and then opened her legs. She rested her hands on the inside of her thighs, her sex open to me.

'I'm not a psycho,' she said. 'I'm not going to harass you, all right? I won't call you in the night or show up at your flat. I just need you to fuck me, okay?'

Sometime later I woke, Louise in my arms, our limbs knotted together like fishing wire. The room was a lot darker, a fine sleet whispering at the window. I hadn't realized how much I'd needed to sleep. Louise must have done too because though I stirred involuntarily her breathing stayed deep and even. Her child did wake her though, and she slipped out of bed and went through to him. I was reaching for my clothes, just about to get up, when she brought him back into the room and fed him, sitting naked in front of me. The light was almost gone. She didn't speak, just sitting there with her child. She looked so beautiful I didn't speak either. In the dark like a ghost mother with her child. I wanted to run my mouth over the scar from her Caesarean, but I stayed where I was. Her baby suckled away happily and I had the impulse to stroke his head. I didn't do that either. When he'd had enough Louise took him back to his cot.

'You're so transparent,' she sighed, getting back into

bed. 'All of you. So easy to tell what you want.' Her hands began to move again, slowly, over my body. 'What a way for a detective to behave. Coming into a girl's house, looking at her like that. I could hardly pour the coffee. I felt like a little rabbit, caught in the headlights.'

'And then the little rabbit jumped out of the headlights, hopped upstairs to the bedroom and took all her clothes off. What sort of way is that for an employer to behave?'

'I guess you're right.' She buried her head in my chest and shivered again. She had become very cold, in just a minute. 'But can this be your fault?'

'I don't mind,' I said. 'I can take the blame, if that's what you want.'

'I do,' she said, sliding on top of me.

'What about this, though?'

'Oh,' she said, her voice getting deeper. The points in her eyes seemed to dance. 'This is totally down to me.'

Chapter Seventeen

I was glad I hadn't taken Jack Draper's money. I was thinking of incriminating him with the police and I'd drunk his special coffee. Then I'd fucked his wife. Twice. It didn't seem right that he should suffer financially because of any of these things. Taking his wife's money had been strange enough, though I did take it.

'I told you,' she insisted, as we sat back down in the living room, me dressed, her in a dressing gown. 'I'm not a nutter. I wanted you. Now I want you to do something else. Much as it would have been worth it I'm not paying you a thousand pounds for making me come. I'm paying you to look into a murder my husband might be guilty of. So here.'

'Okay,' I said, tucking the cheque into my back pocket. 'But making you come is a job I could get used to. And I wouldn't even charge the whole thousand.'

She laughed and blushed a little. 'It was the first time I've done that.'

'Then you have natural talent. Or beginner's luck. And your child is a miracle.'

'You know what I mean.' Her hand went to her wedding ring again. This time, very consciously, she left it there. 'I've wanted to now and then. More for the idea of it than the person, I think.'

'Was that what that was?'

She looked down at her lap. A car droned by outside, like a long sigh of pleasure. 'I don't know. I don't think so. There was something there. You know there was.' Her eyes shifted focus for a second and she looked bemused. 'I never imagined it like that, though. I thought it would be in a hotel, or in a bedroom at a party, in five minutes flat. When I was mad at Jack. I always wondered how I'd feel, afterwards. Whether I'd, I don't know, feel dirty.'

'And?'

'I felt good. Warm.'

'And?'

'And horny.'

'Now?'

'The same.'

I smiled and she put a reassuring hand on my knee. 'Don't worry, I'll let you go.' She left the hand there. 'Do you think you should go?'

'Probably.'

'Yes,' she said.

There was a long silence during which we both smiled at each other and Louise left her hand on my leg. I stood up and she withdrew it, that terrified look returning for an instant before she pushed it aside. Her life, rushing back in. I followed her through to the kitchen where she stood with her back to the door I'd come through.

'Right,' she said. 'Richard will have left his back door open. Can you lock it when you go in? The front door will lock itself.'

'Fine,' I said. 'And you have my number. I left it on the table.'

'Good. Good.'

There was a short, heavy moment, then I made to go.

'You're very sweet, Mr Rucker. In every sense of the word.'

'Mr Rucker?'

'Yes. I think it's Mr Rucker from now on.' Her eyes were timid, asking. She wanted me to tell her something she knew I wasn't going to tell her. I reached for her but she drew back.

'You can just go, you know. I told you, I don't want anything. You don't have to . . .'

'I know.'

We kissed for a long time. I could feel her gown slipping open and me wanting her again. The kitchen table stretched invitingly behind her. But then my eyes fell on a pair of binoculars, hanging from a hook by the kitchen window, and I thought of the photographers besieging her house. If one of them pointed a long lens over the back wall it wouldn't do either of us any good. The angle would have been less than flattering too. I turned and opened the door.

'I'll let you know if I get anywhere.'

'Yes. Thank you. Not for . . . Oh, you know.' She laughed. 'Goodbye.'

'Goodbye, Mrs Draper.'

She put a hand on my wrist.

'Let me know if you find my husband,' she said.

No one seemed to notice that the parcel courier had taken somewhat longer than usual to get a signature. I sat in my car for ten minutes, my hands on the wheel, watching a cat picking apart a starling it had caught. Then I started the car and drove up past the house. I drove through Victoria Park towards Leyton High Road. I parked outside the ground and wandered in through the front gates, following signs to reception. I was in a long thin room split down the middle by a perspex partition. On the other side of it was an office space where three women sat typing, and answering the telephones.

At my approach the youngest of the women stood, and stepped up to the counter. She was an attractive girl with an unconvincing blonde dye, her face a lurid palette of far too much make-up, all the wrong colours. When she spoke to me it was a little unsettling, especially given my disjointed state. As if a Kandinsky had suddenly smiled at me in the Tate.

I blinked the girl into focus, found a smile for her and asked to see Janner. I told the girl that I'd spoken to him earlier, though we hadn't fixed a time. While she phoned up to his office I stood, rubbing my face, looking at the photographs plastering the walls around me. There were past players, past managers, a big shot of the ground in the 40s, heaving with fans, all standing, all dressed in suits and ties. The current squad were up and my eyes moved along them until I was looking at Draper. His big face was split into a confident grin. I looked away. The biggest shot was of the man I'd seen in the Jag on Wanstead Flats. He was standing with the gates of the club at his back, smiling even wider than Draper was, both thumbs up to the camera.

I followed the young girl up a flight of stairs and along a neutral, modern office-block corridor to

Janner's office, which she showed me into before leaving. Janner stood from behind his Ikea desk and shook my hand. I was surprised to see him in a suit and tie, just like the fans of yesteryear, in which he looked about as natural as a pit bull in a little tartan jacket.

We sat and I declined a cup of tea. Janner knew all about Alison now, and he was shocked. He'd also read the *Standard* and couldn't believe the fuss his star player was stirring up.

'Fuck me. *Fuck* me. Super Jack. Not so super to a lot of folk when they read this, eh? There'll be one or two fellas getting a little hot under the collar when they buy the *Standard* of an afternoon over the next few days.'

I looked at him. He met my look with a broad grin.

'Not me, though. For one thing I've never had dealings with Draper before the last five months and for another I'm as tight a Scot as you'll find. And our Mr Korai is worse, he must have some jock in him somewhere. He'd fight the devil for a ha'penny on the flagstones of hell. Give a bung – forget it. As for taking one, my missus is a Presbyterian and if she ever found out I'd done something like that then hell is the place I'd be heading – fast. And before you ask me who Jack *might* be about to name, I've got my thoughts, but then so must every other footballing man in the country. And I'm keeping them to myself,' he added.

I thanked Janner for taking time to see me, and he said that was okay, though he didn't have long. He asked me how I'd known about Alison so early. I looked him in the eye and fed him a line about a tip-off. He made an attractive moue with his lips, but let it go. I told him what I wanted and he thought for a second before giving me a short nod. He was grateful for the advance warning about Draper, he said, and he couldn't see the harm. As he punched some commands into his computer he sighed. He told me that Draper wasn't the only absentee from his squad for the forthcoming game against Crewe – he had two others out with the flu. He'd set his sights on automatic promotion but wasn't sure that was going to happen. He sat back and looked up at me.

'You're not a left back by any chance?'

I thought about my performance on the market the night before last and told him I wasn't.

Janner shook his head with phlegmatic frustration as the printer handed the two pages of Draper's biog to him, which he handed to me.

'I knew he was a risk signing,' he told me, shaking his head.

'But it was his hamstrings that concerned me rather than any psychopathic tendencies he might have. Hey, that'll get managers wondering from now on. Does he have the skill to match his pace and is he likely to carve anyone up? The police were here all yesterday. It's amazing to think that someone you know could actually do that. Not that I'm saying he did, mind. Just that he might. You don't know where the little bugger is by any chance?'

'I was going to ask you.'

'Ha! If I knew that he'd be out on that pitch, believe me, half of Scotland Yard after him or not. I'd make him play if his hands were still red and sticky. I still haven't given up on the Manager of the Month, you know.'

I smiled.

'I tell you what, though. If our Jack didn't do it, and he misses the rest of the season because everyone thinks he did, the fucker who slashed that lass had better hope the police get to him before I do. If they don't, he's a fucking dead man.'

As we walked downstairs I asked Janner if he'd known Alison and he told me no, but he had seen her a couple of times, once at a birthday party for Mr Korai, the chairman. He'd had no idea Jack was ploughing her, as he put it. I followed Janner out onto the pitch where his squad was assembled, all suited up like he was. They were putting together a souvenir programme for when Newcastle came in the Cup. The air was clear and clean and the sun was out, the snow on the pitch already almost gone. The day put me in mind of Shulpa, who seemed to go through each of the four seasons every second hour, with all the permutations in between.

I followed Janner to the centre circle, where a photographer and his assistant were setting up and the players I'd seen training the day before were milling around. The young goal-scorer was there, in a floppy double-breasted number that was a perfect fit – for a rectangular man a good six inches taller than he was. He looked nervous and jumpy, fiddling with the gold chain over his tie. There were also a couple of girls, chatting to each other, wearing long coats that I didn't imagine would stay on once the photo session got underway.

Janner took no notice of me as I went among the players, handing out my card. Seeing them there in their suits, my mind went back to the photograph in Alison's kitchen, and I recognized several of the faces that had been crowded round her. I wondered why Jack wasn't in the shot then realized that he'd probably been behind the camera. Knowing he was seeing the girl he'd probably done it on purpose, to be careful. Not careful enough.

None of the players denied knowing Alison, though all claimed ignorance of her affair with Draper. They didn't need encouraging to speak, all competing as to who had met her first, who'd seen her last, telling me little things about her. Willie, the big centre back, said he'd been at school with her. She was a really nice bird, quieter and far more shy than you'd expect for a Page Three girl, he insisted. She liked to have a laugh but it often seemed like she was pretending, she wasn't very happy. The others agreed. They all shook their heads, assuring me they couldn't believe it, they really couldn't. She was too nice, too nice for someone to do something like that to her.

As for Draper, he kept himself very much to himself, being a bit of a prima donna, and while no one actually said they didn't like him, I didn't get the impression that he was going to walk off with the Most Popular Player Award as well as the Leading Goal-scorer trophy at the end-of-season dinner. I asked them if they thought Draper was the kind of man to do what he'd been accused of. None of them could answer that.

I thanked the players, wished them good luck for their next game and left them to Leyton's answer to David Bailey. The girls were getting ready now, one of them chatting to the photographer, the other seemingly lost in her own thoughts. I'd noticed her looking my way as I'd been chatting to the players – now she was shrugging off her coat, before standing bravely in shorts and a bra top. I smiled as I walked past her but she didn't meet my eye.

Before leaving I had a last chat with Janner.

'The Bosman ruling. It means you can go where you like when you're contract is up, yes?'

'That's it.'

'So why ever sign for any longer than a year?'

'Why? Because you might break your leg and then be fucked. Or else start playing like a ladyboy and binned for that. It gives you security.'

'But Draper only signed for one year?'

'It was all we offered him. He'd have gone for more. He's no spring chicken and we didn't know how it would go – he could have lost his speed, could have easily broken down after a couple of games. Thought it was a mistake a week back, not giving him three years, but now, who knows? I wonder if we'll still have to pay his wages when he's in Parkhurst.'

Back in the office I was met by the same young girl.

'I was wondering if Mr Korai was around. The chairman.'

'Oh no, he's not in today,' the girl said. 'And you definitely would need an appointment to see him. He's busy as sin is Mr Korai. Would you like to see the general manager? Is it about sponsorship?'

'Don't worry,' I said. 'Really. Thanks for your help.' I had a thought. 'Mr Korai, that's the same guy who owns a chain of supermarkets, right?'

'That's him. Done wonders for this place he has.'

'Yes,' I said, 'I'm sure. Thanks a lot.'

A phone rang behind her and the girl turned to

answer it. I smiled goodbye and walked to the exit. A grinning Mr Korai gave me the thumbs up as I walked past him.

Chapter Eighteen

I left my car outside Nicky's closed garage and walked towards his flat, my footsteps crisp on the wet concrete. The night was dark and damp and a gusting wind rattled through the guttering like someone trying to get a note out of a horn. I had my coat on but it was still very cold. A sharp half-moon cut quickly between massive, bulbous clouds like the dorsal fin of a great white in a heavy, grey swell.

No one jumped me.

Nicky had given me his spare key and I used it in the back door before calling the lift. The hallway was almost as cold as the street, and I stood, my hands buried in my pockets. Then, as the lift rose to five, I played over what had happened that day. Her body. Slim, malleable, her sharp elbows against my chest. Her smell. The look on her face, the determined tight look as she moved atop of me, the way her belly felt on mine. Jesus. I wasn't in the habit of screwing the people I had gone to interview. It wasn't the first time that the opportunity had presented itself – hookers will often offer a cop a blow job if he'll turn a blind eye, so to speak – but I'd never yielded to such 'temptation'. Nor had I taken advantage of any of the vulnerable women I'd sat across from over the years, the widows, sisters or girlfriends who were in some way connected to the cases I'd been on. All lost and confused, all in need of a measure of comfort that would bring life crashing into the instant, make the Big Black Reason why I was talking to them go away for a while.

I wondered if that was what I had just done – taken advantage of a confused and needy woman. I didn't think so. Louise Draper had needed comfort all right, but it was she who'd chosen what form it arrived in. She wanted me to take the blame but she knew what she was doing. So I didn't feel bad, exactly, about what had happened. Just confused. Confused as to why then confused when I thought of Shulpa, because when I did I didn't feel any guilt, none at all. Nothing. This was a surprise to me but, I reasoned, it was just something that happened. I hadn't looked for it, I hadn't expected it to go the way it had. It was rounded off and contained, within and of itself. It wasn't about Shulpa, of course it wasn't.

But as the lift door opened I suddenly wondered if I'd have done the same thing had I still been seeing Sharon. Sharon was my brother's fiancée. They were about to be married when he had the accident that left him, and still leaves him, in a persistent vegetative state, or coma. Some years after Luke's accident Sharon and I had been unable to play down our feelings for each other, and had become an item, until the weight and difficulties of the situation got too much for Sharon and she'd bailed out. I hadn't seen Sharon for six months.

The thought stopped me, because I knew the answer straight away. No. No I wouldn't have done what I had. And Louise wouldn't have gone upstairs to wait for me either, because the signals I would have been giving off would not have been the same. So, maybe it had something to do with Shulpa after all but I couldn't understand that. I was mad about her, or at least I thought I was, something that had actually been worrying me. Was I looking for a way out, or a way of protecting myself against the feelings I had for her? It was something I didn't have time to think about.

'Billy, you're here. Thank God. Now what the hell's been going on? He won't tell me. Please, Billy, let me know. I can help, I know I can.'

I'd rattled Nicky's keys, getting them in the wrong lock, and Shulpa must have heard because she opened the door to me. Her face lit into a serious smile and she kissed me, taking my face in both of her hands. She held my hand and led me into the huge living space, where Nicky was propped up on the sofa, three pillows beneath his head and a duvet round his legs.

I was surprised to see Shulpa. I was more so when my eyes fell on Nicky. I took a step back from him. If I'd walked past him on a hospital ward I wouldn't have known who he was.

'Fuck,' I said. 'Fuck me.'

'Pretty, aren't I?'

'You look, I don't know . . .'

'Like the elephant man?'

I nodded. 'Like the elephant man. After he's been given a pretty fucking good kicking.'

'I'm not a nanimal, I'm human bean.'

'No,' I said, 'I've seen the way you go after women. You're definitely an animal.'

'Not much chance of doing that for a while.'

'I don't know. Some women like their men to look a little rough. I've been banking on that for years.'

I moved toward Shulpa but she folded her arms and looked at me.

'Oh,' she said. 'I'm glad you think this is funny, Billy. Look at him. I don't think you should be making jokes.'

'She's right. Don't make me laugh. That is the very worst . . .'

'And you. Look at you. So this is a joke, is it? Your face. It won't be the same. That cut. I can't believe you're laughing . . .'

'Okay,' I said. 'Shulpa, I'm sorry.'

'And him, lying there not telling me the truth. You got mugged, you tried to fight them off, it was just kids. Am I stupid? Why did Mother call me and ask what was happening? I could tell from Billy that it was something more. So, come on, are you going to tell me? Either tell me or I'm leaving, and I don't want to see you again. Either of you. I'm not your baby sister any more, Nicky!'

Nicky calmed Shulpa down and I just nodded when he went through it with her. He was pretty groggy, having just woken up. He told her that he'd borrowed some money from an outfit he shouldn't have. That it had disappeared. Shulpa wanted to know what he'd borrowed it for and he told her for some renovations that needed doing, safety things, that he couldn't afford.

'And they did this to you?' There was a tremor in her voice that really moved me. She was right, this wasn't something to joke about, especially with Nicky's sister there. Nicky looked touched, ashamed by her concern.

Shulpa wanted to know what Nicky was going to do about it. She was all for phoning the police but there was no way that was going to happen. I said I'd already started putting together a solution.

Nicky looked at me, wanting to know if I was serious.

'I spoke to a friend,' I said. 'She's getting us the money to pay off the people we have to pay off. For a few weeks at least. Then we'll owe her.'

'And then what happens?'

'Then Nicky will pay her back.'

'If it was that simple why didn't he just pay the people he owes?'

'They didn't give him enough time to raise it. We've got more time now.'

Nicky nodded. I'd told him I was going to speak to Sal, though I hadn't mentioned that I'd ask her for a loan. He wouldn't have wanted me getting into it like that. If he was surprised he didn't show it. His look said he had no further worries about the matter. I knew the look was bullshit.

'Right,' Shulpa said. 'So. You said the money disappeared. How much was it?'

Nicky and I exchanged glances.

'Come on, you fuckers. I've been here looking after you all day. Why do you treat me as if—'

'All right,' Nicky said. He followed it with a rattle of Bengali.

'Two hundred thousand pounds. What?! You must be mad—'

'Shulpa,' I said.

'Okay. Okay. I just . . . this is incredible. So.' She put her hands on her hips. 'Who's got this? Who took this from you?'

'That's what I'm going to find out,' I said.

'You think you can?'

'Yes,' I said. 'I'll find out. Whether there'll be any of it left, is something else. But I have an idea that finding the person just might be enough.'

I gave Shulpa the keys to my flat, and though she wasn't happy about it she agreed to leave us alone to talk. As soon as she'd gone I told Nicky not to ask her round for a while. He said he'd keep her out of it and thanked me for what I'd done for him the day before. He kept apologizing, telling me that I didn't have to get involved. I thought about what Sal had said, about his reasons for not telling me. He didn't want to admit what he'd done, like she said, but he may have also been worried about what might happen to me. I wondered what he'd think if he knew how I'd spent my afternoon. I sure as hell wasn't going to tell him. Nicky was very protective towards his sister. He pretended to find her annoying, he'd never said a good thing to me about her. But sometimes I caught him looking at her with weary affection. Other times I saw the amused smile he tried to hide as he shook his head, opening another free bottle of fizz for her. I shook my head when I realized that I was more worried about what Nicky would say than what Shulpa would.

I brushed aside Nicky's apologies. I got a few addresses off him, then ran through what had happened with Sal. I told him what she'd said. Nicky nodded.

'And this gives me more time?'

'That's right. You'll owe a bit more at the end but no one will be coming to break your legs. For a while at least. We've got three weeks' worth.'

'But then they will?'

'No. Because I'll have got your money back by then.'

'And if you can't?'

'You mortgage the bar. You told me you bought it outright. If the worst comes to the worst you use that money to pay Sal off and the rest to pay the Maltese. Then you'll be paying the bank more than you can afford for thirty years like most people do anyway. The NatWest, they might send you a stiff letter. They won't break your head open.'

As I spoke I could see a frown taking hold on Nicky's face.

'What's the matter?'

'You said mortgage my bar.'

I looked at him. Carefully: 'That's right.'

'I heard you telling Shulpa that and I was thinking, it's fine, he's just trying to reassure her.'

'Nicky . . .'

'But you meant it?'

I gave him another, measured, look. 'You're going to have to do it, Nicky.'

He shook his head. 'There's no way.'

'What the fuck do you mean?' Sal had said Nicky might not have liked it, but I'd thought he would have seen it had to happen. I couldn't believe what he was saying to me. 'You want to get topped? Is the Ludensian more important than your life?'

Nicky looked at me with the same expression of disbelief, now mixed with patience. 'Of course it isn't.'

'Well then. I can't believe you're saying you're not

willing to mortgage the place. You do know that if I can't find the cash you'll still have to pay off two sets of people . . .'

'Wait. Wait a second. I'm perfectly willing to hock the bar. I'd do it tomorrow.' He shook his head. 'Why the hell didn't you tell me that you were going to ask Sally for money?'

'What do you mean you're willing? So do it.'

'It isn't as easy as that.'

'Why not? Why the fuck not?'

'Because. Because the guy I bought it off . . .'

'What about him?'

'He still owns it,' Nicky said.

There was a silence for a second as I looked at Nicky. I had a cold, empty feeling.

'I don't understand.'

'I'd never have got a licence,' Nicky explained, looking away from me. 'Not back then. I was a dealer, it was well known. My name isn't on the lease. The guy I bought it from, his name is still on that and on the licence, and I put Toby on there too, a few years ago. It isn't officially mine. I can't mortgage it, okay?'

I nodded. I was trying to take in what Nicky was telling me. I'd borrowed money thinking we had something to fall back on. Now I knew we didn't. I saw Sal's face, telling me not to do it, not to ask. If I couldn't find the stash Nicky had lost, we'd have nothing left to pay anyone with. If the Maltese guys came back for Nicky they'd have to get in the queue.

'Well then,' I said, eventually. 'We just better find the light-fingered cunt who took it from you, hadn't we?'

Nicky and I talked for an hour and a half, throwing

ideas around like movie writers developing scenarios. The situation was no different, not really. The man on the flying trapeze still pulls the same moves whether there's a net beneath him or not. I still had to get the money back. Nicky gave me some addresses and some numbers. I asked him who could even vaguely possibly have known about the money. We were still going round the houses when the phone rang.

'Billy. Listen. I'm at your place. There are some police outside. They were waiting for you. I've just got here, I was at a friend's.' Shulpa's voice sounded shaky. I let out a breath. I knew I hadn't got rid of them the first time.

'Were they in uniform? Or not?'

'Not.' Shulpa was obviously nervous. 'A man and a woman. They wanted to come in and wait but I wouldn't let them. Is this about Nicky?'

'No,' I reassured her. 'Just a case I'm working on. It's nothing, what did you tell them?'

'That I was your friend. I had to pick something up.'

'Right. Well, I'd just as soon not speak to them tonight.'

'Okay. Okay, I'll go home then. Do you want to come round?'

'I have things to do,' I said. 'I could be pretty late. I'll probably just stay at my office.'

'Won't you need your keys?'

'Fuck,' I said.

'Don't worry. I'll drop them off.'

'Could you?'

'No problem. Where shall I leave them?'

'There's a fire escape near the back entrance, the

one I took you in, remember? Can you leave them, I don't know, on the third step?'

'Of course. What if I get followed?'

'I don't think you will. Tell them there was a message for you that I'd be back at eleven. That should keep them there.'

'Okay,' Shulpa said. Her voice still sounded like a radio station you were about to lose. 'A shame, though, Billy. It would have been nice tonight.'

I left a second. I heard Louise Draper – can this be your fault?

'I know. I'm sorry. I'll . . . I'll make it up to you. I'll see you tomorrow.'

I handed the phone back to Nicky.

There was a phone box on the street outside the place and I used it. I held the piece of paper in my left hand and dialled the number, looking out through the glass at the third-floor window of a converted Victorian mansion block. I let the phone ring for a long time before replacing the receiver. Then I hung up and walked outside.

I was on Mildmay Grove, near Cannonbury Station. Not far from my office. I'd spent half an hour on Nicky's laptop looking at the Leyton Orient website and then I'd driven over. The night was icy cold now, the pavements glinting beneath the street lamps as though they'd been sprayed with diamond dust. I let the door of the phone box swing shut and jogged up some stairs to the door of number twenty-two. I pulled my hood up and pressed the buzzer for seven, waited, then pressed it again. Nothing. There was a light on in the ground-floor flat, and I hit the buzzer marked one.

'Hello. Who is it?' The intercom crackled like eggs in a hot pan. I was glad. I took a step away from it.

'I'm from number seven. From upstairs. I locked myself out taking some rubbish down. Can you let me in?'

I hopped up the stairs quickly, in case the man who'd buzzed me in felt like checking. At the top I stopped, outside a tatty blue door with a plastic seven glued onto it. Number eight was directly opposite. I pulled my hood down, and put my ear to both doors. Nothing. I reached into the bag I'd taken out of the boot of my car, and pulled out three sets of keys. There were about forty keys in all and I tried them all in the deadbolt, one by one. I got a couple that felt right, but didn't quite fit enough to turn. I pulled out a file and had a go at the likeliest, slimming down a couple of the prongs, and it was better but it still wouldn't move. I stopped when I heard a noise from downstairs – a young couple coming home to a flat on the second floor.

I shone my Maglite into the lock and bit my lip. The Yale would be easy enough to loid, and I knew I'd get the deadbolt eventually if I kept up with the filing. But it was getting near closing time. I didn't want to be standing there with a file in my hand if the occupants of number eight rolled in. I was wondering whether I might have to give up on it when I noticed the window in front of me.

It was an old sash window that wasn't painted shut like most windows in communal hallways tend to be. I ran my fingers round the frame and listened again.

No one else came home. As quickly as I could I un-hooked the latches, put my fingers underneath one of the panes and pushed upwards, slowly. The window moved, not making much noise, a rush of cold air hitting me in the face. I pushed the window up until there was easily enough room for me to climb out.

I stuck my head out first, the chill air running down my neck. I could see why no one had bothered to paint the window closed. The flats looked over a railway line – there was no way to break in from the back. On the other side of the line was a tall row of conifers. I didn't think anyone would see me. Holding on to the underside of the window I stepped out into the darkness, my bag over my shoulder. Then I turned and pushed the window down, keeping my hands on it for balance. I was on a ledge, wide enough to edge along but fifty feet up nonetheless. I looked down onto a back yard, the outlines of a deserted barbecue and a set of stone seats visible beneath me, lit by the rect-angle of light spilling out from the garden flat they were sat outside.

I shuffled along the ledge, careful of the ice, and got lucky – the first window I came to was the bathroom, a louvered set of six frosted panels, the sort that aren't used any more, one of the reasons being that if they haven't been glued they're so easy to get into. They're not usually glued because of fire safety concerns. I tried the top one and it slid out without any fuss. I set it down on the ledge and reached for the second. That, and the rest, came out in minutes, and I laid them all on top of the first, moving as quickly as I dared. I could hear a train in the distance and I wanted to get off the side of the building before it rattled by beneath me, carriages of bored passengers gazing out into the night.

Pushing the bag in first I squeezed into the bathroom without any trouble but slipped when I tried to lower myself to the floor. The toilet seat was down, otherwise I might have got my foot wet. I made a lot of noise and if there had been anyone home they would have easily heard me. I stopped, but I couldn't hear anything.

I saw a thin line of string by the door and pulled it, filling the room with a weak light. I was in a small bathroom with pale yellow walls and a plank floor painted submarine grey. I had a quick look around. I opened the boiler cupboard, went through the medicine cabinet and checked inside the plastic facing on the bath. Nothing. Then I walked out into the hall.

I spent about thirty minutes in Toby's apartment, knowing he was at the Ludensian. The adrenalin rush was unexpectedly high. Maybe I'd have to take up cat burglary instead of boxing. I didn't feel bad about what I was doing. Toby could have found out about the money, he was always at the bar. If he'd taken it the son of a bitch deserved it. If he hadn't, he'd never know I'd been there. He'd come home from his shift and find his flat as he'd left it. I went through the bedroom first, then the kitchen and the living room. Toby lived in a small, sparsely furnished one-bed and, thorough as I was, it didn't take me long. I looked everywhere there was to look. Pillowcases, mattresses, picture frames, drawers, behind drawers, coat pockets, suit pockets, bags, bookshelves, the books on them. I wasn't expecting the whole stash, but if there'd been any spare cash around it might have meant something. Any new hi-fi or computer equipment, the same. But there wasn't. I did discover that Toby was sufficiently worried about hair loss to have a bottle of special shampoo costing fifteen pounds in his bathroom cabinet and I was also surprised by the extent and nature of his porn collection. The only thing of any interest to me was a copy of *Blood on the Tracks* that I recognized because the cover was cracked. I'd loaned it to Nicky, ages ago. It must have been lying round the bar and Toby had borrowed it. I was tempted to take it back but I left it where it was and walked back into the bathroom.

It still didn't mean he wasn't the one. Not that I had any specific reason to think he was other than he was at the Ludensian more than anyone else except Nicky. He'd know the place upside down. So he was just a good place to start. And it felt good to start. I pulled a few squares of paper from the roll and wiped my footprint from the toilet seat.

Outside, on the dark ledge, my foot found some ice and my heart kicked like it was in CPR as my hands grappled at a drainpipe. Blood on the Tracks? Nearly, but not quite. A cat? I was more like a donkey burglar. I made it back into the hallway and closed the window.

When I got to my office I parked in the forecourt and locked the car. There were no police waiting for me. I found my keys by the fire escape and let myself in. It was dark at the bottom of the stairwell, but I knew my way. I walked round to the lift, the orange glow from beneath the black buttons all the light there was. Upstairs there was more. I stepped out of the lift on three, and turned into the long corridor that leads to my office. Through the huge window at the far end of the corridor the moon, turned yellow now, sat like a broken tooth on a bed of dirty cotton wool.

I stopped dead. My hands tensed. Then I smiled. She really was something. You had to give it to her. On the floor in front of me was a pair of shoes. They were black and chunky, lying on their sides. Beyond them was a pair of jeans, left in a heap. My eyes moved up the deserted corridor. I could see a silk blouse, further along. Then, only yards from my door, I could just make out a bra, lying twisted on the floor like a snake that's had two pretty good meals. I walked forward picking each item up in turn, loading them into my arms. Then I stopped again.

Hanging on the handle of my office door was a pair of black, lace panties.

I shook my head, and a grin split my face in spite of myself. I hadn't seen her car. I turned the handle and pushed the door open. The heat hit me in a wave like stepping off a plane in Saudi and on it rode the rich sweet smell of her. She was lying on the sofabed, reading a fat novel she must have brought up with her. All I could see was a pair of eyelashes, blinking at me over the cover. For the second time that day I found myself leaning on a doorjamb.

'Aren't you hot?'

She put the book down and rested her chin on her hands, smiling sweetly. 'It's why I took my clothes off, desperado.'

I smiled back. 'You could have turned the radiator off. Or opened the window.'

'You know, I just didn't think of that. You can do

either if you like. Or else you can just take your clothes off too.'

'Actually, Shulpa . . .'

'Billy!' she said. 'You don't *really* want to talk right now, do you?'

Chapter Nineteen

There were only two messages on the machine, but I didn't get a chance to play them till the morning. It was bright and clear, the trees wet, dripping with the melt from another fall of snow that had come in the night. The first was a voice I didn't recognize, a woman who called herself Cheryl and said she'd call back. I assumed she wanted me to look for a son or daughter. The second was a voice I did know.

'Listen. You know who this is. I bought a different mobile, from a garage. Call me on 01777 377 334. I'm trusting you with this. I don't know if the Bill can track it anyway, but I know they can't if they don't know the number.' There was a pause. Draper was barking out orders as usual but I definitely detected a broad seam of doubt in his voice. *'I want to say . . . thanks. You could have had me yesterday. Listen, if you saw the* Standard *you'll know there are people out there who could be after me. They might have done that to Alison, I don't know. Louise will let you know who they might be. So if you haven't done yet, talk to her, go and see her. Please?'*

Shulpa had left by then. We'd woken early, to the sound of opera. Not a radio but Mike in the café, practising his Italian. Shulpa stretched and smiled.

'This thing's comfortable. But, alas, I have to go to work. Is there a shower here?'

'No, sorry.'

'Oh well, I've probably got time to go home first. Either that or smell of you all day.'

'It's something I've had to get used to.'

'Me too, then. It'll be nice, sitting listening to my ever-so-interesting boss talking about mergers, thinking of you. It might even keep him away from me for a while, the predatory smell of another man!'

'Growl,' I said.

I yawned, rolled out of bed and turned the heating on. It was then that it hit me; a heavy, dead feeling.

'No shower,' I said. 'But one thing I can do is coffee.'

I pulled my jeans on and grabbed a tee-shirt from the bottom drawer of my filing cabinet. I wandered down the hall and put my head into the café, nearly scaring Mike to death. He wasn't used to customers being around at that time. Ally was taking the chairs off the tables. The espresso machine was yet to warm up but half a jug of filter coffee had dripped through and Mike poured me a cup.

'Two, please,' I said to him.

'Two, is it? Working on something last night, were you?'

'Michael. Leave Billy alone. And get that jealous look out of your eye.'

I took the cups from Mike and padded back down to my office. Shulpa was getting dressed. I set the cups down on my desk, refolded the sofabed and dumped the sheets behind it. We can always tell . . . you're pretty damn transparent, you know. Shulpa was looking out of the window, fastening her blouse, taking the first warmth from the slowly stirring monster that was my radiator.

'Oh wow,' she said. She wiped a hand across the condensation on the glass. I picked up my coffee.

'What is it?'

'Here, come here. Quick. Can you see? Down there.'

Shulpa was almost whispering, a childlike thrill in her voice. She pointed through the dripping branches. I looked over her shoulder and nodded. It was the bird I'd noticed. It was ten, maybe fifteen feet away, sitting on a branch, preening again. Shocked almost, I looked at Shulpa.

'I didn't know you were into birds.'

'My dad used to take me.' Shulpa was still whispering. She looked caught out, embarrassed. 'Me and Nicky, when he split up with our mother.' She laughed. 'Nicky used to moan like you wouldn't believe. He hated it. But I love birds.'

I nodded my head, surprised. If I'd had to guess what Shulpa's hobbies would be, birdwatching would have come just above stamp collecting and one below trainspotting. I had a sudden realization that really, I hardly knew her. I liked the fact that she could surprise me that way.

'You never told me. You can take me - what's it called? - twitching sometime.'

'You do enough of that in your sleep. Did you know?'

I looked at the bird.

'What is it? I've seen it before.'

'Really? That means it might be nesting, though I don't think so. I think it's a shrike, but they're rare, so I'm not sure.'

I put my hand on the back of her neck. 'A shrike?'

'I really think so. But you never normally see one in a city. It *is* a shrike. The butcher bird.'

'Nice name.'

'It's beautiful, don't you think?'

The bird stopped, as if it had suddenly realized something. I remembered its call, though now it was silent. 'I do,' I said.

'Oh . . .'

The shrike flew down and away and Shulpa looked devastated for a second. I had an image of her, a little girl holding on to her father's hand, and a wave of tenderness joined the other feelings I had for her. Nicky had told me that his parents had split up, but he'd never given away what he'd felt about it. I thought I saw it all on Shulpa's face. Shulpa kissed me goodbye and left quickly, not touching her coffee.

I called Sal who told me she'd have the money for me at noon. I thought about what I could do for Nicky before then. Not a lot, in the daytime, though I could do some more 'visiting' later on. After going to Toby's last night I didn't really expect to find a bundle of cash under any of the bar staff's beds. I couldn't believe anyone could be that stupid, but I still needed to check. One of his waitresses was new and had asked Nicky to show her his flat upstairs. Also, one of the sous-chefs had handed in his notice. Plus I had a feeling, a feeling about that little shit with the flick knife. There was plenty to think about, but not a whole lot I could do that early in the morning.

I looked at my watch. It was just before eight. If

the police had been outside my house last night it
wouldn't be long before they showed up here. I wanted
to call Draper, but I didn't – I'd do that from a payphone. Hell knows what I'd tell the man about the
progress I was making on his behalf. Haven't got you
off the hook yet Jack but your wife's a bit lively, isn't
she? I also wanted to go and talk to some of Alison
Everly's neighbours, especially the woman who had
found her body. But I couldn't afford to be seen round
there. Instead I shook my head and read through the
biog I'd got from Janner, marrying up names in it with
the information I'd been given by Louise. I tried to
concentrate but I spent a while thinking about her. I
wanted to call her too and I didn't want to call her. I'd
only do it when I had something to tell her. If I called
her now I knew that whatever practical reason I made
up would be rubbish. I knew why I'd be calling her.

Louise Draper didn't have a clue whether her
husband was guilty or not of the murder of Alison
Everly. Her doubt didn't surprise me; it was based on
self-defence. If she believed him and it came out that
he'd done it, she'd hurt even more. I, however, had
come round, with reluctance, to believing him. I just
didn't think he'd done it. He would have had to have
been quick but it was something other than that, something intangible. The way he'd driven off that night,
the way he spoke to me outside my flat. I just didn't
think it was him. I could, however, perfectly understand why he was keeping his head down. His prints
were all over Alison's flat and a policeman had almost
definitely clocked his car. I could also understand why
there had been a tremor in his voice on the machine

that morning. It was because he didn't know whether or not I was going to help him.

And I was his only hope.

I was just about finishing marrying up information when I heard footsteps, in the hall. I glanced up but didn't take a lot of notice. I had been struck by two names, two names that had kept cropping up. A man with a lot to lose and a man with a lot to gain. I wrote both names down in my notebook, as if that would give me something solid, something definite to focus on. With the police looking for me I had to have something to deflect them with. I thought about Draper, wanting to sign with Villa. In my head I went through what I knew of the Bosman Ruling. A player who played out his contract was free to go elsewhere. To another club, who didn't have to pay a fee for him. A small club could therefore build up a player only to lose him to a big set-up, they could be used as an unpaid training camp. I made a note to check it out on the Internet sometime.

The footsteps outside came nearer. They were hesitant, they stopped and moved on, as though the person making them was looking for an office number. For some reason I knew they were looking for me. I was right. Just as I was closing my notebook the footsteps stopped, right outside. After a second there was a light knock on the door.

I assumed it was the police. I walked over and pulled the door open.

'Mr Rucker? You're Billy Rucker, aren't you?' She looked down the hall the way she'd come, and then back at me. Then at one of my cards, held between thumb and index finger in her left hand.

'Yes,' I told her.

'I hope you don't mind me coming to see you. It's Cheryl. Cheryl Johnson.'

I knew I'd heard the voice but the name meant nothing to me. The girl in front of me wore a Burberry print scarf in her hair and she put a hand behind her head to pull it off. Then I had it. She'd been at the football ground, first in a long leather coat, then in a bra and shorts. Now she had the coat back on. She wore a bright pink pashmina shawl over it, knotted at the neck.

'I wanted to talk to you yesterday but . . .' She looked down the hall again. I don't know what she expected to see down there. 'Can I come in?'

'Yes. Of course. Can I get you some coffee?'

'No,' Cheryl said. 'Thanks. I've been up all night. I must've drunk ten gallons of the stuff.'

'Right,' I said. 'Please. Take a seat.'

'Thanks,' she said.

I held a chair out for Cheryl and she sat, crossing long legs, using a sharp pink fingernail to dig out a speck of pencil from her eye.

'I'm sorry it's so hot in here. Take your coat off if you like.'

'I'm fine. I'm freezing actually. You get colder when you don't sleep, don't you?'

I pushed the door to and walked round to the other side of the desk, intrigued. I sat down, opposite my visitor. From thirty feet a.m. and ten feet after dark Cheryl would have been quite a sexy girl. She was in her early twenties with an improbably pneumatic figure pumped up to straining point. Her face was thin and it was a little difficult to say what she actually looked like. Her problem skin was covered in a sub-stratum of only vaguely flesh-coloured foundation that it would have taken Henrich Schliemann three days to get through. It was probably the first time in her life she'd been mistaken for the police. I asked what I could do for her.

'You're looking into what happened to Alison, aren't you? I picked up one of your cards yesterday. I heard you speaking to the lads.'

'Yes,' I said. 'Why, do you think you can help me with that?'

Cheryl was sitting bolt upright in her chair, her hands in her coat pockets. 'You're not the Bill, are you?'

I made a gesture to include my room. 'No.'

'Then who are you working for?'

'Does it matter?'

'It does if you're working for one particular person, yes.' Cheryl gave a nervous laugh, more like a cough.

'I see,' I nodded. 'I can understand that. Well, I'm working for Jack Draper's wife. Okay?'

She tilted her head down and looked at me. 'Honest?'

'Scouts' honour.'

'Then yes, it's okay, if you're working for her.'

Cheryl seemed reassured by what I told her and her fingers pulled at the knot of her shawl. Cheryl had light brown hair with new gold highlights and bright ginger eyes framed heavy with black. Her mouth was narrow, naturally open to reveal teeth that an American mother would have had straightened, giving her quite a tough appearance. She looked like she could take care of herself, but she also looked worried. I could see thoughts moving through her, filtering what she wanted to tell me like a basking shark. She ran her tongue over her teeth.

'Mind if I smoke?'

'Sure.'

'Great.' She drew a pack of Marlborough Lights out of her coat pocket and tried to light one with a Bic. Her hand shook like she had Parkinson's disease.

'Christ, you are cold.'

'Cold? That's not cold. I'm fucking terrified is what I am.'

She left her pack on the table and pulled on her cigarette as if it were her last ever puff.

'So. I take it you knew Alison.'

'Yeah. I did.' Cheryl nodded. 'From different shoots, stuff like that. We was mates. I'm from Leyton like she is though I don't live there now. We was with the same modelling agency. We'd go out sometimes, you know. I saw her at a lot of parties. Models get invited to things, Stringfellows, places like that . . .'

'When you say models, what kind of work do you mean?'

Cheryl gave me a flat, cold stare. 'I'm not Kate Moss. Glamour, mostly. Plus advertising, brochures, bike mags. I met Alison doing that.'

'Right,' I said. 'Right. What was she like? I get the impression she was a pretty quiet girl.'

Cheryl nodded. 'She could be, Alison. Needed geeing up sometimes. She was a bit fucked up. She had this terrible mother, never let her out when she was a kid. It really used to get to her. She used to hit her, the bitch. Alison left home when she was sixteen.'

I was puzzled. The newspapers all said she lived at home.

'Yeah, that's right. She went and lived back there, last year, when her mum got ill. I'd have forgotten about the bitch. But Alison was never like that, she let people use her. She stayed there nearly a year, till about three months before she died. Her mum got well, and I was really pleased when she moved out again.'

'Right,' I said. 'And how well did you know Jack Draper?'

'From parties and stuff. There's a footballer scene, would you believe? I really fancied him actually, but he wasn't interested. Alison was a bit more classy than me if the truth be told, a bit more, what's the word, demure.'

I tried not to nod. 'Did you know she was seeing Draper?'

Cheryl shook her head. 'No way. Big secret that was. I never thought Alison would get into anything like that. *No way.*'

Again I was puzzled. 'Get into what? Seeing someone with a wife? Someone famous?'

'No,' Cheryl said. 'No. Well kind of. Do you recognize me at all?'

It was a strange question that came straight out of the blue. I looked at her but shook my head. I guessed she meant from her modelling work but as I was no longer fourteen I didn't subscribe to those magazines.

'No, you don't look like the sort of bloke who buys the *Sunday People*. Probably read about famines in the *Observer* of a Sunday, don't ya? I was in the *People*, 'bout six months ago. Then a year before that.'

'Modelling?'

'Nah. I had an affair with a player. A footballer.' She

smiled. She had a dirty smile, full of relish. Her teeth were stained with coffee and nicotine. She told me the player's name.

'Sold my story. Remember?'

'Yes,' I said, surprised that I actually did have some sort of recollection of it. 'Weren't you . . . weren't you seeing one of his teammates?'

'Yep.'

'At the same time?'

"S'right.'

'Didn't he deny it, and try to sue?'

"S'it,' Cheryl said. 'Arrogant wanker. Thought he could just fuck me and forget it. We done him right up, we did.'

'We? What do you mean by we?'

'Me and the paper,' Cheryl explained. She smiled again and shook her head.

'How?'

'How? Oh. We didn't have any proof – ' she laughed – 'that he was shagging me. He was real careful. Never so much as looked at me in public. I tried all sorts to get him, even waking up in the night to snap him when he was asleep, but he always woke up and I'd have to shag him again. I told the paper all about what had been going on, but they were afraid he'd sue without any pictures. So the editor phones him and says he's going to run the story anyway and he just laughs and threatens the lawyers. I'm going to sue your fucking teeth out, he said. Then he called me. He didn't know I'd sold the story, he thought someone had just spotted us. He told me to deny everything and he promised me half the libel money. The thing was I was on the mobile at the time, sat in the *People* offices!

We got it all on tape. Everyone cracked up, I can tell you.'

'So, you set it up from the start? Before you met him? You went out with him to sell the story?'

'And I got nearly forty grand for it. It was a lot because there were two of them.'

'And that's what Alison did? To Jack Draper?'

'That's right. She knew all along. It goes on all the time and footballers are too dim to realize. But I have to say that I was surprised that Alison was doing it. She was a bit too straight, and I can't imagine what her mother would have said. But McKenna got her to do it. Somehow he managed to persuade her.'

I hadn't been taking any notes but I reached for a pen.

'McKenna?'

'Yeah, McKenna. I saw her talking to him at the ground one day. That's how I knew it was him.'

'Jack Draper's agent. Jeff McKenna?'

'Right,' she said. 'You know about him, then?'

'Not really. Tell me.'

'I will if you give me a chance. He's the guy I sat up all night hiding from in South Mimms fucking service boring station,' Cheryl said. 'The twat I reckon killed her.'

Cheryl lit another cigarette. She had her hands under control this time. I waited until she'd taken another deep drag and set it down on the saucer I'd pushed towards her.

'It wasn't Draper, then?'

She pulled a face. 'Why would he kill Alison?'

I shrugged. 'He was mad at her, for going to the press?'

'I'd be dead three times over.'

'He just lost it, he went crazy when he realized what she'd done to him . . .'

'Have you met Draper?'

'Yes,' I said.

'Well then. Did he look the type who'd suddenly go crazy? I've never met someone so in control of himself.'

'If he's getting what he wants,' I said.

Cheryl gave me a look that said I was welcome to think it was Draper, she wasn't going to argue. I sat back in my chair. The sun found my window and sent a javelin of light through the haze of smoke, into Cheryl's eyes. They looked like wasps whose nest was on fire.

'Tell me how McKenna's involved? Why kill her? Why would he go after you?'

Cheryl nodded. I knew what she was going to say. 'The two players I was shagging. They were both represented by McKenna.'

'And he set them up?'

'Very clever. It was his idea. I didn't really know any players then. He got in touch with me, after I'd met him at a party. He told me he'd introduce me to a player. Well not introduce, exactly, he couldn't do that. He just told me where the players would be, and which one to go for. Jeff had been getting him pissed all night in this club but he left when I showed up. Just been packed in by his TV presenter bird had Mr Bigshot little-dick defender. I sat next to him and after a while he bought me a drink.'

'And you started seeing him?'

'Yeah. And Jeff set up the deal with the papers.'

'With one of his own clients?'

'Two actually. I met the other one a week later. Jeff thought it'd be a bigger story.'

'And he took a cut?'

'Twenty per cent from me. Probably took a slice from the *People* as well.'

'And you think he did this with Alison? Set Jack up with him?'

I thought about what Louise Draper had told me. McKenna, not inviting her to parties. It sounded like Jack and Jeff McKenna had been close. If anyone would have known about Jack's marital difficulties it would have been him. Maybe McKenna thought he was vulnerable.

'I know he did. As far as I knew, I was the only one Jeff had done it with. Then Alison asked me. She said she was seeing someone though she wouldn't say who, but that Jeff had set it up. She wanted to know if she was getting enough money.'

'Was she?'

'I didn't think so. I told her to ask for more.'

'And that's why he killed her?'

'No! She probably tried to blackmail him – she'd tell Draper if he didn't pay her, something like that. Or maybe she wasn't blackmailing him, she just thought it was wrong. I reckon she said she was going to tell Jack because she was in love with him. That's the kind of girl Alison was; fall in love with the worst man two times over. A married footballer. Either way, Jeff would have been finished as a football agent if his clients had found out what he was doing to them.'

'So he killed her?'

'And obviously everyone thinks it was Jack. And I'm the only one who knows what he was up to.'

'So you're scared?'

'I'm shitting myself. He's a wanker, Jeff is. I was seeing him as well as the footballers, so I know. They were just stupid but he was vicious. He hurt me. He'd have cut me if I hadn't been seeing other blokes. When Alison was killed I thought it was him right off.'

'But you didn't say anything, to the police?'

'I wasn't going to get involved. They'd go and talk to Jeff and he'd know I'd grassed him. He's not the sort of person you grass. I didn't want to go anywhere near the Old Bill. I'd just as soon have stayed right out of it.'

'Until now. Why come to me? Has he threatened you?'

'No,' she said. 'He's not that stupid.' Cheryl suddenly looked very, very scared indeed. 'But he knows what I know. I thought he'd forgotten about me, hadn't heard a word from him. I began to relax. But he came round, yesterday afternoon. He just showed up at my house, 'bout five o'clock. He never did that, he always called. I'd nipped out for some fags and it was fucking lucky I had.' She drew on her cigarette, letting the smoke find its own way out of her mouth as she went on. 'I was coming back when I saw him outside my flat. He had a bag in his hand. He was looking in my windows. I hid behind a van. He rang the bell again and then just sat in his car, watching. I was crapping myself. My car was parked down the street and I got in it. I drove off but he saw me and I had to fucking steam away. I lost him, thank God. That's when I remembered you.'

'And you've been driving all night?'

'I couldn't think of *anyone* he didn't know. All I

could think of was how vicious he was. I sat in a shithole of a pub until closing. Nearly let some twat take me home just so I'd be safe somewhere. But he was foul. I just drove and drove and found myself on the M25. I kept thinking he still after me. My car is a bit distinctive. When I was sure he wasn't I stopped in an all-night place. Didn't have enough cash for a room. I called you and then hit the coffee.' She pulled on her cigarette again, the angry orange a match for her eyes. She looked at the stub between her fingers.

'Whoever said these things are bad for you?' Cheryl said.

Chapter Twenty

I passed CHERYL 1 on the way to the Mazda. It was a canary-yellow Escort with a lot of extra plastic and a stuffed animal suckered to the inside window like a laboratory animal being suffocated. Cheryl was still upstairs. She was terrified of going anywhere in her car and I'd told her she could catch up on some sleep on my sofabed, if she liked.

'Is it comfortable?'

'Yes,' I said. 'It's comfortable.'

'Are there any sheets for it?'

'There are but they aren't clean. I wouldn't bother with them.'

Cheryl told me that she'd probably slept on worse, and I believed her.

There were no police outside my flat when I got there and I was surprised. I'd gone there to tell them about McKenna. I hadn't promised Cheryl I wouldn't. There was no point putting off speaking to them, especially now that I had McKenna's name to give them. I wondered why they weren't there – they'd sounded pretty keen to speak to me. It wasn't long before I knew the answer.

I pulled off down towards Russell Square. I'd decided not to call Draper. I wanted some background

on McKenna but Draper hadn't been too stable yesterday, I didn't know how he'd react. He might have
jumped in a car and got to McKenna before I did. It
was to McKenna's office that I was going, but I didn't
call him either. I wanted to surprise him by just
showing up. I was pumped up to be doing something,
impatient to get across town.

Tapping my feet at a light I thought about what
Cheryl had said, about Alison. She'd been surprised at
what her friend had done and I was too. I'd begun to
build a picture of the girl whose body I'd found and
what she'd done just didn't fit it. I told myself I was
being sentimental. Just because the girl had got herself
killed, it didn't mean she wasn't capable of some pretty
shabby behaviour beforehand. I thought about what all
the players had told me – she was such a *nice* girl –
and shrugged it off as well. They'd probably reacted
the same way I had. Dead people aren't saints. They're
just unlucky.

I took the back way, driving through Bloomsbury,
joining the Euston Road at Great Portland Street. After
twenty-five minutes I was pulling through the forecourt of Marylebone Station towards Lisson Grove. I'd
made good time. I turned off Lisson Grove onto
Broadley Street, still trying to work out just exactly
how to play it. Pretend to be a potential client? An
Albanian refugee with a wicked left foot and a dodgy
marriage? No. What about a potential story – I'd seen
secret FA files which revealed that the Wembley plans
were being scrapped and the new National Stadium
was actually going to be built in Stockholm. I was
putting this idea to one side when I ran into traffic.

The drains were backing up and the streets ran

with slews of cold brown water. The traffic was station-
ary and it stayed that way for at least ten minutes,
even though some of the people behind me did their
best to get it all going again by leaning on their horns.
I was close enough to the place so I parked up. I pulled
the door handle and looked out, the water running
high up over the kerb and onto the pavement.

'Probably a burst water main,' I said to no one, as I
stepped over the dirty river. I locked the car and stuck
five twenties in the meter standing up out of the murky
water.

When I got round the corner onto Salisbury Street
I saw what the real reason for the hold-up was. Three
police cars were blocking the road ahead. A van with
its lights flashing was pulling up from the other end of
the street to add to the problem. I shrugged. I glanced
up at the street name. I was on a row of attractive
Georgian houses, white stucco giving way to red-brick.
I set myself. I counted down the numbers and saw
that I was only three or four buildings away from
McKenna's office. I started walking towards it.

'What the fuck are you doing here?'

She'd been stepping out of the building when she'd
seen me. It was another fine Georgian property, but
this one converted into offices. It had a black smoked-
glass frontage instead of the railings and heavy painted
door of its neighbours. It was number one three four.
McKenna's building. I was only a few feet away from it.

'Well?'

She was wearing the same maroon jacket over a
plain white blouse. She'd stopped on the steps of the
building when she'd seen me and when I heard her
voice I stopped too. We looked at each other, from

twenty yards away. It was a complete shock, to both of us. Like running into your ex at a party. Weird. Neither of us moved. Then DI Coombes marched out onto the street towards me until she was standing a foot away, her hands high up on her hips.

I smiled. 'Hello.'

Coombes stuck her chin out towards me. She was a few notches less than pleased. 'The *elusive* Mr Rucker. Private detective, as I have now discovered since we met. Back at eleven, that little cunt said. Think I enjoy sitting outside your flat? Once again – what the hell are you doing here?'

I didn't know what to say. I was on my back foot but I made every attempt not to show it.

'Well?'

'Oh. DS Coombes. I was going to call you.'

'Were you? How thoughtful. What about?'

'McKenna. Jeff McKenna. Jack Draper's agent.'

'What about him?'

'I was coming just to see him.'

'Evidently. Why?'

'Why? Listen,' I said.

'I can hear you.'

'I'm working for Draper's wife. Louise. She wants me to find her husband.'

'Are you now?' Coombes pursed what should have been her lips and frowned at me, her eyes pinching. Her freckles looked like spats of spilled latte. 'Trying to find him, are we? Find him like you did the other night? Hmm?' I let her go on. 'We got you on CCTV, following him through Bethnal Green. Also, two people said they saw someone looks like you chatting away to Draper in the bar that just happens to be *right outside your house.* Something you want to tell me, is there? Well? Working for his wife? Not him?'

I shook my head. 'He tried to hire me, okay? He'd been getting harassed.'

'His wife told us. And?'

'We got in a fight. I said no, he'd have to do without me. Then I changed my mind and chased round all night to find him.'

'So you must have seen him going into her apartment.'

'Must I?'

'The two noddies who stopped you did and they weren't even looking for him.'

'Policemen are observant, aren't they?'

'Oh yes. So, Draper tried to hire you and you didn't mention this? You didn't think to tell us this?'

'I would have,' I said. 'I was confused, okay? I just wanted to see what went on. If you put Draper in the square without me, what's the harm? I figured you would. I was going to call you after speaking to McKenna.'

'Were you? What do you want to see McKenna about?'

Wasn't it obvious? 'I'm working for Draper's wife. I'm trying to find him, so naturally I want to speak to the man's agent.'

'That all?'

I looked at her, then shook my head. 'No. It isn't.'

'No?'

'Listen,' I said. 'Draper didn't do it. I'm convinced of that.' I looked away from her, to the back-up she had. She must have had the same idea. 'I think McKenna might be involved.'

'What makes you think that?'

'I just found out. It was McKenna who set Draper up, with the press. He took Alison to the *Sun*. He got Alison to start seeing Draper so he could sell the story.'

She was surprised but took it in quickly.

'How do you know that?'

'Girl McKenna used in the past, scared shitless she'll be next after Alison. She came to my office an hour ago. So maybe Alison threatened McKenna that she'd tell Draper what he'd been doing. Make sense? McKenna was stitching up other clients too.'

Coombes looked back towards the building she'd come out of, tried it, then nodded like she was tasting a good Côte Rôte. She let herself look a little impressed.

'And you think McKenna killed her?'

'Maybe, all I know is–'

'Well, we'd better go inside and ask him then, hadn't we? He's at his desk.'

'Right,' I said, a little surprised. 'Right.'

Coombes turned immediately and I followed her. Seeing Coombes was a shock but she seemed to accept what I'd told her. I followed her past two policemen guarding the door and into a small foyer. She headed for the stairs.

'So, you had the same idea?' I said.

'Sorry?'

'That McKenna was involved.'

Coombes didn't seem to hear me. When she got to the top of the stairs Coombes turned left and stopped outside the open door to an office.

'Mr McKenna,' Coombes said, through the door. I could hear activity inside. 'A Mr Rucker would like to ask you a few questions. Is that okay? Yes? Step inside, Mr Rucker, this way.'

I walked past Coombes and into the room, where there were five men in total plus McKenna, at his desk.

'Go on, then,' Coombes said, from behind me. 'Ask Mr McKenna if he killed Alison Everly. Well, Mr Rucker? Go on. Ask him.'

I didn't say anything. I could have asked my question and McKenna wouldn't have denied it. He wouldn't have said anything. The knife in his neck looked to have gone straight through to the desk top. It was standing there, straight and firm. McKenna's head was resting on a huge pillow of deep crimson that had run across the surface, snaking down one of the table legs to the floor.

'Go on,' Coombes said again, behind me. 'Don't be shy. Ask him.'

Part Three

Chapter Twenty-One

Noticing people. Spotting people who are acting differently. Spotting people trying too hard to act the same as everyone else. Seeing the preoccupations sitting just behind the eyes of someone when they're doing something ostensibly normal, when they're talking to you, smiling the big smile. It's not difficult, really, or at least it shouldn't be. Observation: you just have to make it your business, and then when it is your business try not to forget that. Then, after a while, not a lot will get past you.

When you're a policeman it's your job to do this. But there is, however, a problem. Most of the time you are identified as such, and normal circumstances no longer apply. I recently finished reading one of those popular science books that mentioned Heisenberg's Uncertainty Principle and the idea is the same. You cannot accurately measure a system because by measuring it you are interfering. If you tell people you're Old Bill, quite simply they behave differently. If you don't tell them, they often know anyway or their suspicions put them on their guard. People look like they're lying when in reality they're just nervous. People innocent of the crime in question can seem guilty because they've actually done something else, something as mundane as failed to pay their TV licence. And then there are the people who are guilty, but since they either know or suspect you of being on the force, and the knowledge of their crime makes them prepared, they take care to appear innocent as a spring lamb with a good lawyer. As a policeman you have to accept this. Reading the somewhat baffling take on the universe(s) I'd recently finished I got the impression that Heisenberg, one hell of a physicist, would have made a pretty good copper too.

But no longer being a policeman I don't have to worry about what people think of me. I don't often *interrogate* people. I no longer make people feel uncomfortable simply because of the fact of what I do, or represent, and I occasionally have to remind myself how liberated this makes me feel. It isn't often that people mistake me for Bill, so I usually have the liberty of not disturbing the system, of being able to fit in, of being able to observe without changing the status of what I see. It means that I can never get a warrant to search a house, or perform the scientific tests most modern detection now relies on, but it does give me the advantage of being able to watch, to let the truth simply reveal itself like the petals of a spring flower. Noticing the water droplets on the entrance bell of Alison Everly's apartment building is an example of that. It didn't get past me. It amazes me then, when I think of it, how I didn't see any of the rest of it coming. None of it. How I didn't fully realize until it was almost too late, when there was a silver bullet spinning across my living room towards my head. Now that it's over it still amazes me but I realize why. It's all about observation: you have to make it your business and then when it is your business try never, even for a minute, to forget that.

The second part. That's difficult.

Chapter Twenty-Two

One of McKenna's arms was thrown out in front of him, the other one by his side. A long thick trail of red, bordered by crusts of dried black, ran down from the knife that someone had left in the agent's neck. It ran past his ear, joining the tacky balloon of blood that sat pooled on the desk beneath him. Though McKenna's head was resting on it, it didn't look like a pillow. It was more like a cartoon bubble – but minus the words. A pity.

Everyone was looking at me. The room was silent.

'This the sort of thing you used to do when you were one of us, Mr Rucker? Fairly basic error, wouldn't you say – mistaking a murder victim for the murderer? Unless of course you're suggesting that Mr McKenna here killed Alison and then, in a fit of remorse, stabbed himself three times in the back and once in the neck. Boys, I think we've solved it. You can all go home.'

I should have seen it coming but I hadn't. I didn't know what to say. Everyone in the room was looking at me intently, including McKenna. I turned to Coombes. Her head to one side she said, 'So, still don't think it was Draper, then?' I glanced from her to her assistant, the kid who had been in my flat, who looked a little pale round the gills. Then my eyes took in the rest of the office.

The room we were standing in was about twenty feet by thirty. The walls were pale yellow, with frosted glass light fittings plus a series of framed and unframed photos running the entire length of the far wall. Draper looked out of one of them, as well as other faces I knew. The floor was a blocked hardwood, a huge modern rug covering most of it. A long leather sofa was backed against the rear wall, behind a smoked glass coffee table littered with magazines. It was an expensive-looking place, the office of a man doing well for himself.

'Gentlemen,' Coombes said to the room. 'This is Billy Rucker. Former DS and now Private Dick, in every sense of the word. A man who's got a rather strange knack of finding himself in the vicinity of corpses.'

She was talking to two fingerprint specialists who looked a trifle confused before going back about their business, one dusting the window frames, the other using a sideboard to bag and label items he'd found. They seemed oblivious to the fact that between them, lying on a big, bloodstained desk, was the slouched form of Jeff McKenna. Behind him was a set of sliding glass doors, looking out onto a small balcony. The low winter sun was trying to break into the room and half of the floor-length blinds had been turned against it.

Two other men *were* taking notice of McKenna. One went back to packing up a video recorder that he'd obviously just used on the scene while the other was using a tape measure to map the exact position of the victim.

'How many wounds, Ron?'

'Four, ma'am,' the man with the measure replied. 'Three in the upper back, the last one in the neck. All deep, this one's gone through to the desk.'

'A shame,' Coombes said. 'Nice piece of furniture. I wonder what they'll do with it once we've got laddy-boy here bagged and away. Look nice in my flat that would. I wonder if the Habitat people would do me an exchange. I've never seen a sign disclaiming responsibility for corpse damage. Now then. Mr Rucker here thinks that Mr McKenna here is a dangerous killer, so I want you all to be careful. I also want you to take notice of his technique and learn from him. Mr Rucker, the scene is yours.'

Coombes swept a hand out before me and smiled. Her attitude surprised me. The ironic detachment was usually a male thing – who can be the least concerned, the most blasé. Even then I always felt it sat uncomfortably on most officers, who seemed to feel they had to take part in it. But Coombes was enjoying herself. She was making sure she outdid the men, she got there before they did. It certainly seemed to work, they all looked at her as if she were barely human. I could see why she'd made DS in her early thirties.

Coombes moved her hand again so I shrugged and took a step forward. Seeing as she'd invited me, I moved towards McKenna and he stared at me through two vacant eyes, filmy as those on a bass the fishmonger can't sell.

'Don't touch anything, please. Don't want to mix your prints up with any of yours that may already be here, do we?'

Coombes moved to the right of the desk and I mirrored her. McKenna was, or had been, a short, heavy-set man, with dirty blond hair tied back in a ponytail. It was difficult to say what he looked like because his cheek was squashed into the blood beneath it, some soaked into a neatly trimmed goatee, but it was the same man whose face I'd seen in the *Star*. Though McKenna was slumped over his desk, rigor had stiffened him, giving him the artificial appearance of a badly weighted dummy. He was dressed in a black suit, a white shirt without a tie rimmed with blood around a tightly fastened collar. I looked for signs of lividity in his neck but there was too much blood to see. I looked down at the hand by McKenna's side, already discoloured to purple by the blood that was gathered there. I moved round and saw the three stab wounds in his back. The small, dark tears in his suit looked like bullet holes. The wounds looked too small, too insignificant to kill a man, but any single one of them would have done it.

Coombes stood over me as I studied the knife. It was the type used by sushi chefs, but I'd seen ones like it in any number of cookshops and department stores. I could just make out the brand name. The handle was a hard, shiny steel, with indentations for grip, many of which were clogged with blood where it had backed up out of the wound. I looked from it, to the rest of the corpse, before leaning over to the fingernails on the hand thrown out in front of him. I couldn't see anything in them. I looked for signs that his clothing was in any sort of disarray, which might have suggested a struggle. It wasn't. It seemed pretty obvious that he'd let the person in and then been stabbed from behind. He probably died wondering just what the fuck was going on.

Looking over McKenna's body didn't have the same effect on me as seeing Alison's had. Maybe it was some kind of inherent sexism on my part. Or maybe the fact that it was now a crime scene gave me distance, the presence of five police officers all treating it with flat humour or efficient unconcern had dulling any feelings I might have. It might even have been because of Alison – I'd seen her so recently that something in me had prepared itself, re-erected the wall that had gradually crumbled over the last seven years. I had a feeling I hadn't had since it had been my job to look down at inert forms, former people. It was distaste. Distaste for myself.

I stood up, my hands on my hips. 'When was he found?'

'The cleaner opened up at eight this morning,' Coombes said. 'I don't think she was expecting the kind of mess she walked in on. He was alive at six last night, the receptionist saw him.'

I turned to my left. 'What's the smell?'

The DC packing up the camera looked up from his equipment. He was a well-built man in his mid-forties with a full moustache and thin, sandy-coloured hair. He was dressed in tight chinos, a blue short-sleeved shirt and a burgundy tie. He looked at Coombes. She nodded.

'Apart from piss, shit and blood?' he asked in deep Lancastrian tones. 'Gin. Gin and tonic. There was a glass on the desk. Prints all over it. Probably turn out to be the victim's but we've bagged it anyway.'

'I can still smell it, though.'

He nodded. 'There's more on the floor, behind him. Broken shards as well. Another glass. It must have got smashed. We think that one was being used by the perp.'

'Prints?'

'The pieces are too small. And there aren't enough. Perp must have taken the bigger bits with him, when it was all over.'

'Bugger.'

'Bugger indeed,' the man agreed.

'Anything else?'

I turned to the man at the sideboard, labelling bags. He was smaller than his colleague, with large, heavy plastic glasses that gave him more of a scientific look. He had the glass tumbler in his hand, protected by plastic. He introduced himself as DC Carpenter.

'Any more prints?'

'Plenty,' he said. 'We've been over every inch of this place. This guy was an agent of some sort. A lot of people came through here. Prints all over the coffee table, the magazines.' He smiled, and looked at Coombes. 'Don't worry, we've got more than enough for you lot to be going on with.'

'And it'll all turn out to be shit,' Coombes said. 'We'll end up interviewing most of the squad of Tottenham Hotspur and half the cast of *Starlight* fucking *Express*. Right then.'

Coombes unfolded her arms and seemed to come to life. She'd enjoyed playing games with me but now they were over. She asked me if I'd like to revise my little theory about McKenna, and then asked me if I'd spoken to Draper yet or if I knew where he was. I said I hadn't and I didn't. She didn't believe me. Coombes asked me again how I'd learnt that McKenna had sold Jack out and I was about to tell her when three men

clothed in greens filed through the door. They said 'Hi'
to the forensic team and 'Morning, ma'am' to Coombes.
They set a stretcher down by the side of the desk.

Coombes and I watched as the three men
approached the body. Now that they'd mapped his position and filmed him, McKenna could be moved.
They'd get a far better look in the morgue. The most
senior of the three men had another quick look
beneath his eyelids, though, and into his wounds. Then
his two colleagues lifted McKenna upright, one pulling
the knife up out of the desk where its point had just
broken the lacquered surface. The duty pathologist
spent a while pressing the neck, probably looking for
lividity marks like I had, which give away an approxi-
mate time of death. He was gentle, like a doctor
examining an appendix wound. He reached over and
turned the blinds a notch. Then he told his colleagues
to set the corpse back down and he took hold of the
knife that was still embedded in McKenna's neck. He
wasn't pulling it out, though. Instead he grasped it
firmly with both hands, moving it left in the wound
then right, testing the pressure.

'So?' Coombes asked. 'Won't you give us your
opinion?'

I turned from the body, more than happy to do so.
'Isn't it obvious?'

'Tell me.'

I shrugged. 'He knew them.' I glanced towards the
door. 'No sign of that lock being forced. Downstairs
door looked okay to me too. Killed from behind after
making a couple of drinks. Find out which of his mates
drinks G and T. You'll check the phone calls, in and
out?'

'Of course. Anything else?'

'Dunno. When do you think he got it?'

'From initial temperature, sometime last night.'

I nodded. Cheryl had seen him at five. 'Right. Well, whoever did it was careful.'

'Whoever?' A laugh.

'Whoever. Taking the glass like that. He's not some-one who'll panic.'

'Still think it wasn't Draper?'

I thought of Cheryl, sitting in my office. It had all seemed so easy. 'I don't know what to think,' I said.

The men in greens had a bit of trouble getting McKenna onto the stretcher. I don't know why they tried to straighten him, it was never going to happen. As they were wasting their time Coombes turned to me. She looked thoughtful. Something had seemed to soften in her.

'Spoke to your old gaffer after I left you,' she said. 'Ken Clay.'

I saw a fat man with yellow teeth and empty, piggy eyes, all encased in a cloud of Aramis.

'Nice for you.'

'Asked him what kind of man you were. Said you used to be a pretty fine copper.'

I looked at her and shrugged, wondering where this was going. 'I had my moments. Got lucky a couple of times.'

'We all need that. Not sure what to make of you now, though, he told me.' Coombes left a second and her nose and mouth squeezed together. I knew what was coming. 'He told me why you quit. I . . . I'm sorry.' I didn't say anything. 'It must have been hell. Those bastards wanting to get to you and then your brother

243

getting in the way. Christ. Did you have to leave, though?'

'I had to leave.'

'Couldn't you have just taken time out? To get over it. Clay said they would have given you as long as you needed.'

'It wouldn't have been long enough,' I said. 'However long they gave me.'

'Don't miss it, then, this?'

I just laughed.

'What about . . . ?'

I was saved from any further probing by a sound in the hallway. I followed Coombes' gaze out there and saw two heads reaching the top of the stairs. Coombes stiffened instantly. She stepped back like a cornered animal, before shooting me a vicious, warning glance. I didn't understand. But then I saw who it was, stiff backed, approaching the room at a brisk pace. Coombes looked at me, to see that I understood. I smiled. The man walking towards us was Deputy Commissioner John Landridge, the number two policeman in the entire Met. He had a reputation for sticking his oar into high-profile cases, having done a lot behind the scenes on the Jill Dando killing. In my day he was a chief liaison officer at Scotland Yard, and I'd had some dealings with him. Coombes looked terrified at being caught allowing a civilian on a crime scene, especially one with as much media interest as this had. There was, however, nothing she could do about it.

'Morning everyone,' Landridge barked.

We all wished him good morning in reply, nearly all of us adding a sir at the end.

'Good to see you all hard at it. Coombes, isn't it?'

'Sir.'

'Super Jack put another one in the back of the net, has he, Coombes?'

We all chuckled.

'Looks that way, sir.'

'Right then, that makes him our leading scorer this season. Better get him arrested, hadn't we? Should have done that before now. So, what's the state of play here?'

'Just removing the body, sir. The scene's been mapped and filmed, prints taken. Once the body's out we'll seal it. We'll leave someone to answer the phone.' She told him about the glass fragments and the door to door she'd put in motion.

'Good stuff. Carry on, then. Don't mind me, everyone.'

Landridge stood with his hands behind his back, a good six two with a mane of black hair shot with silver. He looked as imposing in his snap uniform as he no doubt intended. He was in his late fifties, but still had a hell of a dynamism about him. As I was the only one apart from Coombes who didn't seem to be racing around, his eyes fell on me. A frown crept onto his face like a cloud across the sun. I could see Coombes wince.

'We've met?'

Coombes stood stock-still. I smiled. 'Yes, sir.'

'Used to work out of . . . Camden? No, Islington?'

I nodded.

'You're working with Coombes now?'

It was sort of the truth, so I admitted it.

'Excellent. Tucker, am I right? Phil?'

'That's it.'

'Yes. Yes. The CC and myself pride ourselves on knowing who's in our force. Put away a lot of nasty Yardies five, six years ago, yes?'

'More like eight, sir.'

'Is it really? My word. Got a lot of good PR points for that if I recall, could do with you doing it again. Oh well, glad to see you're on the team.'

The sun suddenly cut into the room and Landridge put a hand to his face as though he were being interviewed by the Stasi.

'Actually—' Coombes began.

'Wait!' I said.

My cry brought everyone's attention to the stretcher. McKenna had been loaded onto it sideways, in a foetal position, a cushion keeping the knife in place. He was being taken into the hallway, where they'd cover him and secure him to the dolly before carrying him downstairs. The two men at either end stopped.

'Wait! There.'

Something was glinting. I pointed to the far end of the stretcher and everyone followed my hand.

'Look.'

I took a step forward. Everyone was still. Poking out of the turn-up on McKenna's left trouser leg was a piece of glass, dazzling as it was caught by one of the slats of sunlight pressing through the open blinds. Instinctively, Coombes stepped towards it too.

'Leave it!'

Landridge stopped her. He turned to DC Carpenter. Carpenter still had his gloves on. He looked unsure for a second, then went towards the glinting jag, gingerly easing it out. He held it by the edges. It was a thin, triangular-shaped splinter, two inches at its base, three along. Carpenter's wrist turned as he examined it.

'Don't keep us in suspense, man!'

Nobody spoke as Carpenter took the glass fragment over to the sideboard, where he set it down on a length of clingfilm. He opened his case and took out a bottle of dark grey aluminium dust. He uncapped it. He sprinkled a good quantity of the dust over the whole surface of the glass before brushing the dust away. He leaned over and sent a light breath across the surface. Then Carpenter picked the jag up again, carefully. He held it up, his arm at full stretch, until he found the light.

You could see the print from way across the room.

'Bingo!' boomed Deputy Commissioner Landridge. 'Bloody bingo.'

Chapter Twenty-Three

I snuck out of there while Landridge was on the phone to Scotland Yard. I got to the corner but stopped when I heard my name. I turned as DS Coombes hurried towards me, her face pale, and I waited until she'd stopped in front of me.

'Thanks,' Coombes said.

I shrugged. 'Nothing. Don't worry.'

'It could have been my job. I can't believe I let you up there.'

'I won't tell.'

'I'd appreciate it.' She looked back towards the building. I stepped round the corner and she followed me. 'Good job you were there, though. That piece of glass could have got lost on the stretcher, anywhere.'

'Someone would have seen it.'

'Well, whatever. That should settle it, though, don't you think?'

I nodded. 'Can't see any way round it. If the print's Draper's.'

'If?'

'Yes,' I said. '*If.*'

Coombes nodded and folded her arms. '*If* it is, what'll you do, give up on it?'

'I'm working for Draper's wife,' I said. 'I'll still try to find him.'

'And you think you stand a better chance than the combined police services of England, Scotland and Wales?'

'You haven't found him so far.'

'True,' Coombes admitted. 'True.' She'd rushed out without a coat and she shivered, running both hands up and down her arms. 'If you ask me we'll also need the combined police forces of Argentina, Bolivia and Peru if we don't hurry up. That's where I'd be if I was him.'

'Me too,' I said. 'If he has the money.' I had a strange, nebulous feeling. I nudged it aside. '*If* the print turns out to be his.'

Coombes smiled and shook her head. 'Want a bet on it?'

'No,' I said, after a second or two, letting a smile break my lips. 'No, I don't want a bet on it.'

The traffic was light on the Euston Road and I cruised along without any problems until I hit roadworks outside Madame Tussaud's, where a long line of tourists was huddled together in the cold. I remembered going there with my mum and dad when I was ten or so. Parents from all over the world must do it but I could still remember the humiliation when the policeman my dad had told me to ask the time from had turned out to be wax. My dad thought it was the funniest thing he had ever seen, often using it as an example of my stupidity in later years. I wondered how many of the children lined up there now would go through the same thing. I sat watching them for ten minutes. I made it to the underpass eventually, though, and it wasn't long before I pulled off onto Pancras Way, behind King's Cross Station.

Looking at McKenna's body hadn't affected me the way finding Alison Everly's had, but it was depressing. I'd become convinced that it wasn't Draper who'd killed her and I was actually going to do exactly what Coombes had asked – try to get him to come in. If he knew what McKenna had been up to I thought he might just agree. But maybe I was wrong. Maybe Draper really was playing me for a sucker as everyone seemed to think. I hadn't wanted to get myself into this in the first place. I had another image of Alison, what had happened to her, and it made me nearly physically sick to think I might be trying to help the man who'd killed her. I saw Jack again, in Fred's, how cocky he'd been, how arrogant without knowing it. I knew that if he ever went to court for this, that would be exactly how he'd behave. And afterwards too, guilty or inno-cent, it wouldn't affect the way he carried himself. For some reason I saw him with Shulpa, her hanging off his arm. I had a sudden flash of his wife, naked, moving on top of me. I wondered if that would do anything to him and felt small as soon as I wondered it.

I pushed Draper out of my mind and pulled into the small car park behind the George. Twenty-five minutes later I was standing at a payphone in front of the station with a black postman's bag over my shoulder. It was a fairly heavy bag, but I didn't leave it on the floor beside me as I made my call, and it wasn't because the floor was soaking. It was because the bag contained a large number of used twenty-pound notes, adding up to the sum of exactly forty-five thousand English pounds. My shoulder would just have to cope.

I dug my hand in my pocket, pumped two pound coins in the slot and called Nicky. He was on his own. We spoke for five minutes, during which time I told him to do something he didn't want to do, but which I managed to convince him about the importance of. We set a time to meet. Then I told him that I had his mother's birthday present. I took a crumpled Post-it from my wallet and dialled another number.

'Yes?'

'It's me. Don't say my name.'

There was silence for a long while. I drilled my ears into it. Then he spoke again.

'Okay. Okay. Thanks for calling.'

'That's all right. How are you?'

'Good question. I don't know. Fucked off. Bored. I don't get out much.'

'Keep it that way. Where are you?'

There was another silence. 'I don't think I should tell you,' he said. 'They might be listening.'

'True,' I said. 'But that's not why you're not telling me. Have it your way.'

'It's not that I don't trust you . . .'

'It doesn't matter,' I told him. I kept listening for background noise but I couldn't hear any. Jack wasn't whispering, he must have felt pretty safe where he was. I thought I heard voices. 'Now, I've read your biog, and I've seen your wife. Give me your best guess. Out of all the people you could name, who is doing this to you?'

'So you believe it wasn't me? Thank God. Christ, it's all I can think about. The worst to come out of it would be Dave Harvey, my old manager. We used to be mates, but we fell out. He knows I've got stuff on him that'll mean he'll never work again. He's doing well now.'

'But he's not the only one. Those businessmen you named, in the gambling syndicate. They don't sound like they'd mess around.'

'Fuck no.'

'But the only thing I can't see is what good setting you up would do to anyone you were thinking of naming. The threats yes, but not killing Alison.'

'It's obvious. Come on! If it comes from a murderer then what credibility will it have? It'll sound like I'm desperate.'

I nodded. 'And it was you who gave it to the *Standard*?'

'Of course. I'm being stitched up, and I need people to know it. It's working. The *Mirror*'s already calling me the Fugitive . . !'

'It isn't the media you have to worry about. It's the police.'

I hesitated a second. 'So, you think it might be Harvey?'

'I didn't say that. Listen. I've had another idea. I've been wracking my brains and I suddenly thought to call a friend, a friend of Alison's. I just spoke to her, on her mobile. A girl called Cheryl, she worked with Alison. Listen, okay? I knew she was dodgy, from when she shagged Dave Burton and was in the *Sun*. So I asked her if Alison had set me up, on purpose, before we'd even got it together. She didn't want to, but eventually she told me about Alison and that cunt McKenna.'

'McKenna?'

'My agent. My former fucking agent?'

'Former?'

'I'm not using him after what he's done. He stitched me up with the tabloids. He set me up with Alison, can you believer that? Maybe he killed her. Or at least let people know about my book. Billy?'

'I'm still here.'

'Maybe he did it to shut her up, stop her from spilling the beans about what he was doing. Try talking to the greasy twat.'

'I will,' I said. 'Another thing. Tell me about Korai, the chairman.'

'What's he got to do with it?'

'I don't know. Your contract is up, isn't it?'

'True, but why put me out of action? They need me.'

'Okay,' I said. 'Fine. I'm just trying to think of everyone. Keep in touch – just don't say your name. Don't leave messages.'

'Okay.'

'And Jack?'

'Yes.'

'Have you spoken to McKenna?'

There was a pause. 'I called him yesterday, the arsehole . . .'

'On your new mobile?'

'No, a callbox.'

'Good. But don't phone him again.'

'Why not?'

'Just don't call him,' I said.

'What . . . ?'

I hung up.

I called Cheryl at my office, and when she didn't answer and the machine came on I was suddenly and very violently worried for her, though I didn't have any idea what might have happened to the girl. It was just an intense feeling. I was in full sprint to my car when I remembered I'd told her not to answer the phone. I slowed down, walked the rest of the way, then drove up to Highbury. The yellow Escort was still there, as was Cheryl when I put my key in the lock and told her not to panic. She was lying in my bed, her clothes piled on my chair. She hadn't slept, she said, as she sat up, giving me a little hint as to why two healthy young men had got themselves in the Sundays because of her. She was too scared. I stepped into the café while she dressed, taking the postman's bag with me. When I came back I told her why she didn't need to be scared any more.

The room was almost tropical and I opened the window. Cheryl's eyes opened like two Venus flytraps. Once I'd convinced her I was telling her the truth a flood of relief washed out of her.

'Who was it? Was it Jack?' She sounded like a school-boy with a new Playstation. 'He called me just now, I told him, did he go off and–'

'It happened last night.'

'Right right. Christ!' Cheryl nodded to herself, trying to take it all in, immediately calming down again. 'I can't tell you how relieved I am. Oh shit. I could fall asleep right here. Someone killed that vicious little cunt. I still think . . . Well, never mind.' Cheryl's eyes changed focus again, just as suddenly, and in an instant she looked like she was in a hurry. 'Do you mind if I use your phone? My batteries are nearly out.'

'Go ahead,' I said, 'please.'

Cheryl told me she was calling someone she knew at the *Mirror*. When she got through she informed her contact that she had a good story on football agent Jeff McKenna. She listened for a second.

'You know he's dead, right?' I watched her say. 'Yeah, he is. They found him just now. He's been stabbed. And he's been ripping his clients off. I know how. Interested?'

Whoever she was talking to was interested and Cheryl got herself together enough to arrange to meet him, bickering over which restaurant he was going to take her to lunch at. When she'd hung up she had a quick go at her make-up. She wanted to get moving but I prevailed on her to stay in the room long enough to give me the address of Alison Everly's parents. She looked excited as she hurried out: a woman on her way to a good payday.

I set lunch on my desk and refolded the sofabed for the second time that day before sitting down to eat. I wasn't in the least bit hungry. It felt good to just sit at my desk, though, drinking coffee, running thoughts through my head. I stopped for a second as I heard a high-pitched squealing from somewhere, like a chair that needs oiling. I didn't know what it was. I stared at my brother's face, peering out at me from the picture frame. I hadn't been in to see him for a week. I'd go soon, tell him about Nicky. If there was a Nicky left to tell him about. I suddenly had an image of Luke, miraculously waking from his eight-year sleep. I wondered if he'd retain any of the information I'd been feeding him over the years, whether he'd have any knowledge of the lives of the people I knew, most of whom he'd never met. Ally, Mike, Nicky, Shulpa. If he did it would be amazing, it would mean that I really had been communicating with him all these years. If he didn't it would mean that he'd know nothing about me, we'd practically be strangers to each other. I'd lost him once, how strange to get him back only to realize that my life meant nothing to him.

The tax return took my attention but I didn't even come close to picking it up. Unlike last time I had other things on my mind. I now had two bodies to worry about. Now there was twice as much heat on the man I was supposed to be helping. I tried to picture Draper, out there somewhere, his life turned upside down. It was easy enough to see that Draper had a motive for both killings, for McKenna as well as, or independent of, Alison. If he'd killed Alison out of anger at what she'd done then he'd feel the same if not worse towards his former agent and friend. But if McKenna had killed Alison, Draper would still have the same reason to kill him, maybe more. I don't know what he felt for Alison. Maybe he loved her. Maybe he killed McKenna out of revenge. I remembered the feelings I'd had when I'd first met him, how the success that he had oozed from every pore had set me against him. I thought of his voice on the phone that morning, how difficult he was to read. Was he shitting me? Was he? There was no way I could know. Not without finding him. And that didn't seem very likely. If Draper had fooled the police he'd fooled me too. I didn't have a clue where he was, and this was a shame. A big shame. Because I was beginning to think that there might be another, and far more important reason why I should know where Jack Draper was.

The postman's bag on the floor brought Nicky's face into focus. The face he used to have that is. I had two corpses to think about and I didn't want three. I stood up and lifted the bag onto my shoulder and it wasn't that heavy really, far too light seeming to be able to buy three weeks' worth of my friend's life. I carried it over to the door, conscious of what it contained, what it meant, and pulled open the door. The squealing I'd heard earlier pierced the air again. It was coming from outside the window.

The shrike, as I now knew to call it, was almost exactly at eye level with me, three yards out, the closest it had been. Maybe it really was nesting. I turned to go but stopped. There was something else. The shrike had what looked like a small mouse in its talons. It was held beneath the bird's feet and the wet bark of the branch it was perched upon. The bird was still, except for the odd twitch of its head, while the mouse kicked its legs madly and twisted its body to get free from the claws gripping it to the branch. The desperate, reproachful sound cut through the cold air. It felt like the mouse was pleading with me. Terror bolted its eyes open as it looked around madly for a way to escape. I stood still and watched. The bird looked calm, disinterested, scarcely recognizing the fact that the mouse was there, struggling for its life. I saw a hand around Shulpa's neck and a huge, impassive face, turned to me. I rested my fingers on the window latch but didn't open it.

The shrike continued to ignore the mouse as it kept up its fevered kicking. It was never going to make it. It was caught, and it probably knew it, but what else could it do? Suddenly it stopped and lay still, and I thought it had had it, but then it put on another spurt, wilder than the last. It finally got the bird's attention. The shrike turned down to it, almost as if it had seen it for the first time. With two short bobbed movements it had reached down and pecked the mouse's eyes out. I expected the bird to start eating the mouse, but it didn't. Instead it started to look around again, as if it was studying the tree. Its short beak was covered in blood, a drop of which detached itself and fell, disappearing through the branches to the floor below.

I didn't stay and watch the rest. There was only one way it could go. The mouse still didn't give up, weakly scrambling its front legs forward on the branch. It continued to scream until I'd closed the door and walked out into the hall. After that I couldn't hear it any more.

Chapter Twenty-Four

The man who led me through to the vault of a small but discreet security company in Mayfair was a reserved gentleman in his sixties wearing pince-nez style glasses down towards the tip of his nose. He called me sir and helped me courteously even though he probably thought the contents of my bag had come from a building society somewhere, and that I hadn't taken them out of the cashpoint. I was left alone in the room and I loaded the cash into the box, all but the fifteen grand I'd left in my office. The money was old and crinkled but it didn't take up that much room. After I loaded it up my hands felt dirty and I stood, looking at it, before pushing the drawer. In the bag it hadn't seemed that much to get fussed over but now it seemed even less. It was a petty and shabby bundle, an insignificant-looking thing for my friend to get killed over. So I'd better make sure he didn't. Once I'd settled my account I left the place and drove to Westbourne Park.

Sal had told me that that was where the Maltese community tends to be grouped in London these days as well as giving me a rundown on how the outfit Nicky was involved in operated. Westbourne Park is mostly a Portuguese area and you wouldn't know that some of the shops are run by Maltese, as well as a few of the cafés. I sat in one, reading about famines in the *Guardian*. Sal had given me a list of names, some of the people I was interested in, and I went through that too. I thought about some of the other things she'd told me, the way the Maltese operated. I asked her what she knew about a little guy with a harelip and she'd said he was the former favourite nephew, that most people had assumed that even though he was young he'd have taken over. He hadn't and people had been even more surprised when he'd seemed to accept this. Now it wasn't certain he ever would step up. He was wild, unpredictable, they weren't quite sure what to do with him. And he, in turn, was beginning to get impatient.

I sat, watching what was going on. Nothing much was. I wrote down the names of the shops and spoke to a few people. I kept my eyes open but I didn't see either of the two men I was looking for. Just to see what kind of reaction I'd get I asked the café owner, a friendly and loquacious old man with a neat moustache, if he knew either of them. I described them pretty accurately and he wasn't so friendly after that. He told me no and disappeared in the back, not coming out until after I'd left.

It was then that I saw him. A thin guy in a shiny grey suit, with a bang-on mullet and a shaved goatee. He was on his own, carrying a briefcase, walking into a bookies. I waited until he came out, fifteen minutes later, getting a picture of him as he stepped out the door. He looked pleased with himself. The snap on the case was open. It hadn't been before. I watched him walk into a grocer's opposite and when he came out he was carrying the bag in a different hand. I watched him step into a big blue Merc and pull away. I didn't follow him because Sal had told me where he hung out. Instead I walked to Notting Hill Gate, stopping for half an hour in an Internet café.

On the Central Line out to Leyton I sat looking at the three newspapers I'd bought. They all made a lot of Jack's allegations, the *Mirror* indeed dipping its toe into the idea that Jack might not be such a villain after all, running his picture alongside a shot of Harrison Ford in *The Fugitive*. 'Is Jack Draper trying to prove his innocence?' one byline mused. I wondered if they'd be saying that tomorrow, a picture of Jeff McKenna on the front page.

There was also a small piece about the woman who had found Alison Everly's body. Karen Mills. The paper said that it was on her wedding day, and gave a short description of how she'd come to call on Alison. I read it quickly before leaving the paper on the seat next to me.

I called the Everlys from Leyton Station, telling a very cautious, late middle-aged man that while I wasn't a policeman, I was trying to find out who had killed his daughter. I wasn't really expecting him to agree to see me, and I could hear his wife in the background telling him to say no, but when I said I was working for Louise Draper, he wavered. She wants to know if her husband is a murderer, I said. She's devastated by all this as well. There was silence for a second or two before John Everly finally gave me the go-ahead to visit them.

'I think we owe her that,' he said. 'She, at least, has never done anything to us.'

Alison Everly's parents lived in a small bungalow on a clean, modern housing estate, ten minutes' walk from Leyton High Street. I knew, from the newspapers, that up until six months before her death, Alison had lived there too. A limp sun peered through thin cloud like a lazy eye as I came out of Leyton Station and I wondered whether or not to thank it for showing me the jag of glass in McKenna's turn-up. I had the feeling that that jag was not going to make life easier for me. I walked past the football ground, before turning off to the left. I found Borsley Avenue easily enough, and strolled along the line of small, neat bungalows until I got to twenty-seven. I opened the gate and walked up to a brown door with a brass knocker on the front but no bell. A large plastic cross was nailed above it, an agonized Christ frozen in his Passion.

The living-room curtains moved, and ten seconds later John Everly met me at the door. He was a stooped but still very tall, slow man in his late sixties, with no hair to speak of, but long, grey sideburns. He held a soft, warm hand out to me, then asked me if I minded showing him some sort of identification. I told him I didn't mind at all, handing him my card. He squinted at it, shrugged his large shoulders and nodded, before opening the door wide and following me into the hall.

The bungalow I stepped into smelled of new air freshener and old dog food. I could see why when a small highland terrier ran forward from the kitchen and jumped up at me, before John Everly called it down with a wearily affectionate rebuke, bending to take hold of its collar. Everly's voice was old-fashioned, rounded Cockney. He led the dog back to the kitchen where he shut it in, ignoring a couple of barks as he walked back down the hall towards me. He took my coat and hung it on a peg.

'This way,' he said, holding his hand out to the left.

Everly pushed open a thin white door, the bottom of which brushed heavily against a thick brown carpet with lighter brown swirls. He stood in the doorway, his arm across to the door handle, and I stepped past him awkwardly. The room was small, with a bay window and walls covered in heavy cream wallpaper with woodchips beneath. It was also very hot, a gas fire burning a livid orange on the far wall. Mrs Everly was sitting in a high-seated chair in the far corner, a remote in her hand though the TV was off. I don't know what I expected Mrs Everly to look like – I'd given it no thought – but seeing her was a complete shock, which I tried to keep to myself. Mrs Everly was at least five years older than her husband, probably more, and was sitting bolt upright in her chair. While he was a slow, roundabout-seeming man, she sat there rigid but motionless, acknowledging my entrance with barely a movement, the merest tightening of thin, downturned lips. She had a waxen, almost yellow complexion, her eyes covered with large, grey-tinted glasses. Her hair was nylon, unmoving, an improbable purplish-brown. She wore a blue and white checked housedress, a large cross, complete with Christ, hanging down over a flat, almost sunken chest. On the walls surrounding her were other images of Jesus, all in varying degrees of torment. There were none of Alison, as far as I could see. My eyes flicked around them before returning to my hostess.

Mr Everly pointed me to a low sponge sofa and took a seat on a small stool next to his wife. He looked nervous, a weak smile playing on and off his lips like a bulb that won't quite fit the socket. I sat upright, my elbows on my knees, and told the people before me how sorry I was about their daughter. Mr Everly nodded his head quickly and looked down, while his wife just stared at me, her arms spread out on the rests of her chair. The disdain on her face unsettled me. I took my notebook out of my pocket and thanked them for their time. I said I wouldn't be long, I just wanted to find out a little about Alison.

John Everly sat up on his stool. 'And you're working for his wife?' he asked.

'Yes, that's right.'

'And how . . . how is she taking all this?'

I heard her voice: I hate her. I nodded, slightly. 'She's very distressed. I think she wants to know what happened as much as you must.'

'*I* know what happened,' Mrs Everly said.

I turned to Mrs Everly and looked at her, trying not to show my surprise. Her voice was sharp and cold. She was waiting, but I didn't quite know what to say.

'Now then, Violet love . . .'

'I know what happened. He killed her.'

John Everly let out a long sigh. I looked at Mrs Everly and pursed my lips. 'That does seem likely,' I said. 'Yes. But until the police find him they won't know exactly. What I want to do is get a picture of what kind of girl Alison was—'

'You don't understand.' The words were spat towards me. '*He* killed her. Because of what she was like.'

'Right,' I said. 'Well, would you mind telling me what she *was* like. I spoke to some people who knew—'

'She was a little slut is what she was like. She was an evil little slut who sold herself—'

'Violet!' her husband said.

I sat on the sofa, my mouth open before I remembered to close it. I had a roll neck on and the heat from the fire was adding to my discomfort. Everly stared at his wife. Mrs Everly's face was completely blank for a second and then she withdrew into herself, into thoughts there was no point sharing. Her head turned towards me. I couldn't see her eyes and I was grateful for the thick darkened glasses that covered them. Her look was piercing enough.

'Have you any more questions?'

'Well,' I said. 'Yes. Yes. I mean, did you know her friends, who she hung round with . . . ?'

'No,' Mrs Everly said. 'I didn't. Her friends never came here. Well?'

'I'm sorry?'

'Is that all?'

I found that my mind was a complete blank. It wasn't all, I'd made a list of things I wanted to know.

'Yes,' I said. 'Thank you.'

'Right,' she said.

Mrs Everly stood very suddenly and moved towards the door. She'd sat so still that I was surprised by how quickly she moved. She left the room without looking back, and I heard another door opening down the hall, before closing again. I sat on the sofa, stunned by what had happened, how quickly Mrs Everly had gone off like that. I was making a habit of this. I looked at her husband, stooped on his stool, his mouth flickering again, not this time with a smile.

Everly looked up at me. The blood had fled from

his face, leaving it a mottled white. 'I'm sorry,' he said. 'I . . . I'm sorry.'

'It's okay. Really. I understand, it must be hell for you.'

'You're right,' he said. 'It is.' A weight seemed to descend somewhere inside of him, crushing his voice. 'But you don't understand. Don't say you understand, lad. I don't bloody understand so I don't see how you can.'

'No,' I said. 'No, of course not.'

Ten seconds later I was alone in the room. I heard Everly in the hallway, repeating his wife's name. He didn't get a reply. I heard a handle turn, then turn again.

'Come on, Violet.'

There was still no response. I heard nothing for a second and then I heard footsteps and another handle turning. It was followed by three short barks and the scampering of canine feet. The dog rushed into the living room and Everly lumbered in after it, a lead in his hand. The dog turned and saw him, then rushed out to the door. It looked as keen to get out of there as I was. Everly too. I stood up and followed them both outside.

We took a long route to the station, walking beneath lamp-posts just beginning to flicker into life. We didn't say anything until we got to a small park, where Everly bent to let his straining dog off its leash. A bench overlooked a children's play area and Everly lowered himself onto it. I sat next to him.

'Now then. That's better. How can I help you? I'm sorry about before, but the wife, it's tough for her. She's been through a lot, even before this happened.'

I nodded. Cheryl had told me Mrs Everly had been ill. I saw the wig, the colour of her skin.

'Is it cancer?'

'It is,' Everly said simply. The question had caught him off guard slightly but hadn't surprised him. He carried on nodding to himself, his eyes on something far away.

'I see.'

'Of the breast.' He turned towards me as a thought flitted through his mind like an owl across the moon. Then it was gone. 'It started ten, maybe eleven years ago. That's when she had her first mastectomy. Last year she had chemotherapy, then eight months back she had to have another operation. Her ovaries as well, this time. There's not much we can do now but hope. There are some new drugs but we can't pay for them.'

'Right, I see. Well, I'm very sorry I troubled her. It was obviously the last thing she needed.'

'Not your fault. I should have just met you here. Violet, she's got her own ideas about what happened. I can't tell her. She and Alison, they had a difficult relationship.'

The dog was running its hind legs backwards on the grass as an empty crisp packet tumbled past its head. Everly reached into his coat pocket and pulled out a plastic bag. I took the chance to slide my notebook out of my pocket. Everly watched the dog closely, seeming to enjoy its simple, mechanical actions.

Once again I heard Cheryl. She used to hit her, the bitch.

'Difficult how, Mr Everly?'

'Well,' he said. I could see him deciding whether or not to tell me, then giving way as if it just didn't matter any more. 'It was all right for a long time. We used to be a happy family, though it seems so long ago I have to remind myself. Violet was strict. But Alison never gave us any trouble. She was a withdrawn, quiet little girl, good as gold. She was the only child we could have and she made Violet very happy. Until she began to change.'

'Change?'

'You know, boys and things. Wanting to go to discos, the lot. Vi wouldn't have it. I used to tell her that the world was different now, but Vi just shook her head. It used to send the girl crazy. It got worse and worse until Alison left home. Still only sixteen she was and she didn't see her mother for three years after that. I used to meet her in cafés, in the park, places like that. I never told Vi.'

I nodded at Everly, making the odd note. 'Why did she leave?'

'Oh, she'd had enough. I think she could handle the rules, but then there was something else. We'd always been churchgoers but Violet suddenly became very religious, when her own mother died. Alison must have been about fourteen. Here.'

Everly reached a hand into his hip pocket and brought out his wallet. He flipped it open and the face of a young girl greeted me, a studio shot on a mottled blue background. Alison was in her school uniform, a big smile on her face. Her hair was tied back and she had a couple of spots on her cheeks. She still looked very young. I thought of the shot of the little girl that I'd seen in her flat that night, the little nurse with the big smile.

'After that Vi was a lot harder on the girl, though

she'd say she was trying to save her from herself. I didn't know what to do. Alison always got good marks at school, but she began not to bother. Vi started throwing her out of the house, when she came home late and stuff. Drunk, and worse. Then one day Vi found her with a boy. They weren't doing much, just sitting on the sofa, petting. But Vi threw her out and this time she didn't come back.'

'And then you saw her, every now and then. Did you know what she was doing during that time?'

Everly nodded reluctantly. 'Alison had told me she worked in a beauty salon, in town. Maybe she did for a bit, who knows? But then Vi was at the hospital and she saw Alison in the paper. Page Three, like. It got to her, that did. Me too, if I'm honest. Vi brought the paper home and made me look at it. I mean, I loved the girl but doing that. Everywhere I went after that I imagined everyone would be looking at me. 'There's the chap whose daughter takes her clothes off.'

I nodded and was silent for a second. I watched the dog, going about its business as a squirrel looked on from a safe distance.

'And when she came home, was it better?'

Everly cheered up a bit and got ready to stand. 'Yes. I was very proud of Alison then. When I told her that her mother was unwell, Alison came back. She said she'd finished with the way she'd been living, she said she'd repented. Came to church with us and everything. Never went out. It made Vi happy. She believed it, you see. Alison stayed with us for six months or so, taking Vi to the hospital, looking after her. I was still on the cabs then.'

'And you supported her?'

'Gladly, yes. But then she went off again. This fellow had been round a few times to see her. Said he was a friend, but it must have been a bloke from the papers.'

'Long blond hair, a beard?'

'That's him. I reckon you could say he tempted her back into it. Alison said she was going because Vi was better. She said she'd come and visit. But neither of us saw her again.'

Everly's voice cracked and he shut his mouth tight for a second. He looked like he was shivering. After a minute he looked away from me and stood up, walking quickly to the place his dog had been. He bent over with the plastic bag in his hand and then righted himself. The dog scampered round his ankles before chasing off after some pigeons. He called to it, his chiding tones full of something like relief and eventually it came up and submitted to the lead. Everly scratched its head before straightening up and nodding to me. He dropped the bag in a bin. I joined him and we walked through the park, up to the High Street.

Everly wanted to know what was being done about his daughter's murder and I told him he'd have to ask the police that. He said he felt nothing for Draper, whether he'd killed Alison or not.

'It's terrible,' he said, as we shook hands at the tube station. 'But I wasn't surprised, you know? By what happened. There was something about Alison. When the police came round I didn't cry or nothing. Just sort of accepted it.'

'And your wife?'

'Lord, don't ask me.'

'She seemed very bitter about Jack Draper. Did you ever meet him?'

'Never.'

'Your wife seemed pretty convinced that he'd done it. Apart from all the speculation, does she have any real reason to think that? Did Alison say something?'

Everly looked confused for a second and I didn't know why. 'She said she knew he killed Alison,' I explained.

Then Everly understood what I meant and he hesitated for a second. I heard his wife's voice again. He killed her. I saw the pictures round the room and the cross on her neck. He killed her . . . She was a little slut . . . Everly saw me getting it, and he looked ashamed.

'She didn't mean Draper . . . ?'

'Violet doesn't have any theories that would be of any use to you,' Everly said.

I nodded my thanks to Alison's father and he turned to go.

'One other thing,' I said. 'Did you know of your daughter's connections to the football club?'

'Well, I used to take her. When she was little.'

I smiled. 'You a fan, then?'

'Man and boy. Still do some fundraising, stuff like that.' He raised a limp fist. 'Up the "O"s.'

'But you didn't know she modelled for them?'

'Only when I saw her in the programme. That was only in the last few months. I didn't mind that, it was tasteful, like.'

'So you don't know how she met Jack Draper?'

'I imagine at a party, something like that.'

'Right. And one more thing. The chairman.'

'Korai?'

'Yes. How long's he been around?'

'Oh, must be two and a half year now.'

'And he's popular?'

'Put a lot of money into the club, bought some good players. Saved us from bankruptcy near enough. Should go up this year, touch wood. Why do you want to know? Here, you're not suggesting . . .'

I shook my head. 'Thank you for your time,' I said.

Chapter Twenty-Five

I let the rocking motion of the tube lull my thoughts to sleep as I journeyed back into town. The short, constricted life of Alison Everly, coupled with pictures of how it had ended, left me feeling flat and tired, a ball of lead weighing heavy in my stomach, the veins in my arms running with mercury. As the tube pulled into Mile End I looked up at the map opposite and suddenly saw that if I changed trains, I was only one stop away from Stepney Green. I sat up. I knew she'd be there. I knew she'd open the door to me. The doors of the tube yawned. People got off, on. The doors stayed open. My eyes found the sign pointing towards the District Line. I saw her, holding her baby in the fading light. I let the tube doors close and the train take me on to Chancery Lane.

It was already dark by the time I got to the bar. The place was rammed with the after-work crowd, the time of day Nicky really hated. When Toby looked up from a drinks order he said Nicky was upstairs. It was a little strange talking to Toby, having gone through his flat the night before. Toby was busy but he still wanted to know what had happened to Nicky. He sounded genuinely concerned. I said he'd been mugged but Toby looked at me.

'It was those two geezers, from the other night. Wasn't it?'

'You'll have to ask Nicky that, Toby. It's his business.'

'Billy . . . '

I pushed my way through the crowd and ducked under the bar. When I got upstairs Nicky showed me the space underneath the floorboards in the bedroom, where the money had been. He looked inside, as though he might not have noticed the bag, as if it might have been there all along. Nicky was still a wreck, though the fact that he was dressed gave him some semblance of normality. His left hand was bandaged like the invisible man he no doubt wished he was. I didn't tell him about McKenna. I wanted him to concentrate.

'Right, I said, closing up the floor space. 'Got them?'

'Yes,' he said.

'Then let's go. Unless you want to wait here.'

'I'll come, it's my business. But are you sure this is necessary?'

'We have to know who did it, Nicky. That means we have to know who didn't.'

'Okay,' he said. 'But it makes me feel shitty. Even more shitty. Believe me I feel shitty enough.'

'Ignore it. And hurry up. We don't have a lot of time. Think about what those guys said. That's all you can afford to think about.'

'I know,' Nicky sighed. 'I know.'

Nicky's staff have kept their personal belongings locked in his office ever since there had been a spate of petty thefts two or three years ago, kids coming in through the fire escape. When we got to Brixton I pulled up onto the pavement outside a block of flats, the kind that were once all local authority and are now probably about half private. Nicky's new waitress lived in one of them with her boyfriend, a trainee journalist currently working on a night desk.

The girl had been there the night the two goons came in. Nicky had told me she was always asking questions about the business. She was always flirting with him too and Nicky had invited her up for a drink one night, before remembering his rule about not sleeping with his employees. He didn't think he'd left her alone but he wasn't positive, he may have gone to the toilet. Then, the next day, she had come up to fetch him down to the phone, calling through to him as he was taking some money out of the floorboards in the bedroom to put in the tills. Which meant she may have seen something.

I used Nicky's mobile to make sure there was no one at home and then pushed the car door open. Nicky made to get out too but I told him to wait there and call me on the flat number if there was a problem. He handed me the girl's keys.

When we got back to the Ludensian Nicky put the keys back in the girl's bag before she finished her shift. I hadn't really expected to find anything in her flat and that's the way it had turned out. When Nicky came to find me in the flat upstairs he had a bottle of Granddad in his hand.

'Are we going to have to do that to everyone who works here?'

'No,' I said. 'I don't think so. But after what you told me, I thought we'd better. She won't know.'

'It still makes me feel shit.'

'You told me that. How are your ribs? How's your mother?'

Nicky and I sat for a while. Suspecting his staff seemed to have a huge effect on Nicky, it made him looked crumpled, brought down. I'm pretty sure Nicky shouldn't have been on the whiskey but I wasn't going to tell him. I did tell him about my visit to Westbourne Park, though, and about another couple of ideas I had. I tried to pitch my voice light, logical. One idea, I didn't tell him. I kept it to myself, testing it by letting it grow in my mind on its own, unaided. There was silence for a while until I remembered the bird I'd seen that day and I told Nicky how surprised I'd been that Shulpa was into that kind of thing.

He frowned. 'Birdwatching?'

'I know,' I said. 'Beat me too.'

'Actually, when I think of it, she used to go when she was younger.' He paused. 'She used to get taken. I never thought she was really into it herself, though – I don't suppose sitting in those hide things is very good for a Lagerfeld evening dress. You know, there might well be more to my sister than I know.'

'There's a lot more.'

'I don't want to know about that.'

'That's not what I mean, tosser. She tries to hide it, but there's a hell of a lot going on inside her.'

'I know. I couldn't believe how concerned she was about me. She's never given a shit before, or at least I've never thought she has. She tends to use me as a free alcohol service. Maybe it's the influence of your good self.'

'That, I seriously doubt.' I laughed.

We sat in silence again for a long while, drinking

the whiskey. The whiskey was simple and strong,
without contradictions. Images of how I'd behaved
towards Nicky's sister came back to me. God only knew
what he'd say if I told him. It was dark outside but
Nicky only had a small lamp on. The whiskey seemed
to slow the day down. Once again I thought how
strange it was that the only guilt I felt about Louise
Draper was directed towards Nicky, not his sister. I
still hadn't had time to think about what that meant.

I told Nicky that I was going to deliver the first
fifteen grand soon. He nodded. His dark hair fell over
his battered, never-to-be-so-pretty-again face and a
serious look took hold of him. His chin began to
tremble, as he held his glass up to it. He shook his
head, slowly, and I could see him burying his eyes into
the glass as if he could see played out there everything
he'd done, and was now looking for answers as to
how he'd got where he had. He stopped and his head
turned towards me. He didn't look at me, but something passed between us. If he'd been a girl it would
have been the moment when we both knew. I remembered when I'd felt like that with Sharon, how nervous
I'd been, almost wanting to retch. It was a strange
moment. I thought of what Nicky had said about his
school days, how close to Jack he used to be, and I
remembered being jealous, thinking that those bonds
of friendship were the strongest, it didn't matter who
you met later on. I tried to find an equivalent figure.
The only one was Luke. I never had any other close
friends when I was young, not really, people I told
everything to, who I trusted. I was always afraid they'd
come round, and my dad would be my dad, and then

everyone would know. Luke knew already because he was part of it. Only he and I understood.

I was suddenly aware of my watch, ticking. I looked at it, stood up, and put both my hands on Nicky's shoulders, before crossing the room. I turned, waiting for him to look up.

He said, 'I can't believe you're doing all this for me, Billy.'

'I told you. I don't want to hear it.'

He nodded, dismissing what I'd said. He looked round the darkened room as if he were seeing it for the first time. Outside, a woman suddenly laughed, and then was quiet again. 'When this is over, this place is as much yours as it is mine.'

'You never let me pay for anything anyway.' I smiled. I pulled the door open.

'I know, but I'm going to do something. Something else. Give you half of it.' Nicky's voice reached out to me, spiked with slurred pain. Through the bandages and bruising he looked old, tired. 'What am I saying? I'll give you all of it.'

'Nicky . . .'

'Ask me for something, Billy. I've asked you for a hell of a lot. Please, *ask* me for something.'

Nicky was pleading with me. He had become drunk very quickly, the medication giving the booze a kick-start through his body. I looked at him. Sally was right. Knowing what he'd done had been painful enough, after which he'd almost been beaten to death. But even that didn't hurt as much as asking me for help, letting me look right inside of him, to see that part of him that was a fool, a shallow, greedy fool. Now he wanted to do something for me, something to redeem himself.

I wondered if he needed to. I wondered if all this really was going to change the way I thought about him. And if I told him about Louise Draper, would that change what he thought about me?

I was about to tell Nicky again that he didn't need to do anything for me, that his friendship was enough. But I stopped. A thought arrived in me. I don't know where it came from. It just clicked into me like the electricity coming on after a power cut. His best friend from school. No bond's as strong as that. I nodded, very slightly.

'All right,' I said. I folded my arms and looked at him, crumpled, a wreck. 'There is something you can do. And not when this is over as a matter of fact. Right now.'

'Anything, tell me. Billy . . .'

I stared hard into my friend's eyes and pushed the door shut quietly. Nicky looked back at me, his eyes full of hope. I left it a second.

'You can tell me where Jack Draper is, Nicky.'

Chapter Twenty-Six

It was just after eight when I got to Brick Lane. It was dark, a mean, thin drizzle sending the passers-by scurrying along the pavements, bent over like old peasant women. I walked past the converted Truman Brewery and a new, trendy-looking café that hadn't been there the last time I had. Like many areas in London, Brick Lane was changing, just as it had thirty years before, from a Jewish area to a Bengali one. Now there was a new influx; a strange race of pale, limp-looking people in orange sunglasses who never laughed in public and whose sole sense of fulfilment came from finding the right pair of antique trainers. I wondered how long the Bengalis would stick it.

The Bengalis were still in the majority, however. I didn't know how many restaurants there were on the street, though none of them seemed very busy tonight. The waiters standing in the doorways were having a hell of a job enticing anyone to step inside and the street looked tired and flat in spite of the shimmer of the neon signs admiring themselves in the wet pave-ments and the occasional, illuminated waterfall flowing in a shop window.

'You want we have best curry, sir. Please, this way.'

I was hungry enough to take up his offer but I

thanked him and walked on. He may not have heard me, though; I had my hood up against the rain and the eyes of the person I was looking for. I passed another couple of restaurants that also served the best curry in London before slowing down and looking up at the street name to my left. I turned the corner from Brick Lane onto Princelet Street, where a cat darted out from beneath a car. I watched it chase off up an alley across the road, narrowly avoiding the wheels of a BMW.

This was the street. I looked up, above the row of lock-ups behind and opposite me, my eyes moving along a row of restaurant names, speciality food stores and an Asian video shop. It wasn't long before I saw it: RAHIM AND SONS, in English and Bengali, above the window of a wholesaler's on the other side of the road. I stood looking at it for a while before letting a cab go past. I felt tight inside; quiet and calm. For some reason I saw Draper, stepping up to take a penalty. I stepped across the road towards the clothing warehouse.

If Nicky had denied that he knew where Jack was hiding I wouldn't have pressed him. But I wouldn't have believed him. I think he knew that. He looked uncertain for a second because the question caught him cold and he knew I would have seen that. So he told me. I'm not saying he wouldn't have lied if he thought I wouldn't have known he was. Draper would have made him promise not to tell anyone and he was Nicky's oldest friend. But he wouldn't have lied, not with me able to see it.

Nicky smiled when he told me. Memories and whiskey deepened his eyes.

'He was like one of us,' Nicky explained. 'He was always round our house Jack was. My dad thought he was great and my mum adored him. My auntie taught him how to cook, he worked in their restaurant at the weekends. The only white curry boy in Leicester. She said that if he didn't make it in the football game he could always run their place for them. He spent more time with my family than his own. He speaks pretty good Bengali, you know? I swear, when he went to Leeds for his apprenticeship, we had this big party and the women cried like they'd lost their favourite baby. Some of the men looked a bit shaky too. Everyone in my family adored him, and when my dad left he was great. He was only young, just like I was, but he seemed to take charge of us, of my mother especially. He used to make her laugh. My mother didn't know whether or not to stay in the Asian community but I think she saw that as they accepted Jack, they'd accept her as well.'

I nodded, not wanting to rush Nicky. Just as the idea of Alison Everly whoring herself to the *Sun* hadn't fitted with my idea of her, neither did this tale of the local hero fit with what I thought of Jack Draper.

'So,' I asked, 'he's with your mother?'

Nicky smiled and shook his head. 'No,' he said. 'He wouldn't do that to her. Jack was especially close to my uncle, Asif. He never forgot him, getting him tickets to matches he was playing in. Asif's in the rag trade, like my dad, only he does a bit better. Quite a bit. He's got a warehouse on Brick Lane, sells all over the place. He runs it with two of his sons.'

'And Jack's there.'

Nicky hesitated again. Letting on where Jack was hiding was another thing Nicky didn't like himself for. 'Listen, Billy,' he sighed. 'I don't know for sure, I really don't. I swear. But Asif would do anything for Jack, I know that. If I were Jack, I'd go to Asif's place.' I didn't say anything. 'And if I were looking for him, that's where I'd go too.'

Once I'd crossed the street I felt a pair of eyes on me and turned, unable to see who they belonged to. There were still quite a few people scurrying through the rain, all looking like they didn't believe this winter would ever, ever end. A gesture caught my eye, from inside yet another restaurant, where another man was waving me in. I shook my head and stood outside the wholesale place, checking it out, looking at my watch to pretend I was waiting for someone. The rain zipped off my hood. The waiter's eyes left me. There was no sign of life in Rahim and Sons. A grill had been rolled down over the window and the place was dark. Maybe Nicky was wrong. I peered through the grill as casually as I could but I still couldn't see anything, no lights, no noise, nothing.

Down the side of the store ran the narrow cobbled alley the cat had shot up. I moved along the storefront and past the mouth of it. Then I turned back round until I was standing with my back to the alley. I took a glance up and down the street and then turned again. As casually as I could I sauntered down, my hand going to my fly as if I were going to take a piss. I didn't know if anyone was watching me, or even if they'd care if they were. After a couple of steps I moved my hand from my fly to the inside of my coat pocket, where my fingers closed round my Maglite.

The alley wasn't covered but there was no light in it, probably wouldn't have been much more in the daytime. At the bottom was a padlocked gate, about six feet high, opening onto a small yard piled with wooden packing crates. I set the Maglite's aperture to narrow and played the beam over it until I'd found a padlock. I looked back up to the street but the waiter was no longer looking at me. It was too dark. I turned back to the gate. It was seven feet high but there was no razor wire topping it. I was about to go over it when I stopped. I held the torch beneath my arm and tested the lock.

The lock was pushed to look closed but the mechanism hadn't been engaged. I nodded. As quietly as I could I pulled the lock open and pushed the gate, expecting an almighty creak. It didn't make any noise at all. It must have been oiled recently. I nodded again.

I pushed the gate shut behind me, leaving the padlock as I'd found it. I was outside an old but very solid wooden door, pale blue paint peeling, secured by both a Yale and a deadlock. There was a light above the door but it was off. I put my hand over the torch but could see no light coming from behind the door. I took a step back and played the beam on it again. The door was old, and it bowed inward slightly beneath the Yale, where the deadbolt was. It meant that the deadbolt wasn't engaged; that someone was inside. That's what I hoped it meant. I held the torch down, and stepped forward.

I stood for a second, the rain amplified into loud thumps by my hood. I thought about it. Call the police? I could have. No. Instead I removed a long, thin piece of tough but flexible plastic from the inside pocket of my coat. I'd thought I might have had to use it earlier, if Nicky hadn't managed to snag the waitress' keys. I held it in my right hand. I spread my legs for leverage, leaning my left shoulder against the frame of the door. Very slowly, I slid the strip of plastic between the door and the jamb, slowly, slowly, until it met resistance it didn't want to go past. I left it there. Any more and it would make a noise. I stopped and steadied myself, holding the strip in place with my left hand, pressing my right palm against the end that was sticking out of the lock towards me.

I'd only get one go at it. I thought I heard footsteps in the alley but it was just the rain, picking up. I rammed the strip forward as hard as I could, pushing it round into the lock and pulling it back as fast as I could. It made a loud, wrenching noise but within five seconds the door was open and I was in the building.

He was getting up from a camp bed they must have brought in for him. A portable gas fire burnt at the foot of it. There was a small lamp beside him as well as an old TV set, the volume down almost to nothing. He made a lunge to his right, away from me, knocking over a dress dummy, sending a set of steel steps careening away behind him. All around him were racks of dresses, boxes piled to the ceiling. He was stumbling through to the front of the shop when I stopped him.

'Jack,' I said. 'It's me, Billy Rucker. Where the fuck are you going?'

The warehouse was musty and damp, the air laced with curry and something else, far away in the back of it, something I recognized without being able to place. When he'd calmed down, Jack sat on the bed and ran his hands back through his hair, taking long, even breaths. Jack's hair didn't look like it did in the Flex ads. Jack himself looked shocked, relieved.

'Jesus,' he said, shaking his head. 'Fucking hell.'

Even though there wasn't much light I could see that Jack wasn't looking his best. He hadn't shaved in a week and he wasn't the sort of man that suited. It wasn't much of a disguise either. Jack's eyes had the look of a caged animal that hasn't got used to it yet and when he stretched his legs it increased the effect. I stood, leaning against an iron pillar.

The room was big but jam-packed, the dim light of the lamp creating myriad weird shadows from the crates, racks and mannequins. It was warm enough, near the fire. On the bed was one of those big, Afghan hats with flaps at the side, which I assumed Jack wore to cover his face completely. Sitting next to it was a fat paperback, open face down, only a few pages read. On the floor was a pair of old dumb-bells but my eyes left them immediately, fixing on something else. Next to them sat a big holdall, packed and ready. I wanted to know what was in it. Was it just clothes, a toothbrush? Or was there something else? A very big bundle of something else?

I took it all in. Being the fugitive, it wasn't exactly glamorous.

Once Jack was breathing normally I looked down at him.

'Your agent was murdered this morning,' I told him.

How he reacted was important and I didn't take my eyes off him. His look said he knew. But he just couldn't believe it.

'It was on this,' he said, nodding at the small, black

and white tube. 'About an hour ago. That's it, isn't it? That's me. *Screwed.*'

'Did you do it?'

'Fuck off.'

Jack stared at the set to the side of him, *EastEnders* just finishing.

'What are you going to do?' I asked. He didn't answer me. 'Jack.' I spread my hands round the room. 'There really isn't any point to this, is there? Not any more. They won't be calling you the Fugitive tomorrow, not after McKenna.'

Jack turned quickly, challenge in his eyes. 'So what do you want me to do? Huh? Show up at the nearest nick and say "Here I am, it's your lucky day. Lock me up and throw away the key"? I'm being stitched up. I have a life, Billy. I want it back.'

'You won't get it this way.'

'No. No you're probably right.' The challenge that had burst out of him disappeared, replaced by a crushed disbelief. He looked stunned, finished, like a fighter being helped through the crowd after his second comeback. But like that fighter his mind was already looking for a space, an excuse, a way not to believe. 'I'm not just going to let them do it to me. I'm not. Even this is better than the alternative. The food's better, for one thing.' A carton of chicken curry and rice sat on a packing case next to him. It looked tempting. I'd evidently disturbed him as he was halfway through it and he picked it up again. He took a few forkfuls then looked at me.

'I don't need to ask how you found me.'

I didn't say anything.

'I should have just told you. Tailing people, it's your business, isn't it?'

'It would have been easier,' I agreed. 'I can't do anything for you without knowing everything, without talking to you.'

'I understand. I just thought . . . Okay then, now I have to trust you. Do you believe me, that I didn't kill Alison, *or* McKenna?'

'I can accept that for now. But they're both connected to you. As far as I can see you have three choices. First, you could stay in hiding, for ever.' I looked at the bag at his feet. 'Two, face it. If you didn't do it then your prints won't be on the knife that killed Alison or on anything significant at McKenna's, though there will probably be latents at both. You were placed at the scene of Alison's murder but that doesn't mean it was you. So you can give yourself up and hope.'

He was already shaking his head. 'They can fucking find me. Even if I did get off I'd be finished, no one would believe me.' I shrugged. 'What's the third?'

'Help me find out who did it,' I said. 'Who's doing this to you? We both thought it might be McKenna but now we have to think again.'

Jack nodded then shook his head. He told me once more to look at the list of people he was likely to have severely upset with his autobiography. His former manager, a betting syndicate. I asked him to go through his exact position at the club. All the time my eyes kept flitting back to the bag at his feet. I was wondering whether or not to tell him. Tell him that whoever had gone through Nicky's floorboards could well have got him killed. After a while I could see his mind drifting.

'How was she?'

I was still leaning against the pillar.

'Louise?'

She slipped into my mind like she'd slipped into my arms.

'Okay, I think. She's under siege, she's upset, she can't really believe what's happening, but she's okay.'

'Tommy?'

'I don't really know. Louise didn't say either way, which means he must be all right. You miss him?'

'I miss them both. I can't believe . . .' Jack let his words tail off into thoughts as he finished his curry. He shook his head. 'You must think I'm a real prick.'

'Why so?'

'You've been in my house, yeah? You've seen my wife. My kid. You know what I've fucked up. You know what I've put in jeopardy for . . . Shit.'

Draper's mind went even further away until a look of disbelief took hold of his features that he didn't seem aware of.

'You ever do anything like that? Just go off and fuck someone? When you loved the person you left behind? Love them and don't want to lose them?' I didn't say anything. 'I get so . . .' He looked for the word then found it. '*Drawn*. Like a fish on a line. It makes me forget everything, nothing else seems to get in. And then I feel so *stupid*, afterwards. Until the next time.' He gave a laugh. 'And what no one, *no one* believes is that all I want is Louise. Sometimes I think that that can't actually be true but it is. She's all I want.'

'She told me you phone her. I take it you're careful.'

'Yeah, of course. You might have, but the Old Bill won't find me. You had inside knowledge. And you're bright. I sit here, thinking about her, wondering if I'll ever be with her again, like I was before.'

Draper looked up at me, wanting me to tell him everything would be all right. I wanted to get back to the point, and not only because I didn't want to discuss Draper's wife with him. I needed to know who he had told about Alison, who could have possibly known, apart from the girl herself, and McKenna. I also wanted to know his exact position at Orient, his contract, what it was like to play there. I was about to ask Jack, glad to have found him at last. The thoughts in my head were like an intricate game of snakes and ladders designed so you could never reach the end. I kept returning to Draper, just as Coombes had. And then my eyes went to his holdall again. I was trying to put my foot on another bottom rung when Jack stood up and turned away from me.

Jack walked over and dropped the food carton into a bin liner behind the TV. He let out a long breath, his hands on his hips, and stared into the darkness behind me. He shook his head, like an A-Level student in front of Einstein's Field Equation. He turned round to the bed. He reached underneath it and pulled out a big watchman's torch.

'So. You think I should give myself up? That's what I should do? I'd really have a chance?'

I nodded, surprised. He sounded serious. 'Listen. If you didn't kill McKenna they won't be able to pinch you for it. They found a print at the scene but if you weren't there, it won't be yours, will it? As for Alison, I know they have time-of-death problems and there were no prints on the knife. I think you'd stand a good chance. If we get back to focusing on who might have been keeping tabs on you, we just might—'

'You miserable fucking bastard.'

Jack swung the torch with both hands like an axe. It came down on the top of my head, above my left eye. I staggered backwards as my legs buckled like a sprung puppet, sending me down on one knee. The look of dumb surprise on my face must have been pretty comical but Draper wasn't laughing. Did she tell him, did Louise tell him what had happened? I could hear her, getting her revenge on him. But then something came to me. Suddenly I could hear the door wrenching open behind me, a rush of cold. I was about to turn to the sound but I didn't. Jack was bringing the torch down again. He'd heard them. It was why he'd stared behind me, why he'd gone for the torch. I managed to get my hands underneath his swing this time but it still took whatever was left in my legs and sent me down further, half backwards, half to the side, onto my elbow.

Jack was standing over me. Another blow like that would do real damage. But I couldn't move. I had trouble holding my hands up again. A mist descended and I could only just make out Draper through it. Then he flashed clear. He was turning away from me. I watched as he ran towards his bed, past his bag. He didn't stop to take it. He ran over the bed as if it wasn't there, sending the novel bouncing up from it before coming down shut. I watched Draper's back as he carved a path to the front, the way he'd gone before, pulling over clothes rails in his wake. I tried to call him but an aftershock of pain burst inside my temple like a grenade.

It all must have happened in a second. I managed to turn my eyes to the left. An open door, rain cutting in from the night. Two pairs of legs coming towards me. I tried to get my hands up again. The legs got longer and longer until two bodies joined them, shimmering like a mirage, two faces pulling in and out of focus. I felt sick. I saw the two shapes begin to lean down towards me but they never got there. They receded down a dark pulsating tunnel without moving their legs, their arms, anything at all.

They got smaller and smaller and smaller.

Chapter Twenty-Seven

A lilting, jogging motion woke me. I was in the back
of a car, my head on my chest. There were people
close in on either side of me. An iron hand inside my
head took hold of my brain and squeezed. I went away
again, I don't know how long. Then I could smell
expensive leather upholstery beyond smoke and damp
clothing. I could feel the car moving. Another hand,
weaker this time. I was ready for it and I stayed. I kept
my eyes shut and listened for voices, pretending I was
still out. There were none, just a radio tuned into
Five Live. A football match was beginning. The crowd
sounded like desperate flies buzzing inside a forgotten
bait box.

I drifted in and out until the sensation was replaced
by something else. Simple, understandable pain. The
car moved on, slowing, turning. I didn't know where I
was, who I was with. I could feel my hood, crumpled
and wet against the back of my head. I thought of my
Recco system, pulsing radar signals out to anyone who
would be searching for me. I couldn't think of anyone.
I had just opened my eyes a touch to see what I could
see, when something strange happened. The sounds
of the crowd on Five Live spread out, moving beyond
the radio. I thought it must have just been my head,

now throbbing like the crossbar after a Stuart Pierce penalty. But the noise persisted, getting slowly louder. Wider. Then the car came to a halt and there was a rattling sound. I opened my eyes wide to see a set of gates draw back, gates with a crest emblazoned with four words bold above them. Four big words.

LEYTON ORIENT FOOTBALL CLUB.

The car stopped round the back. They got me out and shook me awake. I'd been in a Jag, a black Jag. I tried to get my bearings, checking for ways out, the nearest police. I couldn't see anyone. They were all inside the ground, a rising, swarming sound to my left. I was still pretty groggy. My head rushed as I was taken hold of and walked towards the sound, a low, swooping bass now, then beneath a sign that told me it welcomed Home Supporters. I didn't feel welcome. Neither of the men looked at me. I thought about a stumble, then a feint to the right followed by a sprint. There was no way. They knew the place, and they hadn't been hammered over the head by a footballer who thought he'd been sold out. I let them take me along, trying to pretend I was worse off than I was, just in case.

I was flanked by two men, one the chauffeur I'd seen out at Wanstead Flats. My arms were held as we bypassed the turnstiles and turned to a large gate that was opened by two orange-coated stewards who both nodded and stood aside. The gates shut behind us. I asked where I was being taken but didn't get an answer. I was helped up two flights of stairs inside a concrete shell, the noise coming from above my head now, intensifying with each step, accompanied by our shuffling footsteps like a jazz drummer using the brushes to back a wailing horn. We were joined by the smell of hotdogs, cigarettes and instant coffee all drifting around us in the cold damp air. The stairs were dark, I held my head down to make sure I hit the steps. But then we emerged at the top of the stand, the noise going up one last, important notch and I stopped. A brilliant floodlit pitch emerged below us, making me blink, sending my head reeling. It was amazingly light, full of scurrying figures. Again, arms took hold of me. They were tight under my armpits but they needn't have bothered. A break for it? I wouldn't have made ten feet.

There were plenty of people around but nobody noticed my discomfort except for my two guides. They were all looking the other way, down at the action. I was sat in the back of the stand. Once again the two men joined me, one either side. Neither of them was as big as the Maltese guy I'd seen in Nicky's but I soon realized that size isn't really important: when the chauffeur opened his coat to show me the square butt of an automatic I nodded respectfully. Neither of the two men spoke, preferring just to stare straight ahead and wait. I wasn't in a very creative mood so I did the same, until my head began to throb again and I held it in my hands, looking down at the grey concrete beneath my seat.

I shivered with the cold and pulled my coat round me. I took several deep breaths and my mind became a little clearer with each one. I breathed deep into my haziness until all of it had broken up, like a dam down a fast river. I made myself think. What had I got myself into, how could I get out of it? While I was outside, surely I was okay? I looked up, ahead of me. The stand I was sitting in was along one side of the ground – I was looking down at the office buildings I had entered on my last visit there. Above the offices a row of glass boxes were lit up to reveal seated figures, protected from the noise and the cold. Above them was a modern stand with bright blue plastic seating and clean steel supports. Another stand to my left was similarly new while the one it faced behind the opposite goal was thirty years old at least. A small clutch of away supporters huddled together in the rain. I looked around me. The stand I was in was half full, most of the fans down near the front. It was a covered stand and for this I was very grateful as a driving rain lashed down on the players like a flight of javelins, lit by the angry phosphorescence of the floods. The pitch was neon bright, green as a Subbuteo table.

In spite of the rain I was surprised to see that the ground was about two-thirds full. The benefits, I assumed, of a promotion battle and a dead model. I sat for five minutes, breathing damp and chips and smoke and hope on the cold night air, staring at the spectacle before me as my head straightened. The swell of the crowd filled it, cut by the voices of the players on the pitch. They were the same men I'd seen only yesterday, in the centre circle. I tried to pick out some faces but I found it hard, and not because of my state of mind. They all looked different. Now they were a team. They ran and chased, harried for each other, each of them serious, focused. They carried the hopes of what looked like about eight thousand people with them. Were they the same men? I remembered looking back at them having their photos taken, beyond to the empty rows of plastic seats, the shabby advertising hoardings, the stained concrete terraces, all empty. I was reminded of Sal's gym. This was another place that needed life and energy. But unlike the gym, which relied on people taking part, this place needed spectators; shouting, singing, stamping their feet, swearing, straining, urging. Without them, these guys were just so many men standing around in cheap suits and fake gold jewellery like so many second-hand Porsche dealers. With that image in my mind it seemed very bizarre that these thousands of people should come here, putting their faith in them every week, especially on a piss miserable night like this.

My eyes went to the people in front of me, all leaned forward in their seats, stamping, chanting, and to the stand to my left, united in song about their heroes. Again I saw the players, the nippy teenager in his elder brother's suit, fussing with his tie chain. It struck me that football was a self-sustaining prophecy, a god created by its worshippers, endlessly feeding on one thing and one thing only: their desire for it to exist. Yesterday it looked like the spell was broken. But now the magic was back. In the lower divisions the magic wasn't so strong – you could see the rabbit going into the hat, the silk scarf poking out the end of the sleeve. People like Janner had to keep it alive. It was a tough job, with the competition from television and the big boys poaching his would-be stars when their contracts ended, nicking the club's fan base from right under its nose, enticing kids from within earshot of the ground to support teams in towns they'd probably never ever go to. I realized what a bonus someone like Draper was to a place like this, like Tom Cruise doing Rep in Wakefield. Because in spite of everything, his arrogance, his ambition, Jack Draper had just exactly what the people surrounding me came to that football ground for.

The stand half stood as the ball flew over the bar, then relaxed. Applause. I was shunted out of my thoughts when the man to the left of me moved aside to let another man take his place. I looked up to see the thin, impassive figure of Mr Korai.

My head hurt, not made any better by the butt of the automatic in my thoughts. I nodded to myself, and looked at Korai as he settled himself. He didn't look too comfortable, out here in the stand. I thought about all the things I'd found out about him, from the Internet. His two goons had sat up a bit. They looked a little more tense than they had before. Korai himself didn't look at me and nor did he say anything to begin with, simply sitting there, engrossed in the game below us, as if he'd simply sat down next to a stranger. I folded my arms and set my face, my head tilted towards him. Korai was a tall, bone-thin man in the same cashmere coat I'd seen him in at the training ground, a blue and white scarf tied very tightly round his neck. His head, I noticed, seemed too big for his body. On it he wore a trilby, beneath which two peaked, white eyebrows sitting over dark, almost black eyes, gave his face the look of a hawk, an effect added to by a strong beak-like nose. His skin was the colour of a strong latte, his eyes dark as a chess player's, unmoving. I turned away from him. Still, he didn't speak. Was this just the chairman's way of giving me a freebie, giving me a lift as well? I'd rather have paid, even though the price was probably outrageous.

The chairman and I both watched the proceedings until the young black lad with the lightning bolt shaved into his scalp took the ball past a lethargic-looking left back, only to see his shot tipped round the far post by the keeper. Korai clapped his gloved hands together but still looked distanced. His face became thoughtful, the peaks of his eyebrows meeting.

'Do you think we have another star in our midst?'

Korai's voice was high-pitched and shrill. Overly educated, more English than an Englishman and therefore faintly comical. He'd turned his head to me, his expression telling me he really did want to know the answer to his question. He was smiling.

'Maybe.' I shrugged. 'I'm no expert.'

'Neither am I, neither am I. Which is why I employ Mr Janner there. But I was told you were impressed by the boy. The striker. You picked him out at training, I was told.'

His sing-song enthusiasm stopped me. I pursed my lips. 'Anyone can see he's talented.'

'Indeed, you are right.' Korai nodded vigorously. 'But has he *got* it? Got it like our Mr Draper has got it?'

'Who knows?'

'Who indeed, Mr Rucker, who indeed? Mr Janner, hopefully. I put a lot of money behind his ability to know. A great deal of money.'

My eyes flicked to the pitch as the ball was punted downfield by the opposition goalkeeper, straight out for a throw. I looked back as Korai turned his body towards me. I tried not to let his cheerfulness unsettle me. It's easy to be cheerful with two bodyguards either side. I edged back slightly. He'd used too much after-shave, the kind you get in barbershops.

'I, by the way, am Vish Korai. Although I think you know that.'

'Oh yes, I know it.'

'I understand you had a slight accident,' Korai said. He looked slightly pained. 'I want you to know I wouldn't have told anyone to harm you.'

I looked at him. 'I'll take your word.'

'I understand that you discovered the whereabouts of our ghostly employee Mr Draper. You led my fellows there. Unfortunately,' he raised his voice to the men either side of us, 'neither of them thought to chase after him!'

My mouth opened and closed. An aftershock of pain welled behind my eyes like the crowd rising before the ball went over. When it was gone I moved my head from side to side. 'So it wasn't him you were after?'

Korai laughed. 'Him? *No*. You, Mr Rucker, you! Why should I go chasing round after Super Draper? What good would Super Draper do me now, huh? It's not as if he can play, is it?'

Korai turned to the pitch again and tutted when one of his players passed the ball behind his colleague and it rolled out towards the advertising hoardings next to the dugout. For the first time that night I noticed Janner, as he burst up from the bench to tell Willie what *he* thought about it. The centre back held his hand up and his head down. In contrast to his coach's outburst, Korai sat back and gave a short, dismissive laugh.

'Stupid bloody game, don't you think? This soccer?'

I looked at him, surprised. I shrugged my shoulders and shook my head. 'I have to say I like it,' I said. 'When it's played well.'

He laughed again, louder. 'Not bloody here!' He sounded like a long-suffering fan.

'No, you're right, not here right now.'

'No. No. Ah, but it will be!' Korai said. 'It will be! Believe me. Not long now. It will be, here or at a different ground.'

'Different?'

Korai waved a dismissive hand at me. 'This one is small. Too small for what I want.'

Korai winced again at another woeful error, this time a back-pass that had the keeper scurrying out to clear it just in time. He shook his head. I understood how he felt. This wasn't exactly an ennobling spectacle. He held a finger up to me. 'No, I'll never really take to it, this nonsense, not like you all do. My interests, outside my work, are primarily musical. Classical music. For me you see this is work. It's about investment. Just the *right level* of investment. To get us up. No more than necessary. Then more next season. I don't want to waste resources, overspend . . .'

'Why did you bring me here?' I said.

Korai stopped his pleasant spiel and sat back again. He looked thoughtful, understanding, and he nodded. Then his look changed in a second. Suddenly he thought I was particularly stupid.

'Well now. Well now, yes. The point? Let me think. I see a man looking at my players in training. I think you are a scout, a spy, but I'm wrong – Janner tells me you are looking for my player. Then I hear you've been asking questions about me. Here, other places. Everywhere I go, I feel you. Today I even had one of our fundraisers *demanding* to see me. About his daughter. This is the final straw. He seemed to be implying something. I cannot have this. She was murdered, as I believe you know. He wanted to know what I knew about it.'

'What did you tell him?'

'That I knew nothing, naturally. And that while I sympathized I didn't appreciate my name being mentioned in connection with her death.'

'I can see why you wouldn't. I can see that.'

'Meaning?'

'A high-profile man like yourself. It would be embarrassing for you if people started saying you had had Alison Everly killed. Very embarrassing. And even more so if you got arrested for it.'

If my words got through to Korai I couldn't see it. He was still looking at me but there was nothing in his face. It was motionless, like the bird I'd seen, just before it struck. While Korai didn't give the slightest hint to what he was feeling I had the impression that he wanted to reach over and peck my eyes out. He turned to each of his 'helpers' and, very politely, told them to leave. They climbed over the seats in front of them casting warning shots at me over their shoulders. They climbed over more seats and sat five rows down. Again Korai turned to me. His voice was English ice.

'Why would I kill a girl I've never met, Mr Rucker?'

'Let me ask you a question. What did you pay for Jack Draper?'

Korai took the question with surprise but he nodded, his eyes closing then opening slowly. He rubbed his hands together and spread his lips into a grimace, revealing Cohiba-stained teeth capped with gold. Then he shrugged. 'Oh, next to nothing. Everyone assumed he was finished. Less than a quarter of a million. Not peanuts for us – the rest of the squad didn't cost that much put together – but I trusted Mr Janner's opinion . . .'

'What's he worth now?' I said.

He looked like he'd never even thought about it. 'Janner tells me two, three.'

'Million. Yes?'

'Certainly.'

'Big profit, if you sold him, no? Transfer fees aren't dead yet. And it's probably more than two or three, these days. Big shot in the arm for a club like this. You could get three or four very promising youngsters for that. Except, oh, let me see, just one thing. One *slight* problem.'

'Which is?'

'An obvious one. You don't own him, do you? He's free as a bird. You can't sell him. While you were right to take a chance on him you made the mistake of only giving him a year's contract. Which means that he can leave at the end of it and pick up big wages elsewhere, from a club who won't have to pay to sign him. Not pay you a single penny. Bit galling that, no? You take a financial risk on Draper, you pay him more than you normally pay, you get him fit, you get him playing well, you build your whole team around him and what does he do? He says so long and thanks for the career and walks straight into the Premiership. Unless, of course, you can persuade him not to leave somehow. Where did you get the cat's head, Mr Korai?'

My host nodded appreciatively but the smiling was over. He locked his fingers together and then pushed his gloved hands forward until I could hear them crack.

'Why would I want to sell him?' he asked dismissively. 'Surely you realize that Draper is worth more to me getting us promoted. Why would I want to make my star striker go into hiding at this crucial time for us, when we need him? I want him on that pitch.'

I was about to answer that when Squires floated a corner over and Willie the centre back sent his elbow into the side of his opposite number's head, before holding up his hands in amazement when the whistle blew. The player stayed down and Willie shook his head as he was booked. The clash sent a shock wave through my own head, but I didn't really mind it. I'd wanted to sit next to Korai and say what I was saying to him. I didn't like the way it had happened but his boys had saved me the trip.

'I don't think you knew he would go into hiding after Alison was killed. That was not what you expected.'

'What do you mean?'

'You're used to getting what you want,' I explained. 'I think it frustrated you that Draper kept refusing to sign. Well, didn't it?'

'You seem to know everything.'

'You tried to scare Draper into it with photos and a late Christmas present on the back door, but you got no response from him. Then you somehow found out about his affair with Alison and you saw your chance. You had her killed, that's my guess. Your idea was to blackmail him. When she was dead you would tell Draper you'd let the police know about his affair with her if he didn't give you his signature. That would really land him in it. You stood to get your team promoted *and* make two million pounds at least, by selling him straight after. A motive if ever there was a motive. The only problem was you didn't know about McKenna, and his deal with Alison, and the *Sun*. You had Alison murdered, thinking you could hold Draper's affair with her over his head, only to see the next day's papers drop Jack in it anyway. Your plan backfired a little, didn't it? If you'd left well alone he may have gone on a free transfer at the end of the season but at least he'd have been out there tonight, wouldn't he? And it looks like you need him, doesn't it?'

The crowd fell silent like a storm that suddenly drops to nothing. All that is, but the tiny pocket in the far right-hand corner who jumped out of their seats in an instant frenzy of orange and yellow, as if a conductor had suddenly pointed his baton at them. A tannoy announced that Crewe's scorer was one Jes Lee. His friends were congratulating him as he made his way back to the halfway line.

'All going a bit pear-shaped, isn't it?' I said. 'I bet you're sick as a parrot.'

'Listen,' Korai hissed. He had swivelled right round to face me and his hands were clenched into fists. 'Ask me if I'd kill someone to keep what I have here. To make it better. Go on, ask me.'

'Well, would you?'

He snapped his fingers. 'Like that! This isn't just a couple of million I've got here, all wrapped up in Draper. This club is going to be huge. Look at Chelsea, at Fulham. Do you know the demographic of this area? The East End is hip now, it's cool, though God knows why anyone with any money would ever want to live amongst these people. In five years time the streets of

Leyton will be lined with Range Rovers – it's already happening!'

'You seem to be agreeing with me,' I said. 'You had every reason . . .'

'Maybe. But I didn't. How would I know Draper was fucking some little newspaper whore?'

'You had *me* followed. Following Draper would have been easy. You have resources, Mr Korai.'

'So why not just blackmail him with the knowledge, why kill her?'

'Because he would have just taken the affair on the chin or denied it. He wasn't the first player to be stitched up and he won't be the last. And he really wanted to leave. But threatening him with a murder rap? He'd have signed his name quicker than a B-list celebrity on a children's ward.'

'You're a clever man, Mr Rucker. But there is one thing you're forgetting. McKenna. Why kill him too?'

'Revenge, for spoiling your little plan, that's my guess. Or else, now that Draper's prime suspect he may as well go away for it, and killing McKenna adds to the pressure on him. Better him than you, eh?'

'Okay. But one more thing, a minor irrelevance. Proof.'

'If you did it, I'll find some. Me or the police.'

'I have already spoken to them. They weren't quite so incisive as your good self. Have you mentioned your little theory to them?'

'Not yet. But I will. They're a bit obsessed with Draper at the moment.'

'A bit like this lot, eh, Mr Rucker?'

Korai turned from me to the crowd who, finding no one on the pitch worth shouting about, were singing the praises of their errant hero. The chanting rang out loud and clear from all areas of the ground, cutting through the rain. They weren't singing 'Super Jack', though. Not 'Super Jackie Draper', the chant that had followed Draper from West Brom to East London. They sang,

'Super, Super Mac.'
'Super, Super Mac.'
'Super Mac the Knife.'

Korai listened, his blank look underlined with something a step or two beyond hatred. But it wasn't for me. His mouth was open in amazement at the crowd as the chanting went on. I know what he was thinking and I felt it too. I saw Alison, her body, her hair, how empty were her eyes. I wondered if somewhere in that ground, her father was listening to this.

'Charming, aren't they?' The chairman's mouth moved as if it were full of anchovy paste. 'What lovely people. I was brought up round here, you know?' He wasn't looking at me. He was looking at the people who came through his turnstiles every week, but he wasn't really seeing them. 'Leyton boy from the age of nine. Went to the local school. John Stanley Comprehensive, it's still there. About ten minutes' walk from here.'

He stopped for a second as he went back there, his eyes full of images. I didn't have to ask him what he was seeing.

'What a place we found when we came here to this country. To this city, this backward city. We were nice people. Quiet people. I had never ever known violence before. But we had to put up with a lot of it, a lot of Paki bashing, as they called it. Funny that, seeing as we came from Singapore. Not that that made any difference to them. I had my ribs broken one day, you know? Four ribs, after they caught me on my way from school. Top of the class Paki boy, they didn't like that. That was the worst time but there were many others. Punching, swearing, tipping things on me. I didn't walk past this place, not when there was a game. My mother was spat on in the shops. Literally spat on. And not by children, by other women. You know we never sat in our front room because of the stones through the window? My mother used to dream of moving, though she never did. She died just as I was making my way. Some women stop outside dress shops but my mother couldn't walk past an estate agent. And now people flock to the area, an estate agent's dream!'

Korai's voice reached up high and sharp. He gave a short, guttural laugh and shook his head vigorously, trying to get it back together.

'Then why?' I said.

'Why?'

'You're rich now. Why, all this?'

'In a minute you'll see,' he said. 'Look around you.'

I did, but I didn't know what I was looking for.

'White people,' he said. 'The sort of people who don't mind the likes of me "but I wouldn't want my daughter to go out with one". You know?'

I shook my head. 'It's not just whites. Look, I can see—'

He waved me away, his eyes glinting. 'The young ones, no. I admit. But these older ones. I remember them, you see? They don't know it but I do. These old ones. I see them. Eating the overpriced food I sell them that rots their guts, buying replica kits in the shop for their grandchildren that cost me nothing. Fifteen pounds each, to see this rubbish! You know how much we made from each 'real' fan of this club when I bought it?'

'Tell me.'

'Ninety pounds in a year, including season ticket, food etcetera. Not much.'

'Not much.'

'Last year it was *two hundred eighty*. You know how much a season ticket to Arsenal is?! And there are more of them, many more fans now. If we go up this year, more again. And then more, more fans, more money from each of them. And the more we win, the more they pay, the more they cheer! Do they have nothing else in their lives but this, this *game*? They don't realize that when their team wins, they have less money! The FA Cup, for instance – if we do well there are more games they have to pay for. And if we don't win? In two years' time I build a big supermarket right in front of your eyes!'

Korai was gripping my arm. I put my hand on his wrist and nodded towards the pitch, where the 'O's had got a penalty, Squires having gone down after another run.

'So, I want to tell you not to meddle with me. That's why I got you here. Little dog, chasing my coat tails. I killed Alison Footballer-Fucker? Prove it. And you better do it quick because if the newspapers start saying it, you be careful. If I can kill her, are you so special?' His fingernails were digging into my arm. He didn't seem to realize. I looked up to see his two friends, staring back at us. Beyond them Willie stepped up. The lad had wanted to take it but had been told to stand aside. Willie sent it low, to his left. The keeper got a hand to it but the ball crossed the line. The place erupted and almost immediately the halftime whistle blew.

Korai put his lips right up to my face and raised his voice.

'You won't destroy all this for me. As you say, I have resources, Mr Rucker.'

Two of them were looking at me.

'I have many, many resources. You hear me?'

'I hear you,' I said.

Korai nodded his head then stood. His friends stood too. I saw a skinny little boy on the ground, schoolbooks scattered, fifteen holers going in, hard. I watched him walk down to the touchline. He didn't look back at me. While his minders held an umbrella over his head the little boy with the broken glasses marched all the way round the pitch, waving at the supporters, a bright white grin splitting his old, cracked face wide. There was no sign of the anger, the bitterness. He shook hands with some of the fans and threw his scarf to them. He held his arms in the air and danced a foolish jig to the tinny sound of the club song, blaring out of the tannoy. A sea of blue danced with him, whipped up by strange winds. By the time he got to the tunnel the whole of the crowd was standing.

They loved it. They ate it up.

Part Four

Chapter Twenty-Eight

Jack Draper must have found a new hiding place because when I got up next morning the slightly too dramatic girl on *London Live* was still reporting his absence and the police spokesman was beginning to sound like he really, *really* hated his job. The news-reader also mentioned that Draper's team, Leyton Orient, had only managed a one-one draw last night, making me glad I'd gone home immediately after Korai had left me. Orient were now fourth in the table, drop-ping down from second due to results elsewhere.

Early that morning I called the mobile number Draper had given me but there was no reply from it. I gave it one last try before leaving my flat and this time it was answered.

'Hello. Hello.'

The voice belonged to an old Glaswegian.

'Hello,' I said. 'Is Jack there?'

'Jack, I don't know any Jack. Well, I did once but he's been dead ten years. And who would you be?'

It was then that I realized the man was very, very drunk. I asked him where he'd got his phone from.

'Oh,' he said. 'A young fella give it me. He didn't have any change but he said I could have this. Last night it was. Said I could have it. Not that I've anyone to call, mind. But it's been fine talking to you.'

'And where are you, exactly?'

'Where? I'm right here, you daft bastard.'

The phone went dead and when I tried the number again it just rang.

The rest of that morning I spent in Westbourne Park, being as obvious as I could be about asking some very blunt questions no one wanted to answer, making sure a lot of people got a good look at me. I'd given up on Nicky's staff. I thought I knew who had taken his money. I took the roll of film I'd shot in Westbourne Park down to Carl to develop. All the while I had a nice bruise just above my left temple that made my head look like a leaking battery. It stopped me getting in the ring but Sal told me that it was a good chance to work on my speed so I was back on the rope, getting my footwork better than Gene Kelly's. We didn't talk about the only thing there was to talk about. Taking quite a few more painkillers than the side of the pack suggested got me through the day.

I had lunch with DS Coombes. In the afternoon I took an express train to Leicester, telling Nicky that I wanted to go through some security arrangements with his mother and father. I didn't spend long there. I hadn't been back in my flat for more than an hour when Louise Draper called. She wanted to know what was happening. She had heard about McKenna and was now certain her husband was guilty. I didn't tell her that DS Coombes had called me to say that the thumbprint on the shard of glass I'd spotted definitely did come from Draper. Louise wanted me to go round and give her an update, and I did go. I also had another look round her house, and did see there what I'd thought I remembered. Louise's sister was with her, as was her neighbour, the doctor, being there for her, but they both left when Louise told them that we needed to speak. And we did speak, though not about her husband. She said things to me and I said things to her, and sometimes we said them at the same time, to each other.

I spent Saturday with Shulpa. She called to say that though her boss wanted her to go into the office she was blowing him off. He'd got mad but so what? I remembered what Nicky had told me even before Shulpa had moved to London. She never stayed in a job very long, before getting bored. It seemed like the pattern was beginning to repeat itself. Still, legal secretaries were in demand and she could always temp, which would probably suit her more anyway. Or else her boss was so cracked on her she could just do whatever she liked and not have to worry. That wouldn't have surprised me either and I admired Shulpa for not being a pushover.

Shulpa complained that we never actually spent any time just being together, talking. I said I was free until late afternoon and asked if she wanted me to come over to her small flat in West London. I wasn't surprised when she said why don't we meet in town? We grabbed lunch in a café by Holborn Station. Shulpa was astonished at the still-vivid state of my forehead, asking me how it had happened. I didn't tell her that the man she'd practically grown up with had done it. I said I'd slipped in the gym and she tutted.

'The things you get up to when I'm not there,' Shulpa said.

Shulpa and I talked about nothing as we ate, until she fell silent.

'Are you okay?' she said, eventually.

'Apart from a headache, sure.'

'You seem a bit withdrawn.'

'Do I?'

'You're not your usual, adoring self. You do adore me still, don't you?'

'I do. I absolutely do adore you. I adore you too much as a matter of fact. It's creating problems for me. I seem to spend all my time thinking about you. It's as if a mist has fallen over my eyes, created by your beauty.'

'Yeah, right.'

'It's true. You mist me, you get me very misted.'

We were quiet again and then Shulpa tentatively mentioned Draper. Shulpa asked me various questions about the police, whether or not I thought Jack had killed the people he was supposed to have. I shrugged.

'Ask Nicky,' I said. 'He knows him far better than me. You probably know him better than I do actually.'

'But you've been working for him, haven't you?'

'Uh huh.'

'Why didn't you say? Nicky told me,' she added.

'I didn't think. I have a lot of cases, I didn't realize. Sorry.'

'It's okay. So, is he guilty? Of killing that girl? And his agent? It's pretty amazing.'

I shook my head. 'I don't know for sure. I did actually find him but he legged it before I could speak to him. I'm not sure I'm working for him any more to be honest. I think he thinks I ratted on him.'

'How?'

'By telling some people where he was staying.'

'And you didn't?'

'Of course not. Though I would if I was certain he did kill Alison and his agent. Anyway, you knew him pretty well when you were younger, didn't you? Do you think he could kill anyone?'

'It was a long time ago.'

'I know, but even so, if you had to guess?'

Shulpa frowned as she thought about it. Nicky had been positive that Jack didn't have it in him to kill anyone. I looked deep into Shulpa's dark eyes. 'Yes,' she said after a second or two, her voice very even. 'Yes, I actually think he would be capable of that. Do the police have a lot on him?'

'I don't know,' I said. 'They've got enough to want to talk to him pretty badly but I don't know if it's enough to send him down.'

Over coffee I brought up the subject of Nicky. Shulpa hadn't asked me about him – probably wanting to have an afternoon free of worry, or else we'd done a good enough job convincing her that we'd got it sorted. When I told her he was on the mend Shulpa wanted to know what was going on about the money he'd lost. I told her I was working on it. Then she wanted to know if Nicky had got his mortgage sorted.

I hesitated. I seemed to spend all my time lying to this girl. I decided I should tell her the truth. It was only fair to warn her.

'No,' I said. 'He can't get a mortgage.'

'What?' Her fork stopped outside her mouth and her eyes opened.

'He can't get one. He doesn't officially own the Ludensian.'

'So . . .' Shulpa took it in quickly. 'What are you going to do?'

'Find the money he's lost.'

'What . . . what if you can't?'

I looked at her, hard. 'I'll have to ask the Maltese guys he was dealing with not to kill him.'

Shulpa looked back at me. Then she gave a dismissing, metallic laugh. 'They won't do that. They won't really kill him, will they?' I didn't say anything. 'Billy? I mean, what good would it do, it wouldn't get them the money, would it? And it would end all chances of getting it, no?'

Shulpa was trying to convince herself, not me. I remembered the look on her face when Nicky and I had been making elephant man jokes – the fear, the concern.

'No,' she said. 'It doesn't make sense. Of course they'll threaten him but they're businessmen, they'll just keep demanding money. They won't kill him.'

I looked at Shulpa, the way she was avoiding my eye, diving back into her meal, the way she'd brushed the idea of them killing Nicky aside so quickly. I didn't tell her she was wrong, that the Maltese most certainly would kill her brother if they didn't get what they wanted.

After I'd paid, Shulpa said she didn't mind what we did, as long as we didn't have to talk about anything horrible. I thought for a second then took her to one of my favourite places, to Sir John Soane's house, which was only round the corner. I told Shulpa where we were going and she said great, asking me what we'd find there. I told her that John Soane had gone all over the world collecting artefacts. His former house on

Lincoln's Inn Fields, just behind Holborn, is a mini British Museum, literally stuffed with Greek marbles, Roman statuary and countless other rare antiquities. They are all squashed into an elegant Edwardian terrace alongside some beautiful, classic English furniture. The impression you get is bizarre and surreal, as if Charles Dickens had gone on *Changing Rooms* with Pliny.

When we got there the museum was surprisingly quiet. Shulpa seemed suitably wowed by it all, especially when one of the trustees explained the various political figures thinly disguised in a set of Hogarth cartoons, hidden behind some panelling. She was even more impressed when he told her what the paintings were worth. I'd been to the house a few times, though I still found things to interest me. It wasn't until we walked down to the basement, however, with its strange light and flagstone floor, where most of the bigger pieces are, that anything really struck me. And did it strike me. I turned a corner and came face to face with my ex-girlfriend, Sharon. The girl my brother had been engaged to when he had the accident that had left him in a coma. The girl who, were he ever to come round, he would think was about to marry him. The girl I'd taken from him even as he lay there, who I'd thought would be the last girl I'd ever want to be with.

Sharon was standing beneath a small arch, looking upwards at the ceiling. She wasn't moving. My face flushed instantly and I stopped in my tracks. I couldn't help gaping at her and I could hardly speak. Shulpa stopped at my side.

'What's wrong?'

Sharon was naked. It was then that I remembered going there with her, how we'd come down to the basement and I'd had exactly that response. How I'd teased her. I hadn't seen Sharon's body in more than six months and there it was. An exact replica in smooth, polished, two thousand-year-old marble. Exact, breathtakingly exact, so exact I could feel my body responding to it the way it responded to Sharon. Sharon had laughed. I don't look like that! You do! My God! I'd tried to get Sharon to take her clothes off to prove the point and we'd both ended up laughing so much as I tried to strip her that we'd been asked to be quiet, or leave.

'What's the matter?'

'It's nothing. Really.' It wasn't nothing. Something inside of me had responded in a way that was immediate and visceral. Images of Sharon flashed into me. I told myself that I should have applied my restaurant rule to museums too.

'Are you sure? It doesn't look like nothing. What is it?'

I tried to explain to Shulpa and she gave me a measured, hard look. I sighed. 'It can be difficult having exes,' I said. Shulpa looked off to the side. 'I didn't mean to see this. Did I? You never know when the past is going to hit you.'

'I know,' Shulpa said. 'Don't think I don't know that.'

'I mean, you've had other relationships, do you ever think about them?'

'Yes.'

'So you must know what I mean.'

'Yes. I do. But you don't have to spell it out, Billy.'

We were both very quiet for a while, looking at an

Egyptian sarcophagus, both studying the myriad tiny figures carved into the granite. Shulpa wouldn't meet my gaze.

'You never talk about them,' I said. 'Maybe you should.'

Shulpa put a hand on her hip. 'I've had a lot of boyfriends. You want a list?'

'No, but if there was someone really special . . .'

'What about you? You've told me about her.' Shulpa turned and waved her hand dismissively at the statue of Pallas Athene. 'But there must have been others. And you only told me about your Big Love Affair with her as a way of warning me off. And don't tell me I'm wrong, I'm not stupid, Billy. You like me, we have great sex, but take it any deeper? You don't want that, do you? The word rebound could have been coined for the way you are with me. This is the first time that we've ever even just gone somewhere.'

'Shulpa . . .'

'So, sorry I didn't tell you about the ones before you, I just didn't think to. But let me see. There was Michael, a trader, who I met when I was twenty. I was only young then and even though he was kind of a nerd he impressed me with his Porsche. After him, let me see, a one-night stand with some guy whose name escapes me and another with the bass player in an indie band that was going to be big, he said. Then I was fucking this bouncer who was a bit thick but he got me in wherever I wanted and always had a lot of coke around as well as having an *absolutely enormous* cock . . .'

I held my hands up. 'Okay, I'm sorry. I'm sorry. It doesn't matter . . .'

'No, let's get on with it. I've got plenty more, believe me. But you have a go first. Anyone else you want to tell me about? Let's get it all out in the open. I want every last snog since you were twelve. Or did you start earlier than that? Don't miss anyone out, I'm very jealous, Billy.'

'I'm sorry. I am,' I said again. 'Really. Come on.'

Shulpa stood in front of me, both hands on her hips now like the urn behind her. She'd got really fired up, in seconds. An old American woman was cringing in the corner, trying not to listen. Shulpa glared as she shuffled out, leaving us alone in the small basement. Then Shulpa glared at me, her eyes burning. I just stared back. I thought she was going to go off again but suddenly her eyes lost their focus.

'Oh, I don't mind you being jealous,' she said. 'It's a compliment, actually. And we should talk about our pasts.'

I nodded, slowly. 'Yes,' I said. 'But I'm sorry. As for Sharon, you could be right, about why I told you about her. I'd never really thought . . .'

'Her?' Shulpa turned round and sauntered back over to where Sharon's double was positioned beneath the arch. She walked round and studied it, nodding.

'Not bad. But I've got better tits than that and you know it.'

She struck the same pose as the statue, and I laughed.

'Or do you? Shall we take the Pepsi challenge? Shall I prove it to you?' We'd left our coats upstairs and Shulpa's hands went to the bottom of her cashmere roll neck.

'Shulpa . . .'

'I think you need to be sure, Billy. You need to be absolutely certain.'

This time I *was* asked to leave the Soane Museum. We both were. We were, apparently, lucky that the curator didn't call the police. Shulpa and I were told never, ever to go there again.

Chapter Twenty-Nine

I called DS Coombes on her mobile from Holborn
Station after seeing Shulpa onto the tube. We'd spoken
yesterday and after finally managing to persuade her
that my way of handling it was the right one, we'd
agreed what to do.

'Are you there?' I asked her.

Coombes' voice was tight as a ten-pound line
pulling a twenty-pound pike. 'I am. With fifteen other
officers in support, all on my say so, with nothing to
back me up but this idea you've had. Are you sure he's
in there?'

'He has to be. You've seen no movement, no one
coming in or out, who even vaguely could have been
him?'

'No one.'

'Which means he's inside.'

'Or I'm going to make your life a real misery. But
if he is there I still think we should just go up and grab
him . . .'

'Trust me. You can always jump on him if he goes
anywhere. You sure the place is covered?'

'If he's in there and he tries to leave, we'll know
about it.'

'Well then. Wait, for now.'

'We're ready to go! Get over here. Let's do this now.'

'Later,' I told her. 'There's something I have to do first.'

The tiny St John club was rammed when Nicky and I got there just after eleven, rammed because, though the place stays open as late as four, after a while they stop letting people in. The day hadn't been as cold as it had been of late and the night was similarly mild, tattered straggles of low cloud uplit a browny orange against the dark sky like orange juice laced with rum. We'd parked Nicky's car on Charlotte Street and after taking the postman's bag out of the boot we walked south to the area north of Oxford Street that isn't officially Soho, which people are beginning to call Noho. Nicky was nervous. He walked quickly and I had to tell him to relax, to calm down. Probably to keep his mind off what we were about to do he asked me about Jack. He told me the police had interviewed him. I told him about finding him, and about Korai. Nicky asked me what developments there had been and I told him about the print on the shard of glass that I'd spotted in McKenna's office.

Nicky stopped. 'That's it, then, isn't it?'

'I don't know,' I said.

'It is. It is. He's fucked. He'll go away. Christ.'

'Well, I know he's your friend, but it does look like he did it. What other explanation can there be?'

'No,' Nicky insisted. 'He didn't. He can't have. I grew up with him and I just know it. I . . .' Nicky shook his head.

'What?' I asked. 'What?' He turned to me. We were almost where we needed to be.

'Later,' he said. 'Later. Let's do this first.'

Nicky and I turned left off Wells Street onto Boswell Mews, a narrow lane full of post-production suites and casting agencies. I was pretty sure, actually, that I'd been to the St John before. If it was the same place, I knew it to be a small bar-cum-club that stays open late, which you're supposed to be a member of to get in. The couple of times I'd been no one seemed to take much notice of this. I'd seen a lot of Mediterranean-looking guys in there but had assumed for no good reason that they were Greek. The name should have alerted me, I suppose, but I wasn't convinced that I'd ever actually known it. It was just that little club off Wells Street. Now I knew that it wasn't a Greek place: it was where a certain group of Maltese entrepreneurs hung out. Nicky had been contacted by none other than the head of the Maltese outfit in London and told to go there that night – and to bring fifteen thousand pounds with him. He'd obeyed these instructions, but not the last one they'd given him. He was told to go alone.

A small wooden sign above the door and a low rumble from upstairs flagged the entrance. The door was a thick, grey steel and was shut, but it opened before we could hit the buzzer. The rumble grew louder. I followed Nicky up a dark staircase that immediately turned to the right, where I knew the bar to be. We emerged into a small room full of smoke and noise. People were standing at a bar to the left, others were hunched round cheap-looking tables full of beer glasses and steel ashtrays. I nodded and confirmed to myself that I had been there. It was the same little dive. It looked like a skanky pub frequented by old lags in a run-down part of town rather than an in-the-know West End drinking joint, with worn stools and flimsy tables sitting on a dark red carpet patterned with grime. Only the fact that it was full saved it. I was in yet another place that needed people.

There were a lot of people there right now but in spite of the crowd the place had a flat, slow-paced feel to it, everyone sitting for the duration now. They were mostly men in their thirties, some Maltese-looking, some not, some with girlfriends but most in groups of three or four. People who just wanted a place to drink late. A slow Ron Sexsmith track sat on top of the hubbub like a dust sheet thrown carelessly over an old chair.

The bar was a small L with just enough room between the wall on the left-hand side for three stools. When Nicky and I had managed to edge through the crowd jostling for service, the man on the nearest stool saw us and stood down from it. He began to tell Nicky that he hoped he had a present for him when he saw me. He stopped in full flow.

'You,' he said. 'It's fucking you. Look, Alexander, Nicky's brought his bodyguard along.'

The thin guy with the unsuccessful facial hair who I now knew to be Christopher Ameli looked pleased to see me but it was an amazed, what-have-we-got-here? pleased, rather than a nice pleased. He stood with his hands on his hips. He'd had his mullet clipped, the sides shorter, making him look like a prize poodle at the local fete. Not an effect he was probably aiming at. He had a cigarette in his mouth, which stayed there as he spoke. He was addressing the man on the stool along from him, his big friend, who was going through some receipts with a calculator, oblivious to the noise around him.

Friend was wearing the same Prince of Wales check suit he'd worn to the Ludensian three weeks ago, the collars of a black silk shirt wide over the lapels. He, too, looked surprised to see me but he wasn't giving anything else away. He'd probably shaved that morning but dense stubble still sat heavy on his huge, bell of a face like a burnt field, running almost up to his eyes.

The big guy turned instantly to one of the two barmen. The guy was in his early fifties with a flat, hard face void of any expression at all. His dull eyes were cutting straight through me. They were eyes that hadn't just seen it all, they'd seen it all twice. They had it memorized.

The bell tolled. 'Is this him?'

The eyes didn't let me go. 'Yeah, 's him. Spent all day yesterday in the cafés, asking questions. The bookies too. Has anyone seen a big guy, and a thin guy with a beard? This is him.'

'Right. I see. You.' Alexander swung his face towards me, his voice vibrating with its own echoes above the din. 'Get out of here. We'll talk to Nicky on his own.'

'You already did that,' I said, just loud enough to be heard. 'You can still see the words on him. I'm not going anywhere. Or if I do I'm taking this with me.' I took the bag from Nicky and held it up. He stood beside me, his arms folded. 'And you can kiss goodbye to fifteen grand. You won't have another chance to get it. You're not fucking us around any more.'

The bell didn't move but a crack appeared in it, something like a smile but mixed with disbelief. No, he isn't really saying this. Two huge arms rested on the bar as the face leaned forward.

'So, you saw what we did to Nicky here, and you were jealous, yes?'

'Why don't you give that up?' I said. 'There's no girl here for you to grab. Cut the stupid threats and talk to me. I'm not going anywhere. Now, you haven't even offered us a drink. Which, after the way you've behaved, is the least you could do.'

The other barman had disappeared through a door into the back. All three of the men in front of Nicky and me seemed a little confused, not quite knowing what to do. They looked, collectively, like a volcano that was about to blow, but they each needed one of the others to start things off. The little guy went first. He pushed the stool aside. He had his knife out before he'd taken a step. I met his eyes. I tossed the bag at him as he came forward, unsighting him, and I sent a foot out towards his knife hand. People behind me moved back. I heard a 'Fuck!' as a pint went over. The huge guy was standing but his thin friend was in his way. My foot found the wrist and his blade clattered off into the crowd. I used the same foot in his groin but I was too late to turn as the old guy came over the bar, jumping right onto me, sending me backwards and down. There were more shouts of disbelief. I pushed the guy off and tried to get up. I had help. Two hands like the claws of a crane reached down to my throat and launched me back against the bar. He'd found a way through. I caught Nicky to the side. I saw a hand the size of a cabbage going backwards. I thought I was going to have to watch it come forwards again but it stopped. The eyes of the man holding me had edged to the right.

'What is this? What is this happening?'

The shrill high voice cut through the smoke. Someone had killed the music. The room was still. There was a wide semicircle around us. The sound of the voice put me back in school. I twisted my neck round as far as the hand at my throat would allow and I saw her. She'd come out of the door behind the bar and marched round the side. Everybody stopped.

'In the back, now,' she said. 'How dare you do this in my club? In the back. I'm sorry, everyone. Go on with your drinks. A misunderstanding. Please. You, you look like you spilled your drink. Another drink for this man, Peter. Please, everyone.'

The bar gradually returned to normal, heads being shaken, stools being picked up. Ron Sexsmith kicked in again from the top with 'Secret Heart'.

The back room was the same size as the bar. If they'd wanted to expand they could have more than doubled their space but they obviously didn't. I got the impression that the St John was a bit like Sally's gym, the tip of a very deep iceberg. I looked around. The carpeting was the same as next door but brighter, not showing the same wear. Old brown leather sofas lined three of the walls with low wooden coffee tables in front of two of them. Nicky and I were sitting on the sofa furthest from the door we'd gone through, looking up at a desk. It was a big, metal thing like a navy officer's, squatting in the exact centre of the room, looking like it should have been further back. Behind the desk sat the woman who had no doubt saved me from the broken nose I'd so far managed to avoid at Sally's. The man who had nearly given me it was sitting on the sofa on my left, while the thin guy stood with his back to the thick oak door, the low rumble from next door seeming to come through from his belly. Three other men I'd never seen before had followed us into the room and were sat on the sofas looking at us. They all seemed to know who we were.

The woman on a raised chair behind the heavy grey desk was no taller than five two. Her name was Miriam Ameli and she was, as Sal had told me, the head of the Maltese outfit in London. Miriam must have been seventy-five but she could have been anything up to ninety. She was stringy, her faced crumpled and parched as a dried pea, her short hair, dyed way too black, sitting on her head like a skullcap. She gave off strange, contradictory signals the way some old people do, looking both incredibly frail and utterly immovable at the same time. She wore a single string of pearls over a black cardigan, a delicate gold cross bobbling at her grizzled throat. She was looking at Nicky. She looked at him with irritation and distaste, as if he was half a worm in the apple she was eating. Without taking her eyes off him she lifted an arm from beneath the desk and waved it at me.

'We told you to come alone. How dare you bring this man!'

Nicky sat up. 'Alone? After last time?' His voice was a shaky roller coaster, propped up by thin wooden supports. 'No chance.'

The old lady shook her head, confused. She brushed Nicky's point aside. 'But that only happened because you tried to be clever with us. What did you expect? And why have you been doing this? I don't understand. Did my husband ever give you trouble? You did what he asked and it was fine – and you made a lot of money. Why am I different? Why do you try to cheat me? What did you possibly think you could get from cheating me?'

It was a good question, and I answered it for Nicky.

'Nothing,' I said. 'He could get nothing by cheating you and that's why he didn't. The money was stolen.'

'I told them that,' Nicky insisted. 'I told them but they didn't want to know. Those two. They didn't want to hear it. I wouldn't cheat you, Mrs Ameli. I would have to be very foolish to cheat you. The money was taken from my flat at the bar.'

'What do we care what happened to it?' The little guy had pushed himself off the door. I liked the way he made up for his lack of size, by including every inch of the room in what he was saying, like the star of a musical. He was coming closer. 'We made a deal, you *owe* us. Your problems are your problems. So, are you going to pay us? Or would you like us to terminate our relationship right now?'

'Wait!' Mrs Ameli brought her hands down flat on her desk, which complained with a deep, booming sound. Her voice betrayed an irritation with her nephew that I was pleased to hear. I thought about what Sally had told me about him. That he was impatient to get his turn, that he thought he should have got it when his uncle had died. He looked at the old lady and shook his head, stepping back again.

'It is as my nephew says,' the woman said, her voice calmer, remembering to include him. 'We really don't care if you were stupid enough to lose the stake. What is that to do with us? You must see that we want paying. But it looks like you know this. What have you got there?'

Mrs Ameli's eyes fell to the floor beside me. I'd retrieved the bag from the bar and it was sat at my feet. I picked it up, casually, and popped the clasps.

'Fifteen grand,' I said, as if I'd just thought of it. 'We managed to scrape it together. Nicky was going to keep paying you somehow, until he was square with you, but I've persuaded him not to. This is the last you're going to get and you're lucky to get even this. It isn't Nicky who's doing the cheating, it's the other way round. You want it or not?'

'Are we going to listen to this?'

'Be quiet!'

The old lady was looking at me steadily. She let out a breath and turned to her nephew then back to me. She'd snapped at him again and it had embarrassed her. She knew I'd made her do it and she didn't like the fact. She folded her arms.

'You like Maltese cafés, I hear.'

'The ones I've been to in the last few days, sure. I'll have to pay a visit to the island sometime.'

'I would recommend it. And you like asking questions about us, not very subtle ones at that. Do you think you can threaten us with the police, something like that, so we let your friend off? Tell them where we operate, who we deal with? Is that what you are trying to do? I have to tell you that we have some very good police friends, it wouldn't do any good.'

'I don't doubt it.' I shook my head. Out of the corner of my eye I could see her nephew, angry that his aunt was letting me play with her. He couldn't see any point to this. 'I'm not going to threaten you with anything.'

'I'm very glad. But then what were you doing there?'

'Hanging out. Trying to help my friend here.'

'You seem very attached to him.' One of the men across from me smirked. 'But help him how?'

'By seeing if some rumours I'd heard were true. Rumours that would help back up an idea I'd had.'

'Rumours. I like a nice gossip at my age. And were they true?'

'I think so yes. In fact, I'm sure of it.'

'Pray tell.'

'You mentioned your husband, Mrs Ameli.'

The word husband from my lips changed the air in the room. Everyone tensed, became focused. Mrs Ameli was still folding her arms but she sat up. The game had taken a direction that wasn't funny. Her very deliberate look said, 'Careful, tread carefully.'

'You kind of took over things when he died, didn't you?'

'I don't know what you mean. This club? Of course.'

I nodded. 'I've spoken to some people who knew him, in a business sense. He commanded a lot of respect. He'd treat a man fairly, I was told. He would, wouldn't he?'

The old lady nodded. 'If the man didn't try to cheat him. He had rules and if you played by them you had nothing to worry about.'

I nodded back. 'He treated Nicky fairly. Did a lot for him. And you continued to be fair, no?'

'Get to the point.'

'The point is, Nicky is not being treated fairly now. Hasn't been treated fairly.'

'I've told you. His problems are not our concern. Asking for my money to be paid to me is as fair as I get.'

'Even if you already have it? Even if you stole it from his bar, only days after delivering it to him?'

Miriam Ameli's mouth opened and her hands gripped the front of her desk. She bucked forward in her seat. Her eyes shot open like I'd put a thousand volts through her.

'You be very careful. How dare you say that I—'

'Not you, Mrs Ameli. Not you.' I nodded to the door. 'Him. Your nephew. The man who's been carving out a nice little space for himself recently, striking out on his own as it were. Him. Nicky's not paying you any more because he already came and took it.'

I think he was too stunned to move. I'd had half an eye on him, expecting that knife he was so fond of to flash out as soon I'd said what I had. But he didn't react. Everyone was looking for him. He looked back at them as if they were mad.

'It was why he was so keen to finish Nicky the other night,' I said, turning to the bell. 'You had to stop him, no? Because he didn't want Nicky figuring it out. He wanted to kill him, and write off the cash, because he knew you were never going to get it. He knew where it was.'

'I am definitely going to kill *you*. That is absolutely certain, my friend.'

'Here,' I said, throwing the bag to him again. 'Take a look inside.'

He caught the bag one-handed, barely moving. My

eyes were full on him now. He was like a horse in blinkers, one thought only. It was rising in him but he was careful to check it. He was very calm. I think he knew he couldn't lose his cool. Being accused of something does that to you. Everyone in the room was still looking at him. It wasn't accusation on their faces, but they weren't exactly with him. He let out a snort of derision and shook his head.

'Well?'

The old lady had pushed her chair aside and was standing, looking at her nephew.

'Well?'

'It's rubbish. He's just trying to bullshit us.'

'I mean, what's in the bag?'

'The money, I hope. At least it better be. Not that I am going to forgive this shit.'

'Open it!' she told him.

Her nephew put the bag down on the arm of the sofa and snapped the clasps. I could see him thinking, trying to get there before he saw it. His hand came out with a roll of bills.

'Five grand,' I said. 'There are three of them.' He pulled them all out and set them on the arm of the sofa. Then his hand went in another time and he was holding a blue folder. Everyone's eyes followed it. He looked at it with contempt, as though he was amused. Then he opened it decisively and flicked through the pictures that were in it. I'd had them blown up to A4. He tried to hide his shock as he went through them quickly. Then he shook his head.

'What do these show? They show nothing.'

'They show you going into a bookies,' I said. 'Then a café and a supermarket. And a casino. With a bag that gets heavier each time. You don't normally do collections on your own, do you? I was told that. Always in pairs. The last picture shows you at a safe-deposit place. I bet it's not one you usually use, if you use one at all. It's in Mayfair, Mrs Ameli, Johnson Security. Heard of it?'

I could tell she hadn't. She had stepped forward and was taking the photographs from her nephew. He looked pale, sick. He started to protest his innocence, telling her it was bullshit.

'I was told he was doing it by a friend of mine who knows about such things,' I explained, as the old woman looked at the pictures in her hand. 'Striking out on his own. They "let" him win at the casino and at the bookies. The shops and cafés just pay him extra. But I knew you wouldn't believe me until I could prove it. No one likes paying him extra but they do it because they're afraid of him. They think he's going to be next after you, that's the impression he gives. That's why they don't complain to you, because of what he'd do if you didn't believe them, or if he got control anyway. He's been playing his own game all over town and he's done it again with Nicky. He's the only one who knew where the money was. He was the only one who went up with Nicky into his flat. He went up with Nicky, didn't he?' I turned to look at the big sombre face to my left. He was breathing through his nose, a steady intake getting slowly quicker. I left him and looked at his boss again. She'd looked at the pictures and was starting again at the beginning. 'Ask them, they won't deny it. And I reckon that if you go to Johnson Security there you'll find the money you want, and some. If you don't, come back to us. But you will. So, don't talk to me about fair, Mrs Ameli. Talk to him. Because if this is a game you call fair, we're not playing any more.'

Christopher Ameli was studying his aunt's face as she looked at the photographs in her hand. When he could tell that yes, she believed it, he came for me. He didn't get very far. His cousin grabbed the back of his hair and stopped him. He pushed him onto the three men all getting up from the far sofa. Ameli struggled with them and screamed at me but they soon shut him up. When she'd finished looking at the pictures in her hand Mrs Ameli folded them in half and turned to Nicky and me. She picked up the rolls of bills still lying on the arm of the sofa and stuffed them back in the postman's bag. She handed it to Nicky and then turned to the man standing next to her.

'Get them out of here,' she said.

Chapter Thirty

Nicky couldn't believe it was that easy. We'd stopped round the corner from the place, Nicky leaning against the wall of a bank, the relief beginning to flood into him. He was limp as a rag doll.

'What if they go to his security box and the money isn't there?' he said to me.

'It will be. I saw him going in the place. He looked like he went there a lot, by the way the owner dealt with him. There'll be more than a couple of hundred grand if you ask me. Enough to satisfy them. Anyway, we'll know in a day or two. If you want my guess you won't be hearing from Mrs Ameli again.'

Nicky held his face in his hands and then laughed. 'Unless she wants me to wash another bundle for her.'

'To which your response will be?'

'Hey, if the money's good . . .'

'Don't,' I said, pointing my finger at him. 'Not funny. Don't fucking *even*.'

We stood for a while longer as Nicky got himself together. Then Nicky began to look uncomfortable. As I made to move off he stopped me.

'I'm going to tell him,' Nicky said.

'What?'

'Draper. I'm going to tell him about the evidence,

the glass. I have a number for him.' I stood up straight, my hands on my hips. 'I knew you found him. I spoke to him yesterday. I told him that you wouldn't have sold him out.'

'I would have, but I didn't.'

'I said you must have been followed.'

'I was.'

'Well, I'm going to tell him. I have to. He's a friend. Like you did all this for me.'

'I understand.'

'Do you?'

'If you know he didn't kill that girl. What do you think he'll do?'

'I don't know. I just promised I'd call him if I heard anything. I wanted to tell you first.'

'Okay,' I said. 'Just do it from a payphone. And disguise your voice, use a handkerchief or something.'

'I will.'

'Right then.'

Nicky and I stood looking at each other. He looked hollow. I turned to go.

'Billy,' he said.

'Yes.'

'I've been weak. This whole thing. I hate to think . . .'

'What?'

'I don't know. I just . . . I'm sorry.'

'I know you are, Nicky. I know.'

I figured the tube was faster than a cab so I jogged to Oxford Circus where I followed signs for the Central Line westbound. I had to be quick, if Nicky was already calling Draper. I used a cardphone on the platform to tell Coombes I was on my way and she said she wouldn't wait more than half an hour. I said she wouldn't need to. When the train roared out of the tunnel I stepped forward then sat on it for twenty minutes, tapping my feet, going through it. I hoped Nicky just called, that he stayed away. After six stops I pushed the doors apart and hiked up the escalators.

Coombes had said she'd be in an unmarked white van opposite the flats and when I got to the place there was only one van there. I gave a couple of taps on the side of it. Then I walked round the back. The back doors swung open and Coombes' face appeared. She held the door for me and I took a quick look over my shoulder before stepping up inside.

They were four of them in the van, Coombes and three men, two of whom were unknown to me. One was in headphones, testing some listening equipment at the far end while another was reloading a camera. The van smelled of coffee and piss, and I looked round for the bottle they'd been using, so as not to go anywhere near it. The guys had obviously not made concessions to the fact of Coombes' presence and why should they? If they had to go they had to go. I wondered if Coombes used it too, or if she had her own. I didn't think I wanted to know. As I stepped inside Coombes made room for me.

'At last!' she said. 'Right then. You ready?'

'Absolutely. Got the rear door covered?'

'Sure have. Couple of men spent all day pretending to be gardeners, now just lurking in the shadows. And we're not the only unit out front either. See that pimp mobile?'

Coombes shuffled aside further to let me look through the small surveillance hatch in the side of the vehicle, which on the outside appeared as a panel of smoked plastic. Across the street I could see a long white stretch limo lounging just outside the front of the six-storey building we were parked opposite, all its windows black.

'Cool, huh? Who'd believe that that thing was full of coppers, eh?'

'Your budget must have gone up since my day,' I said.

Coombes asked me to go through my theory with her once again and I did. I didn't take long, she'd had the full version. Coombes nodded a couple of times and when I finished she told me that yes, just as she'd thought when I'd run it by her yesterday over the phone, it was bullshit. It didn't matter, though, she said, when I started to explain it again, because even if it was she still got to nab Draper – if he was up there. That was all she cared about. I said whatever and asked her if she'd brought along the shard of glass we'd found at McKenna's. She reached in her bag and handed it to me, telling me not to take it out of its evidence bag. I looked at her like, I don't need to be told that and she looked back with I know that but I still have to tell you. Coombes had described the piece to me in detail over the phone but I still wanted to look at it myself.

'You can't believe what I had to go through to check that out,' she said. 'The forensics bods thought I was joking. If I lose that I am absolutely fucked.'

I turned the shard round in my hand, and nodded. 'It was worth it,' I said, as I handed it back to her.

The surveillance officer in the headphones moved

towards us and the young officer Coombes had appeared with at my flat told me to lift my shirt up. He took a small pack and a series of wires from his colleague and helped attach the wire to me. He didn't look too pleased about it, probably wishing he was the one going in. He certainly wasn't very cheerful, but maybe it was because his already spawn-like acne had taken a turn for the worse. He looked like an extra dying from something nasty in an early episode of *Doctor Who*.

'You sure this is right, ma'am? I mean, I know he used to be an officer but now what is he? There must be a rule against this.'

'There's probably a whole book of them somewhere.'

'Then surely—'

'Just shut your mouth and get that wire on him. It's the perfect public/private partnership. Your Mr Blair would absolutely love it. You're not even charging us for your services are you, Mr Rucker?'

'It's on me.'

'Well there you go. Talk about cost effective. Right. You ready?'

I pulled my shirt down and closed my coat.

'Can we have a level test, please?'

'Sure. How is this? Okay? Okay?'

'Loud and clear,' the man in the headphones said.

Coombes' eyes were bolted open like a speed freak's. She loved this, she was clearly an adrenalin junky. I tried not to let her hyped state affect me. I turned the handle and pushed the door, enjoying the cool rush of fresh air. As I did so I could hear Coombes' wired voice priming the rest of her team, over her handset. I stepped down from the van. Again from Coombes' handset I could hear her team responding. 'Thank God! About bloody time!' I stopped for a second and took a breath. I shut the doors of the van quickly and put my hands in my pockets. I could no longer hear any voices but suddenly I could feel them all around me, watching, waiting, I could feel the tension in the air.

I made myself stand still for a second and told myself to chill out. It was a mistake, I should have just got on with it. Doubt seeped into me. I suddenly wondered what the hell I was going to do if the hunch that had germinated inside me three days ago was wrong. The hunch that had stretched and grown ever since, however I'd tried initially to ignore it, then to stamp it out, to dig at it, to poison it with doubts. What if Coombes was right, what if it was bullshit? As I stood at the back of the van, waiting to play my hand, I found myself agreeing with her: it couldn't be true, it just couldn't. And if it wasn't how would I react? I knew the answer. I'd feel very, *very* stupid, but that feeling would be nothing compared to the other emotion I'd know. It would be nothing at all compared to the relief.

I'd stepped out of the van onto a small street between the King's Road and the Fulham Road. The air was thick and damp. I gave a short tap on the back door and pulled my hands out of my pockets. Then I crossed the street towards a long row of handsome red-brick mansion blocks, stretching up and down the road in both directions, the kind that used to be townhouses. They were clean and uniform, well lit, with white cornices and window ledges mostly lined with boxes that in the summer would have been brimming full of pinks and geraniums. Now they were mostly empty. I let a cab pull past and I walked over, not being able to stop myself looking up towards five. I remembered the last time I'd been there, how I'd done the same thing. A struggling winter sun had sat on the window like a broken yoke. Now there was a light on, a small square of dull orange pressing through the blind.

I crossed over quickly, not wanting to be spotted. I had Draper's face in my mind. I didn't want him clocking me. I didn't want him making a break for it. If he tried that there was no way out. He'd be caught. That would be it for him, especially now the police had his print. No doubt. They'd catch him and they'd charge him and he would go away for a long, long time. I had the feeling I'd had once before, only now it was stronger. Draper only had one hope. Even if he didn't know it, and I didn't like it, that hope was me. I shook my still-painful head. It was much easier to work for people you liked. So much easier. I didn't like the way Draper thought. I didn't like the way he behaved. I didn't even like his silky fucking haircut and for some reason I also had something against his razor rash. But I had to help him, just as I'd had to help Alison, even if, by doing so, I was kicking up the worst kind of shit. Because they had chosen me. You can't decide who chooses you.

Coombes had arranged for the heavy wooden entry door with its pretty stained glass to be on the latch so I didn't have to wait for a drunk woman to open it for me or pretend to have locked myself out taking the rubbish down. I pushed the handle. The hall light was on. I was in a neat and old-fashioned foyer, reminiscent of a small private hotel, with a delicate walnut table to my left and a series of wooden mailboxes screwed to the wall. There were mirrors on both sides and ahead of me I could see an old single lift with a wood-panelled door. I slid it open and then eased back some polished metal caging. I rode the lift up to the fourth floor where it stopped with a loud ping. I stepped out into a narrow darkened corridor and then walked along a thick, paisley carpet until I'd found the fire escape. I shut the door quietly and hopped up two flights to five.

I took a long deep breath and made myself go through it one last time. No, there was no way round it. None at all. I walked up to the corridor and past the lift. I put my ear to the door of flat twelve, holding my coat so that it wouldn't rustle. It was the second time in two days that I'd done this, hoping to hear signs of Jack Draper. This time I could hear movement but no voices. Feet padded back and forth and I thought I could hear the snap of some latches, like those on a suitcase. I nodded. I kept my ear to the door as I knocked, briskly.

In an instant, the movement stopped. Still, no voices. Nothing. I knocked again, a sing-song kind of put-you-at-ease knock, a non-threatening, hey-how-are-you? knock. There was a movement. I stepped back as I heard footsteps approaching the door.

'Who is it?'

'It's me.'

'Who?'

'It's *me*. It's Billy Rucker.'

Silence. More. Then, 'Billy.' Very flat. 'What are you doing here?'

'Open up and I'll tell you.'

'Just a minute. I'll . . . Just a minute. I'll be there in a sec. Just a minute.'

The footsteps retreated and I heard more. Then they came towards me again and the latch turned.

Jack Draper wasn't holding any threatening objects in his hand this time. But he did look nervous. He stared down at his feet, giving me a chance to look at him. It was a surprise. His hair had been cut, clippered short to a number three. It suited him, so maybe something beneficial *was* going to come out of all this. Unlike his hair, his beard had continued to grow, now actually quite suiting him too, as well as being a pretty effective disguise along with the crop. He could pass for someone else at a pinch. As he had in Nicky's uncle's warehouse, he looked pale, scared, but it was more intense now, even more desperate, as if he'd just been told some very bad news. Again, I nodded to myself.

Draper shook his head wearily. He sort of laughed. 'I should have known you'd find me. Nicky said he hadn't told you but I still should have known. You did it before.'

'It was harder that time, but I managed it. And you thought I'd betrayed you.'

'I know. I'm sorry. You can see why, though, can't you, the people outside? I only realized that you'd probably been followed later on. If you *had* told the Bill, it would have been them coming through the door, not you, wouldn't it?'

'Exactly.'

'So I'm sorry I clobbered you. Christ.'

'It's okay,' I said. 'It doesn't hurt as much as it looks like it should.'

'So,' Jack said. 'Tell me. Was it the police? Had they followed you?'

'No.' I shook my head. 'It was people working for Vishnan Korai.'

'Korai?'

'He was after me. He wanted to tell me to get off his back.'

'Because?'

'Because I'd been looking into him. I'd thought maybe he'd had Alison killed as a way of bribing you to sign your contract.'

'Jesus. And did he? Is that what happened? Korai? So he was sending me those pictures. He never gave any hint . . .'

I looked over my shoulder. I could hear the lift starting its descent to the ground floor, from four. Someone must have called it.

'Why don't I come inside?' I said.

The room I stepped into was a small one, with dormer windows covered by taut white roller blinds. It had probably been the maid's quarters originally or else the nursery. The walls were woodchip painted duck-egg blue, while a thick green rug stretched almost to the edges of some light, sanded floorboards, probably the original pine. A portable TV set, off, sat carelessly on the floor and a clothes rail stood underneath the window, quite a few of the wire hangers on it empty. To my right, a modern, Japanese-looking sofa lined the near wall. Beyond it was a tiny, over-bright kitchenette lit by a line of small halogen bulbs fixed to the ceiling. At the back of it was a single door, which was closed, but which I knew opened into a tiny bath-room. My eyes took all this in very quickly before turning to my left, to the bed.

To Shulpa, who was sitting on it.

Shulpa had her hands in the pockets of the Prada blazer she was wearing. She was sitting up very straight. Her face was expressionless. Draper looked from me to Shulpa, then back to me again.

'Oh shit,' he said. 'This isn't what you think. I've known Shulpa years and she just offered—'

'You don't have to lie to him, Jack,' Shulpa said. 'He won't mind. He's not really into me anyway. Jack's right, Billy, we have known each other a long time. For ever, really. And there wasn't anything going on between us for ages, but there is now. It just happened. I'm sorry.'

Draper looked confused. He ran both of his hands back over his head, looking like he was expecting to find more hair there. He was worried I was going to hit him. 'I shouldn't have come here,' he explained. 'I shouldn't have dragged Shulpa into this. I didn't know where else to go. She said the police hadn't bothered her about me and told me to come over. I didn't expect anything other than a place to kip. I . . . Jesus.'

Shulpa was looking up at me, still very calm. Her head nodded, almost imperceptibly. 'I should have told you, Billy. That he was here. I just didn't know what you'd do. I really wanted to help Jack – I know he's innocent – and I didn't know how you'd react. I'm sorry. As for me and Jack, how we feel. I know you and I have had fun but you don't really mind, do you?'

No, I don't mind. Not in the way you think. Behind

me, the lift began again. Coming up. I reached behind me and pushed the door to, hearing the Yale click.

'You mentioned Korai,' Jack said. 'So you reckon . . . ?'

'Which airport were you thinking of going to?' I said.

Both Shulpa and Jack stared back at me. They were frozen, like Sharon was in the Soane Museum. They looked like they'd stay that way for ever. 'I would suggest an internal European flight for which you won't need passports. No, better still the car ferry or the Eurostar, where you can just drive through and hope they don't spot you. Then buy a false passport someplace, it isn't hard, and fly out of the EC from somewhere Jack isn't known. Portugal maybe, or Turkey where the controls are useless. Somewhere like that. You *are* leaving, aren't you?' I looked at the empty hangers on the rail beneath the window and my eyes skirted round the room until I saw the end of a suitcase, pushed beneath the bed Shulpa was sitting on. I nodded, my eyes turning to her. 'What did Cat Stevens say? I hope you find nice clothes to wear? So, which is it, ferry or airport? Have you told your wife, Jack?'

At the mention of Draper's wife, his face changed. The pain on it was mixed with confusion and helplessness. I wasn't giving him a hard time but he felt he had to justify himself.

'They know it's me!' Jack said. 'They know it. I've got to skip. It wasn't me but there's no way out, not now, the police have found some sort of print . . '

'Nicky just tell you that, did he?'

Jack stopped, and nodded. I turned to the girl on

the bed. I hadn't told Shulpa about it because I didn't want Jack skipping before now, which he would have done as soon as he knew it was hopeless. I'd known Nicky would tell him.

'That why you wanted to spend some time together?' I asked Shulpa. 'So you could pump me for news on how things stand for Jack?' Shulpa didn't nod. She just looked at me. I shrugged. 'You could have just asked. I'd have told you. So, you're leaving, Jack? Leaving everything. I can understand why. You'd be in the nick anyway so you wouldn't get to see Louise or Tommy. She wouldn't wait for you and by the time you got out he'd be a young man. A stranger. He's fine, by the way. So yes, you're fucked, it's true. But to tell you the truth I can't be bothered with all this protestations of innocence crap. Not any more. You must have done it, McKenna at least. There's no other way round it, is there? Well, is there?'

Again Jack's hands tried to delve into hair that wasn't there. He started to pace. He looked like a man in a straitjacket. I could see his knowledge of his own innocence begin to wane. Did I do it? Maybe I did? I must have? Everyone thinks so, they found my prints . . .

'You know I walked in on her?' I said.

Draper knew instantly what I was talking about and he stopped in his tiny tracks. He turned to me, stunned. His eyes shivered. He stood with his mouth open, waiting for me.

'I saw her too, Jack, just after you did. Can you see it? Can you see her? The look in her eye, the shock, the surprise, all laced with terror. Well?'

Draper didn't answer. I was looking straight into his eyes at me, at Shulpa.

'Did you imagine what it must have been like for her? When it happened. Yes? I did too. I kept trying to imagine how she struggled, how shocked she must have been when it started, then what she felt when she knew it was over, that she couldn't stop it. What must that have been like? And that knife, Jack, can you see it, in her face just standing there, can you?'

'I didn't do it. Please. I'd do anything. I didn't. She looked . . . I never would have done that to her.'

Draper had slowly sunk to the sofa where he was sitting, his head in his hands, shaking like there were a hundred funnel webs scurrying over his body.

'It's too late, Jack. You can say what you like.' There was a phone up against the wall by the kitchenette and I walked over to it. I picked up the receiver. 'I'm going to call the police. I didn't think it was you either until this piece of glass. I thought it was Korai, I even thought her mother had done it out of some religious zeal. But it wasn't them. I'm sorry, Jack.'

'Put the phone down, Billy.'

Shulpa had taken her right hand out of her jacket pocket. She was holding it in front of her, towards me. In it was a small, shiny silver gun, barely bigger than one of those cigarette lighters. But it wasn't a toy. I set the phone back very gently. I kept my eyes on my former girlfriend. I say former, we hadn't officially split up. Somehow, though, I didn't think we'd be able to get past Shulpa having both slept with her former lover *and* pulled a gun on me. The two murders, maybe we could have lived with them, but I thought actually that it was probably better just to let things go. We just drifted apart really, oh and she threatened to shoot me. Plenty more fish in the sea. Jack, who hadn't been watching Shulpa, saw the way I was standing. When he turned to look at her his mouth opened.

'Shulpa . . !'

'Don't worry, Jack. It's okay. You didn't kill those people, you're not a murderer. I believe you even if he doesn't. If no one does. You're not going to prison. Billy's right, we're leaving. He isn't going to stop us.'

Jack didn't know which way to turn. He held his hands up. 'Shulpa, relax okay. Listen. This is making it worse for me. Why don't we all calm down? Fuck, where did you get that thing? It's okay, Billy, she won't use it. She just cares about me . . !'

'Oh, she'll use it all right.' I had my palms stretched even though she hadn't told me to; the innate etiquette of the aimed-at. My eyes turned to Jack. 'She won't have any qualms using that. Not her, no. She doesn't have any qualms at all about killing people.'

Jack slowly froze again as he looked at me. He knew what I was saying. What I was beginning to say. Shulpa knew it too. Her hand trembled. She brought her left hand up to steady the butt of the little automatic.

I ignored it and looked at Draper. 'What did you feel for Alison Everly, Jack?'

He was surprised. He shook his head. 'Christ, nothing, I liked her, she was really sweet. But it was just sex . . !'

'You wouldn't have left your wife?'

He shook his head. 'God, no . . !'

'But when you started seeing Louise it was just sex too, wasn't it?'

Draper looked ashamed. 'Yes.'

'And then you fell in love with her. Shulpa, that must have really hurt you. Christ. You were practically engaged. You loved him so much, didn't you? He was everything, especially after your parents split. You'd do anything for him.' I gave a laugh. 'Jesus, he even managed to turn you on to birdwatching.'

'How the hell did you know that?'

'I saw the books in your house, Jack, and the binoculars. Nicky said your dad never took you, Shulpa. Your dad told me the same thing. Your mum told me what you were like after Jack left. Jack was everything to you, wasn't he? He still is. Did you kill Alison as part of this plan, to make Jack leave with you, or was it just rage, from hating her. Did the plan come after? Which way round was it? Well?'

The two people in front of me had very different expressions. Both had gone ashen, but only one was looking at me with pure, white, gut-deep hatred.

'I thought it was me who was trying to forget someone, not you. I should have known. You were trying to fuck yourself into loving me, into forgetting Jack. From the moment we met. You know it's bad for you, don't you, that feeling you get when you think of him? You know it makes you want to do things? Even this afternoon, you were trying not to love him. Weren't you? At least you have tried over the years. But it didn't work, did it, it never ever worked.'

'It never came close. But don't you tell me that. I knew it was her you wanted. All the time. I found the pictures of her. Prissy bitch. I knew you were thinking of her when you were having sex with me.'

'I wouldn't have thought of her while I was so much

as touching you,' I said. 'But come on, tell me. Why did you kill her? Was there a reason you can say, or did it just happen, happen when you realized that not only did Jack not want you for his wife, he didn't even want you on the side. He'd rather bang a sad Page Three girl who just needed the money because her mother was ill, who needed to do it but didn't even want to.'

Shulpa's hands were both shaking now. 'You thought he'd be suspected of killing Alison and then he'd leave with you. But he didn't. He thought he'd get round it, he could beat it. So you killed his agent as well, to add to the pressure on him. You shouldn't have used a glass from Nicky's bar,' I said. 'I recognized it, that little tinge of blue. It was different from McKenna's glasses. The piece even had a couple of letters of the brand name on it. You took it from Nicky's after being there with Jack one night, didn't you? You came to London for him. You'd probably propositioned him, and he'd turned you down. What was it, Jack, did the way she looked at you freak you out? You sent letters to Louise, the one who'd taken him from you. You did that thing with a cat. You were following him, stalking I think they say. But if you'd killed Louise you would have been a suspect right off. So you thought you'd land Jack in it, so that the only out he had was you, someone with enough money to get away somewhere with. Someone who loved him enough to put herself on the line for him.'

The more I spoke the more alone Shulpa seemed. I was reminded of Louise Draper, on her sofa like Alison. Draper's whole body was moving away from her, without him even realizing. He looked like he'd had a stroke. Shulpa eyes were bolted on to me, tears running down her cheeks in two continuous streams.

'Is . . . is he right? Is what he is saying true? Did you frame me? Is this all because of you?'

'I loved you.' Shulpa turned to him. 'I . . . love you. You don't know. No one knows. I'm normal. I'm not bad. Why did you want her? You could have come to me. That slag. I saw you with her. I saw you. I was going to send pictures to your wife of her and then I thought no, you still won't want me. So I tried to make you need me. I'm not bad, I'm in love. If you loved someone like this you'd know . . . ' She turned to me. 'Why did you have to get in the way? There wouldn't have been any more . . . deaths. We'd have been happy. We could have gone to Pakistan, we have friends there. We would have gone for ever. Why did you have to do this to me, Billy?'

It wasn't just the change in her eyes as she finally saw it all slipping away. I'd seen her arm beginning to tense. Thinking back on it I have Sal to thank, as I have for a lot of things. The speed work that was aimed at making me faster sliding a hook from my friend Des: the rope, the hoops, the step. Six months of it had left its mark. I fell to the left as her finger closed. The gun snapped like a Christmas cracker and the wall behind my head spat as I hit the floor. I jumped to my left as the gun snapped again. I heard them trying to get in the door. I looked up to see the gun again, pointing straight at me. I seemed to be looking at it for hours. But Draper was on her before she could fire. He got her arm down but she bucked with her whole body and brought it up again. Draper threw himself on her. They fell off the side of the bed, struggling, a mess of legs and arms. The door burst open. As the officers rushed into the room I heard the little gun, muffled now, say pop again and then again.

Chapter Thirty-One

I didn't enjoy playing Nicky off against himself, against his friend, against his sister. I didn't enjoy anything about my acquaintance with Jack Draper. One thing I really didn't enjoy was the conclusions I've had to make about myself.

I think I've discovered that I'm a jealous man. A suspicious man. Nicky says that in the past, before I met Shulpa, he'd often mentioned that his sister used to go out with Jack Draper. He tells me that he spoke about it on numerous occasions but I don't really remember this. Possibly, not having met her or knowing I'd be involved with Shulpa, I didn't take it in. But when I met Draper I knew it, without admitting to myself that it was affecting the way I felt about him. I was instantly wary of Draper and from then on I was wary of her. It was probably because I could never understand why Shulpa hung out with me when she was the girl she was, and here was this hip famous dude who had everything I assumed she would have wanted. It wasn't as simple as that, though. I'd under-estimated my girlfriend. Shulpa didn't want a man like Draper, she didn't want what he stood for, all the things he was that I wasn't. She just wanted Draper himself.

The jealousy I felt for him meant that I soon started

asking myself questions, though. Draper had started playing in London and she had come there too. The way she'd gone into my office, obviously looking to see if she could find anything. There was a look in her eye sometimes that told me she had lost something, she would never be happy until she found it again. I've realized that I must be a jealous and suspicious man because it wasn't long after Alison Everly's death that the strange thought that Shulpa had been involved in it had come to me.

I pushed the idea aside, proof only of my own paranoia, and I pushed it aside again. I'd gone off to visit Alison's parents, I'd chipped away at the thought that Korai was involved, all so that I wouldn't have to see what was in front of my face. It was only when I realized that it was Shulpa who had taken the money from under the floorboards of the Old Ludensian that I knew what had happened. Then, I had to accept it. She'd taken the money before killing Alison. She'd needed it to lure Jack away, so that she would be his only escape route. Then, when she had it, just over two hundred thousand pounds, she set about making him need her.

But knowing it was Shulpa didn't help Nicky. Even if I *was* sure that it was she who had stolen from him, I still had to get the Ameli crew off Nicky's back. As they'd told us, if Nicky had lost it, what was that to do with them? I tried to get Shulpa to give the money back, by assuring her that Nicky would die if I didn't find it, but she'd refused to believe that they would kill him. She wouldn't face it. She couldn't accept that she, in fact, was killing him. Either that or she didn't care. Other than getting Shulpa to hand the cash over the best way I could think of was to accuse one of their own of doing it. Christopher Ameli gladly stepped into the frame. The rest of the stuff I said about him was true and I figured he could take this on his shoulders too. Protesting his innocence of the matter wouldn't have cut any ice, not after what I'd told them. Even if Miriam Ameli wasn't absolutely sure, she would have found enough money in her nephew's secret stash to more than compensate her.

When I went to see Sally at the George, two days later, to pay her back the money Nicky owed, I told her what had happened. Sally told me that Christopher Ameli had disappeared.

'Back to Malta?' I asked her.

'There or somewhere a little further away,' Sal had replied, with a shrug.

Even though I knew Shulpa had had ample opportunity and motive to lift the cash from Nicky, it still amazed me that she'd do that to her brother. I couldn't be *absolutely* sure it was her until I found it. I thought it would be in her flat, in her travel bags even, and I assumed that the police would come across it. But they didn't. Nor did they find any safety deposit keys on the premises. I was glad. How would it have made Nicky feel? I let it slip to the back of my mind, knowing that it wasn't important, not really. What was important was that my friend was off the hook that he'd thrown himself on. That and the fact that his sister had been found out to be a murderer and had been shot, twice. That she was critically ill. I was more than happy to let its whereabouts remain a mystery.

The days following were hard for me but harder for Nicky. His relief turned to horror when I phoned

him and told him what had happened, that Shulpa was
in an ambulance on the way to A and E. I met him
there. I didn't tell him that Shulpa had taken his money
but the fact that she was a double murderer was a big
enough blow. At first he refused to believe it and he
wanted to know why I'd begun to suspect her. I should
have just said jealousy but I told him little things. The
birdwatching – I'd seen binoculars and field guides in
Jack's house. Her father confirmed that he never took
her and his mother told me that Jack did. The fact that
she lied about it for no reason made me think. When
I found Jack in his uncle's warehouse I'd smelled something, something familiar. I didn't want to know it
was Shulpa's perfume but I had to face up to it. The
paperback that was sitting on Draper's bed was the
same one Shulpa had been reading in my office that
night. Then, when I'd recognized the glass fragment
as coming from the Ludensian, I realized that Shulpa
wasn't just in contact with Jack, helping him out. She
was right in the middle of it. In Leicester I'd found a
box in Shulpa's bedroom with her old diary. The intensity of her feelings for Jack was obvious, as was her
rage when he left her. I already knew by then but it
cemented the reality, made me see why doing what
she had had seemed logical to Shulpa.

There was also Alison's body. The person who had
killed her hated her so passionately that Alison hadn't
just been murdered. It went further than that. Her
body had jealousy written all over it.

But none of it was proof, and Coombes couldn't
have done anything if I hadn't gone in with a wire and
got her to confess. Draper would have gone away for
it – either that or Shulpa would have come forward to

save him from prison. I didn't know whether or not she would have done that. I guessed not. She wouldn't have been any nearer to him either way.

In the days that followed the events in her flat I spent a lot of time in a hospital in Hammersmith, with Nicky and his parents. Both of the bullets that had come out of Shulpa's gun while she was struggling with Jack had gone into her. One wasn't serious, a flesh wound only, but the second had punctured her kidney and had stayed there. She'd been operated on as soon as she'd arrived at the Hammersmith unit and was still in intensive care after three days. The fact that the police had been right on the scene must have helped her, but as it was the doctor in charge didn't know which way it was going to go. I stayed with Nicky, explaining again and again why I'd done what I had. Sometimes he could understand it and sometimes he couldn't.

'Would it have been so bad to let them leave?' he asked me finally. 'Would it have been so bad to let her get away with it?'

'Yes, Nicky it would,' I said to him. I told him about finding Alison, what she had looked like. 'Yes. It would have been so bad.'

It was while I was just sitting there with him, trying to make him see that it would never have ended with Jack and Shulpa riding off into the sunset, that I had a thought. I suddenly realized how I could find the money Shulpa had taken. It was simple. I thought back to the night that she was shot. I'd trooped out of the place onto the street, following Coombes and the stretcher down to the ambulance. Amid all the lights and noise a bewildered minicab driver had shown up.

He'd been called by Shulpa. He'd had to prove that he wasn't an accomplice by showing all sorts of driver ID, and calling his office, but in the confusion no one had asked him one very simple question: where had the cab been booked to. I remembered the name of the firm and after waiting around an hour on a fold-out chair in a cramped and smoky office in Fulham the driver came in, straight from an airport job. When I asked him he said he remembered very well where he was supposed to be heading that night. He wasn't likely to forget that call in a hurry.

'Well?'

'To Clerkenwell,' he said.

I spent three hours in the cellar of the Old Ludensian before I found the canvas bag stuffed with notes, packed at the bottom of a box of old plates Nicky didn't need any more. All she'd done was move it, not wanting, I presumed, to be seen with it by Nicky. The money had been there all the time, it had been right there when the mirror had got smashed, only down the road when Nicky had been attacked. It had never ever left. It would have been funny if it wasn't funny.

I didn't tell Nicky. And it wasn't because I didn't want to let him have the money. Did he need to know that his sister had sold him out, that she would have let him die to get Jack Draper? I didn't think so. Shulpa was through the worst, so the doctors were saying. If she'd died I would have told him – what difference would it have made? But one thing Nicky kept saying to me as we sat outside intensive care, waiting for news of her, sometimes holding hands with his mother, was how much he realized that he loved Shulpa. In spite of everything. How he would visit her, try to be there for her, if only she would make it through. When she did, I knew I shouldn't take that love away from him. Or from his mother. From either of them. Even from Shulpa, who was going to need it. I was worried that Shulpa might tell Nicky, thinking he still needed the cash, and when she was well enough I asked to see her. She wouldn't speak to me, or her family. The only person she did want to see wasn't there. DS Coombes agreed to give a message to her from me. Just tell her that Nicky is safe, I said. Coombes was curious as usual but she just nodded.

Shulpa was tried for the murders of Alison Everly and Jeff McKenna and given two life sentences. Nicky and I stayed very brittle with each other throughout the trial and for a long time after. I spent time on my usual cases, down at the gym, visiting my brother. I even ran into Sharon there. Over coffee I told her all about what had happened. It was great to see her and we've since met each other there a couple of times. I keep nearly calling her, asking her out for a drink, and I keep hoping that she's nearly calling me. Who knows, maybe one day one of us will do it. Someone who did call was Louise Draper, and I went to see her, to tell her how things had gone. I hadn't called her and I was a little nervous. I offered her a refund but she wouldn't take it. The doctor was there with her again but this time he only went through to the kitchen. Louise told me that Jack had begged to be allowed home but she'd had enough of it. No more. She was getting a divorce and planning to marry her neighbour as soon as it was through. She'd even appeared in the *Express* to explain her decision. A picture showed her and the doctor arm-in-arm, above an article about being brought together by pain.

On the way back I drove through Hoxton Square again, just as I had the night I'd first driven down Stepney Green. I found myself slowing and I found myself parking, and then I found myself standing in front of Alison Everly's door on the fourth floor. I'd taken the door from someone coming out. Alison's flat was shut up, cold and quiet, but there was no police tape covering it. Nothing to show, no flowers or anything. I put my hand on the door and just stood, staring at it, not really thinking of anything other than the fact that it somehow felt right for me to be standing there. I must have been there five minutes when I felt a movement beside me, and turned to see a woman walking up.

'What do you want?'

She was a plump woman with a small face, in her early thirties. Her voice was cold and suspicious.

'Nothing,' I said. 'I just . . . I sort of knew the girl who lived here. I know what happened to her.'

'Oh,' the woman said. 'I knew her too. Alison.'

'Yes.'

'She was nice.'

'Yes. I came to think so.'

'They called her a slut. But she wasn't. Her mother, she needed money for her mother.'

'I know,' I said. 'I'd kind of thought. But I'm glad someone else thinks it.'

'She wouldn't have done it otherwise. I found her.'

'You . . .'

'I found her body. It was horrible. I was supposed to be getting married. I found her in the morning.'

'And you were getting married. That day?'

She almost laughed. 'That day. It was a blessing in disguise for me actually, if not for Alison.'

'Yes?'

'He wasn't right. I don't know. He was a bit of a snob about Alison, the time they met. When I saw him later, I could just tell. Sometimes you can, can't you, for no good reason?'

I thought of Shulpa, and of what Sally had tried to make me see about her.

'Yes. But sometimes you can't,' I said.

Karen Mills invited me in and we talked about Alison. She said she hadn't known about Draper, but she did know Louise wasn't happy. On the table was a copy of the *Express*, opened to the picture of Louise and her new love. Karen laughed.

'It serves him right,' she said. 'The bastard. Even if he didn't do it. It serves the smarmy bastard right. I hope it really hurts him. I hope he realizes what he's gone and lost. What you get when you treat people like that.'

I said goodbye to Karen and thanked her for the tea she'd made me. I didn't know, actually, how Jack felt about losing his wife. Maybe he didn't have time to think about it. He was a big star now. Jack was on the back pages of at least one paper every day and had been signed up for exclusives by most of them. His one-to-one interview with Martin Bashir had been a ratings smash. His first game back for the Mighty 'O's was against Newcastle in the FA Cup. People wondered if he was fit enough after what he'd been through but

Draper got both goals in a dramatic last-minute victory that had nearly raised the roof. After the game the Newcastle chairman had immediately expressed an interest in Draper, following Chelsea who had already come in for him. Everyone would have to wait, however, because, according to the pundits, Draper was waiting until the end of the season for his contract to run out. Then he would be a free agent. Then he could ask the earth from anyone.

I didn't speak to Jack. He didn't come to the hospital. Coombes' effort to get him charged with Shulpa's attempted murder didn't get anywhere. Draper never called to thank me for getting him out of the jam he was in, and nor did he mention my role in any of the interviews he gave. But one morning a package arrived by bike at my office. It was two tickets for that night's FA cup clash, the next round, against a first division side now managed by his former friend and manager Dave Harvey. I thought it was a beautiful slice of irony and immediately phoned Nicky. Things seemed a little easier between us now that it was clear Shulpa was doing fine, though she was still refusing his visits. Nicky was more than willing to go out to East London with me.

'Toby can cope,' Nicky said. 'He's kind of got used to being the boss now anyway.'

We got there just before kick-off. Nicky and I did our bit for Mr Korai by buying a couple of overpriced hotdogs before taking our seats in the stand, where Jack Draper's name was being chanted by a capacity crowd. He was their obsession and they were letting him know it. Shulpa never felt anything more for him. As the game got underway I thought to look for Janner

367

but I couldn't see him. I did see a guy I thought I recognized, though, sitting where Janner should have been. I asked the woman next to me what was going on. She explained that Janner had been given the boot, even though Orient were now back in the top three. His place had been taken by a former England star in his first managerial role. She was going to tell me more but was taken by a passage of play, Draper going in for a header that got tipped over the bar. Nicky and I got drawn in too. His play really was mesmerizing. If Nicky used to be the same standard he wasn't any more. Jack was a class apart and not only with his feet. He exuded something, an arrogance if you like, his chest out, his silky hair shining in the floods. He had it. I had to admit, he really had it. The goal he got just before halftime was a beauty. A simple turn, a neat curl. The goalkeeper didn't even move.

Leyton Orient were drawing one-one with ten minutes to go when Jack Draper's career came to an end. Dave Harvey had stood up from the bench and ordered a substitution. Harvey was being investigated following allegations Draper had made in excerpts from his autobiography printed in the *Evening Standard*. He brought on a player not listed in the programme, who, it later transpired, had only just been signed by his club. The player looked a little overweight to me, and I couldn't work out why Harvey had brought off the man he had, why he was bringing on a defender at all when his team were the bigger club and could easily have won the game. Apart from Draper, Orient didn't look much. But I soon realized that the visiting manager knew exactly what he was doing. The tackle, if you can call it that, rang round the ground like a gunshot. You could tell that it would take Draper six months before he could even stand, let alone kick a football. His leg snapped in two like a dry twig. It wasn't the shape any leg should be. As the medics ran on people around me looked away. The other players went green, walking up to him then turning away. A silence fell over the ground like a pall. The woman sitting next to me held her hand up to her mouth and I thought she was going to be sick. The ref showed the red card and the substitute left the field to a chorus of boos. Jack Draper screamed like a baby as they lifted him onto the stretcher. You could hear him all the way down the tunnel.

The crowd stayed subdued for ten minutes. I hadn't even noticed that Draper had been replaced by the nippy teenager. Gradually the atmosphere got back to normal. The kid found a lot of space at the back, the other team being down to ten men. He was fast and keen, definitely lightning. He got applause for a run that ended in a corner. Two minutes later he won the game with a brilliant burst of pure speed that sent him past the last defender, and a neat bit of skill that took him round the keeper. The place erupted. The woman next to me was jumping up and down. At the end of the game Vish Korai came out onto the pitch and held the lad's arms aloft. Both had smiles on their faces wide as empty goalposts. The crowd went crazy. They loved it. They ate it up.

And the money? It's under my floorboards. I'm wondering what to do with it.

ADAM BARON

Shut Eye

PAN BOOKS £5.99

The first Billy Rucker novel

Teddy's first assignation with a male lover is also his last. The married airline pilot lies dead in his London flat – his torso scarred by the sharp shards of the shattered champagne bottle left protruding from his abdomen.

Ex-copper turned private investigator Billy Rucker joins the case on the exhortation of Teddy's brother, a well-know Tory MP. And for Rucker it's the start of a long, lonely trail through the city, clutching a grainy black and white photograph with a gut-gnawing suspicion lurking at the pit of his stomach. Until the phone rings and asks for a meeting – and suddenly the name of the game is fear.

'It's Rucker's disillusioned monologue that makes
Shut Eye stand out among the myriad of formulaic thrillers,
and adds up to an accomplished first novel'
The Times

'Classy debut thriller, with crunchy London backgrounds . . .
Forecast for series is excellent'
Literary Review

ADAM BARON

Hold Back the Night

PAN BOOKS   £5.99

The second Billy Rucker novel

It is the hottest summer since 1976, but private investigator Billy Rucker is doing okay. Tracking down missing teenagers in a city the size of London requires skill, patience and more than a little luck. And luck certainly seems to be on his side when Mrs Bradley asks him to look for one of her twin daughters, Lucy. Because just that morning, while searching for another missing person in Camden Town, Billy had caught a glimpse of her. So all he need do is hang around and sooner or later Lucy will appear.

However, it is exactly when Lucy *does* appear that Billy's luck most definitely runs out. And Billy is left at the centre of a murder investigation – with only one way out.

'Urban noir has arrived in London,
and Adam Baron is one of its finest proponents'
Independent

OTHER PAN BOOKS
AVAILABLE FROM PAN MACMILLAN

ADAM BARON
SHUT EYE	0 330 37063 4	£5.99
HOLD BACK THE NIGHT	0 330 39117 8	£5.99

JAMES HUMPHREYS
SLEEPING PARTNER	0 330 48095 2	£5.99
RIPTIDE	0 330 48098 7	£6.99

ANDREA BADENOCH
MORTAL	0 330 36925 3	£5.99
DRIVEN	0 330 36926 1	£5.99
BLINK	0 330 39283 2	£5.99

All Pan Macmillan titles can be ordered from our website,
www.panmacmillan.com or from your local bookshop
and are also available by post from:

Bookpost, PO Box 29, Douglas, Isle of Man IM99 1BQ
Credit cards accepted. For details:
Telephone: 01624 677237
Fax: 01624 670923
E-mail: bookshop@enterprise.net
www.bookpost.co.uk

Free postage and packing in the United Kingdom